HAWKSMEAD

Books 1 & 2, Bridge to Eternity & Breaking through the Shadows

Romola Farr

WILDMOOR
PRESS

The illustration 'Breaking through the Shadows' is by
Lucy Perfect and is her copyright.
lucyperfect.com
instagram.com/lucyperfect

BRIDGE TO ETERNITY

Hawksmead Book 1

Romola Farr

WILDMOOR
PRESS

PROLOGUE
September

The legal speed limit for vehicles travelling along the Old Military Road was sixty miles an hour and he was breaking it. If a car rounded a corner in the opposite direction it would end up in a ditch because this driver was not in the mood to slow down for anyone.

The sound of cannon fire blasted from his top pocket and he reached for his phone. He took his eyes off the road to read the text, grunted, and handed the phone to the person seated beside him.

The passenger glanced at the short message, looked up and saw they were approaching a humpback bridge.

'You're going too fast.'

There was another round of cannon fire and both took their eyes off the road to look at the phone's screen. The message was clear and unequivocal. It was time to return home.

'Watch out!' yelled the passenger.

The driver lifted his eyes from the phone. Ahead, two people, holding hands, were blocking the mouth of the bridge.

He jammed on his brakes and skidded.

To regain control he took his foot off the pedal and steered the only course acceptable to him, hoping the inevitable impact would not cause too much damage to his van.

CHAPTER ONE
October – The Previous Year

Audrey Willatt crossed her legs and smoothed the skirt of her dress. The view out of the carriage window was exquisite but with every passing mile, the knot she felt in her gut grew tighter. She was leaving her home in the south of England and heading north to a Victorian pile she had bought a few months after her husband died, situated on the fringes of a bleak moor.

'The next station is Hawksmead,' stated the recorded voice from the train's speakers. Audrey stood and pulled down her folded coat from the rack above her seat and slipped it on. She picked up her handbag and followed a few passengers down the carriage to her two large and way too heavy suitcases. She felt the train slow as she lifted the heavier of the two from the rack and placed it down by the doors. She went to collect the second case and was momentarily taken aback to see it within the firm grip of a tall, well-dressed, elderly gentleman. She had spotted him when she had changed trains in Derby, and wondered whether there would be an opportunity to make his acquaintance. There was something about his posture, the way he carried himself, that appealed to her.

'May I help you get your bags off the train?' he asked.

'That's very kind of you. My mother drilled it into me never to pack more than I can easily carry. She would not have been impressed.'

The train slowed and came to a gentle stop. The door adjacent to the platform was opened by a fellow passenger pressing the illuminated button, and Audrey took her first breath of fresh moorland air.

'You get off and I'll carry the cases to the platform,' the Good

Samaritan said.

Audrey didn't argue and stepped from the carriage. The stranger followed her and placed the first suitcase at her feet.

Towards the rear of the train, the guard blew his whistle. Audrey felt tense as she watched her helper climb back into the carriage to retrieve the second case. She knew this was the really heavy one.

The guard blew his whistle again.

The man held onto the door frame as he eased his way off the train and with some relief on his face placed the suitcase at her feet.

There was another long blast of the whistle and warning beeps as the door began to close. The stranger turned and almost leapt through the narrowing gap. The door slid shut and Audrey waited, expecting to see the man's face at the window, but the train moved, gathered speed and soon she was standing alone with her suitcases on the empty platform.

CHAPTER TWO

Tina Small hated carrying clients in her white VW Golf, but it was part of the job. She was usually good at relaxed chit-chat but on this occasion she had something to hide and the elegant woman sitting beside her as they drove through the former mill town was tugging at her usually immune, estate agent's conscience. How had she let this happen? She should have sent a taxi. She had broken her own golden rule and allowed Audrey Willatt to penetrate her tough enamelled veneer. Never like a client, her boss had warned her, and she never had, until now.

'Has the sale of the boarding house provoked much local interest?' Audrey asked, breaking the long silence.

Tina felt the blood rushing up her neck and spilling out across her cheeks. Thankfully, she had applied plenty of make-up so, with luck, her client wouldn't notice. Blushing was for losers and she had worked hard to train her brain not to do it. At one point she'd gone to a hypnotist but, ultimately, it was Tina's determination that had won through – until now. Her body felt hot as blood, pumped by guilt, flooded into surface veins, undoing years of hard work. She was a blusher and always would be. Fortunately, her hot ears were hidden by her blonde hair, but she could not hide her discordant breathing.

Her mother had suffered from panic attacks for years. Was this one? She had to get a grip. She knew she was smart, too smart to go to university.

'Why should I waste my life and money going to a school for grown-ups when I can get on with my career right now?' she had told her disappointed parents.

Now, twenty-one and with three years' working for what she had helped become the area's leading sales and lettings agency, she was experiencing her first major trauma.

It had seemed casual enough at the beginning when Trevor Harper, Tina's boss, dropped a huge bunch of keys, the largest she had ever seen, on her desk and beamed down at her. 'We got it! If we get an offer and it's accepted by the executors managing the estate, it's double commission for you, Tina, my girl.'

'Nice tie,' she responded as she scooped up the heavy bunch and pulled open a cupboard door to retrieve the agency's digital camera; its wide-angle lens giving properties a scale they often didn't deserve.

'So, what's the address?'

Trevor stopped thumbing a text on his phone, looked at the designer label on his tie and replied, 'Hugo Boss'.

'Not the tie. Where am I going?' She slipped into her new Ted Baker raincoat.

'You know, the old school boarding house, just off the High Street. The one that's been empty for years.'

Tina froze. She hadn't seen it coming. She'd been so busy selling new-build properties on an estate gracing former fields to the south of the River Hawk, she'd not heard about her boss going after the old school boarding house. If she had, she'd have ducked the job and made sure her lazy colleague, Max, had the pleasure; but now, standing with the keys in one hand and the camera in the other, she couldn't back down.

Somehow, she forced a cheery smile. She liked working for Trevor. He was happily married and never tried it on with her. He was also ambitious, and she hoped one day to be offered a partnership in what she expected would become a long chain of estate agents.

She walked to her VW Golf, worried about the task ahead but too proud to confess her fears. There was absolutely no way she could wriggle out of spending at least a couple of hours within the forbidding building and retain her pride.

She sighed as she slipped into the black leather driver's seat and clicked her belt. She checked her phone for messages before slotting it into its hands-free rest. And then she had a thought. She reached for her phone and searched online for Hawksmead and articles about the old school boarding house. Over lunch, one Sunday, her maternal grandmother had taken great delight in detailing the shocking goings-on that had led to the boarding house gaining its reputation for being haunted. To Tina's surprise, her father had got up from the table and, without a word of explanation, had walked to the end of the garden.

After much badgering, her mother had told her about her father's big brother. 'He should have been a day boy but, for some reason, your grandparents thought it would be less disruptive if he boarded. Every day, he rode his bike from the boarding house up to the main school on the moor. One morning, he was hit by a car and killed.'

'How come I've never heard of him?'

'There wasn't much child psychology in those days. Your dad was only five, and his parents thought it best if he forgot he ever had a brother. He was not taken to the funeral and all photos were hidden away.'

Frustratingly, Google could find nothing about the events of fifty years ago. It didn't matter. Tina knew enough and it churned her perfectly flat stomach. She took a deep breath and fired up the car's engine. She told herself it was just an old building like any other. She'd be fine. When was anyone ever hurt by a...? She couldn't bear to even think the word.

She slipped the lever into first and released the handbrake. Her car always gave her a great sense of personal pride, but not today. She checked her side mirror and pulled away from the kerb with a feeling of dread she hadn't experienced for a long time. Despite photographing and measuring up numerous empty properties and never being bothered by mice and spiders, the history of the old school boarding house chilled her to the core.

Driving across the moor with its beautiful golden hues caressed by the September sun did not calm her troubled thoughts. The humpback bridge that was the northern gateway to Hawksmead came way too soon and within a further minute she was parked in a short drive that led to a porch with a tiled roof and a large oak door. She picked up the camera from the passenger seat, took a deep breath, and went around to the boot to retrieve a tripod.

She looked up at the imposing, former annexe to the abandoned school out on the moor, and decided to shoot the exterior once she'd photographed all the interiors.

Finding the right key amongst so many on the large bunch took time and Tina was all for giving up when the aged lock gave, and the door creaked open. She stepped inside and was almost overwhelmed by a sense of impending doom. The hallway was dark, despite the hour, and eerily silent. Wooden panels caked with dark brown varnish lined the walls. The floor was a mix of well-trodden terracotta tiles and patches of cement filler. Ahead was a wide oak wood staircase leading up to a half-landing, with a corridor to the left and a short flight off to the right.

Tina looked at her phone and selected one of her favourite play lists. If she was going to have to work in this miserable old building with its well-deserved reputation, she wanted to fill her head with Sam Smith, not with squeaking hinges. She inserted her ear buds and entered a world of silent tears, accompanied by the melodic pleading of *Stay With Me*.

The air in the cavernous hall had its own peculiar smell – not typical of an old house. It was pungent, and she feared it would linger in her nostrils long after she'd escaped. But that wouldn't be for several hours, even when using her super-fast ultrasonic measurer. She had no idea how many rooms there were but, judging from the exterior and the number of keys on the bunch, she was going to be alone in the house for way too long.

Determined to suppress her fears, she twisted the telescopic legs on her tripod and fixed the camera to the screw fitting. Looking at the screen on her phone, she terminated Sam Smith mid-song and welcomed Ed Sheeran's *Thinking Out Loud* into her head. After a few bars she terminated him, too. The music had to be more upbeat. She laughed at her choice and joined in the singing of One Direction's *Story of My Life,* a song she was too cool to like even when she was a teenager.

Nearly four hours of photography and measurements later, after jumping at her own shadow more times than she would admit to her boss, Tina felt boundless relief as she finally stepped out of the former boarding house. She closed the heavy front door, ensured it was locked and carried the camera across Hawksmead High Street to get a good angle on the entire structure, the last building before the High Street became the Old Military Road. It felt good to be outside, breathing in air that was sweet and fresh. Fortunately, whatever horrors lurked within the corridors had been quelled by a constant flow of her favourite music, piped into her ears.

It was early afternoon by the time Tina returned to the estate agency. Without saying a word, she hung up her raincoat and slumped down in her desk chair.

Trevor wandered over. 'Did you take all the measurements for the floor plan?'

She nodded. She'd never felt like this before as her mood was invariably buoyant.

'It's quite a place, isn't it?' he said.

She looked at him for the first time since getting back to the office. 'Nobody's going to buy it unless it's to knock down and they can't do that as it's Grade II, so it's going to stay empty.'

'You'll find some angle. There are people out there with more money than sense. And it's going for a bargain price. Of course it will sell.'

'I don't think so. It's the scariest and most depressing property I've ever been in. You do know its history?'

'Rumours and hearsay. It's just a building that needs revitalising. A little TLC. Anyway, I know you'll do your best. Get it online as soon as possible.'

Tina created the floor plan, which covered four storeys, and then turned to her camera. She transferred all the photos from the chip onto her computer's hard drive and set about selecting the best shots.

She was half-listening to Trevor's phone conversation when she saw it. She leapt up from her chair and backed away from the computer, her eyes fixed on the screen.

'I'll put it to the vendor.' Trevor ended his call and came over to her. 'What is it?' The swirling screensaver blocked the image. He moved the mouse and the image that had shocked Tina came back into view.

Trevor put his head close to the monitor. 'It's the Victorian glass. There's always a slight ripple and it's created an optical illusion.' He looked at Tina. 'Add in the clouds and you have another online hoax like the mystery ghost girl in Shropshire, or wherever it was.'

'Except, that wasn't a hoax.' Her voice caught in her throat.

'Every ghost picture online is either an elaborate scam or an optical illusion. You don't even believe in God, Tina. How can you believe in ghosts?'

'My grandmother is from Wern in Shropshire and that girl actually existed. They even know her name.' She knew she was starting to sound shrill.

'Really? Let's keep it real.'

She slumped back into her chair. 'Are you sure you want me to post this picture online, optical illusion and all?'

'Go back before the light fails and shoot the house from a different angle.' He took control of her mouse and deleted the image.

'Could you please delete it from my memory, too?' she asked.

CHAPTER THREE

Audrey Willatt opened the VW's passenger door as Tina hurried around to the boot to retrieve her cases.

'It's bigger than it looked in the photos,' Audrey said. And bigger than she remembered, aged fifteen, sitting in her parents' car waiting for them to return. She looked up at the imposing building and felt doubt creeping in as her bones caught the first chill of winter.

Tina hauled the two large suitcases out of the Golf's boot and placed them by the entrance to the driveway. 'I'll be off,' she said.

'Aren't you going to show me around?'

'It's bought and paid for, Mrs Willatt. It's all yours. My job is done.' Tina jumped into her car, but Audrey held the driver's door open.

'I think you're forgetting something.'

Tina dropped her head. 'Okay, I should've told you but it's not a legal requirement.'

Audrey waited for Tina to explain but the young woman seemed unable to find the right words.

'Relax,' Audrey said. 'It was up to me to have the building surveyed, but I chose not to. Unless the house is regularly flooded by the River Hawk or is about to be demolished by a new railway line or trunk road, I cannot imagine what it is you haven't told me.'

Tina licked her lips and looked beyond Audrey to the red-bricked pile with its dark windows and neglected garden. She gasped.

Audrey turned around to see what had caught her attention.

'Can you see it?' Tina asked.

'See what?'

Tina looked away from the building. 'Nothing. It was just a passing cloud reflected in the Victorian window.'

Audrey waited for Tina to continue, her patience wearing thin with the increasing cold. 'I'm getting chilled. Either tell me what's bothering you or come inside and show me around.'

Tina took a deep breath and looked down at her immaculate nails.

'You're going to tell me,' Audrey continued, 'so, you may as well get on with it.'

Tina looked up, resignation written across her blushing face. 'It's haunted. I was going to mention it, but – '

'You didn't want to scare me away.' Audrey looked at the exceptionally pretty young woman sitting in the driver's seat and wanted to give her a hug. She liked the way Tina presented herself. The pride she took in her groomed appearance and pristine German car. She didn't blame her for keeping quiet about something that Audrey knew didn't exist. On a more realistic level, even if the property was riddled with wood rot and rising damp, the house was still a steal at the price Audrey had paid.

'Terrible things happened in that house a long time ago,' Tina said, in little more than a whisper. 'I should have been honest. I should have told you its history.'

'I see. Well, as it was a school boarding house, I expect there were plenty of crimes committed in the name of education.'

'I should have said something. I'm so sorry.'

'It's an old house with a sad past. That's all there is to it,' Audrey said. 'Nothing to feel bad about.'

'I've got to go.' Tina closed her door and fired up the engine. She slipped the gear lever into first and was about to pull away when Audrey banged on the roof.

Tina lowered her window. 'What's the matter?' She looked desperate.

'Excuse me, am I a ghost?'

Tina stared up at Audrey, doubt in her eyes. 'I don't understand.'

'Do you think I'm a ghost, too?'

Tina did not respond, puzzlement creasing her brow. Audrey held out her hand which Tina touched with her fingertips. 'You're not a ghost.'

'Correct. And, as I am not a ghost and cannot walk through walls, perhaps you would kindly give me the door keys?'

'I'm so sorry. I'm not thinking straight.' She scrambled for her bag and pulled out the large bunch of antiquated keys. 'There are quite a few internal doors and they all have locks.'

'Why don't you come in and show me?' Audrey felt the weight of the keys in her hand.

Tina looked up at the top window, and Audrey saw the fear in her eyes.

'It's okay, Tina. Your job is done.'

'Let me take you back to the station,' Tina blurted. 'I'll put the house back on the market. No commission. You don't want to live there, Mrs Willatt. Believe me, you don't.'

'Goodbye, Tina. Please call in whenever you're passing.'

Audrey watched Tina drive off, spinning her front wheels as she accelerated way too fast. For a few brief moments, she contemplated reaching for her phone and booking a taxi to take her back to the station. Now she was finally standing by her new home, the enormity of her situation hit her, coupled with an almost overwhelming wave of loneliness.

She was a widow, sixty-five, slim, stylish, awash with life insurance cash and shivering, not from the chill moorland breeze or the threatening clouds, but from the enormity of the task she had set herself. What had seemed a good idea at her home in Kent now felt entirely foolhardy as she stood alone, by the imposing house with its tragic past, missing her wonderful husband. But it had been her decision; her choice to rip up the inevitable future that had lain before her in Sevenoaks and strive to lure out the truth that lay within the walls of the old school boarding house.

~

September 1965

This is the secret diary of Robert Oakes

DO NOT READ UNTIL 2065

I am thirteen years old and frightened. I am not very bright. When stressed I cannot get the words out. My parents took me to a doctor. He recommended vigorous physical exercise in an outward-bound school. He said it would cure me of my stutter and help me with my school work.

It took five hours for my father to drive my mother, sister, and me to the fifteenth-century former monastery. As we drove onto the humpback bridge, which spans the River Hawk, I got my first glimpse of my uncertain future rising up out of the moor. Why do all boarding schools have to be so frightening? Why can't people be friendly?

My father parked our car near the front door. School had not officially started so there was lots of room. I wanted to fail the entrance exam but it was so easy, even I couldn't achieve that dream. A woman called Mrs Barry opened the door and guided us through the various corridors to the headmaster's study. On the way she told my parents that I wouldn't be entering the school through the main entrance once they had gone. Junior boys had their own entrance where they could change their shoes and take off muddy sports clothes. She didn't speak directly to me but to compensate my mother gave me reassuring smiles, except she wasn't really smiling. We were told by Mrs Barry that Mr Gibbs was a mountaineer and had climbed Everest or tried to. Frostbite had got the better of him and we were not to be surprised by his hands, which every boy has to shake after lunch.

Mrs Barry knocked on the headmaster's door and walked in without waiting for a reply. The room was large for an office. My first thought was that he needed the space to wield his cane – surprisingly, it was my mother's first question. Brilliant news!! There is no caning – they have many other punishments that Mr Gibbs said were much more effective.

Mrs Barry left, and Mr Gibbs invited us to have a guided tour. He went into the history of the school; how it was once an abbey and then a hospital for people with highly infectious diseases before being converted into a school in the 1920s. Being an outward-bound school, there are lots of activities apart from rugger, hockey and cricket, such as climbing the high ridge, canoeing on the River Hawk, camping on the moor and at least half a day each week working on the school farm that provides much of the food eaten by the boys. My parents nodded politely. I shivered. All I hope is that I survive until Christmas when I can go home. Mr Gibbs took us back to our car, weighed down at the rear by my heavy trunk. He held out his hand to me and, for the second time, I had to shake his hard, stubby claw. I felt sick.

My boarding house is a tall building a mile away from the school, across the river in the local town. It has many locked doors that Matron said once housed workers for the local cotton mill. She showed my parents and me up to my dormitory at the very top of the house, which I share with three other boys. My sister was forced to wait in the car as Matron said her skirt was too short and would attract unwelcome attention from older boys. It's freezing in the house and it's not even fully-autumn yet! The cold truly bites into my legs. Part of the school uniform is that we have to wear corduroy shorts, whatever the temperature outside. My father helped me lug my heavy trunk up the stairs to the top room. My mother, under Matron's guidance, helped me unpack, as Matron says that all the trunks are stowed in the attic until the end of term. Luckily, I can keep my tuck box under my bed.

The moment came that I dreaded and feared almost more than anything in my life. My mother pulled her coat around her neck and I could tell that she wanted to return to the car before she started crying. Matron said that I could have a few minutes with my parents to say goodbye and then I was to go and see her. Outside the house, the cold gripped me – not the wind off the moor, but the unwelcome chill that emanates from every brick within the building.

Mummy gave me a hug and a kiss on the cheek and a pack of stamps so that I could write as often as I wanted, and she would write to me. My father gave my shoulder a squeeze and said, "Chin up old boy. You'll be fine. And remember, what I told you – think what you want to say and then say it – clearly. Don't stutter. If you do, other boys will pick on you and make fun." My sister hugged me and had to be prised off.

How could they leave me here? What have I done? Thirteen weeks lie ahead, but what sort of condition will I be in by the time I go home for Christmas?

I watched as the rear car lights disappeared into the rising moorland mist. I wanted to run, but there was nowhere to go. I have never felt so alone. I have no money as the school keeps my allowance and just gives me five shillings each week to spend on tuck. I went to Matron's private room. I knocked on her door, and she actually gave me a smile when I entered. She's quite old, at least forty. She told me about the bed sheets which I have to change once a week. We're allowed to change our shirts and underwear on Wednesdays, and on Sundays so that we look smart for chapel. Jockstraps are washed after every game. I hate the look of my jockstrap. It's so ugly and way too big. Matron said that she encourages showers to be taken as often as required, but each boy must shower every other day.

More new boys arrived, and Matron gave us jam sandwiches in the house kitchen. We sat there, silently eating, eight condemned boys thinking of home. The rest of the new boys coming to the school sleep within the main school building out on the moor – we're the lucky ones, Matron told us with a smile. I don't think any of us felt lucky.

After tea, we were allowed into the Common Room to watch television and to read a book. We watched The Man From UNCLE, but I couldn't follow the plot – my mind was hundreds of miles away.

Other boys arrived, older boys who turfed us out of our comfy chairs and called us names. We decided to go up the squeaky stairs to the loft room. In the dim light emitting from the bare bulb, we chatted and got to know each other. They all seem resigned to their fate, as though this experience is something that just comes with life. I know I'm here because it's my fault. If I were cleverer and didn't stutter, I wouldn't be here. This school is for boys whose parents are at their wits' end, or that's how it feels, although some of the boys seem to be really smart. I'm doing my best not to stutter and to avoid words that begin with 'W'. That's my worst letter. Sometimes my mouth goes into a spasm and my face contorts just trying to get out the word "where".

In the bed next to mine is a boy we have nicknamed 'Mini'. We're all small, but he's even smaller. I think we're going to be good friends. His real name is Small – that's funny. We all laughed – I hope he didn't mind. There's a boy called McGrath who's trying to take control of the dorm. I don't like him very much – I hope he doesn't read this. If he finds out how I really feel he'll probably give me a fat lip. The fourth boy is Phillips. His middle initial is 'L' but he won't tell us what it stands for. I don't have a middle name, but I already have a nickname – B.O. – short for body odour. They got the idea from the TV when a woman whispers into a man's ear telling him he has B.O. and that he needs deodorant. I shall write home and ask my mother to send me some. Mini told me that it's after my initials which are burned into my tuck box. But my initials are R. O. – Robert Oakes. Of course, Bobby, which my sister calls me, is short for Robert and Oakes is my surname. I've only been here a few hours and I'm B.O. – I expected a black eye but not that. I'll probably get used to it, but I'm still going to ask my mother to send me deodorant – just in case.

If you are reading this diary in a hundred years' time, ignore the printed dates. I want to be a writer and my English teacher at my prep school said that writing down thoughts and events helps to keep them in proportion – makes them more bearable. It helped Scott of the Antarctic to write down what was happening, especially as he knew in his heart that they were all doomed.

Am I doomed? I feel it.

CHAPTER FOUR

It took a while for Audrey to find the right key and a bit of courage to push open the heavy oak door and enter the dark, echoing hallway. She searched for a light switch and was rewarded by the flickering of a neon strip, incongruous within the Victorian setting. She dragged her suitcases into the hall and pushed the front door to until she heard the latch click in its keep. Immediately, she was subsumed by a pervading silence and a biting chill.

She waited a few moments as her eyes adjusted to the artificial lighting and to stiffen her resolve. Ahead, she knew from the plans she had seen on the agency's website, was a kitchen and laundry facility.

Leaving her bags in the hallway, Audrey went behind the stairs and followed a dark corridor until she entered a large kitchen which clearly had not seen much modernisation since the Second World War. She found a Bakelite light switch and sent power along old wiring. Neon tubes hummed and flickered into life, illuminating a white tiled room with an ancient cast-iron coal-burning range and a separate hob with six gas rings.

On the far side of the kitchen, below high windows was a deep, ceramic butler sink with separate hot and cold brass taps. Audrey turned on the hot tap, and icy water ran over her fingertips. Next, she checked the hob – there was gas, but no spark to ignite it. She made a mental note to buy a long-stemmed lighter. Prior to completion of the sale, she'd insisted the gas hob was checked by a heating engineer and was pleased to see a gas safety certificate left on the heavily marked, wooden worktop.

The lights flickered, and for a moment Audrey feared she

would be spending her first night in darkness. She had not wasted money having the electrical wiring checked as she knew it would not pass muster and needed to be replaced in its entirety.

Off the kitchen in the laundry room, she discovered two 1980s Bendix washing machines. She remembered as a child, her mother had been particularly proud of her Bendix. Audrey tested them both for power and was pleased to see the glow from two dim red lights. She opened the doors and checked the drums. In one, she found a few blue-and-white rugby socks and some strange-looking under garments. Audrey held one up to the light.

'Interesting. A jockstrap. I think you've come to the end of your useful life.'

She emptied all the old clothes out of the drum and onto the floor, closed the door and set both machines to a rinse cycle.

Next, she turned her attention to the boiler. It was a vast oil-fired Paxman, at least fifty years old. Although it had been serviced prior to completion of the sale, the engineer stated in his report that it was not fit for the twenty-first century, and he could not supply a safety certificate. Audrey decided to wait until morning before trying to fire it up. She would definitely need heating when winter set in.

Leaving one suitcase in the hall, Audrey grabbed the lighter of the two and reached for the burnished handrail. Perhaps it was the additional weight of the heavy bag, but each step she took was accompanied by a creak of welcome – or warning – by the old wooden stairs. At the top of the first flight, she was presented with a wall-mounted sign with aged gilt letters stating that the lavatories were to the left. She turned right and headed up a short staircase that led to a long corridor. On her left was a closed, panelled door. She turned the knob and pushed, but the door held fast. In the gloom, Audrey found another light switch, and filaments within a dusty bare bulb hanging from a plaited flex, lit up to provide a dim glow. Out of her handbag, she withdrew the heavy bunch of keys and sighed at the quantity.

'We have the front door, and possibly the back door.' She inserted the third key on the bunch and gave it a twist.

'Well, thank you. Somebody has applied logic.' She turned the knob and swung the door open, its dust-encrusted hinges groaning.

Fading daylight, through sun-damaged, moth-eaten drapes, revealed a room that was clearly once the house's grand drawing room. A magnificent, marble fireplace, long since cold, stood against the left wall and was one of the room's few original features. Bare floorboards, bowed and worn by years of pounding by pupils, squeaked with surprise as Audrey crossed to the window. She attempted to pull open the perished curtains, but the frail material came away in her hands. With her back to the window, she examined the room, deciding whether to make it her base, her bedsitting room.

She looked up and admired the ornate ceiling, with its plaster rose and fancy cornicing, and wished she was sharing the experience with Duncan. Missing him came in waves, and it was at moments like this she felt the pain of loss the most. She yearned for his relaxed company, his wit, his wisdom and, most of all, his love and, she admitted, his love-making. Her sons would not wish to think about that aspect of her life, but Audrey was not prepared to say adieu to one of life's great pleasures quite yet, although many of her women friends seemed to relish the moment when they could shut down that particular department. Their loss of desire puzzled Audrey; hadn't they worn the same mini-skirts she had in the 1960s? Hadn't they stripped off their bras and danced through the summer of love smoking pot to Scott Mackenzie? Hadn't they spent Saturday afternoons in record shop listening booths swooning to The Beatles, The Stones, The Troggs and The Kinks? How could their tastes have changed so much? Was bridge really better than an enthusiastic husband, even one bolstered by Viagra? Audrey sighed. She loved her friends, but she didn't miss their endless talk about money, house prices, and ticking off the next item on their bucket list.

The low sun was casting angular shadows across the stark walls as Audrey stared at the fireplace. She could almost hear the chatter of boys, sent away by their parents to an outward-bound school, far from home and far away from anyone who really cared. She shivered at the thought and determined to get on with moving in. She felt the drawing room was too big for a bedroom but ideal for a sitting room which, of course, the original architect had designed it to be.

It took another hour and fifteen minutes of heaving her suitcase and examining various former dormitories before Audrey settled on a room at the top of the house that still had a working ceiling light. Bare floorboards led her eye to a tiled, cast-iron fireplace with a scorched grate. There were four narrow iron beds with thin stained mattresses and a sash window with flaking paint and panes coated with dirt. Although there were no curtains to speak of, Audrey was not concerned as only a passing falcon would be able to spy on her thin frame.

She opened her suitcase, pulled out fresh sheets and made up a bed nearest the door. She searched the room for blankets and found a pile in a high cupboard above a bookcase full of classic-looking dusty tomes, clearly overlooked by cleaners for decades.

She selected a blanket from the pile, and when shaking it out, she noticed a faded crest identifying the school: Hawksmead College. She placed the blanket on her top sheet but decided one was not going to be enough. She pulled down several more that she discarded as they had moth holes but found one in the middle of the pile that looked good enough for the time being, until she could buy a duvet. She was just unfolding it when she heard something drop on the floor. She looked down and, to her horror, saw her gold wedding ring roll along a floorboard towards the window. Unable to move fast enough, she watched it reach a gap between the boards and slip from sight.

She dropped the blanket and rushed to the spot where the ring had disappeared. She put her eye to the gap, but the light was too poor for her to see. She got back up and looked around for her handbag. In it, she retrieved her phone and went back to the spot where she had last seen her ring. She turned on the phone's torch and shone it between the boards. Light reflected from several sixpences, shillings and decimal coins that had obviously met the same fate as her ring. Although the narrow light beam did not pick out her ring, she was confident it would be safe until she could get the floorboards lifted.

~

This is the secret diary of Robert Oakes
DO NOT READ UNTIL 2065

The first morning, this morning, I got out of my warm bed into the chilly air and hastily put on my new school uniform. I took my new blue wash bag to the washroom and cleaned my teeth. I found my hat and gloves and made my way down to the bike shed where my father had deposited my second-hand bicycle, which he'd bought for twelve pounds and we'd transported on top of our car. I knew my way to the school because I could see it across the river, rising forbiddingly out of the sodden moor. A few new boys from my dorm and the dorm below, looking as fearful as I felt, also gathered their bicycles. In the dim, dawn light, we pedalled past the old cotton mill towards the humpback bridge and into a terrifying new world. My mother's last words to me were to keep my chin up and to make friends with the other boys. I'm trying.

Today involved finding our way to the various classrooms, including the science block and the biology lab. We were handed books and tools such as a slide rule which Mr MacIntosh, the maths master, said cost thirty shillings and would be charged to our parents' account. I like the mechanics of the slide rule with its clear-plastic cursor but the multitude of numbers makes my brain hurt. I was already floundering, and it was not even lunchtime.

Sorting out the pecking order seems to be what the bigger boys want. There's no real structure within each year, so who tells whom to do what is decided amongst the boys. Everything seems to be about toughening us up.

Lunch – hooray, we thought. We walked into the great hall which is lined with long wooden tables and matching benches. Grace was said in Latin by the headmaster, who then clapped his fingerless hands and we all sat down. To welcome the new boys, the older boys ordered us to go and collect food for them and then they shouted at us for only carrying two plates, one in each hand. More experienced boys know how to carry two plates in one hand. I don't think my hand is big enough. By the time I sat down to eat, it was time for pudding. I was pushed off the end of the bench and ordered to get the gypsy tart and custard. I tried to carry three bowls, but I couldn't. When I got back to my seat to eat my first course, my plate had been taken away. I went to get pudding, but I was told I was too late – it was all gone. I shook my head and laughed to myself but kept my mouth shut. I could feel the stuttering coming on like a table lamp with a bad connection. At the end of the meal, the headmaster stood and clapped his stubby hands again.

"Today, we welcome new boys to our fraternity. There is much for them to take in and so I trust and expect older boys to offer friendly advice and a helping hand. Hawksmead College is more than a school – it is an institution where boys become men and we are unremitting in our pursuit of that aim."

Those were his words exactly as he spoke them. After lunch, I had to shake his hand again. I expected him to remember me, but I'm just another new boy.

This afternoon a trial was in store – games! Except, rugger is not a game. Games are fun, and rugger is not fun. We put on our sports kit and football boots and ran out to the rugby field. The sports master, Mr Tozer, gave us a brief rundown of the rules, which seem very confusing to me. I was placed at full-back, the last defence to stop someone scoring a try. A boy whose nickname is Elephant – he has size thirteen shoes – came running towards me. Mr Tozer told me to fall on the ball, but I knew that if I fell on the ball, Elephant would fall on me. I kicked the ball, and it spun off the field. Elephant gave me a push, which was better than being squashed. I don't like rugger. I much prefer football. Mini told me that I can get out of playing rugger by volunteering for extra work on the farm. I wasn't sure until I saw a boy called Kirby emerge from a scrum with a bleeding mouth and scratches on his cheek. Why am I here? *WHY?????*

On our second morning, the new boys in my house had to go to the sanatorium. We were told not to pee when we woke up, so all of us were bursting by the time we had cycled over the bridge and along the Old Military Road to the school some bright spark had placed in the middle of a damp moor. The school nurse gave us each a glass jar and we had to pee into it right in front of her. I filled mine to halfway but, Pearson, a big boy in the dorm below, kept on peeing until the jar was full and over-flowed. The nurse was not happy. I thought it was very funny until I was called into a room where there was an old man called Doctor Jefferies. He told me to drop my shorts and underpants and then he felt my balls. I have never been so embarrassed.

~

Audrey closed the front door of her new home and stepped out to find a place to eat. The bunch of keys given to her by Tina weighed heavily in her handbag and she made a mental note to remove the ones she needed to open her front door.

Daylight was dwindling fast as she walked down her gravel drive. There was no gate at its mouth but Audrey saw the old steel fixings where a gate had once been positioned. She turned around and looked back at her new purchase. It was a detached, imposing residence, set in its own walled garden, and would once have been the home of a wealthy merchant before being turned into a boarding house for mill workers and then pupils attending the school out on the moor.

She decided to explore her garden while there was still enough twilight to see. The grass was high after a wet and warm summer, but excessive shrub growth had been cut back prior to sale. Audrey liked gardening, but the extent of the work to be done to restore her new garden to its former glory required the skills of a professional and, more importantly, professional equipment. She admired the old brick wall that bordered her property and the mature trees that gave her house privacy. Not that she wanted to exclude people; quite the opposite, she wanted to attract the curious and, possibly, the guilty.

The damp, long grass had soaked her shoes and feet, but Audrey was not worried as she stepped from her drive into Hawksmead High Street. To her right stretched the Old Military Road that cut through the moorland wilderness; to her left was a pavement leading to Hawksmead Methodist Chapel, an early Victorian construct in red brick and stone, with a modest spire. The church would, no doubt, have been built to provide a place of worship for mill workers; not too grand or beautiful, but a physical presence to remind hardworking weavers that God was all knowing, all powerful. Audrey liked visiting churches and looked forward to hearing its bells on Sunday morning.

She may even attend a service, more for the communion of fellow parishioners than for kneeling in the presence of a constructed deity. Lying in on Sunday mornings was in her past. Sitting in bed with a cup of tea and sharing the Sunday Times with her husband, reading articles to each other, was one of the many joys from her marriage she missed.

She continued on down the High Street which was lit by Victorian lamp posts emitting sodium-coloured light. The air had a damp chill, and she made another mental note to buy some warmer clothes. Hawksmead was a small town, exhibiting enough human life to make it thrive and affording Audrey ample opportunity to say "Good evening". In many ways, walking alone made it easier for her to talk to strangers than if she'd been part of a couple; also, being of a certain vintage, passers-by were not as wary of her as they would usually be of a stranger in their midst with a distinctly southern accent.

The bow window of a news agency caught her eye, and she stopped to look at the goods on display; a mix of practical items for the office, including a variety of hole punchers, plastic folders, treasury tags and a wide selection of staplers. There were also a few plastic toys for young children, including hideous masks for Halloween. What attracted Audrey was a selection of handwritten postcards stuck in the window. She was not looking for anything in particular, but she always enjoyed reading cards advertising products and services. She opened her bag, removed her spectacles and used her phone's torch to read some of the messages. One in particular interested her and she sent a short text to herself, noting the phone number.

She went into the shop and purchased a gas-powered candle lighter, which she popped into her handbag as she carried on down the High Street. Across the road, she was pleased to see Merlin's Hardware Store. On the sign was a drawing of a bearded man holding a long staff above a marketing slogan: *A Wizard Way to Work*. Was this the one corner of the world where Harry Potter had yet to reach? Audrey laughed and continued on. Apart from a few awkward exchanges, her approaches to passers-by were rewarded with plenty of welcomes and good lucks.

'I hope you'll be very happy here,' said a tall Irishman, with a crooked back and a walking stick. 'Have you bought on the Hawk estate?'

'No,' Audrey replied.

'I hear the sound-proofing is non-existent and owners are already complaining about mould. My firm tendered for the construction, but we were undercut by a Russian outfit with an Olde English-sounding name that fooled the council. Or, perhaps it was cash in brown envelopes that swung the deal in their favour. Affordable homes? That's a joke. I protested, got a campaign together, and then had an accident. You go figure.'

Audrey was momentarily taken aback by the onslaught but regained her composure. 'My new home is the old school boarding house at the top of the town.'

The Irishman's mouth fell open, and Audrey waited for him to comment. What came out was a mirthless cackle followed by a loose cough. Struggling for breath, he carried on making his observations.

'So, you own the old school boarding house? I thought the Russians had it. Well, you do surprise me. We considered turning it into flats, but it's not really viable for conversion. I expect the Russians planned to burn it down, but you trumped them. Anyway, I wish you all the best, but be careful walking down the stairs. The floorboards are very uneven.'

'Is that how you hurt yourself?' She was beginning to regret starting the conversation.

'The executors for Hawksmead College invited a number of contractors to take a look around and bid for the property – including the Dryomov brothers. I tripped at the top of the stairs that go down into the main hall, but I could've sworn I felt a Russian paw push me from behind.' He lifted his walking stick, which was made of aged oak with a rounded end that fitted into the palm of his hand, and held it out to Audrey. 'Take this.'

She made no move to take the stick.

'Those Russkies don't give up easily. Keep this near you when alone in the house, and use it if those vodka swilling bastards ever cause you any trouble. And, believe you me, they will.'

'I think your need is greater than mine, but thank you for the insight – very much appreciated. It's been a pleasure to meet you Mr – ?'

'Hyde.'

She offered her hand. 'Audrey Willatt.'

'My advice to you, Mrs Willatt, is sell to the Russians and get the hell out.' He left her hand outstretched and hobbled away.

~

A few days have passed since my last entry and I'm beginning to get used to the way things are done. My father was in the army during the war. He said that being in the ranks with thugs was more dangerous than fighting the Japanese. He got away from them by joining the Military Police. I don't want to join anything. I just want to go home.

Each morning, I wake up in our freezing dorm, quickly pull on my clothes and go down to clean my teeth. My toothpaste is all used up. Other boys steal it. I went into town and bought Eucryl tooth powder. They don't like that. Nobody steals it. I'm learning.

Mini and I are becoming good friends. We cycle to school together and generally try to watch out for each other. People like him. They don't like me so much. I still don't know how to use a slide rule, and that is really bothering me. Mr MacIntosh is not friendly. He doesn't hit us, but to be called a numbskull is not nice – but, it could be worse.

Today, I went to a woodworking class and met some older boys. I always try to sit to one side of a class and near the front. Bad boys always sit at the back, and my theory is that the master will look over me to the trouble-makers at the rear. But woodworking is different as it's a room with loads of workbenches that we have to share. Our first task was to practise using the tools, such as the vice, the lathe and various chisels. I could hear whispering behind me. At first, I thought they were joking, but it started to get a bit heated. Mr Cooper, the master, seemed preoccupied at the front, using a lathe to carve a candlestick-type of lamp. He was making a lot of noise but even he turned when he heard a high-pitched scream. I looked around and saw a boy with his cheek slashed open – blood was pouring down his chin and onto his shirt. The room went quiet. A boy holding a chisel tossed it onto the bench and claimed it was an accident.

Mr Cooper told me to get help. I ran out of the room and into the corridor. I saw some older boys and ran up to them, but they pushed me away before I could stutter a word. I ran out of the building and across an open area towards the headmaster's study. I tried to open a door, but it was bolted on the inside. I thought about the boy bleeding to death because I couldn't get help. I ran around the whole building, searching for a way in. The only door I knew for sure that would be open was the main entrance. I could hardly breathe when I pushed open the heavy front door. I tried to remember the way to the headmaster's study.

I was running down a corridor when my English master shouted at me to stop running. I was so relieved, I went up to him and tried to find the right words. All that would come out was 'Help!'. The master gripped my arms and looked into my face. I think he could see how worried I was. I managed to tell him what had happened. He hurried off, and I sat on a bench. I didn't know what to do. I thought rugger was bad enough, but this was serious. When I was eight, I got attacked by a dog and needed stitches. I looked at the scar on my wrist and knew that the boy would have a very long scar on his face. What would they do with the other boy? I haven't seen him since. I don't think it was an accident.

The woodworking class was the last of the day. I was too scared to go back and see all the blood. I met Mini for tea in the main dining room, or refectory as the school calls it. He told me that Mr Cooper had been in a panic. He tried to stop the blood and was cursing me for taking so long to get help. Mini told me that some boys in the school are not normal. They've done something bad and their parents had a choice of their sons either going to a government approved school called Borstal or an outward-bound school, if the parents could afford the fees. The judges think that exercise will sort out the boys; reduce their anger and violence. I don't think my parents realised this when they agreed to send me here. Now, it really is a matter of getting through to Christmas.

CHAPTER FIVE

The Falcon had no pretensions of being a gastro-pub, but Audrey liked the look of the sandwiches and put in an order. Ted and Heather, who were the licensees for the popular chain, had managed to create a personalised environment. Although the decor clearly followed the brewery's company lines, extra little touches were distinctly Hawksmead, especially the old framed photographs taken of the local cricket team, the rugby club, and summer fetes held in the grounds of Hawksmead College. Audrey was particularly drawn to a monochrome photo of a school play and asked Ted why he had it in his pub.

'Ah, well, I wasn't always a publican,' he confessed with a smile. 'Believe it or not, when I was a boy at Hawksmead College, I did not plan to spend my days pulling pints and rolling out the barrels.'

Audrey slipped on her spectacles and examined the photo more closely, which was entitled: *Cyrano de Bergerac*. She looked at the tall, imposing publican.

'I know what you're, thinking,' Ted said. 'You're wondering how a slim, handsome, young actor became a florid, stout-of-girth landlord. Well – ' he indicated the pub, 'this is now my stage and my customers are all my players, bit parts, one and all.' He laughed at his own joke.

'Tell her who you played,' called out Heather, Ted's wife, as she carried used glasses back to the bar. She was the exact opposite of Ted: slim, petite and blonde.

'I'm sure the lady can determine simply by looking at my handsome visage,' Ted responded.

Audrey turned and examined the black-and-white print more closely; the name of each character was printed below the teenage actor playing the role. 'I don't think you were Cyrano – you don't have the nose. I don't see you as Comte de Guiche or Le Bret. And you're much too commanding to have played one of the pastry chefs.' She moved her head closer to the photograph and looked into the eyes of Roxane, the focus of Cyrano's passion. After a few moments, she put away her spectacles and approached the bar. 'You'll have to tell me.'

Ted slid a gin and tonic across the polished rosewood counter. 'It's a G & T to welcome you to our fair town.'

'Thank you.' Audrey picked up the glass and only put it back down when it contained nothing more than crushed ice and a slice of lemon. She patted her chest. 'That was a surprise – but very good.'

'Here's another surprise.'

Audrey looked across at a man sitting on a bar stool, his face red and bloated.

'Most people think Roxane was played by a girl. After all, she was very beautiful – but *he* lacked the necessary.' The man used his artisan hands to outline a pair of breasts.

Ted looked at the large clock on the wall with Roman numerals. 'Isn't it your bedtime, Vincent?'

'Have you not heard? They closed the mill more than a quarter of a century ago. There is no longer a morning horn calling workers to the looms. These days, I wake up to the gentle sounds of Ken Bruce on Radio 2.'

'Barman!' Audrey called, with a laugh in her voice. 'The same again for my friend.'

Ted grunted and exchanged a look with his wife as he pulled another pint of The Edge.

'What happened to Roxane? The boy who played her?' Audrey asked, moving closer to the old soak. 'You appear to know a lot about him.'

'Where are you from, lady?'

Audrey hesitated for a moment. 'Kent. Sevenoaks to be precise.'

'Been here long?'

'A few hours. I've bought the old school boarding house at

the end of the High Street.'

Ted placed the pint of ale in front of Vincent and removed his empty glass.

'To you, good lady,' Vincent said, lifting his tankard. 'May your time in our fair town be pleasant.' He put the glass to his lips and opened his gullet. After three long pulls, the pint was gone, and he slammed the empty tankard back on the counter. He controlled a rising belch then through red-rimmed eyes he focused on Audrey. 'The old school boarding house – if only walls could talk.' He almost slipped off his stool, but regained his balance as he stood to give a mock bow.

'Madame. Before you stands – ' This time he failed to suppress the belch and grimaced as beer mixed with stomach acid surfaced into his mouth. Audrey waited for him to swallow and recover. 'Madame. Before you stands Cyrano de Bergerac – poet, musician, philosopher, swordsman – and Roxane's one true love.' He wiped away an escaping tear and sniffed, hard.

'It's fifty years, Vincent. It's time you came out of character,' Ted said from behind the bar.

'How can I? I loved her. We all did. None of us will ever forget what happened.' He meandered to the door.

'He's too smart for his own good,' Ted commented to Audrey. 'Clever, gifted, but he's allowed an unfortunate incident to cloud his entire life. Real shame.'

Audrey watched Vincent pull open the door and stagger into the chilly night. She turned to Ted and ordered a half pint of The Edge. With her drink for company, she selected an oak booth and settled back into the old, red leather padded bench. A few moments later, Heather delivered a plate of pork and applesauce sandwiches.

'Is that going to be enough?' Heather asked.

'I'm not a big eater.'

'Unlike me. What's the secret?'

'Fear. Fear of putting on weight at my ballet school and fear of putting on weight as a photographic model.'

'Then you've got a bit of catching up to do. Let me make you another round. Or, I've a lovely Bakewell pudding aching to be eaten. It looks like a squashed cowpat but it's delicious. I'll save you a slice.' Heather winked and headed for the kitchen.

Audrey took a sip of The Edge and thought about where she was at the age of sixty-five. In story terms, she was at the beginning of her third act of a life she regarded as very fortunate. She considered the many forks in the road and the decisions she had made along the way and wondered what her story would have been if she had taken another route. More and more these days, especially since the death of her dear husband, Audrey would reflect upon her life.

'Last orders,' called Ted, which Audrey took as her cue to set off for her new home. Before taking her leave, she returned to the cast photograph from *Cyrano de Bergerac*, hanging on the wall.

'Christian. You played Christian.'

'Handsome but thick!' laughed Ted, as he loaded glasses into an automatic washer.

Audrey said goodnight and, a little reluctantly, left the warmth of the friendly pub. The walk up the High Street was chilly, dark and, much to Audrey's relief, uneventful. By the time she got back to the old school boarding house, there was light rain. She wondered how a building, on the edge of a small, pretty town could look so remote and desolate.

Snapping on the dim lights, Audrey paused in the large entrance hall and looked up the flight of wide stairs ahead of her. The air was still. What was she hoping to achieve? She closed the door, and the bang echoed around the hall. Any noise felt better than the silence. She walked through the hall to the rear corridor and on to the old kitchen where she made herself a hot milk drink, courtesy of her newly purchased gas lighter and a travel-sized milk pan. It was one of a few practical items she had brought with her, together with a travel-sized kettle, an old Philips FM transistor radio, and essential supplies including teabags, a pack of Rich Tea biscuits, a small tin of cocoa, and a pint of milk. Fortunately, the giant-sized refrigerator still worked, albeit without an interior light.

In the laundry room, she took another look at the boiler and was tempted to try and fire it up. Chilled air emanated from the tiled walls, and Audrey was in no doubt she was in for a long, cold, draughty winter. But she needed daylight and a mind refreshed with sleep before attempting to get the boiler going.

Standing in the kitchen, sipping her hot drink and looking at the faded white wall tiles and terracotta floor with its old fitments for appliances long since removed, Audrey felt a strange kind of contentment. She had come to Hawksmead on a mission and was determined to see it through, but she knew even the best-laid plan could take her in a new, unforeseen, direction. Keeping her mind open to fresh possibilities had helped to make her life interesting. She'd enjoyed her first evening in The Falcon and was intrigued by Ted. He had a wonderful, positive outlook that could only come from someone who had the imagination to enjoy the very best that life brings. He had been an actor but, like so many in that profession, he'd had to branch out. Ballet would always be Audrey's first love. She had often gone up to London by train from Sevenoaks to watch the wonderful prima ballerina, Darcey Bussell, perform, loving her stunning technique and effortless grace. Sometimes, Audrey's husband had joined her but he'd not been a theatre lover and often a long day in the office was followed by a long snooze in a very expensive Royal Opera House seat.

At the bottom of the stairs, steaming mug of cocoa in hand, Audrey looked up into the dark above and thought about the man she had met with the injured back. In the belief that houses reflect the spirit of the owner, she put on a brave smile and placed her foot on the first step, which groaned in protest under her weight. Very soon, she would appreciate that the old house creaked and howled at any excuse, whether it was from her weight on the stairs or from the wind that would often cut across the moor and whip the angular building on its way through the town.

Despite switching on all the lights, the impregnable shadows conspired to play tricks with her mind, helped by the accompanying creak of the floorboards. She wanted to hurry up the stairs to the cosy refuge of the top dormitory room, but she didn't want to spill her hot drink, so the climb was eerily creepy and slow. The house was cold, and although at this time of night, since the death of her husband, she always felt alone, she also felt a kind of presence that almost gave her comfort. Her rational mind laughed at herself, and she was smiling as she entered the top dormitory. Maybe she had been mad choosing a room so far from the nearest lavatory, but it was easily the cosiest. In time, she would move to another, larger room but, for now, this one suited her best.

She slipped out of her clothes and took masochistic pleasure in the cold biting into her thin flesh. She kept her vest on and slipped her nightdress over the top. Her phone was her link with the outside world, and she looked around for a plug socket for her charger. She found a Bakelite socket that was on the lighting circuit, designed for turning on table lamps from a wall switch, but her modern plug was the wrong size for the small, rounded holes. She moved a couple of beds and located a single, wall-mounted socket that had the contemporary rectangular holes. She plugged in her phone, turned off the centre light and climbed into the narrow bed with its strangely comforting lumpy mattress. She took a deep breath and laughed at her situation; she was lying on an old iron bed in a freezing room in a creaky house in an unfamiliar town and had not a clue what was going to transpire over the coming weeks.

With her eyes closed and the room lit only by a full moon, Audrey wrapped the thin blankets around her frame and drifted off to sleep. A cloud blotted out the moon, and the dormitory became almost pitch black.

A few minutes later, she stirred and opened her eyes but couldn't see a thing. She rolled onto her side and let sleep envelop her once again.

The moon reappeared from behind the cloud and cast a small, human shadow on the far wall.

~

She was standing outside the prefects' room, quaking in her

buckled, patent-leather shoes. The door opened, and Diana's piercing blue eyes stared down at her. Diana was head of house and not someone Audrey had ever warmed to despite her popularity with the other girls – her prowess at lacrosse having secured the winning goal in the inter-house competition.

'Come in,' Diana said, holding the door open.

Audrey had heard what happened to girls who were called to the prefects' room and felt the tears spring to her eyes. Somehow, she made her twig-like legs carry her body into a room she had never seen before. Through her blurry vision, she saw worn armchairs, an old oak coffee table with stains going back years, black-and-white framed photographs of winning lacrosse teams, and exquisite photos of the school's prima ballerinas. The door closed behind Audrey, and she heard the key being turned in the lock. Now there was no escape.

There were four prefects in the room including Diana; Sarah Woody, known as Swoody, who Audrey knew was brilliant at tennis; Elizabeth, the school's current prima ballerina since playing the lead role in *Coppelia;* and Victoria, a wonderful singer, who had melted the hearts of many of the girls' fathers when she took the role of Maria in *West Side Story*. Audrey was in awe of them all and terrified in equal measure.

Diana pulled a wooden box to the centre of the room and stared at Audrey who was trying not to wet her knickers.

'Step on the box.'

Audrey looked at the box and wished that she'd told the truth. But she'd had to protect her friend. Marjorie was on a strict diet. She was banned from eating sweets. Fat dancers were not allowed at the school where girls often went on to perform with the Royal Ballet.

'Step on the box,' snapped Diana.

Audrey moved her feet and felt wee trickle down her leg. Not much – she'd already been to the lavatory – but enough to make her feel even more self-conscious.

She climbed onto the box and stood there, not knowing where to look.

'Sing your name, girl,' Victoria barked.

'I don't understand,' Audrey said.

'Sing – Your – Name.' Diana repeated Victoria's command.

Audrey tried to sing her name, but it came out as a croak. All the girls laughed. It was a fake laugh to humiliate her.

'First position!' Elizabeth demanded. Audrey looked blank. 'She doesn't know the first position. Ha, ha, ha.'

Audrey shuffled her feet to create a hundred and seventy-degree angle – ballet's first position.

'Third position!' Elizabeth ordered.

Audrey moved her feet to second position.

'The girl's a fool. She really is dim. How long have you been here, Audrey?' Elizabeth asked.

'Nearly two terms,' Audrey said in a quavering voice.

'Fourth position.'

Audrey shuffled her feet and received a mocking round of applause. She could not believe her face could get any redder.

'Why have we summoned you, Audrey?' Diana demanded.

'Because I told a fib.'

'No! Because you lied to a prefect,' Swoody snarled. 'Do you know what happens to liars, Audrey?'

Audrey shook her head.

'Well, you're going to find out.' Swoody leapt out of her chair and reached for a heavy book which she held out to Audrey. 'Put this on your head.'

Audrey took the tome and carefully balanced it on her head. The dense pages made it very heavy. She had to stand completely still to stop the book from falling. But she managed it. Diana checked her watch.

'Now sing a song from Oklahoma,' Victoria commanded.

Audrey croaked out the first verse from the opening number, and all the girls laughed. The book fell from Audrey's head.

'Oh dear. You were so close, Audrey,' Diana said. 'Now you have to do it all over again.' She handed the book to Audrey who placed it back on her head.

'Fifth position,' ordered Elizabeth. Audrey tried to move her feet without the book sliding off her head.

'If the book falls off your head again, you'll be punished

much more severely,' Diana said with glee.

Audrey felt the book sliding down the back of her head.

CHAPTER SIX

Tina arrived at the estate agency early in the morning. Magdalena and her cleaners were just leaving so she was relieved not to have to punch in the alarm code as her nail extensions had caused her to set off the alarm on more than one occasion.

She was early because she couldn't sleep. Her usually impervious conscience was bothering her. She liked Audrey; there was something good about the older woman that had cut through to Tina's heart, and she didn't feel happy leaving her alone in a house that had such an awful history.

She headed for her desk and to her surprise saw two keys she recognised attached to the agency's identification tag. Trevor must have found them in the locked key cupboard and decided that they should be given to the new owner. She checked her watch. She had time.

The VW Golf came to a quiet halt in Audrey's short drive. Tina turned off the engine and sat for a moment, not wanting to leave the warmth and safety of her comfy car for the creaks, groans and worse that lurked within the old house. She opened her bag and looked at the two house keys. She could simply post them through the letter box but that would not put her mind at rest. Of course, there was an alternative solution: Tina had Audrey's mobile number. It was 7:45 a.m. so Audrey should be awake. She tapped her screen and waited to be connected but it went straight to voicemail. Audrey must be one of those rare people who actually turned off their phone at night.

Tina opened her car door, eased herself out, and closed it quietly. She walked to the front porch, took a deep breath of cold morning air, and pushed the old porcelain button. From inside, she heard the bell ring. She waited. She imagined Audrey hearing the bell, getting out of bed, and hurrying down the stairs into the hallway.

She listened for any sounds. The door remained shut.

Tina imagined Audrey waking, taking her time and being very slow as she walked down the stairs.

Still the door remained shut.

After more than four minutes, Tina rang the bell again. She was getting cold standing on the doorstep, and even the scary house was becoming a little more inviting. She gave the bell a long push and then slid one of the keys in the lock and opened the door. Immediately, she was overwhelmed by the gloom of the hallway.

'Mrs Willatt? Audrey? It's Tina, from Harper Dennis.'

She listened.

Nothing.

She walked towards the base of the stairs and called again. No response. She looked back at the open front door and thought about the safety of her little car.

'Audrey!'

Tina knew the house well from having measured it up and decided to head for the kitchen as that was on the ground floor. The sun had not made much of an impact on the day so she dug in her bag for her small, rubber torch of which she had quite a few stashed in her car. Many houses had unlit areas and hidden hazards, so a strong, lightweight torch was an estate agent's essential tool of the trade.

Tina opened the door to the kitchen and saw the jar of cocoa sitting on the worktop. As she stood there, holding the door, pondering, she heard the piercing scream of a child, cut off by the crack of a rifle or the snapping of wood. It was an ugly sound, one that she'd never heard before, and it chilled her blood.

She slammed the kitchen door and leant against it. Her hand shook as she opened her bag and took out her phone. She had a signal, not a great one but good enough. Should she call the police or her boss, Trevor? The police would take at least ten minutes to arrive and Trevor even longer. She put her ear to the kitchen door and heard the front door slam shut. Was she trapped? In her chest she felt her heart, pounding. She took a deep breath and pulled open the door. The corridor looked long and dark.

'Hello?' She tried to instil confidence in her voice. 'Audrey?'

She hurried along the corridor into the hallway.

The front door was shut. It must've been a draught. The temptation to escape into the safety of her car was almost over-whelming. She looked up the stairs to the first landing.

'Is anyone there?'

She climbed the stairs, each step creaking under her weight. Nothing about the house felt right. She was desperate for the loo and hurried down the corridor to the washroom. She pushed open the door and looked at the long line of closed cu-bicle doors. A ripple went up her spine and she shivered. She could wait. She wasn't that desperate.

She returned to the top of the stairs and looked down the long corridor that led to the dormitories.

'Audrey?'

She climbed the few steps and ran to the stairs at the far end.

She called again. She looked back down the long corridor and decided climbing the stairs was her only choice. She hurried to the second floor and was halfway up the flight to the top floor when a voice stopped her dead.

'Who is that?' it called.

Relief flooded through every vein in her body.

'Audrey. Mrs Willatt. It's Tina. May I come up?' She did not wait for a response but hurried up the stairs to the top land-ing where Audrey was waiting, wearing slippers and a dressing gown.

'Good morning, Tina. What a surprise.'

Tina did her best to control her breathing and held out her manicured hand. In her sweaty palm were the two front door keys on a ring with the estate agency's tag.

'I found these in the office, Mrs Willatt. I rang the doorbell but when there was no reply, I was concerned.'

'For *my* safety? You look scared witless.'

'I wanted to make sure you were all right.' Tina felt far from all right herself.

'That's very kind of you, Tina. As you can see, I have survived my first night.'

Audrey took the door keys out of Tina's hand. 'I'll carry these rather than the heavy bunch you gave me. Would you like a cup of tea?'

Tina was desperate for a cup of tea, desperate for the loo, but even more desperate to leave the house.

'I would love to, but I have an early viewing.'

'Perhaps another time. I'll see you out.'

Tina walked back down the stairs, ahead of Audrey. 'May I ask a question?' she said.

'Of course.'

'Why did you pay so much for this house?'

'I put in what I thought to be a derisory offer.'

'You could have gone in much lower,' Tina said, taking care not to trip in her heels.

'I wanted the house. I didn't want to lose it. Does that surprise you?'

'I can think of a couple of people it did surprise.' She walked down the long corridor, followed by Audrey and stopped at the top of the final flight of stairs.

The front door was wide open.

Audrey shivered. 'A chilly morning. I'm surprised you left the door open.' She walked down the stairs to the entrance.

Tina stared at the open door, then followed her down.

'Thank you for bringing the keys.' Audrey smiled at the young estate agent.

'No problem. I hope you'll be happy here.'

'So far, I've been made to feel very welcome.'

'By whom?' Tina looked back into the cavernous hallway.

'By the house. I think it's happy to see me.'

'I must go.'

'Please come again. My door's always open.'

Tina gave Audrey a tight smile and walked, as quickly as her heels would allow, to her car. She pressed her fob and the alarm beeped.

'I'm planning a housewarming tea party,' Audrey called from the porch. 'You must come – bring your beau.'

'I will. I promise,' Tina replied. She gave Audrey a cheerful wave and then her situation went from desperate to critical. She really needed a pee.

'Audrey? Sorry to bother you, but can I use your loo? It's the cold air.'

'Of course.'

Tina almost ran back to the front door.

'I'll come with you,' Audrey said.

'Thank you. I didn't want to go alone.'

Audrey laughed and closed the front door. Tina followed her up the stairs and down the corridor to the washroom.

'Audrey, are you just putting on a brave face, or does this house really not bother you?'

'It doesn't bother me one jot.' Audrey opened the door to the washroom and held it for Tina, who stopped dead.

'What is it?'

Tina couldn't move. Every cubicle door was wide open. If she hadn't been bursting, she'd have run screaming from the house.

CHAPTER SEVEN

Audrey watched Tina back out of the drive and then hurried to the lavatories; the cold air was affecting her, too. She selected a cubicle and sat down, leaving the door open. Although the old wooden walls were scrawled with insults, rude words and even ruder drawings, Audrey came from tough enough stock not to be intimidated. When she pulled the chain with its decorative porcelain handle, the rush of water was a comforting sound.

She decided to test the showers, which were located around a corner from the lavatory cubicles and washbasins. They were in a large open area that had several shower heads and drains, affording no privacy. She imagined how vulnerable young boys must have felt when using them. Audrey kicked off her slippers and hung her dressing gown on one of many old iron hooks. She turned a knob and leapt back as icy water was forced out of the old brass showerhead. The boiler was off, and she was not in the mood for a cold drenching.

She wrapped her dressing gown around her shivering body and slid her feet back into her slippers. She pulled open the door and hurried down the corridor. The house felt especially bitter, so getting the old boiler going was now a priority. At the top of the stairs, the sole of her slipper caught on an uneven floorboard. Her foot came out and the vast void of the open staircase came to meet her. She flailed the air with her right hand searching for a purchase and her fingers found the burnished dome of a finial at the top of a newel post. Audrey swung round on her slender arm and slammed into the handrail and balusters. The weight of her upper body lifted her feet from the stair tread and she could feel herself going over the banister. She screamed.

No!

This could not be it. This was not why she had come to this desolate house.

Somehow, she managed to regain her balance and sat on the stairs, shaking with fear. She reached up for her slipper and made a mental note to fix the uneven floorboard. She knew she had been lucky, unlike Mr Hyde, whom she had met last night, hobbling along the High Street, condemned to back pain for the rest of his life.

The nameplate informed her it was a *Paxman Autonomic Oil-Fired Boiler*. In a stained and cracked plastic folder was an instruction manual, but Audrey did not have her glasses. In Sevenoaks, her father had installed an oil-fired boiler and she remembered watching him fire it up. She found the water stop-cock and aligned the handle to the pipe. The tap to the oil pipe was very stiff but, using the old jockstrap to protect her hand, she managed to twist it open. It took a further eight minutes of experimentation before she heard a frightening roar coming from the furnace. Toxic fumes caught in her throat, reminding her to open the exhaust flue. Satisfied with her handiwork, she looked through the thick glass viewer at the ferocious power of the flames.

The shower room was still freezing cold as she slipped off her slippers and hung her dressing gown on a hook. She turned on a tap and, surprisingly quickly, the room filled with steam.

Luxuriating in the warmth of the hot streams of water, she considered her situation. She had come to Hawksmead for a reason, but first, she must deal with practicalities, such as buying food from the local shops, and arnica for her recently acquired bruises.

She turned off the water and dried herself as quickly as she could in the rapidly cooling shower room. She shuffled into her slippers and pulled on her dressing gown as she walked back into the main washroom area. She noticed that the old mirrors were all steamed up, and was about to wipe a mirror clear when she changed her mind.

'Probably for the best,' she laughed, picking up a comb for her wet hair.

If she had wiped the mirror, she may have noticed the reflection of a young boy in corduroy shorts, standing by one of the lavatory cubicles.

~

This is the secret diary of Robert Oakes
DO NOT READ UNTIL 2065

It's over two weeks since I last made an entry on these pages. My mother writes to me all the time and manages to fill her letters with lots of news. I am at fault, not my parents. If I were half as good as they are I wouldn't be here. I look up to them in every way. I haven't mentioned the chisel fight as I know my mother would panic – but what can she do? It's down to me to find a way through.

Something bad has just happened. McGrath wanted to read my diary. I said it was just thoughts. He snatched the book away from me and looked at the front which says – 'diary'. He started to read this, and I threw myself on top of him. Mini helped me get back my book, which I've now got to hide to stop him from reading my private thoughts. Anyway, Matron came in to make sure that all was well and gave us five minutes before lights out. I pulled my diary out from under my pillow and was just about to write when a fist came out of nowhere. McGrath punched me in the eye for not allowing him to read my diary. He just punched me once, but it really hurt. Matron is coming so time to hide you, my friend.

When I woke up this morning my eye was still hurting. All today, boys have pointed and laughed at me. I don't look good. My actual eye is blood-shot, and there is swelling and purple bruising all around it. I'm not going to punch McGrath – he wants to be my friend. He said he's sorry, but I know he'll punch me again if I annoy him. Perhaps he is one of the violent boys that should be in an approved school? I don't know. I just try to ignore him.

I have some good news! I don't have to play rugger anymore. The farm has an abundant potato crop and needs extra hands. The work is cold, back-breaking and dirty, but at least I don't have Elephant landing on top of me. I'm also excited about the cows. I could get to work with them and learn how to milk. I wrote home to my parents, and Mummy said that Daddy had worked on a farm at the same age as me. She said that cows are big and heavy and to take care. Elephant is big and heavy – I'm not worried about the cows.

CHAPTER EIGHT

Word spread rapidly around the small town that the old school boarding house was now occupied by a widow. People who had avoided the building ventured to take a look, with some even bold enough to ring the doorbell, keen to meet the brave woman who'd taken on the place.

Audrey was surprised by her new celebrity and quite enjoyed being the focus of attention. Perhaps her showbiz inclination from her time as a dancer and model was bubbling to the surface.

Lying in the narrow bed, with its worn springs, she felt welcomed by the house, even comfortable. She had been dreaming of her husband. They were both in their twenties, and she wanted to hold onto the feeling. But, as with morning mist, it evaporated the more she was awake.

Audrey was making tea in the kitchen when the doorbell rang. She glanced at her watch and saw it was only a few minutes past eight o'clock. Smiling at the prospect of a visitor and hoping it would be Tina, not just the postman – with whom she'd already spent quite a while chatting on the doorstep – Audrey hurried to the front door. She pulled it open and was surprised by the size of the person blocking out the morning light.

'I'm here to make you offer.' His voice was gruff and distinctly unfriendly.

'And you are?' She knew full well that he must be the Russian property developer that Hyde had mentioned on her first night in Hawksmead.

'My name Spartak Dryomov. You heard of me?'

'By reputation. Currently, I am not in need of any services.'

Audrey was surprised. She had expected rough, peasant features but standing on her doorstep was a bulked-up Rudolf Nureyev, the famous Russian ballet dancer whose beautiful, chiselled face still made her heart beat a little faster.

'I buy house. Cash. Today, if you like. More than you pay.' His blue eyes and dirty blond hair perfectly complemented his cheekbones, and Audrey fought the urge to reach out and touch his face.

'Why now? You had plenty of time to buy it before?' she managed to ask, slightly more forcefully than she had intended.

'I wait for price to drop, then you steal it from me.'

'Now you're being ridiculous. I think you should be on your way.' She attempted to close the door but the weight of the Russian leaning against the aged oak was too great.

'You hear my offer. That is polite.' He fixed her with his blue eyes.

'I'll tell you what is polite. Not ringing my doorbell at eight o'clock in the morning without an appointment and not holding my door open in a threatening manner.'

Spartak lifted his hands and backed away.

'Sorry lady. I don't want to offend. My mistake. I am not yet used to English way.'

He strode down her drive to a white van parked at the end, opened the passenger door and climbed in. The engine revved.

Audrey waited for the van to leave before re-entering her house and slamming the door shut. She knew the Russian could be dangerous, but she did not feel in the least bit intimidated; just annoyed with herself for finding him attractive. He had sex appeal, there was no denying that. She hurried upstairs to the top dormitory room and selected practical clothes for the chill morning.

She returned to the washroom to sort out her hair and make-up. Her dear mother had taught her never to go out of the house without first applying her face. Of course, when she was young, a little mascara usually sufficed but now, skills she'd picked up as a fashion model received more and more employment. Another skill she had learned as a model was speed, and surprisingly quickly, she was smiling at passers-by as she walked down the High Street.

The little brass bell above the door tinkled as Audrey entered the front office of *The Hawksmead Chronicle*.

'Call me Mystic Meg, but I know exactly who you are, Mrs Willatt,' Andy Blake said, a tall man with sandy hair and a beaming smile. 'How may I help you today?'

Audrey slid a sheet of handwritten paper across the counter. 'I'm having a tea party to warm my new home and I would like to invite the whole town.'

Andy whistled through his crossed front teeth. 'Ooh, that could be risky. Hawksmead is a good town, but there are some unsavoury elements – not that I'm xenophobic. But, you have no idea who you may be inviting in to case the joint, so to speak.'

'They're welcome to case my joint. There is, literally, nothing to steal.'

'Interesting point of view,' Andy said. 'I'll put your advertisement in for free if you'll agree to *The Chronicle* writing an article about you. Perhaps a photo of you standing by your new home?'

'Are you sure that makes good economic sense?'

He laughed. 'If I had good economic sense, I would not have given up my chartered accountancy practice and followed my true love of journalism by saving *The Chronicle* from folding.'

Audrey held out her hand. 'You have a deal.'

Andy shook her hand. 'I'll be sending my son, Tony. He's the best journalist this side of the River Hawk. If you have time to do the photo this afternoon while it's still light, I could get the article in for the next edition, together with your invitation. Unless something actually happens in this town in the next day or so, you may well make the front page. I can see the headline now – *Haunted House Has New Resident*.' He laughed at his own joke. 'That should attract a few readers. I may have to increase the print supply to the library.'

So far, thought Audrey, as she walked back up the High Street, her simple plan seemed to be working out. Of course, it didn't mean she would achieve what she set out to do, but at least the ground was being prepared to give it a good go. And, if her plan failed, as was most likely, she would return to Sevenoaks and meet up with her old friends again for bridge, and swimming at *St Julian's Country Club*.

Giant-sized meringues in the bow window of the Olde Tea Shoppe caught her eye and, on impulse, she decided to go in. It was quite busy with customers but a table by the window came free. Whilst waiting to be served, she watched the small world of Hawksmead pass by. After a couple of minutes, she looked in her handbag and took out her phone. She wanted to give her new home a good going over before the housewarming tea party and searched online for a cleaning company.

The tea shop door banged open, and a young mother with a double buggy tried to push her way in. Audrey leapt up from her chair, leaving her phone on the table. She held the door open, as the young mother manoeuvred the buggy between the tables and chairs.

'Thank you so much. I thought, while he's asleep, I'd stop off for a coffee. I may even get to drink a hot one.'

Audrey looked at the sleeping baby and at a pretty toddler, wide awake, sitting in the buggy beside him.

'You've bought the old school boarding house, haven't you?' continued the mother.

'Is it that obvious?'

'I'm married to Tony Blake. His dad owns *The Chronicle*.'

'Then you must join me.' Audrey indicated her window table.

'If you're sure. By the way, my name's Eden – as in the famous garden.'

'Audrey Willatt.'

'And this is my little Princess Georgiana – after Prince George.'

Audrey parked the buggy whilst Georgiana was helped by her mother onto a chair. Out of her large holdall, Eden produced a book and a small pack of crayons.

Audrey sat down at the table and looked at the sleeping baby. 'What's his name?'

'Officially, it's Charles.'

'After the prince?' Audrey tried to keep the smile out of her voice.

'The prince? Oh, you mean William's dad? No, not at all. It's after Princess Charlotte. But we couldn't call him Charlotte, so Charles was the next best. Anyway, as soon as I saw his little scrunched-up face, I knew it had to be Charlie.'

'He looks a little pale.'

'Yes, he's not himself at the moment. He had a restless night. I thought a walk out would do him good.'

Audrey looked around for someone to serve them and saw a handsome woman emerge from the kitchen, who waved and smiled. She approached the table, pad in hand. 'Hello Eden, how lovely to see you. How's your dad?'

Eden turned to Audrey. 'My dad and Eleanor dated in the seventies, but she dumped him when she went to London to sing with the English National Opera. He's never got over it.'

'I'm quite sure he has,' Eleanor said. She took Eden's order for cappuccino, and an apple drink and chocolate chip cookie for Georgiana.

'I would love a pot of tea,' Audrey added.

Eleanor peeked at the sleeping Charlie. 'He looks a bit pale.'

'He's not himself,' Eden responded.

'Back in a minute.' Eleanor headed for the kitchen and disappeared through the swing door.

'I love babies,' Audrey said. 'Would you mind if I held Charlie?'

'If he starts crying, don't blame me,' Eden said with a smile.

Audrey got up from her chair and gently eased Charlie out of his buggy seat. He slightly stirred when she held him in the crook of her arm. 'I think he may have a temperature.'

'It was up a bit when I took it this morning. I gave him Calpol. That usually works.'

Charlie's eyes opened, and he arched his back as though trying to get away from the daylight. His little cry was dry and pained.

'He did that arching thing this morning.'

'Mummy, wee-wee,' Georgiana announced, wriggling in her seat.

'We've just got her out of nappies,' Eden declared.

Audrey touched the top of the baby's head with her finger-tips and a great sense of foreboding shot through her body. 'His fontanelle is raised.' She looked at the baby's mother. 'Eden, listen to me. Call your father-in-law or your husband and get them to drive you and Charlie straight to hospital. Don't waste any time. Call now.' She saw the colour drain from Eden's face.

'Are you a doctor?'

Before Audrey could respond, Eleanor emerged from the kit-chen carrying a carton of apple juice and a cappuccino, which she placed on the table, ensuring that the cup of hot coffee was away from Georgiana.

'Sorry to bother you, Eleanor, but would you mind taking Georgiana to the loo?' Eden asked getting up from her seat.

'Come on princess.' Eleanor lifted Georgiana from the wooden chair. 'You're getting heavy.' She looked at Audrey holding the baby then carried the little girl to a toilet at the back of the tea room.

Eden grabbed her bag, hanging by its straps on the back of a chair and searched in its deep recesses for her phone. Audrey noticed her shaking hands as she scrolled through contacts for a number.

'What do you think it is?' Eden asked, without looking at Audrey.

'I'm not a doctor, but he needs to be checked over.'

'It's meningitis, isn't it?' She wiped away an escaping tear and spoke for a few moments into her phone.

Audrey handed the stiff little body to his mother. Within a minute an Audi, driven by Eden's father-in-law, pulled to a halt outside the window. Audrey opened the tea room door, and Eden hurried across the pavement to the waiting car. There wasn't a child seat, but Audrey believed that the danger to Charlie from the bacteria coursing through his bloodstream was far greater than the risk of a car crash.

Or maybe she had overreacted and sent mother and baby off on a fool's journey? She hoped that was the case because the alternative was a parent's worst nightmare.

She returned to her chair and sipped the cappuccino Eleanor had made for Eden. Her thoughts had been tugged back many years to a Tuesday afternoon when she had taken her first-born son to the local GP surgery. Typical of many new mothers, Audrey had bought every baby book she could lay her hands on. From her own research and motherly instinct, she knew that something was wrong with her baby but she allowed the doctor to reassure her.

The following day, her husband, Duncan, stayed at home to nurse their son whilst Audrey read and reread her baby books. There was no internet and nobody else to talk to. By the evening, both Audrey and Duncan were convinced that their son was seriously ill. They called their local surgery and a young general practitioner came to their house. Dr Manson examined the sick child, especially his chest area.

'I'm not sure what it is but I think you should get him checked out,' she said, writing on a pad. 'Drive to Farnborough Hospital, now, and give them this note. I'll ring and let them know you're on your way, and then I'll let myself out.' She picked up their phone.

Duncan drove Audrey and their son to the hospital, where they were greeted by a junior doctor in his late twenties, who was accompanied by an older nurse.

Ten minutes later, they were approached by another doctor. 'Mr and Mrs Willatt, we believe your son has meningitis,' stated the registrar, not wasting time introducing himself. 'But, to be sure, we need to do a lumbar puncture. I recommend you wait here.'

Audrey and Duncan sat and waited, stood and paced – few words passed between them.

Another ten minutes dragged by and then the junior doctor emerged from the treatment room. 'We have sent the sample we took from your son to the lab for testing, but we are convinced he is very poorly with meningitis. We have given him antibiotics while we wait for the results of the test; they should come through before midnight.'

Pneumococcal meningitis was confirmed, and Audrey and her son were placed in an isolation ward, away from other babies. At about 3 a.m., "industrial strength" antibiotics arrived at the hospital, and a drip was set up to administer the medicine. Not being able to find a vein in the baby's arm, the drip went straight into his little head.

Saturday afternoon, Ms McFall, a consultant paediatrician, spoke to Audrey. 'Your son is very sick. The next twenty-four to thirty-six hours are critical. If he survives, he is at risk of losing most, if not all, of his hearing and vision.'

Audrey looked out of the Olde Tea Shoppe window to the pavement, where just a few minutes before she had seen the young mother holding her sick baby. She heard excited chatter as Georgiana, followed by Eleanor, rushed from the toilet, and picked up a napkin to dab her flooded eyes.

'Mummy! Mummy!'

Eleanor scooped Georgiana up into her arms. 'Mummy's had to pop out with your little brother. She wanted you to have fun, so she said we could play with you.'

Audrey saw the girl's lower lip tremble as she took in this bad news.

'But where is Mummy?' Georgiana was now fighting to free herself from Eleanor.

'Georgiana, come and have your apple juice and then I'll tell you a story about a very pretty little girl who became a princess,' Audrey said.

'And I'll get your cookie,' Eleanor added, hurrying to the kitchen.

'What's her name?' asked Georgiana, sucking up apple juice through her straw.

By the kitchen door, Eleanor sang in full operatic voice: *'Her name is Georgiaaaaaaaaana.'* The patrons in the tea room stared at Eleanor in amazement.

Georgiana's mouth dropped open. Audrey looked at the toddler and arched her eyebrows, questioningly. 'And what is the name of the little princess?'

Almost in unison, the whole room sang: '*Georgiaaaaaa-aaana.*'

'Georgiana!' laughed Georgiana.

~

Hello reader in 2065. What is your world like? Have you heard of the Beatles? I like pop music. My mother likes Elvis – have you heard of him? My parents bought *Wooden Heart*. There's a lot of wooden hearts in this school, I can tell you. I hope people are nicer in 2065. It can't be much worse, at least not much worse than life in Hawksmead College for unwanted boys. I know I'm not really unwanted. My parents love me, and I love them more than anyone in the world. I do keep crying – in private. Nobody must see. Nobody must know. Not even Mini, who is now my best friend in the world.

My eye is getting better, but it's a good reminder to ignore McGrath. He's given up trying to be my friend and now just likes to make fun of me whenever he has an audience. "W...w..w.hat's the time, B.O.?" In class, he's particularly unkind, although the masters know better than to ask me a question. I don't understand why people are like this. Why does school have to be such an assault course? What have I done wrong? I'm good at English and love writing stories. The English master (Mr C) is the one teacher who doesn't make fun of me. He says nice things to me, especially when correcting prep. Prep is work we have to do outside of class in our own time. It's not exactly homework as we are very far from our homes.

I was happy today for the first time in a very long while. I got ten out of ten for an essay in English. Mr C asked me if I wanted to be a writer. I said yes, of course. My mouth was so dry with excitement that I decided to go to the drinking fountain. I turned the handle at the side and dipped my head down to the cold water. Somebody kicked me! I jumped back and looked around to see who it was, but nobody was there. A pinging sound caught my attention. I looked at the drinking fountain and saw a squashed airgun pellet in the bowl. I looked at my leg, and it was turning dark blue. The skin had split and was bleeding. Was someone trying to kill me? I looked all around me and then up at a window in a top dorm. A boy was pointing an airgun at me. I couldn't see his face. I raised my hands as I'd seen TV cow-boys do when faced with a Colt 45. I heard another crack, and some dust shot up near my feet – and then I could hear them laughing. I turned and ran back into the school building. The thought of reporting the incident never crossed my mind. They'd get me for sure if I did.

Fight! Fight! I was in the bogs, that's our name for the school lavatories, when the cry went up. I didn't want to see what was happening, so I stayed locked in my cubicle. It was Wilkins squaring up to Turnbull. I could hear the punches and the anguished cries. Both sounded hurt. Then I heard Matron who clapped her hands and told the boys to clean up and to report to her in fifteen minutes. She said that both would be deprived of hot cocoa and Wagon Wheels for a week – maybe longer if they didn't behave.

A lot of blood gets spilled in the bogs, mostly from people dropping shampoo bottles and not picking up all the broken glass. Shaving is also a hazard for some. A great "joke" is to nudge someone's shaving arm, hear them curse and then watch the blood flow. I have entered a mad world!!

Whoever you are, wherever you are, as you read my story, I hope your life is good. One day, I will be free of this place. One day.

CHAPTER NINE

'Hello Tina, it's Audrey.'

Tina was pleased but worried when she heard Audrey's voice on the estate agency's landline. 'Are you all right? You should have called me on my mobile.'

'My request is so mundane I didn't want to interrupt you negotiating a big sale.'

Tina laughed. 'Are you really inviting the whole town to your tea party?'

'Please tell me you'll come.'

Tina hesitated.

'I'm hoping this tea party will fill my new home with happiness and love. By the way, what can you tell me about a Mr Dryomov?'

Tina didn't know how to respond.

'Tina? Are you there?'

'I've not met him but, according to my boss, Trevor, he put in a ridiculously low offer. Fortunately, the estate's executors turned him down and then you came along offering a fair price, which is why we almost snapped off your hand.'

'Interesting. Now, re the tea. I've got the catering all sorted but I need a cleaning company. Is there one you can recommend? I've looked online, but as soon as I give my address they all lose interest.'

'Magdalena. She has an excellent team of Polish cleaners who won't be in the least bit bothered by your, your – ' Tina couldn't say the word. 'I'll text you her number.'

~

Today, I herded cows for the first time. They are BIG!!! I didn't realise quite how big, and their udders are enormous. I have to admit that when I was under a cow attaching a pump to the four teats, I was scared. When the cow mooed, I leapt back and fell off my stool. And, when a cow moves, there is no stopping it. And if it kicks – watch out. She can break bones. I love the heat that comes from cows. I am always so cold that I like to be close to the animals as steam is actually rising from them. I did taste the warm milk but I prefer it chilled or hot – warm feels strange. Tomorrow, I'm back in the potato field, and I know that I will get bone cold but it's so much better than having my nose broken on the rugby field.

I didn't cry today. That's progress. Or maybe it's because of my friend, Mini. We go everywhere we can together. Some boys call us "queer", but I don't really know what they mean; we just like being close. I don't stutter when I'm with Mini. He's taught me that in the right circumstances, I can be normal. I'm not different. He's given me confidence and although I can still feel a juddering in my brain, and I still fear the letter 'W', I am more confident, but still not confident enough to raise my hand in class.

Mini has told me that the school play is *Cyrano de Bergerac* and boys rehearsing for the play will not have to go camping on the moor for three days. Mr C, my English master, is producing the play. I like him, and I know he likes me because I'm good at English. But he also knows I stutter when I'm nervous. I managed to get hold of a copy of the play and read about Roxane who charms handsome Christian and his sword-fighting friend, Cyrano. The only role I have a hope of getting is Roxane. At my prep school, I was always cast as the girl. Of course, in Shakespeare's day, boys similar to me would always play the girl. I have found a speech that I think will help get me the role. I know I can act if I can just not stutter. Of course, if there were a part for a stuttering actor I probably wouldn't get it! Mini has helped me learn the lines. I thought if I learned a speech, it would impress Mr C that bit more. Also, it's so easy to trip up over words when reading from a book. Mini thinks I have a good chance. He's a tremendous support. Without Mini, I would have run away a long time ago.

I've auditioned! I stood in line and was surprised that nobody made fun of me. Perhaps they were all too nervous. Eventually, it was my turn to walk on stage. I have read the whole play several times and rehearsed my lines with Mini so there was no risk that my mind would go blank. As I stood on the stage in the grand hall, I knew that this was my one opportunity to do something special, be someone special. When I looked out into the hall, I felt Roxane imbue my body, and I became her – and she was perfect. I spoke her words, flawlessly, without a hint of a stutter, and it was the greatest feeling I have ever enjoyed in my life. When I finished, Mr C stood and clapped.

"Well done, Oakes. The best audition of the day."

I felt so good when I heard those words.

"But, I can't give you the role because I cannot take the chance on you not stuttering."

When I heard those words, I felt Roxane leave me.

"I won't stutter, sir. All the while I am Roxane I won't stutter. Please trust me, sir. I won't let you down."

Mr C asked me to read another speech which I hadn't learned. My whole body almost shook with fear as I looked at the lines. But then I felt Roxane's confidence flooding through my veins, and when I turned to speak, I knew that she was within every corner of my mind. And I got the role! I am so excited. Mini is also excited for me, although he is sad that I won't be going with him on the moor for three days. I'm sad about that too, but being Roxane fills me with happiness, with a joy I've not felt before.

CHAPTER TEN

Audrey couldn't help waking early each morning. Although the biting cold that blew through the old windows and corridors did not encourage her to get out of bed, the pressure on her bladder ensured she was downstairs making mint tea before 7 a.m. most days.

She hoped that by opening up her lath and plaster walls to the whole town, there was a chance that somebody would let slip information about what had gone on in the old house, even if it was second or third hand. Her husband was no longer with her; her grown-up sons had their own lives to lead, and she had nothing but old age to look forward to. If the nagging voice in her head was ever to be quelled, she had to act now. She owed it to her younger self. Occasionally, she had been a bit frightened of the dark shadows and accompanying creaks, but she would not be deterred.

Saturday arrived, and even for Audrey, who had been blessed with many special occasions during her adult life, it was a big day. She stirred the bag around in her mug and admitted to herself, as she sipped her herbal tea, that she was acting cool but did not feel it inside. She was nervous and wished her husband could share the responsibility. Too many people coming to her house scared her but too few scared her even more.

She took a shower, and whilst drying her hair she noted, with pleasure, the high standard of cleaning. The lavatories would be available for both men and women, which certain guests may find awkward, especially if some men decided to use the "piss wall", an apt description Audrey had seen scrawled above the antiquated urinal. But, it had been a boys-only school and so there was only one set of lavatories.

The rest of her house was also spick and span, thanks to Magdalena and her team of Polish young women working all Thursday and Friday to lift the inevitable dust that had fallen since Audrey had moved in. While the girls were packing up their equipment, Magdalena had taken the opportunity to chat to Audrey. She was tall and, in Audrey's eyes, a complete knock-out with high energy and business savvy.

'Dirt,' Magdalena said, 'is never in short supply. Cleaning is boring but essential. Work is plentiful as dirt cannot be cleaned, cheap, from a call centre in Bangalore. If they want to steal my clients, they have to come here and scrub, and there are no better scrubbers than my girls.'

She kissed Audrey goodbye and wished her much happiness with her new home and life.

'Come to my party tomorrow,' Audrey said.

'I would love to, but we have two big jobs in Undermere for local council.' Magdalena opened the front door. The air was cold, but she didn't seem to notice. 'Bye-bye, see you soon. Have good party. You should charge entrance fee at door – make money.'

Audrey stood in her porch and watched Magdalena walk to her van but, before climbing in, she turned and called out to Audrey.

'Say goodbye to your grandson for me. He didn't say much, but he looks like you – typical English.' Magdalena laughed, waved, and climbed into the driver's seat.

~

I learned something today that has shocked me. Mr Gibbs asked all the new boys to go to the biology lab. I saw a projector sitting on a bench and was immediately excited. I love films, and looking at projection equipment is especially exciting. Mr Gibbs entered the lab, and we all immediately went quiet and stood by our stools. I cannot take my eyes off Mr Gibbs' hands. They are so horrible to look at and even worse to feel. He closed the door and, with his first sentence, he shocked and embarrassed us all. I cannot remember exactly what he said but here is the gist. I hope it's at least a hundred years before anyone reads this.

"Good morning, boys. Today, we are going to learn about the re-productive process – not of frogs, which I know you have been study-ing in biology – but humans – you and me – how we got here. Now, the temptation is to snigger and laugh, but this is a serious subject, and unless you enjoy five-mile runs followed by a five-minute cold shower, I suggest you button your lips until I ask for questions."

He ordered a couple of boys to pull down the blinds over the win-dows and asked me to turn off the lights. He went up to the projector and switched it on. A blurred image appeared on the white wall across the room which Mr Gibbs brought into focus. The picture was of a naked man. Mr Gibbs picked up a ruler and pointed at the man's penis and his scrotum. He told us that this was the man's equipment for making a baby. Every boy in the room felt inadequate. The next picture was of a naked woman, but we hardly had a chance to look at her before Mr Gibbs moved on to the next image. It was an outline drawing of a man with his penis all hard and at an angle. Mr Gibbs said that when the man is ready to make a baby, his penis gets hard because of the extra blood flow. The next picture was of an outline of a woman's insides, and it showed her vagina, her womb and her two ovaries, out of which she hatches an egg or two every month. The man and woman have to time it right in order for the man to fertilise the egg. At that point, I was completely lost and turned to look at Mini. Even though it was quite dark, we were able to see each other. Both of us were thinking – why would we ever do that? And then Kirby put his hand up and asked that very question.

"When a man loves a woman," stated Mr Gibbs, "he wants to help her make a baby, and in order to do that he has to inject her with his sperm. The sperm are like wriggly tadpoles that are carried in fluid into her womb, and the lucky sperm is the one that manages to stick his head into the egg first."

"What happens if other tadpoles stick their heads into the egg, too?" asked Kirby on behalf of all of us, as we were all wondering the same thing.

Mr Gibbs said that only one sperm was allowed in and that all the others would be rejected. It was at that moment I vowed never to get married. I don't know what convinces anyone to do what Mr Gibbs showed us. Another boy asked how long it would all take, and Mr Gibbs thought that forty-five minutes from beginning to end was normal. Kirby, who seemed particularly interested, held up his hand to ask another question.

"Sir, what makes the man's penis go hard, and once it's hard what makes it go soft again?"

Mr Gibbs rubbed his stubby fingers together and considered his reply.

"The man's wife makes the penis go hard, and once he has ejaculated into her, his penis quickly returns to its normal flaccid self."

There was one question I wanted to ask and, for the first time in many weeks, I put up my hand.

"Please sir, how does the man make himself ejaculate?"

Mr Gibbs rubbed his stubs even harder as he considered my question. I felt my cheeks going red, but luckily the room was fairly dark.

"The man moves back and forth within the vagina, and at the appropriate moment, his semen ejaculates from his penis and the sperm swim as fast as they can towards the egg. That is how we all come into this world. The key points you should retain are that it is only something that you need concern yourself with once you are married. Some boys and men like to practise the ejaculation experience on their own, but that is not why God gave you a penis. It is not a toy to be played with. It is a tube to facilitate urinating and when you are married, to help your wife make a baby."

"Sir, is it true that if a man pees into his wife's vagina, she will die?" Kirby seemed to have a lot of questions.

"No, that is not true because it can't be done."

"But if he did, would she die?"

"It is impossible for a man to urinate with a full erection, so the question is not relevant."

And with that, the blinds were lifted, and Mr Gibbs asked Campion, a chubby boy who is particularly clever, to carry the projector back to the headmaster's office.

I am amazed that any babies get born at all. The thought of my father doing that to my mother is impossible to imagine. It is so horrible, I vow in this diary never ever to do that.

CHAPTER ELEVEN

The first part of Saturday morning, Audrey utilised her limited calligraphy skills making signs:

Kitchen / Tea Room

Lavatories

Common Room

Dormitories

The local florist had placed vases of flowers in every dormitory room to cover any remaining musty smells.

Eleanor had closed her Olde Tea Shoppe following the Saturday lunch rush and had come to help Audrey serve tea.

'But, won't you lose business?'

'I've stuck a sign on the door informing my regulars that if they come up here they can partake in a free tea.' She cast an eye over the vast quantities of sandwiches, pastries and cakes in the kitchen. 'I have to admit, your caterers have done a good job. Logistics could be a problem, but not as long as people form an orderly queue.'

Tony Blake from *The Hawksmead Chronicle* appeared in the doorway with his camera. He was tall, wiry, almost gangly. Audrey hoped that she had been wrong about the meningitis. Any humiliation was a thousand times preferable to another baby undergoing the treatment her son had endured. She tried to read Tony's face, willing him to give her good news.

'Charlie's going to be all right,' he said with a big grin. 'It was touch and go for a while, but all is well now.'

Audrey was shocked by her reaction. Tears welled up, and she had to blink hard to prevent the excess rolling down her cheeks.

'Eden brought him home this morning,' Tony continued.

'You saved his life, Mrs Willatt. You saved his life.'

Audrey could not find the words to respond.

'Would you like a cup of tea? No charge.' Eleanor smiled. 'We need to celebrate.'

'Yes. Brilliant. I heard there's free cake, too.' Tony turned to Audrey. 'Would you mind if I took a shot of you in front of your house? Dad wants to do a big feature on the party. It could run for two issues.'

'Go on Audrey. Now is not the time for modesty,' Eleanor chivvied. 'Don't worry. If anyone comes, I'll pour the tea. After all, I am a professional.'

Audrey walked with Tony to the end of the drive and he positioned her in front of the tall, formidable boarding house, and beside a makeshift poster Audrey had taped to a piece of board.

Free Tea & Cake
All of Hawksmead, Welcome

The words were underscored by an arrow pointing to her front door.

Several passers-by stopped to watch the photography.

'Please come in,' Audrey beseeched, 'and help me warm my new home.' Glances and smiles were exchanged, and an intrepid few turned into a trickle and then a stream.

'If we have another child,' Tony said, as they walked back towards the house, 'we're calling her Audrey – if she's a girl, of course.'

'But it's not a royal name.' Audrey tried to disguise how deeply moved she was.

'Well it should be. And, if it's all right with you, we would very much like you to be Charlie's godmother. Neither Eden nor I are particularly religious but, after what's happened, we want to be – and we want to get Georgiana and Charlie christened. Please accept.'

Audrey wrapped her arms around the young man. Even if her plan didn't work out, coming to Hawksmead had already rewarded her in spades.

Young families, couples, individuals, Tony's father, Andy, and many others, crunched down the gravel drive. In the kitchen, people shuffled along the worktop counter, placing sandwiches on rigid card plates before receiving a cup of tea poured by Eleanor. At first, the chat had been a little forced but as the flow of people increased, the noise in the large, antiquated kitchen, with its hard, echoing, surfaces, became phenomenal.

Children gathered platefuls of fairy cakes and American-style muffins. And near to where Eleanor was pouring tea, there was a choice of soft drinks in cartons with straws stuck to the side.

'Few newcomers to the town,' Eleanor said to Tony, as she poured her umpteenth cup of tea, 'could have made a more positive impact than Audrey has done on our small community.'

The cacophony of chatter and laughter in the cavernous hallway pleased Audrey no end. It was exactly what the old house needed, but she was not sure how much she liked being the focus of such considerable attention. When she outlined her plans to develop the property, plans she had no intention of seeing through, she was surprised by the reactions, which were invariably supportive.

'You've set yourself a mighty challenge,' stated Colin Turner, a tall, gruff man with a florid face and a solid frame. 'But there's not one person in this room who doubts your determination to turn this miserable old building into a new and exciting asset for our town; one that will benefit all the people.' In his left hand, he was skilfully balancing a large muffin on top of an impressive pile of sandwiches. 'I missed lunch, owing to a poor round of golf, but was comforted by the thought that I would encounter a very good spread here. As you can see, disappointed I am not.'

They were approached by a stout woman with a distinctive rather than pretty face. 'I'm the mayor,' she said. 'I don't normally wear this much bling.' She gestured to the heavy gold-plated mayoral chain hanging around her neck. 'Except when I listen to rap, of course!'

Both Audrey and Colin Turner laughed.

'You're quite a celebrity, Mrs Willatt,' continued the mayor. 'And despite missing an afternoon of jam making, I couldn't not come and meet you. Most people give this house a very wide berth, even crossing the street, so I'm surprised you've got such a crowd. I've bumped into many people I know, and we all hope you'll do this every year. You've created a forum where neighbours who pass each other on the High Street with barely a smile are now firm friends.'

Audrey offered to give guided tours around the house, but party guests seemed reluctant to leave the comfort of the large groups, which disappointed her, although she didn't know what nuggets of information she expected to discover.

'The Falcon has landed,' Ted said as he eased his way up to Audrey, who was trapped in the corridor between a crowded hallway and an even more crowded kitchen.

'How lovely to see you, Christian!'

He laughed and did a cursory bow.

'I suppose your wife is minding your business?' Audrey had quite warmed to the publican.

'That's the reason she's so pale – she will not leave the inn. Of course, the invisible ball and chain around her ankle may have something to do with it!'

'And, you have your regular barflies to consider,' Audrey said.

'It was much better in the old days when the law made us close. This all-day opening is killing on the feet!'

'Would you like a guided tour, for old time's sake?'

'It's more than fifty years since I was last here. I was glad I was a local boy and not a boarder. I'm surprised anyone survived this place. Some didn't, of course, but that's a story for a very different day. Now, as the Americans say, I'll give the tour a rain check as I have just seen an old codger I've not spoken to for a while. So, thank you for making today happen. It's brought all sorts of unlikely people together.'

'I've not seen Cyrano de Bergerac, yet. Do you think he'll poke his nose in?'

Ted took a deep breath and looked intently at Audrey. 'The Michaelmas term when Vincent played Cyrano was brutal, and he suffered, particularly. It opened a fissure to his heart that alcohol has yet to heal.'

Ted eased his way through the throng to the hallway and Audrey made her way back to the kitchen, her thoughts far removed from polite chatter and tea cakes.

CHAPTER TWELVE

'Tina. How many times do I have to say it? You're a good driver with great motoring skills, but you drive too damn fast.'

Tina had made it clear when she first dated Sean that he was always going to be a passenger in her car. Now they were late for Audrey's tea, and he was complaining once again.

'Don't start. I'm not in the mood,' she snapped. 'I never drive too fast for the conditions or beyond my capability. Why can't you accept that?'

She waited for Sean to respond, but he seemed to be having difficulty choosing the right words.

'Sean, do you accept that I am a safe driver?'

She waited.

'Do you trust me,' she pressed on, 'to get you from A to B, safely?'

'Yes, of course I do.'

'Then why do you keep stamping your foot on a non-existent brake pedal? It's annoying *and* distracting.'

She turned into Hawksmead High Street and drove past the Falcon pub.

'Is it just going to be tea, or will there be booze, too?' Sean ventured to ask.

'What is your problem, Sean? Does Derby County mean so much to you, you can't even miss one match? They're playing again next week, for crying out loud.'

'I was just asking if there was going to be anything to drink? Did I mention football?'

'You didn't have to.'

They sat in silence, both pairs of eyes fixed on the road.

Look at that,' Tina said, indicating the number of cars parked near Audrey's house.

There were no parking restrictions on Saturdays in Hawksmead, which was good, but they would still have to park some way off and arrive on foot, as every parking space seemed to be taken. Although she exercised regularly in the gym, Tina hated walking. She had also spent quite a bit of time polishing her lovely VW Golf. Now, nobody would see the results of all her hard work; a shining trophy of success at such a young age.

She pulled the handbrake on, and Sean opened his door and leapt out. He hurried around the rear of the car and managed to open Tina's door before she pulled the interior handle. Sean's love for Derby County and his desire to rush around opening doors for her were beginning to be a bit of a turn-off.

'But he's drop-dead gorgeous, Tina,' said Suzanne, an old friend she had not seen since they'd had an embarrassingly drunken snog at the school leavers' party. 'And he's lovely. What's your problem?'

'He's twenty-eight and earns half what I do. He's got no ambition. He ducked uni and only trained to be an inventory clerk to earn enough beer money to go out with his mates. It's not a future.'

'But you ducked uni too,' Suzanne responded.

'I ducked uni as part of my strategic plan to get ahead, not through lack of ambition.'

'Fine. You make the dosh, and Sean's your handsome plus-one.'

'But what happens when we marry and have children?'

'Oh my God, Tina – you're pregnant!'

'No, no, but I'm thinking ahead.' She had met Sean on a job when he was carrying out an inventory for tenants who were leaving a property, and she was measuring it up for a speedy sale. She had fancied him on sight.

'You've always been good at thinking ahead,' Suzanne smiled. 'While the rest of us were trying to pick the next X Factor winner, you were planning your career path.'

'Exactly.'

'So, what's the typical career path for an inventory clerk?'

Tina took a deep breath. 'There is no career path, that's the problem. It's the kind of job middle-aged people do when all else has failed. I want Sean to reach for more; to set up his own inventory company and be the employer. There's almost no competition in Undermere, and nothing in Hawksmead. In London, checking-in and checking-out tenants is taken very seriously, and there are loads of inventory companies; but here, it's much more relaxed, with landlords often doing the work themselves. Sean has a chance to corner the inventory market; but despite my less than subtle hints, as long as he has a bit of cash in his wallet, he's happy.'

'He's happy because he's got you,' Suzanne said. 'Tell him, he can't keep eating your gorgeous cake and having it too.'

The two young women looked at each other and both burst into fits of giggles.

'That came out all wrong!' Suzanne hiccupped, and it brought on another bout of giggles. When she had just about recovered, she fought to speak through tear-filled eyes. 'You know what the answer is?'

'What? Restrict the cake?' They both doubled-up with un-controlled laughter.

Suzanne searched her pockets as mascara tears streamed down her cheeks. Finally, she found a small pack of tissues and was able to wipe her face and give her nose a massive blow. 'Right. No more talk of cake. The answer is, *you* focus on earn-ing the big bucks and, when a sprog arrives, Sean stays home to do the childcare. Problem solved.'

They hiccupped in unison but were too exhausted to laugh.

Tina clicked her VW fob, and the indicator lights flashed con-firming that her shining beauty was locked. She took Sean's hand, and they walked at a brisk pace along the pavement to-wards the boarding house. Tina was not dressed for the cold – she never was; style was always her driver. As they approached Audrey's new home, she sneaked a peek at the top window and was relieved to see only clouds reflected in the pane.

'We should go up there,' Sean commented, much to her surprise.

The two crabbed their way between a Range Rover and Honda and, as they approached the open front door, were confronted by a cacophony of voices coming from the house.

'Oh my God, the whole town is here,' Tina declared.

The hallway was jam-packed and it took quite a lot of excuse-mes and close encounters for Tina to lead Sean through the chattering mass to the rear corridor and into the kitchen, where they entered the queue for sandwiches and cake. At the far end, Audrey and Eleanor were pouring cups of tea. They seemed surprisingly calm, Tina thought, bearing in mind the amazing number of guests.

'Tina!'

Tina pulled her eyes away from the array of fairy cakes and cream puffs and beamed across at Audrey, giving her a manicured-and-varnished thumbs-up. After much sideways shuffling, the young couple arrived at the tea station, and Tina introduced Sean. In return, Audrey introduced Eleanor.

'I thought you'd know each other,' Audrey said.

'Tina does not yet fit the profile of the average customer at the Olde Tea Shoppe,' Eleanor responded. 'Which is either the retired or young mums meeting other young mums with their children.'

'Mrs Willatt,' Sean said. 'I've passed this house a thousand times and always wondered what it was like inside. Is it okay if we explore?'

'Finally, somebody wants to look around. Please go into every room. Nowhere is out of bounds. Have fun. Fill the house with your youth and love.'

With a beaming smile, Sean took Tina's hand.

'Why don't we explore after we've had tea and cake?' she said, pulling back on his arm.

'There's loads of food. It'll still be here when we get back.'

Tina felt dragged by Sean as they weaved through the party guests towards the stairs in the hallway. For a moment, they were blinded by a flashbulb.

'Audrey's a really cool lady,' Sean said, keeping a firm grip on Tina's hand.

'I know this house backwards. I measured it up for sale. I don't need to explore it.'

'I bet she was really hot when she was young.' Sean almost hauled Tina up the stairs to the half-landing. He looked at the faded sign pointing to the lavatories.

'Maybe later,' he said.

'Well, maybe now for me. I'll follow you up.' Tina extracted her hand from Sean's and headed for the lavatories. She didn't really need to go, but she had to get away from him.

CHAPTER THIRTEEN

Sean climbed the few steps to the first floor corridor. It was surprisingly dark, despite the glowing bulb hanging on its plaited flex. He looked at a beautifully inscribed sign on one of the doors: Common Room.

'Common Room – for common people?' He laughed at his own joke, turned the knob and pushed open the door.

He wandered into the drawing room and took a few moments to admire the original plaster cornicing and marble fireplace.

'Impressive.' The door swung to behind him.

Ensuring he was alone, he went down on one knee. 'Tina, me darlin', would you do me the great honour – ' He shook his head and laughed and got back up onto his feet. 'No, she'll think that way too uncool.'

He wandered over to the Victorian sash window and looked through the grimy panes to the walled garden below.

'Would you like a wagon wheel?'

Sean spun round. He felt the hairs rise on the back of his neck as he searched the room for the source of the young voice.

~

Hello dear reader in 2065, I hope wherever you are, whatever you are, that the world is treating you kindly. If it is, it's made a lot of improvements. Poor Mini, it's time for him to leave for three days' camping on the moor. It's been raining hard for the last few days. I told him that he had to keep warm and laugh at every discomfort. Daddy says that laughing at a problem diminishes it. Mini is stoic; he may be small – he is Small! – but, he is strong and popular. I'm going to miss him – and I'm going to be alone in the boarding house, which I'm not looking forward to because it's quite spooky at night. Matron will be here, so I should be okay.

Today, we started rehearsing. A boy called Hart is playing Cyrano and he is very good. He doesn't like me, as a person, but when I become Roxane, he changes towards me. I'm a good actor. As Robert, I stutter, but when I am Roxane, it's like she's taken over my mind and body. I am her. I love her. She is beautiful and clever and sweet.

I have made a new friend. Paolo Ynsfran is from Paraguay in South America, and he is playing Roxane's duenna – a sort of older chaperone for Roxane. He is very nice, and I like him a lot. I have about eleven hundred lines to learn, but Hart has about eighteen hundred. The play has five acts, and Roxane is in four of them. I love her so much. I want to be her forever. I am so excited about the play.

Mr C fired a starting pistol during rehearsal for a battle scene, and it gave me such a shock that my knees buckled under me. He was cross that I'd over reacted, but I could tell that he regretted his words. At lunchtime, he said that he was giving us the afternoon off to learn lines and to rest. I didn't know what to do. Roxane knows all her lines. She is confident in a way that I will never be. As I was walking back to the bike shed, Mr C called out to me from his car and invited me to go home with him for tea. He drives an MG 1100, the same as my mother does, so it's nice to get into a familiar car. I like Mr C because he says kind things.

We drove to a house on the outskirts of Hawksmead. It's a nice place, smaller than my home but very cosy. It's nice to be in a homely environment after being so cold but, in a way, it made me yearn for home even more. He made a pot of tea and also put out biscuits and a jam sponge cake. He's not married and looks young. We had a good conversation about the play and how it was coming along. I am impressed by his plans for the set and am so excited to be part of something so big and so special. I sat on the sofa, and Mr C put the tray with the tea things down on the coffee table. I didn't stutter once. Not once. He made me feel so comfortable and he really does like my Roxane. He kept talking about her. It may be hard for you to believe, but people see me differently now. When they look at me, I think they see Roxane – I don't mind why people are nice. I just want them to be nice. I don't want to be punched or shot with an airgun ever again.

We talked about films and TV programmes, and although Mr C sat a bit close to me on the sofa, I enjoyed the sponge cake. After tea, he looked up film times in the local newspaper, and he took me to the cinema in Undermere. We went to see *Lawrence of Arabia*, but I didn't like it. It's full of cruelty. Towards the end, I asked Mr C if I could go into the foyer to make a phone call. He was reluctant to let me go, but I promised to wait for him by the box office. I rang home. I had enough pennies to make a call, and my mother called me straight back. She was so pleased to hear my news about the play and was absolutely thrilled when I told her about Mr C taking me to his home for tea. She promised that she and Daddy would drive up to see the play on the Saturday night. I am so excited. This is my dream. I am going to be an actor. I am not going to stutter ever again.

When my mother said goodbye and I put down the receiver, the film had ended, and Mr C was waiting for me. He said he was going to take me out for a meal before driving me back to the boarding house. We went to a smart restaurant in Hawksmead and I had Chicken Kiev. Mr C used his fork and knife to carefully pierce the chicken as he was worried that I would press too hard and squirt juice all over my shirt and jumper. He had a glass of wine, and I had apple juice. For pudding, I chose apple pie and custard and almost scraped away the bowl, it tasted so good.

Mr C drove me back to the boarding house and said hello to Matron. He reminded me that rehearsals were to start at 9 a.m. As all the boys are away, there is no chapel service. I shook Mr C's hand and thanked him for the most amazing afternoon. Matron was really nice to me too. She made me hot cocoa and gave me a Wagon Wheel which I said I would save as I was still full of apple pie. We watched some TV, but I fell asleep. She woke me up and walked with me up the creaky old stairs to my dormitory room. I like her. I don't know her name. We just call her Matron. I don't think Mr C even knows her name as he calls her Matron, too.

After three intense days of rehearsal, *Cyrano de Bergerac* is really taking shape. On Sunday night, the boys returned from the moor – cold, ill, bedraggled and much the worse for their experiences. I looked for Mini who thinks he has flu – or pneumonia, as he can't stop shivering. The showers are full of boys trying to get warm and clean off all the grime from the moor. In the Common Room, the talk is of two older boys who are missing. Part of the training was canoeing on the River Hawk, but the heavy autumnal rain has swollen the river, and they can't be found. Mini said that the river swept the boys down to the humpback bridge where a man saw them trying to grip the slippery stones.

CHAPTER FOURTEEN

Tina pulled the chain and watched the force of water swilling around the decorative toilet bowl. She opened the door and crossed to the washbasins, conscious of a tall, blond man washing his hands a few basins to her left.

'This is a first for me,' he said.

Was he talking to her? She was not a hundred per cent sure.

'I'm not used to sharing with woman.' He looked at her.

Tina smiled. 'It's a first for me, too. Some of the graffiti is quite fruity.'

'My name is Spartak.' He approached her with his hand extended. 'It is clean. I give you my word.'

Tina laughed and hastily dried hers on a paper towel. 'Tina Small.' They shook hands and she almost jolted from the electrical charge as her fine bones were encased by his palm.

'Yes, I know who you are. I wanted to buy this house.'

She froze for a moment, her mouth slightly open. 'The Russian brothers.'

'Please do not judge me too harshly. My brother is like bull in tea shop.'

'I had heard.'

'Well, it is very pleasant to meet you. We are looking to develop more land, more old houses. Point me in right direction, and I will make you rich.'

'It was very nice to meet you, too.' She turned away from him and headed for the door.

'Nothing illegal or immoral, I assure you. All I want is advance warning, so I can get my chicks in row.'

'Ducks,' she corrected him.

'I apologise. I am not being entirely honest. I would like

to take you out for drink because you are the most beautiful woman I have seen since I come to UK.'

Tina looked at the man who was almost twice her age and felt an overwhelming wave of desire, which shocked her. She couldn't help but compare her boyfriend, Sean, and his lack of ambition with this sexy man whose sculpted looks were complemented by his drive to enrich himself, a quality Tina profoundly understood.

'I bet you say that to all the estate agents!' The door opened behind her, and she jumped out of the way.

'I hope I'm not interrupting anything,' said a young man with a smirk. He headed straight for the urinal, unzipping his fly en route.

'Time for me to go, I think,' Tina said, and she slipped through the door which swung to behind her. She eased her way through the throng to the top of the stairs and looked down into the hallway, which was buzzing with chatter.

'I'd like us to live in a grand house like this,' whispered Sean into Tina's ear as he wrapped his arms around her waist from behind.

'Then you'd better start earning more money.'

'Don't worry – I've got plans. Follow me.'

He almost dragged Tina up the short flight of stairs and down the long corridor to the stairway at the end.

'Where are we going?'

'To meet your little ghost boy.'

Tina pulled back on his hand. 'It was just the clouds reflected in the glass. An optical illusion.'

'Really?' He led Tina up the next flight of stairs to the second floor. Boards creaked with every step they took. 'It's a bit chillier up here.'

'Can we go down?' Tina almost begged.

Keeping a firm grip on her hand, Sean climbed the final flight of stairs to the top landing. He let go of her and walked across to the window. 'Wow. Great view from here. You can even see the old school on the moor. Glad I didn't go there. It looks like a bloody prison or a lunatic asylum. Hey, I've got an idea. Why don't you go back down and take a photo of me at the window with your phone? See if I look like a ghost.' He laughed.

Tina didn't bother to respond. Instead, she entered the top dormitory room. Audrey's clothes were neatly folded on the narrow beds. On the windowsill was a glass vase with a generous bunch of lilies. Outside stood the oak tree, its leaves turning red and gold.

Sean came up behind her.

'Why is she sleeping in here? There's a much bigger room downstairs.'

'Sean, we've gone as far as we can. '

'You're right. Let's get out of here.'

'You go on ahead.'

'What about tea? Do you think she'll mind if we leave?'

She dug in her bag and pulled out two twenty-pound notes. 'Here. Take a taxi.'

He looked at the money then at Tina. 'What's going on?'

'Go home. We'll talk later.'

'Are you dumping me?'

'I'm sorry.'

'This is bollocks. I'm not leaving without you.'

'Please, Sean.'

'What if I can't get a taxi? They're always busy on Saturdays.'

'I'm sure you can cadge a lift off someone.'

'It's this house. You've lost your mind.' He snatched the cash out of her hand. 'Call me tomorrow when you're thinking straight again.' He swung the dormitory door back on its hinges so that it bounced against the old plaster wall.

Tina sat on Audrey's bed and put her face in her hands. She sneezed. She looked up – her eyes were swimming. On the windowsill the petals of the Spirited Grace lilies had opened and were emitting their intoxicating fragrance.

She delved into her handbag and set about repairing the damage her tears had inflicted on her cheeks. Less than happy with her work, she put her powder compact away, got up and opened the door.

Her heart skipped a beat.

Across the landing was a lone figure standing by the window. 'We meet again,' Spartak said. He came over to her and she instinctively slid her arms around his neck. All thoughts of Sean evaporated from her mind as she tilted her head back and their lips touched.

CHAPTER FIFTEEN

'Bugger that,' said Colin Turner, the local councillor and buildings' surveyor Audrey had met earlier. 'He's full of hot air. Don't let him bully you. If you have any trouble, Mrs Willatt, let me know, and I'll rally the Hawksmead cricket team. He wants to put up a bunch of boxes on this site, but not while I'm on the planning committee.'

'We hope you'll be very happy in Hawksmead. This party was a brilliant idea,' said the councillor's wife. 'If you fancy a game of tennis, my local club has indoor courts.'

Before Audrey could respond, Colin cut in. 'And, if you need any advice re building works, give me a call.' He handed her his card. 'No charge.'

'Hi, I'm Jason.' Audrey turned to look into a lean, tanned, wrinkled face, offset by blue twinkling eyes. 'Thank you for the great tea. It's been a wonderful get-together for the town.'

'My pleasure. I am so pleased you could come.' She shook Jason's outstretched hand.

'Do you play tennis?' he asked.

Audrey was slightly taken aback by the question. 'Yes, a bit. It seems to be a popular sport in Hawksmead.'

'I bet you're good. I belong to a great club with air conditioning.'

Audrey put her hand up to her nose to contain a sneeze. 'Excuse me. It's the lilies. My nose is buzzing.'

'We should have a game.'

'That would be lovely.'

As soon as Jason was out of earshot, a woman – stick thin with hooded eyes, an ever-present smile and exquisite taste in clothes – kissed Audrey on each cheek and half-whispered in her ear. 'He's married. We widows must watch each other's backs.'

Audrey laughed. 'I knew he was married. A pity. He reminds me of a boy I went out with when I was fifteen. Very handsome.'

'What happened to him?'

'After a couple of weeks, I gave him a frank talk.'

'Why? What had he done?'

'Oh, absolutely nothing, except being liked by my dear mother. As soon as she said, "Oh, he's nice," I knew it was time to kiss him goodbye.'

'By the way, my name's Maureen.' She held out her bony right hand which Audrey shook. 'If you're not otherwise engaged on Monday evenings, perhaps you'd like to join our bridge set? We alternate between each other's homes; make sandwiches, coffee, et cetera. You do play, don't you?'

'Of course. That would be lovely. But perhaps when I'm a bit more sorted. Although I do already have the sandwiches,' Audrey laughed.

As if a plug had been pulled out in an old enamelled bath, tea party guests and new friends came to say goodbye and offer return invitations. Audrey was greatly admired for taking on the big old house, especially given its grim reputation.

It was the dome of his bald head that attracted Audrey's attention, then his white dog collar. Head thrust forward creating a slight stoop, what could have been quite a stern appearance was mitigated by smiling blue-grey eyes and a confident and friendly shake of Audrey's hand.

'Mrs Willatt – Longden, Reverend William.'

'Are you from the church next door?'

'Yes. To answer your unspoken question – why is a man of eighty-five still in the pulpit? I derive my income from my pension. I do not need to draw a stipend, which helps the Methodist Church. You should come and join us for tea and biscuits when you have a moment. We are raising money to sort out the rising damp that is so affecting our walls.'

'I would love to,' Audrey said. 'Churches fascinate me and, sometimes, I am almost tempted to believe.'

'Since the departure of my wife, Lily, I rattle around in the church manse. Come and visit, no prior appointment necessary – or you can find me at the church, ten a.m. every Sunday. Non-believers are most welcome.'

'I think I may have heard your bells.'

'That'll be Saint Michael's down the road – Church of England. We only have one bell, and it's cracked.'

Tina uncoupled her hand from Spartak's at the top of the stairs that led down into the hallway. There were still a few party guests, holding glasses of Prosecco.

'Tina!'

She looked down at Audrey and a tsunami of blood flooded her cheeks. She gave a little wave and hurried down the stairs followed by Spartak.

'Thank you, Mrs Willatt, it's been a wonderful event.' She kissed Audrey on each cheek.

'Please call by anytime.' Audrey turned to Spartak. 'Thank you for coming, Mr Dryomov. Are you here to make me an offer?'

'Not to buy but to renovate. I have very good team of hard-working men. Here is my card.' As if he were a conjuror, his business card appeared between his fingers.

'Thank you.' Audrey took the card. 'I'll be in touch should I need a quote.'

'And also,' Spartak said, 'if you change your mind and would like to sell, I know we can come to price that will keep smile on your face for a very long time.'

Audrey looked at Tina. 'I saw Sean storm out a little while ago. I hope everything's all right.'

Spartak put his arm around Tina's shoulder. 'Everything's just fine, Mrs Willatt. We must go. I thank you for tea. It exceeded my most optimistic expectation. I believe, when a good thing is presented to me on a plate, it is rude not to accept.' He steered Tina through the hall and out of the front door.

By the time the final tea party guests said their goodbyes and stepped into the chilly air, it was dark. Audrey made a special point of remembering names and faces but her attention was continually drawn to a tall man, wearing a herringbone jacket and silk tie, whom she had seen earlier chatting to Ted, the publican. She was sure he'd been watching her almost as keenly. She smiled to herself – it wasn't only Tina whose endorphins were on the march that Saturday afternoon.

The penultimate guests left and the gallant stranger from the train extended his hand. 'Malcolm Cadwallader, widower. A bit of a mouthful.'

She slipped her hand in his and a frisson of excitement ran through her. 'Audrey Willatt, widow. How nice to see you again.' She felt his warm, dry skin as she looked up into his eyes. 'You disappeared before I could thank you properly.'

He smiled and released her hand. 'I'd left my car at Undermere station, so had to get back on the train. This excellent tea is more than recompense for my small service.'

Why was a widower much more attractive than a divorcee? Audrey pondered. Perhaps it was the finality of death as opposed to the baggage of divorce that made Malcolm so appealing to her. She liked the way he had dressed for the occasion, and she liked his posture. As a former ballerina, Audrey always admired good posture. She also particularly admired the shape of his head with its balanced cheekbones and jaw, and how his blond hair gave him a hint of boyish youth.

'Willatt – a truly distinguished old English name,' Malcolm stated.

'It was my husband's.'

'Of course.'

'Cadwallader?'

'The last and greatest King of Wales. Seventh century, so the DNA is a bit thin!'

Audrey laughed. She settled her blue eyes on his and felt sixteen again.

'Has anyone told you that you're the spit of Audrey Hepburn?' he asked.

'You're too kind. I do have a bit of Dutch – like her.'

'Really?'

'Van Staaten.' Audrey inwardly smiled as she considered the slender link that connected her family's genes with the Netherlands. 'My great-grandfather was the painter Louis van Staaten.'

'I'm astounded!' Malcolm paused. She watched him gather his thoughts. 'I was selling a few items that belonged to my late wife at Fielding's, the auctioneers, when I saw this amazing watercolour of medieval buildings lining a canal in Flanders. The reflections of the barges in the water are second to none. I stayed for the auction and paid about seven hundred and fifty pounds; more than I've ever paid for a painting, but it gives me enormous pleasure.'

'If he'd painted in oils, it would have cost ten times as much.'

'You must come and see it.'

'Do you have etchings, too?' Audrey's marriage to Duncan had been successful from every angle and had produced two wonderful sons and two grandchildren. Why was she even toying with the possibility of a new romance?

Malcolm smiled. 'I paint a bit. I like to go up on the moor. Some of my best ideas have come to me in that wonderful wilderness.'

'What kind of ideas?'

'I was in marketing. I'm good with words; creating concepts for advertising campaigns – that sort of thing. Sadly, I do not possess your great-grandfather's artistic gift.'

They talked, in the dimly lit hall, oblivious to the debris around them and to Eleanor, who was hovering in the corridor that led to the kitchen.

'Do you like walking?' Malcolm asked.

'I do.'

'Have you walked the Ridgeway, yet?'

'I can see it from my bedroom window.'

'If you like, we could walk it together. You should definitely climb it before winter sets in.'

He entered her number into his phone and they said goodbye with another charged handshake. Audrey closed the front door as Eleanor emerged from the corridor. For a moment, the two women looked at each other.

'It's this house,' Audrey said. 'It seems to turn people on – or maybe it's the lilies.'

'I've lived in Hawksmead a long time, but he's the first man I've seen who comes close to getting my cake to rise,' Eleanor said, laughing. 'If you don't want him, send him down to the Olde Tea Shoppe. Tell him there's a cream meringue waiting for him.'

Both women guffawed.

'Why is he so attractive?' Audrey asked herself as much as Eleanor.

Eleanor pondered for a moment. 'It's our time of life. We've got our homes, we've had our families – we're no longer looking for a go-getter, a high achiever. What matters to us now are shared interests, shared pleasures, a kind character – and if there's a decent body thrown in, then that's a bonus.'

'He's very slim.'

'And has a young voice. Definitely not a smoker,' Eleanor added. 'Right, let's get on with sorting out this mess.'

'I absolutely won't hear of it.'

Rather than clearing up, they shared the remains of a bottle of Prosecco, then gave each other a sisterly hug before Eleanor said goodbye and stepped into the night.

Audrey let the door close and heard the latch click into its keep. She slid home the heavy bolts at the top and bottom, and sighed. She was alone – and didn't much like it.

There was a creak behind her.

A shiver rippled through her body.

She turned. 'Hello? Anyone there?'

Upstairs, along the corridor, she heard a door hinge squeak. Then a floorboard creaked and creaked again. She waited. She wanted to run. She was in an unfamiliar house, in an unfamiliar town, and every nerve was telling her to get out. How she yearned for the cacophony of recent chatter.

The footsteps were definitely male and getting nearer. She took a deep breath, determined to remove all tremor from her voice. 'Who's there? The party's over. It's time to go home.'

'Mrs Willatt?'

The source of the voice appeared on the half-landing.

Audrey let out a sigh of relief. 'Sean. What are you still doing here?'

'Sorry. I fell asleep.' He walked down the creaking stairs into the hallway. 'Has everyone gone?'

'Yes. I thought you had, too.'

'I came back. I wanted to speak to Tina. Did you see her?'

'I did.'

'Did she say anything about me?'

'No. We only had a brief conversation.'

'I tried her phone, but it went straight to voicemail.'

'I'm sure all will be fine in the morning.' She pulled back the heavy door bolts.

'I heard a voice, earlier. But no one was there.'

She reached for the door latch.

Sean stood very close to her and almost whispered in her ear. 'He sounded very young.'

'It must've been one of the children having fun. The chimneys act as echo chambers.'

'He asked me if I wanted a wagon wheel. A wagon wheel? Why would I want a wagon wheel?'

'A Wagon Wheel is a chocolate coated biscuit sandwich,' she said, drily, and swung the door open. 'The wind's picking up. Do you have a car?' She held the door as cold air refreshed the hall.

'No. I'll walk down the High Street and pick up a taxi at the railway station.'

'I hope you get things sorted out with Tina. She's a lovely girl. Really smart and go-ahead.'

'That she is. Goodnight, Mrs Willatt.'

She closed the door and bolted it, again.

For a moment she allowed the pervading silence to envelop

her. 'Being a widow sucks, Duncan.' She wiped away an escaping tear.

The kitchen looked pretty good, thanks to Eleanor's sterling work. Cling film covered plates of uneaten sandwiches and cakes. Although there was still plenty of cleaning up to be done, Audrey had all the time in the world to sort it out in the morning.

She flicked on various feeble lights as she walked through the house, no longer needing the bunch of keys as she had unlocked every internal door. She had loved seeing so many people talking and laughing and sharing in the excitement of being together within a building that they had often crossed the road to avoid. In fact, she had almost forgotten why she had hosted the tea party in the first place.

Audrey noticed that the lights were on in the old drawing room and went to switch them off. Hot water pipes clanged together as if hit by a hammer.

She held her breath, her ears pricked for further sounds. Could there be someone else still in the house? The pipes clanged again – and she breathed out.

She went back downstairs and entered the laundry room. Despite its age, the boiler still pulled its weight, and with the help of a separate pump sent hot water through the old lead pipes. Audrey turned a knob and, protected by the thick glass window, saw the flames die back to a single pilot light.

She made a mug of cocoa, ate a couple of leftover sandwich triangles, and climbed the stairs to the half-landing. She focused her mind on Malcolm and tried to ignore the creaking floorboards that were accompanied by the wind's pitiful moan.

'Can I really fall in love again at the age of sixty-five?' She spoke the words out loud. 'Is it really possible?'

She walked along the corridor to the washroom and wondered whether she could ever again feel the same kind of love she had felt for the father of her boys. Or could it only ever be affectionate companionship? No, what she felt within her slim frame was not affectionate companionship but a sensation that took her back to when she had happily given up her virginity, to the accompaniment of Procol Harum's *A Whiter Shade of Pale*.

She laughed and pushed open the washroom door. 'Girl, there's still life in the old bones yet.'

Following her usual swift ablutions, Audrey carried her cocoa up to the top dormitory room, flicking on and off lights as she went. She smiled when she saw her single bed with its old school blankets. A lily, taken from the bouquet, had been placed on her pillow. She guessed it was Tina. What had she got up to with the Russian? She shivered as a cold draught rattled the ill-fitting window.

CHAPTER SIXTEEN

The clock in St Michael's Church struck the midnight hour as Kirill Dryomov pulled his white van to a halt. His big brother was going soft, becoming English, more of a doe-eyed spaniel than a Russian bear. Not Kirill. His face, as opposed to Spartak's handsome features, looked like it had been flattened by a shovel, the result of too many fights. If people crossed him, he punched them. Man or woman – it didn't matter. His brother may not have the stomach to deal with the old stick, but Kirill most certainly did. It was a simple matter of honour, or deep-down resentment grown from a lifetime of playing second balalaika to an older brother who was popular with women and their mother's clear favourite.

Across the street, the old school boarding house almost glowed in the street lights. He could break in now and throttle the scraggy English woman's neck. He'd enjoy that. So far, he'd killed two people in Moscow and hurt quite a few since he'd followed his brother through passport control into Britain's open arms. Of course, as his brother reminded him, the British police were not quite so easily bribed as the police and public officials in their home town of Kaluskovye.

He opened the rear doors to his van and removed an old axe.

Tina had spent the evening with Spartak following Audrey's tea party but had decided not to stay the night in Undermere's four-star White Hart Hotel. Her parents were cool about her sleeping with Sean but would definitely kick up a fuss if they knew she'd chucked Sean and had sex twice with Spartak all in the same day. Perhaps it was time to look for her own place.

The Old Military Road from Undermere back to Hawksmead seemed especially dark as the headlights on Tina's Golf strained to probe the blackness. She had no desire to live in a city or a large town but there was no doubt that the countryside at night could be really spooky. The wind was picking up off the moor, and the stark branches against the midnight sky looked like something out of a horror film. When she had broken up with her first boyfriend, Gavin, her brother had taken her to a special screening of *The Scars of Dracula* to try and take her mind off the heartache. Images of Christopher Lee as the blood-sucking count flashed through her mind.

The moon came out from behind a dark cloud, and the angular trees lining the road ahead looked especially eerie in the silvery light. Tina wished she'd stayed with Spartak in the hotel bed; the thought of snuggling up with him seemed a very good idea, but it was too late now to turn back.

A dark shadow scampered across the road and Tina slammed on her brakes.

Damn!

It was a fox, she was sure, but her nerves were playing tricks with her mind. Ahead, the road turned to the right, a typical blind bend. Tina straddled the middle of the road to take the optimum line and then she saw something up ahead.

Almost beyond the range of her headlights was a small figure, the moon casting whoever it was in its strange, cold light. She stamped on her brake and came to a stuttering walking pace.

She checked that all her doors were locked. Through her windscreen, she saw the figure standing in the road, staring at her. He was wearing a coat, which was flapping back and forth in the gathering wind.

Fear stirred her guts, then a blinding light killed her night vision. A large vehicle blasted its horn behind her. Terrified of an impact damaging her pride and joy, Tina floored the accelerator.

The wind was turning into a gale as spots of rain splattered onto her windscreen. She knew the vehicle behind could crush her little car, but she was driving straight at a helpless child. Adrenaline coursed through her body as she debated which ditch to swerve into. And then the road veered sharply to the left by the turning to the former school. The boy miraculously became a fence post and the long flapping coat was a gate swinging back and forth in the increasing wind. Tina swept past, spurred on by the headlights tailgating her Golf. Was the boy just a trick of the moonlight? She swiftly arrived at the humpback bridge and knew she was going too fast, but if she braked hard, the vehicle behind could propel her into the river.

She screamed as her car almost took off at the apex and thumped down on the far side, a real test for her German-made suspension. She pulled the wheel and managed to prevent the Golf from crashing into the stone wall that lined the side of the bridge.

The vehicle was still following close behind, so Tina pressed her accelerator and headed for Hawksmead High Street. She was going way over the speed limit as she left the Old Military Road, and almost didn't notice the flash of a speed camera competing with the full-beam headlights in her rear-view mirror.

Audrey's house came up on Tina's left and she skidded to a halt by the entrance to the drive. The vehicle following swerved around her, slowed, blasted its horn, and sped away. It was a Range Rover similar to Spartak's. Why would he be following her to Hawksmead? He said his home was in Undermere.

Tina didn't know what to think. Her whole body was shaking. Loads of impatient people drove Range Rovers. As for the boy standing in the Old Military Road with the flapping coat – it had just been her imagination, and no more real than the big man standing in Audrey's driveway, with oak leaves swirling around him, and holding what looked like – in the glow from the streetlights – an axe.

Was she going mad? Was this a dream? A nightmare? A Hammer horror? A few hours earlier, she had been consumed with desire in the top dormitory room, and now she was consumed with fear. What was the house doing to her? Nothing had gone right since she'd first entered that hateful building.

She ground her beloved gears and fought to find first. Her

clutch plates connected, her front tyres squealed, and she roared off with her mind in turmoil.

~

Audrey awoke with a start; she knew she'd been dreaming but couldn't remember what it had been about. The room was pitch black and very cold. Outside, it was clearly blowing a gale. She pulled the sheet and blankets more closely around her shoulders, wishing that she'd bought a duvet. More annoyingly, the half-drunk mug of cocoa was causing unwelcome pressure on her bladder – or, perhaps it was the Prosecco. She did not relish the cold, dark walk to the lavatories and wondered whether she was too young to have a Victorian potty tucked under her bed, as she'd seen her grandparents do when she was a little girl.

She closed her eyes and tried to slip back into sleep but, after a few seconds, she knew she had no choice but to get up. She flung back the covers and felt with her toes for her slippers. She debated putting on her dressing gown but decided that would slow her down. She stood and reached for the doorknob, which she turned. Out on the landing, a little of the sodium lighting from the High Street gave her enough illumination to find the light switch. The house was quiet; eerily quiet, Tina would say, whereas for Audrey, she felt that her new home was at peace. She was still getting to know its many little ways but, as she walked down the shadowy stairs, she was excited about the man she had met for a second time and the possibilities that lay ahead. Finding the truth about what happened in the boarding house fifty years ago suddenly seemed of secondary importance.

She came to the half-landing and felt along the wood-panelled wall for the switch. She turned on the light and smiled. Debris from her tea party littered the floor and surfaces, reminding her of the delicious touch of Malcolm's hand.

The washroom, with its hard floor and walls, was particularly cold as Audrey sat down in one of the cubicles. Her mind relaxed with her body and sleep overcame her. Her head flopped forward, waking her with a start, but even in those few seconds of sleep, she'd had a dream about a little boy, that felt stark and very real. She shivered in the cold cubicle, her thin nightdress providing little protection.

Audrey washed her hands and looked at her reflection in the mirror. She gave herself a wry smile; she knew she looked good for sixty-five, but she was no longer a pin-up, a top Lucie Clayton fashion model; a dolly bird who earned lots of cash wearing clothes designed by Mary Quant.

At the age of seventeen, she had been selected, together with four other models, to fly to Australia and attend sporting events wearing Mary Quant's latest collection. It had been a big story at the time as one of the models was the girlfriend of a member of the sixties' pop group The Monkees. Audrey had loved all the attention. Her parents had seen her on the evening news, flying off with the other girls to Australia where they were treated like film stars. The trip launched her modelling career and put a lovely sum of money in her bank account. The only downside was leaving her new boyfriend, Duncan, whom she'd met at a party in Sevenoaks. She and Duncan had clicked immediately. He was witty and cheeky, a cool dresser, physically fit and very classy. When she had kissed him goodbye at Heathrow Airport, she had secretly been thrilled to see his tears.

Audrey still felt tired but yearned for the comfort of dawn so left the lights on as she made her way up the stairs. She opened the door to her bedroom and switched on the light. All was as she had left it before heading for the lavatories.

She slipped between the sheets of her bed and was comforted by the cold cotton encasing her. She looked up at the bare bulb illuminating the room and thought about her life and the reason why she had moved to Hawksmead. She knew she mustn't lose sight of that but other plans, other desires, were now jostling for her attention.

She closed her eyes and could see the light bulb's feeble beam through her eyelids as sleep took her back to her ballet school in the heart of the Sussex countryside. She was on stage, holding hands with Curly McLain, singing *People Will Say We're in Love*. And she really had been in love with Curly, or rather Lauren, who had been Audrey's "pash" since she'd first arrived at the boarding school, aged eleven. Audrey had fought to get the role of Laurey Williams in *Oklahoma!* the musical, just so that she could spend as much time as possible with Lauren. She'd even written home to her brother and begged him to lend her his favourite six gun and holster so that Lauren as Curly would look like a real cowboy.

It was a sad day for Audrey when she left the ballet school aged fourteen. Her parents had been advised that short tendons in her legs prevented her from progressing as a ballerina. She was in the front passenger seat of her father's large Mercedes car, driving back at the end of the summer term, not relishing the prospect of attending a local school where she would be the new girl.

'Fourteen is an exciting time in your life,' announced her father, out of the blue.

'Is it?'

'Yes, very exciting, especially as you will now be at a day school,' continued her father as they drove through the beautiful Sussex countryside. 'Do you like The Beatles?'

'Of course. Everyone does.'

'Who's your favourite?'

'You know who,' Audrey said, wondering why her father had raised the subject. He liked Doris Day, The Seekers and German beer-drinking songs – why was he asking about The Beatles? But Audrey was happy to think about them, although she didn't have enough money to buy their LP.

'It's Paul, isn't it?' asked her father.

'Of course, who else could it be?'

'Mummy says a lot of her friends like John.'

'All the girls in my school love Paul.' Audrey did not tell her father she had written to Paul, declaring her love. She didn't know his address but felt sure that *Paul McCartney, The Beatles, Liverpool*, written on the envelope would definitely get her letter to him. Her old pash, Lauren, would always hold a special place in her heart, but there was no doubt that Paul was now her new and forever pash.

'Boys like girls, and it's important that you understand the whole process.'

'What process?' She was relieved he could not read her mind.

Her father had to scrape a hedgerow to prevent a head-on collision with a mini being driven at sixty miles an hour in the opposite direction.

'Blithering fool!' he shouted. Audrey hoped the scare would change the subject.

'Shall I put the radio on?' she asked.

'In a minute. I just want to clarify a few things. Boys and girls, as you may have noticed, are different in many, many ways. Girls are pure, and boys are — '

Audrey waited for him to finish the sentence. 'Boys are not pure?' she offered.

'They may be pure, but they do not have pure thoughts.'

'How do you mean?'

'Boys have a – a penis, and it can have a mind of its own.'

'A penis has a brain?'

'Not exactly, but it does control the brain.'

'Does yours control your brain?' Audrey asked, warming to the conversation.

'Good God no!' said her father, his cheeks flushing under his fourteen-year-old daughter's gaze. 'Not at all. But, you are now of an age when boys see that you are budding, and that can be awkward.'

'Budding?' Audrey asked, genuinely perplexed.

'You know… bras and things.'

Audrey looked down at her budding breasts. 'You mean my bosom?'

'Well, it's not quite a bosom yet, but they *are* budding.'

Audrey was pleased that her father had noticed the rapid change that had happened to her during the summer term of 1964. 'You think boys will notice?'

'Most definitely, and they may want to see them… without a

bra.'

Audrey felt a frisson of excitement at the thought of showing off her bosom. 'I don't mind.'

Her father took his eyes off the road in alarm. 'You jolly well should!'

'I don't mind at all,' Audrey said, really beginning to enjoy the conversation. 'What harm can it do?'

'It's what it leads to.'

'Leads to?'

'Boys will not stop there.'

'Where?'

'At your… your breasts.'

'They won't stop at my breasts?' Audrey asked. 'Where will they go?'

'They'll want to go where they should not, and that is how we get unwanted babies. Do you understand?'

Audrey understood. She'd had full instructions from girls at her school on exactly what boys wanted and what she should let them do and what she should not. But she was really enjoying giving her father the run around, so feigned ignorance.

'Daddy, where will boys want to go?'

'If you let them, they'll want to go south.'

'South? I don't understand.'

Her father took a deep breath. 'South. Where your knickers are.'

'My knickers? I don't think you've got this right, Daddy. Boys like to kiss and, sometimes, touch tongues. Why would they want to go to my knickers?'

'I can assure you they do.'

'But why?' Audrey asked. 'What's there to interest them?'

'Best discuss it with your mother. I want to listen to the news.' He turned on the radio.

'*…that is the end of the news. And now the shipping forecast, issued by the Met Office on behalf of the Maritime and Coastguard Agency…*'

Audrey looked out of the car's side window as the BBC's Home Service shipping forecast warned of gales in Rockall,

Malin, Hebrides, Bailey and Fair Isle. She knew exactly why boys wanted to go south.

'It's going to be a lovely day,' her father said. 'You should go swimming.'

'Will you buy me a bikini? One-piece swimsuits are so boring.'

She looked at the road ahead as the bright sun sent shafts of light through the canopy of trees.

Audrey opened her eyes and was surprised to see that the sun was up. At this time of year, it must mean she'd overslept. She thought about her dream and smiled to herself, before throwing back the blankets and swinging her feet to find her slippers.

Her phone beeped; she picked it up and checked the screen. It was a text. She read it; she read it again and tapped in a short reply. She hurried out of the dorm but, at the first turn on the staircase, she slipped and stumbled. She removed both slippers and carried on, her bare feet at the end of long, slim legs slapping the stairs as she rushed to the washroom.

She stepped into the cavernous shower area and turned her head up to the large rose. Shafts of freezing water cascaded over her face and naked body. She wanted to wake up; she wanted to be sharp; she wanted to be at her best.

CHAPTER SEVENTEEN

It's a few days since I last wrote my thoughts down, so I have quite a bit to tell you – and it's not happy news. On the Monday morning after the weekend break on the moors, the whole school was brought together for morning chapel. Every member of staff looked very solemn, and for the first time, the headmaster seemed unsure of himself. We didn't sing a hymn, but he went straight into an announcement.

"Christopher Wilkins and David Turnbull were canoeing as part of their Duke of Edinburgh Award. Both lost control of their canoes and were tipped into the water. Their bodies were found by the police, and their parents have been informed. It was a tragic accident, and although it may be considered ill-advised to have ventured onto the river, the ethos of our school is that risk is a part of living."

I whispered a prayer of thanks to Roxane for sparing my life. Mini said that neither boy was wearing a life jacket as it was too difficult to use the paddles with one on. Mr Gibbs then informed us of future events and that Monday was to be a normal school day.

Disturbingly quickly, we all got back into our usual routines as winter truly set in, despite it being early November. Snow covered the moor and farming duties involved cleaning out the barn and helping with the cows. No more potato picking – hooray! I have got used to the regime, and thanks to Roxane and playing a major role in the school play, I have earned the respect of even the nastiest of boys. The older boys in the boarding house still call Mini and me the queer twins but it seems to be done with some affection, as long as we take their turns to clean out the bogs. I don't mind. It's all about surviving to Christmas, and I'm happier than I thought possible in this place. And I like myself a bit more – Mr C says that I have genuine talent and that if I keep practising I will rid myself of my stutter. I hope so. Mini says it's all in my mind, and we laugh.

~

Malcolm, sitting in the driver's seat of his Honda Civic, looked at his phone and checked the local weather forecast for the day ahead. It was going to be sunny in the morning, but an icy blast was heading in from the east bringing rain from mid-afternoon. He thought about his wife, Mary, who had been the belle of Hawksmead. He remembered the first moment he'd seen her when he was aged sixteen. David Winstanley was having a gathering at his house. There were quite a few girls aged fourteen and Malcolm was entranced by their female forms. Mary was five foot four inches tall, slim and sweet, and Malcolm promised himself that one day he would marry her. But it took two more years at boarding school, three years reading English at Oxford, and two years of working and living back with his parents before he met her again, by chance, in Hawksmead High Street. In fact, she saw him coming before he saw her and she called out his name. He was immensely flattered that she remembered him at all, let alone his name. She'd been up at Edinburgh University studying for a Philosophy PhD and was home for the summer holidays. They chatted about mutual friends until Malcolm plucked up the courage to ask for her phone number.

Nearly fifty years on, driving his Honda Civic to Audrey's house, he felt the same intense excitement. He'd fancied Mary in every way a man desires a woman and was pleasantly surprised by the same surge he felt coursing through his veins when he first saw Audrey. Of course, life was more complicated these days, but at least he could text an invitation rather than having to summon up the nerve to invite her out on the phone.

She was the first Audrey he'd ever met – it was an unusual name for the post war generation. He admitted to himself that he was nervous and had taken great care with his appearance, but getting the balance right between looking smart and being comfortable was not always easy. Today, he'd had to dress for warmth but, at the same time, he wanted to wow Audrey. He could be considered too old for her at the age of seventy-five but his fitness, coupled with his excellent mind, wiped a good twenty years off his slate – at least, that's what he told himself.

The doorbell rang, and Audrey almost skipped down the stairs. She reached the half-landing and looked into the cavernous hallway, taking care not to catch her shoe on the offending floorboard.

'Just coming!' She hurried down the final flight and did a quick self-check of her clothes as she crossed the hallway, kicking aside used paper plates and plastic champagne flutes. She grabbed her coat, hat and gloves off a coat stand she had bought from a local bric-a-brac shop, and pulled back the bolts.

She opened the door to a tall man, silhouetted by the autumnal, early morning sun, and to the head of an axe embedded in the thick oak panelling.

'I see the axe man cometh,' Malcolm said indicating the axe cleaved into her door.

Audrey stared at the axe open-mouthed.

'Any idea who did it?' he asked.

It was the first axe she could recall seeing, outside of a film or on TV, and it scared her. She licked her lips and tried to control her breathing. 'I think it may have something to do with a certain Russian property developer.'

'You must let the police know.'

Audrey tried to free the axe.

'May I?' Malcolm placed his hand gently on her shoulder.

She smiled up at him and stepped aside. He used the length of the handle to lever the axe head free from the aged oak. 'At the very least, it's criminal damage,' he said.

She took the axe and placed it in her hallway. Letting Malcolm help her with the axe was a perfect ice-breaker. She must make sure to thank the Russian, she thought, smiling inwardly at her forced levity.

'Usually, I don't worry about double-locking, but I think I will now,' Audrey said, rummaging in her handbag for her keys.

She made sure that the door was fully locked and slipped her hand through Malcolm's arm. They headed off down the short drive, past Malcolm's Honda, to the main road.

Turning right, they walked in happy silence along the footpath towards the River Hawk.

'I've not been this far out of town,' commented Audrey as they turned a corner in the tree-lined road and she caught sight of the narrow, humpback bridge.

'There's no path over the bridge,' Malcolm said. 'We'd better walk in single file. I'll go first.'

'Why should you go first?' enquired Audrey, enjoying Malcolm's company more with every step.

'I'm older than you and taller. The oncoming cars will see me more easily.'

Audrey smiled and let go of his arm as they walked to the apex of the stone bridge. Malcolm continued to the far side. She paused and looked down at the fast flowing water. Malcolm hurried back to join her.

'We're living dangerously, standing like this.'

Audrey squeezed his arm. 'It's beautiful.'

'You should see it when it's in flood – it's savage.'

Audrey looked through the trees lining the riverbank to the faint outline of a distant building rising from the steaming peat bog.

'Hawksmead College – now closed, of course. It's where the boys who boarded in your house used to go every day for lessons.'

'Let's go up there.' Audrey gave him her brightest smile.

A car crested the bridge and braked hard to avoid them.

'Anything to get you off here!' Malcolm took Audrey's hand and led her down to the north side of the river.

~

There's been a terrible accident. I'm almost too sad to write it down, but you've helped me a lot, you person reading this in 2065 – your understanding has given me courage when I needed it most.

This morning, it was particularly cold on the moor. Condensation on the window panes had frozen on the inside. I dressed up as warmly as I could then Mini and I went down to the shed to collect our bikes. My teeth chattered as we pedalled. The cold went through my gloves, and my bare knees have never been so blue. There was a dense mist across the moor, and the school formed only a faint outline. As we approached the humpback bridge, the road looked like a black satin ribbon. Mini came alongside me, pedalling hard. As we cycled together onto the bridge, without warning, our wheels slid out from under us, and we landed hard on what I learned to be black ice.

We were both in shock, our knees bruised and bleeding. What had happened? It took a moment or two for us to be aware of a car coming towards us, sliding uncontrollably on the ice. I rolled as close as I could to the side of the bridge but Mini was not so quick. The car scooped him up, and I heard his bones crack as he was crushed between the bumper and the stone wall. The MG 1100 was badly damaged, and I'd never seen a schoolmaster cry until that terrible moment.

The police asked me what happened, but no one at the school wants to talk about Mini. I will write to his parents, but I don't know what to say. Do I say that I have lost a friend? Do I tell them that I loved him? What will they think of me? Will they think I'm queer? At night, I look at Mini's bed, and I can't stop crying. His mattress has been rolled up, and all his personal knick-knacks removed. McGrath calls me a baby, but I don't care. Mini is dead. He's dead and I loved him so much.

~

The Old Military Road was fairly straight. A high hedgerow to the left blocked their view, but to the right were ploughed fields giving way to peat moorland.

'It's been a while since I walked along this road,' Malcolm said. 'Usually, I'm in my car and I forget how beautiful it is out here.'

'Crataegus monogyna,' responded Audrey, indicating the hedgerow.

Malcolm laughed. 'Common hawthorn. Did you study Latin?'

'I know the Latin name for a few plants, but at my ballet school French was more important. It's the language of dance.'

Twenty minutes later, they passed a rusting triangular sign warning motorists that a school was up ahead. A few minutes' further walking and a side road opened up to the right with a sign on the far corner announcing in weathered letters: *Hawksmead College*.

They turned right and walked along the narrow road, bounded by hawthorn hedges that required trimming after bounteous summer growth.

'Did your parents send you to Hawksmead College?' Audrey asked, happy to have her hand warmed by Malcolm's crooked arm.

'No, it was a boarding school for troubled boys, designed to build character through a variety of physical challenges. At least, that's what it said in the prospectus. Anyway, it was way too alternative for my parents. They sent me to more of a classic British boarding school in Kent. A sort of poor man's Eton with a uniform less grand but still with detachable stiff collars. It now has girls, but in my day, it was cold, sadistic, and I hated every moment.'

'But your schooldays were still the happiest days of your life. No?'

Malcolm burst out laughing. 'I hope the happiest days of my life are still to come.'

Audrey squeezed his arm as they continued walking towards the old school, breathing in the damp moorland air and relishing its mix of odours.

'I was a fag,' Malcolm stated, 'and earned ten shillings for the privilege.'

Audrey laughed. 'In other words, you were a personal servant to an older boy?'

'Yes, to the head of house. A good-looking boy called Stuart Feltwell. It was a poisoned chalice because I was accused by my peers of passing on information to him. I didn't reveal anything, but other boys thought I did. Feltwell was kind to me, but he liked his privileged position too much and made sure that no junior mistook his friendly demeanour for weakness. His beatings were a regular occurrence and inflicted for the tiniest transgression. It was an alternative form of bullying.'

'Sadly, bullies do quite well in our world,' Audrey said.

'Like your Russian friend.'

'He's the first Russian I've ever met, and he reminds me of Rudolf Nureyev. I loved him when I was a little girl. He was beautiful and courageous.'

'As are you! My apologies. That was a bit forward.'

Audrey couldn't contain her smile as a warm glow engulfed her body.

Malcolm stopped walking and turned to her. 'You must inform the police.'

'I may be wrong blaming the Russian. He looked much more interested in bedding my estate agent than embedding his axe in my door.'

'Interesting.'

They stood close together as they shared the view of rolling hills with their scattered clumps of trees.

'It is beautiful,' she said. 'But it must have been a frightening, lonely view for a young boy arriving for the first time at the big school. Is that the ridge you promised to take me up on?' She pointed to a high ridge in the distance.

'Yes. We must go up there before it gets too cold.'

As one, they started walking again. Their easy, relaxed chatting carried them along the country lane towards the remote edifice of the former boarding school. On their right, they came to a couple of houses built in classic 1980s architectural design.

'There was much argument about the construction of those two properties,' Malcolm said. 'People felt that it was the thin end of a nasty property development wedge. But they needn't have feared. Once Hawksmead finally lost its textile mill, there really was no pressure on housing – until recently, of course. Now, the council can't wait to show its credentials by giving planning permission to anyone with a trowel... or, indeed, an axe.'

'Well, the axe is mine, now.' Audrey laughed, expressing far more confidence than she actually felt. She slowed, took a deep breath of damp moorland air, and cast her eyes over mile upon mile of open countryside, criss-crossed with ancient stone walls and peppered with tiny, remote cottages. 'My mother taught me many things, but perhaps the most valuable was the ability to relish the moment.'

'I am most definitely relishing this moment,' Malcolm responded. 'People talk about companionship in old age, but this walk with you has wiped fifty years off my clock.'

'And fifty years off mine too – and some to spare,' Audrey laughed, giving Malcolm's arm another squeeze.

The sun had already reached its high point of the day and was now slipping behind a chimney stack rising above the imperious, empty school building. The immediate grounds were unkempt, with weeds carpeting the gravelled drive and apron. The mighty walls had, for the most part, succumbed to ivy and other climbers, encasing the old school in a green straitjacket. The windows, a mix of architectural styles, revealed no life within; copper pennies on the eyes of a dead body.

'I can only imagine the horrors that once lurked within,' Audrey said, more to herself than Malcolm.

'It was the era. Children were clay to be moulded, especially young boys, far from home. Discipline was the byword. There was no warmth. No affection. No love. Just hardship.'

Audrey looked at Malcolm and was surprised to see tears sparkling his eyes.

'Anyway,' he continued, 'it's closed now. No more suffering.'

They stood, side-by-side, in the shadow of the empty building.

Audrey broke the silence. 'What's to become of it?'

'There's talk of turning it into a hotel and conference centre, but the cost of conversion seems to be prohibitive.'

'They should tear it down and give the land back to nature.'

'Little chance of that. Parts of it are fourteenth century.'

'Perhaps we should head back. It's getting a bit chilly.' She shivered. 'I could make us soup for lunch.'

'Why don't we go to the Old Forge? They do a very tasty set meal.'

'Sounds lovely.'

They walked at a steady pace along the country lane that led back to the Old Military Road. With every passing year, Audrey believed it became harder to turn good acquaintances into real friends, but she hoped that Malcolm would prove to be an exception. She'd lost the only man she'd ever loved and had felt like ending her own life to free her of the pain. If she hadn't had family who loved her, Audrey was sure she would have taken the easy way out. Now, little more than a year after the funeral, she wanted to live every minute of every day she had left.

It was early afternoon by the time they reached the Old Forge Restaurant with its low beams, inglenook fireplace and scattered diners at the coffee stage. In the rear yard, Audrey had spotted a man in spattered chef's clothing enjoying a post-lunch cigarette.

The manager put on a good show of being pleased to see them, but Audrey knew the chef would be annoyed at having to cook for latecomers.

'Are you going to buy Hawksmead College too? You clearly like big houses,' Malcolm asked, offering Audrey the bread basket.

She smiled and took a hunk of wholemeal. 'Is it for sale?'

Malcolm poured red wine into their glasses. 'It's so relaxing being retired. Not having a deadline is one of the best things about growing old.'

'Having children aged me. I was young when my first boy was born and then when my youngest went to university, I looked in the mirror and saw my mother's face.'

'Well, she must've been a beauty.'

Audrey smiled and lifted her glass in a salute to Malcolm.

'Why did you move here?' he asked. 'Why Hawksmead of all places?'

'I heard it was home to a handsome widower.'

'Touché.' Malcolm lifted his glass.

'I was lonely in Sevenoaks. My lovely husband had moved on and left me rattling around in the family home. I needed a reason to get up in the morning. I had a bit of spare cash and thought that I would turn an unloved building into one that was full of warmth and laughter.' She took a sip of wine to hide her lie.

'Your tea party was an inspiration and a wonderful success, but warmth and laughter are quite a challenge to achieve in a building as austere as the old school boarding house.' He reached for his glass of wine but took a sip of water instead.

'Actually, I think it's going to be quite easy,' Audrey said. 'Many people come to walk the Ridgeway and to enjoy the wonderful moorland scenery. I intend to convert it into a hostel and offer cheap, simple, accommodation. Perhaps, if you're not too busy, you'd like to help me.'

Audrey's mind was in turmoil. Was that a lie or the truth? Was that a marriage proposal or a business offer? They looked at each other; and for a moment, neither had a word to say.

After simple but tasty rural fare, Malcolm got up from the table and appeared a little unsteady. 'Please excuse me; I need to see a man about a dog. Red wine during the day has twice the effect.'

Audrey watched him straighten his back and walk with purposeful strides to the men's lavatory. She looked across at the manager and squiggled the air with her hand. He nodded and brought the lunch bill over. Audrey offered her debit card and the manager slotted it into the wireless card reader. After tapping in her pin, the card and receipt were handed back to her. She slipped both away in her handbag.

She spotted Malcolm emerging from the men's lavatory and pretended to read messages on her phone. Out of the corner of her eye, she saw him approach the manager.

'I'd like to settle our bill, please,' she heard him say.

'You're too late. Madam has already paid.'

'Could you let me know how much it was?'

'Madam gave me explicit instructions not to.'

Audrey put her phone away in her bag as Malcolm approached the table. He was followed by the manager carrying their coats.

'Audrey,' Malcolm said, his tone reproachful. 'What have you done?'

She gave him her full megawatt smile. 'It's a small thank you for a wonderful day.'

The late afternoon was still fine as they walked along the quiet streets of Hawksmead, each lost in their own thoughts but relishing the other's company. A chill breeze had picked up, giving them both the excuse they needed to wrap an arm around the other. At the far end of the High Street, they waited for a white VW Golf to speed by, driven by a pretty young woman Audrey realised was Tina, before crossing to Malcolm's Honda, parked in her drive.

'Come to my place for tea.' Malcolm said.

'Are you suggesting that I accept a ride with a strange man and drive off to some mystery location?'

'I have homemade damson jam, and an original van Staaten eager to make your acquaintance.'

CHAPTER EIGHTEEN

Malcolm parked outside a classic early Victorian terrace of three cottages as Audrey's phone beeped in her handbag. She took it out and looked at the screen.

'It's Tina, the estate agent who sold me my house. She wants me to text her when I'm home, safely.'

'Well, well, well,' Malcolm said. 'To think at the age of seventy-five, I cannot be trusted to preserve the honour of a young woman.'

Audrey laughed and they both got out of the car. She closed the door and looked at Malcolm's pretty garden with its wooden pergola spanning a path of Yorkshire paving stones leading to the front door. To the left was a small rose garden with neatly tended beds, all ready for the harsh winter to come.

'It's exquisite, Malcolm,' she said, genuinely moved by the beauty of the cottage and setting.

'It's a bit small for me, height-wise,' he said, joining her. 'But Mary set her heart on the place and, since her passing, I've not found a good enough reason to sell, apart from the occasional bumped head.'

He swung open the white-painted wooden gate and indicated for Audrey to walk up the path to the front door, painted light blue with mottled glass panels. He followed her, fishing in his pocket for his keys. He unlocked the door, immediately causing a loud beeping noise. He eased his way past her to an understairs cupboard and tapped in a code on an alarm pad. After a couple more beeps, the annoying sound ended.

'Come in, come in,' he said and closed the front door behind her.

She looked at one of several framed photos lining the narrow hallway.

'Did you take them?'

'Yes, in the days when film ruled the photographic world.' He switched on the hall light. 'I've not taken to digital.'

'Is that Mary?' Audrey gestured to a portrait of a honey-blonde young woman.

'Yes. I wish I'd used black and white film stock. After fifty years, the colours are not what they should be.'

'She's beautiful. I can see why you fell for her. What happened?'

He looked away. Audrey waited. There was a heavy silence which Malcolm eventually broke. 'Breast cancer. It's not a subject I care to give oxygen. Tea?'

Audrey smiled. 'You read my mind.' She looked again at Mary's portrait then slipped off her walking shoes before following Malcolm into a small but perfectly furnished sitting room. The rear wall was now an archway to a dining area, and beyond, Audrey could see through French windows to a beautifully tended little garden with a centre patch of lawn, a wooden pergola, and assorted shrubs and bushes in neatly weeded beds.

'I'm impressed. You have an exquisite home, so different from my boarding house.'

Malcolm turned on more lights. 'And here is your great-grandfather's painting.' He gestured to a landscape watercolour of a windmill, artisan cottages, boats with rust-coloured sails, and coal-carrying barges moored to the bank of a wide river. 'He was an absolute master. Look at his reflections in the water. Not sure which river it is, but the region is definitely Dordrecht. Would that be right?'

'I think so.'

'It's what I look at when I eat my breakfast.' He entered the kitchen, and Audrey heard him filling a kettle. A few minutes later, he placed a plate of buttered crumpets on a mat depicting a comedy fox hunt, which was one of six protecting the dark, rosewood dining table. He took two fine porcelain plates out of a sideboard and a couple of silver butter knives from a drawer.

From another drawer, he removed two white, lace-trimmed napkins.

'I'll get the tea.' Malcolm disappeared into the kitchen.

Audrey stood by the French windows, staring into the garden. She imagined Malcolm and Mary as a young couple, sharing the excitement of their new home, all those years ago. She thought about Duncan and their first flat in Beckenham, bought for five thousand pounds. They'd been so happy.

'Tea,' announced Malcolm. He placed a porcelain teapot on a stand.

'Your garden is a perfect tonic for all the ills in our world.'

'That depends. Now it looks good as I've put it to bed for the winter but come spring and summer, it's a constant battle between man and nature.'

Audrey laughed.

'I intend to plant vegetables next spring so that I get some return for all the hours.' He pulled out a rosewood dining chair with a tapestry padded seat and Audrey took her cue to sit down. He sat on her right at the end of the table and offered her the plate of crumpets.

'Jam?' Malcolm indicated a porcelain pot, with matching lid and cut out section for the teaspoon.

'Mmm, truly scrumptious. I'll need another long walk.'

'Your stairs,' Malcolm said, reaching for the teapot, 'will ensure you keep the weight off. Where are you sleeping?'

'I'm in a room at the very top of the house. Did you not go up there at my housewarming?'

'Er, no, I didn't venture far. Isn't it a bit out of the way?'

'I like it. Something about the room appeals to me.'

Tea turned into high tea and then an early light supper. It was gone ten p.m. by the time they got into Malcolm's car and drove back to Audrey's new home. He swung into her driveway and as soon as he'd brought the Honda to a halt, he leapt out and opened the passenger door. She looked up at him and couldn't help admiring his tall, slim frame and surprising athleticism. She climbed out of the car into the distinctly chilly night and allowed him to escort her to her front porch. They reached the door and she turned to face him, residual light from the High Street giving his contours an ethereal glow. She slipped her arms around his neck and their lips met. Within moments a gentle kiss turned into one that was full of passion under a three-quarter moon floating in an almost clear sky.

Audrey was surprised by her awakened desire and wondered if there could be a happy future with this handsome man, an eventuality that had definitely not been in her game plan.

'Come in for a nightcap,' she whispered.

'I'm driving.'

'No need to hurry up in the morning. I make good mint tea.'

Malcolm eased his body away. 'Let's go back to my cottage. It's warm and cosy.'

She kissed him, gently.

Audrey heard Malcolm firing up his Honda as she closed the heavy oak door and flicked on the dim hall light. The house was quiet and seemed content but stark compared to Malcolm's lovely cottage. The floor was still littered with debris from her tea party. She smiled – but her face froze when she saw the axe leaning against the wall, and she quickly looked away.

CHAPTER NINETEEN

Tina had an early viewing of a property in the morning, so had decided not to stay the night with her new lover. She always drove too fast, but despite campaigns by various parent groups, Hawksmead did not have speed humps or cameras apart from the one near the humpback bridge, for which Tina would, in all probability, receive a penalty ticket. She was still shaken from her experience after the tea party and was convinced that she was now seeing ghosts, thanks entirely to her involvement with Audrey's house. Grade II it may be, but she wished Spartak had bought it and razed it to the ground. Their relationship had survived the first twenty-four hours – he had sworn on his mother's grave that it wasn't him who had chased her in a Range Rover – but her parents were unhappy that she had missed their family Sunday lunch to spend the day with him.

She had decided not to take the Old Military Road back to her parents' home in Hawksmead but the much longer and less lonely arterial route. She entered Hawksmead at the southern end of the small town and rejoiced in seeing the street lighting. Her spirits lifted, she pressed the accelerator and roared up the empty High Street. As she cut across the white line in the centre of the road to make a perfect entry into Woodland Rise, her retinas were blanched by full-beam headlights coming from a vehicle speeding in the opposite direction.

Malcolm felt good as his size ten shoe pressed down on the accelerator. He hated wearing spectacles, but even he succumbed when driving at night, and now his lenses were magnifying the glare of approaching headlights. Instinctively, he swerved hard to his left but his side mirror slapped the approaching car's side mirror with a combined speed of ninety miles per hour, smashing them both.

Tina leapt out of the car she loved and had just damaged for the very first time. How could she have been so stupid, and who was the idiot driving in the middle of the road? She looked across the street and recognised Malcolm as he got out of his car. Why was he driving so fast? Had something happened? Weren't old people meant to just pootle along?

'Are you all right?' Malcolm called.

'Yes. Are you?'

They gave each other a thumbs-up.

Tina pulled off a loose section of mirror and got back into her car. Instead of turning left into Woodland Rise and heading to her family home, she continued up the High Street, at a leisurely pace, and brought her car to a gentle halt. She stepped out and shivered, not from the chilly night air but from gut-wrenching fear that enveloped her as she looked up at the old school boarding house, eerily silent in the sodium-coloured street lighting.

She felt a painful twinge of guilt for selling the great unloved pile to Audrey, and wanted to be sure that she was all right. The man with the axe may have been no more real than the boy with the flapping coat, but Malcolm speeding away was definitely not a figment of her imagination.

The moon came out from behind a cloud and added to the spectral ambience of the house, as droplets of water crystallised in the midnight air. And then she saw him – his young, pale face clearly lit by the moon, looking down from the top landing window.

Tina stood motionless, caught in the boy's stare, her eyes locked on his until a cloud passed in front of the moon and released her from the boy's grip. She had Audrey's mobile phone number. Should she call and warn her? But what would that achieve? She jumped back into her car and spun the front wheels on the damp tarmac.

~

Something has happened which you may not believe. I'm not sure I actually believe it myself. Two nights before the opening of *Cyrano de Bergerac* and my parents coming to see me in the play, I woke up in the night, bursting for a pee. As you know, my dormitory is at the top of the boarding house and, to get to the bogs, I have to walk down two flights of narrow, wooden, creaking stairs that make a terrible din no matter how hard I try to be quiet. The way is lit by dim, yellow, night lights that create a strange glow in the freezing air. Shivering with cold, I stopped at the half-landing. To my left were the wide stairs that went down to the main hallway. From nowhere, a boy approached me. He was smaller than me and, in the gloomy light, I was convinced he was my friend Mini. I said hello to him, forgetting he was dead. The boy did not respond. He came up to me and stared into my face. It wasn't Mini. I mumbled an apology, but the boy just continued to look at me. Then he turned, and I watched as he went down the main stairs into the hallway and disappeared from view.

Bursting, I rushed to the bogs. It was only when the pressure was off, I realised that when the boy walked down the stairs, there was absolute silence – not one floorboard squeaked.

I left the bogs and walked slowly back to where I had seen the boy. I looked down into the hallway and then rushed upstairs to my dorm, caring not a jot about the noise I was making. When I was safely in my narrow bed and had the sheet and blanket over me, I finally took a breath.

CHAPTER TWENTY

Audrey emerged from the kitchen and walked along the corridor, back into her entrance hallway, steaming mug of cocoa in hand. She deliberately avoided looking at the axe and took her time climbing the creaking stairs, turning on and off lights as she went. Her mind was completely consumed with thoughts of Malcolm. She hardly knew the man but would have slept with him on their first date, as she did after just one date with her husband. Of course, that was in the Swinging Sixties when miniskirts and marijuana, peace and love filled her world.

In the top dormitory room she took off her clothes and pulled on cotton pyjamas. Lying between the sheets under thin boarding-house blankets, she felt way too excited to sleep and wished she'd accepted Malcolm's offer to return to his sweet cottage. If she rang him now, she knew he would drive over and collect her. She looked at her phone, which she had plugged into its charger, and debated calling him. What a day she'd had. How life changes on a sixpence. Her reason for coming to Hawksmead suddenly seemed almost inconsequential to the desire she felt for a man that three days ago she'd known only as a Good Samaritan who'd helped her with her bags.

She eyed the row of tired old books, sitting on the top shelf within the bookcase. They looked untouched for many a decade, apart from a large encyclopaedia that had a small thumbprint in the thick dust.

Decision made, she flung back the bed covers and swung her bare feet onto the scarred floorboards. For a moment, her hand hovered over the phone. She took a deep breath and sighed and turned her attention to the faded spine titles above long-dead authors' names.

Dust made her sneeze as she flicked through the various tomes and then she looked at the child-sized thumbprint.

She pulled on a thick lambswool sweater and had to use two hands to lift the heavy encyclopaedia off the shelf. The worn cover was locked with a small brass clasp. She blew as much dust off the book as she could and sat across her bed leaning against the cold, yellowed wall. She opened the tome and flicked a few pages and then her heart raced with excitement, for in a large, jagged, cut-out section was another book. On its dark blue leather cover was written *1965* in faded gold. She eased the little book out of its hiding place and looked at the flyleaf:

This is the secret diary of Robert Oakes
DO NOT READ UNTIL 2065

Audrey's heart missed a beat as she turned to the first entry, written in pencil in a neat, carefully rounded, schoolboy's hand. She read the first sentence, and all thoughts of Malcolm and her new life evaporated from her mind.

I am thirteen years old and frightened. I am not very bright. When stressed I cannot get the words out. My parents took me to a doctor. He recommended vigorous physical exercise in an outward-bound school. He said it would cure me of my stutter and help me with my school work.

Audrey read the diary straight through but paused to wipe her eyes on her bed sheet before reading the final two entries.

Roxane has saved me again. When I am her, I do not think about Mini. I think about Christian, speaking beautiful, poetic lines to me that were written by Cyrano. I think about misplaced love and how we are all too frightened to reveal our thoughts. But I don't know what my thoughts are. They are very confusing to me. I like being Roxane, I like dressing up as her, and I like people thinking I'm pretty. When I look in the mirror and see Roxane, I feel the best I've ever felt. No wonder they call me queer!

My performance of Roxane received a standing ovation. Not once did I stutter when I spoke my lines. My parents are staying in a hotel in Undermere and seem really proud of me. Last night, I went to bed happy for the first time in a very long while. But something woke me in the early hours of this morning. For a moment, I thought I heard Mini calling me. I tried to go back to sleep but, scared of wetting my bed, I decided to go down to the bogs. When I reached the half-landing, the way looked clear in the dim lighting – and then I saw him, Mini, standing in the hallway looking up at me. I felt a great pull inside me to be with him.

Silently, the boy climbed the stairs and came towards me. It wasn't Mini. I could see tears in his eyes and rope burns around his neck as he reached out his hand. Icy tendrils stroked my cheek before I found the courage to escape to the bogs and lock a cubicle door. Who is he? What does he want? I wept for my friend Mini as I shivered and waited for the sound of boys getting up for the new day.

Once the washroom had emptied, I cleaned my teeth and rushed up to the dorm to get dressed. Down below, I heard the distant chatter of boys leaving for chapel, and Matron starting her Morris 1000. Then the boarding house fell quiet. On my pillow was a letter from my mother; inside, I found a crisp one-pound note. My parents had come to say goodbye, but Matron couldn't find me and told them I'd left for breakfast.

I am writing this through my tears. Mini has gone, Roxane has deserted me, and I am back to the stuttering, blubbing boy I truly am. I know my parents love me, but I wish they'd taken me home.

Someone is coming up. I can hear the stairs creaking. Time to hide you, my friend.

Audrey hugged the diary as if it were the boy himself. The dormitory room was freezing cold, and condensation on the old window panes had turned to ice. She pushed back the bed's sparse covers and slid her feet into her slippers.

This is the secret diary of Robert Oakes
DO NOT READ UNTIL 2065

Tears poured from her eyes as she wept for the boy who had written his private thoughts in the very room in which she slept.

Exhausted with emotion, she saw the encyclopaedia, with its cut-out section, and decided to put the diary back in its secret home where it had lain hidden for fifty years. She touched her fingers to her lips, passed the kiss on to the diary's leather cover and returned the encyclopaedia to its place on the shelf. She turned off the light and went to the window, and was about to close the fraying drapes when the moon emerged. Through the frosting pane and cold air, she could just make out the humpback bridge and the meandering black serpent of the River Hawk.

CHAPTER TWENTY-ONE

'Fifth position,' ordered Elizabeth. Audrey tried to move her feet without the book sliding off her head.

'If the book falls off your head again, you will be punished much more severely,' Diana said with glee.

Audrey felt the book sliding down the back of her head and woke up before it hit the floor.

Through the window she could see the first signs of dawn. Her sheets were sodden. She had no choice but to get out of bed and roll them up. She peeled off her clinging pyjamas and put on her dressing gown.

Lost in thought, she went down the wooden stairs barefoot, no longer noticing the accompanying chorus of creaks and squeaks. She stopped at the half-landing and looked down the stairs that led to the hallway. This was where Robert Oakes had met the ghost boy. Who was it he'd heard climbing the stairs to the top dormitory room?

Audrey entered the washroom and dropped the rolled bed sheets on the floor together with her pyjamas. She hung her dressing gown on one of many old iron hooks and used her usual cubicle. Her breath billowed out in the cold morning air. She pulled the long chain with its porcelain handle, walked into the communal shower, and checked there was a towel hanging on a hook. She turned on the water and jumped clear before the icy spray could soak her. It took about three minutes for the water to get warm and by then, Audrey's thin body was shivering with cold. She turned her face up to the spray and thought about Robert Oakes standing in her shower, scared, cold, lonely. How bereft of love he must have felt that first day of school. From her own experience, she knew that most parents want to do the very best for their children, little realising that they may be handing them over to people with hidden vices.

Warmed through, she stepped out of the shower and quickly wrapped herself in her towel and dressing gown. She walked into the washroom and cleaned her teeth; the mirror above her was misted with condensation.

In the kitchen, while the kettle was coming to the boil, Audrey popped the damp sheets and pyjamas in one of the old washing machines, poured soap in the dispenser and switched it on. She wished she'd worn her slippers as the tiled floor was numbing her feet. Looking around for salvation, she spied two old rugby socks she'd found in the washing machine when she first arrived, and put them on.

The oil-fired boiler had been on low all night to ensure she had hot water for her shower. Now, it had to pull its weight and heat the freezing house. She turned a knob and was pleased to see the roar of flames through the thick viewing glass.

'Not that it will do much good,' Audrey said out loud to herself as she re-entered the kitchen and made a cup of mint tea.

Warmed from her drink but still scantily attired, she climbed the stairs up to her dormitory room, completely lost in a world that had existed in her house fifty years ago.

She opened her bedroom door and stopped dead. Her breath came in short snatches, and her body shook as blood drained from her face.

On the floor lay the encyclopaedia together with all the books that had rested on the shelf for fifty years. How had they fallen on the floor? Audrey had never watched any films about ghosts or poltergeists, not out of fear, but because she could not suspend her disbelief. And yet, on the floor lay the heavy encyclopaedia and all the other books. Perhaps there was more to the supernatural than she'd given credence.

She knelt down and opened the encyclopaedia and was relieved to see the diary was still in its hiding place. She picked it up and placed it on her pillow. She looked at the high shelf and saw it was broken in two. Examining it closer, she saw the ends were riddled with tiny holes.

'Woodworm – not a poltergeist.'

There was a creak behind her.

She didn't look. Her heart pounded. How she wished Malcolm was with her. Screwing up all her courage, she turned to face she knew not what.

Caught in a draught between her bedroom window and the window across the landing, the dormitory door was swinging gently back and forth on its old hinges. Audrey laughed with relief. She looked at the boy's diary sitting on her pillow and slipped it out of sight, underneath.

BANG!

Audrey jumped. The door had slammed shut. She closed her bedroom window and took a deep breath.

'Get a grip, girl.'

She grabbed a few, trusty, practical items of clothing and quickly got dressed. Handbag in hand, she was about to leave when she had another thought. She removed the diary from under her pillow and contemplated returning it to the cut-out section within the encyclopaedia, but decided to pop it into her bag.

She looked around the room, now messy as a teenager's. 'I'm here, Bobby. You're going to be all right.'

CHAPTER TWENTY-TWO

The travel kettle came to the boil. Audrey popped a Yorkshire teabag in a mug and poured on the boiling water. She was fired up. She had a plan. Her hand went to turn on her Philips radio to listen to Radio 2, but she did not press the button, preferring the sound of her own mind rather than the distraction of lively chat.

She blew her tea and thought about Robert and his friend Mini, who had been killed on the humpback bridge; and the two older boys who had tried to claw their way out of the swirling torrent. She thought about the boys' parents, especially Robert's, and could not contain the tears that rolled, unchecked, down her cheeks. She also thought about the ghost that Robert had seen. Who was he? Was he really a ghost? Do they actually exist? She sipped her tea.

Audrey slipped on her coat and her wool-lined hat and gloves. She looked at the axe leaning against the wall by the front door in the hallway, turned the latch and pulled the door open. A great hulk of a man was standing on her doorstep – and her mouth dropped open.

'Good morning Mrs Willatt,' Spartak said. 'Thank you for excellent tea party. It was kind of you to invite us all.'

'How can I help you?' She tried to sound calm.

'I believe you have something of mine.' His voice was gruff and deep and – Audrey thought, much to her annoyance – incredibly sexy.

'I've told you, my house is not for sale.'

'I hear you. I have come for axe.'

'Axe? Explain yourself.'

'My little brother got over excited, and –'

'Left an axe embedded in my door.' She indicated the deep cut in the old oak.

'I sincerely apologise for distress caused.'

'There was no distress on my behalf. Your little brother is the one with whom you should be concerned. I suggest you keep him on a tighter leash.'

'I give you my word he will not trouble you again.'

'Good.' Audrey stepped through the doorway forcing Spartak to step back. She turned her back on him and closed the door.

'What about axe?'

'Apology accepted.' She used her key to double-lock the door and turned to face the handsome Russian. 'Now, you'll have to excuse me as I have a busy day.'

'It's my axe. You cannot keep it.'

'And my door will not heal.'

'It has sentimental value. I ask you to return it to me.'

Audrey removed her phone from her bag.

'Who you call?' he asked, looking less sure.

She ignored his question as she swiped the screen.

'Please. All I want is axe.'

She scrolled through her contacts and selected one. She put the phone to her ear.

'I will return when you are less busy.' He spat out the words as he stormed off down her short drive towards his van, where another man was sitting at the wheel.

'Hello.'

'Malcolm, it's Audrey.' She listened to his happy response. 'I have an errand to run this morning. Could we meet for a late lunch? I'll give you a call.'

Tina, seated in her car across the street, watched the van pull away, forcing a taxi, about to overtake, to brake hard. She was in a state of shock. She had wanted to check that Audrey was okay, following the clash of mirrors with Malcolm, and to take up her invitation to drop by for coffee. She had not expected to see her new boyfriend, or the man in the driver's seat of the van.

Realisation dawned. She had broken up with Sean and slept with a Russian whose brother, she now realised, was probably an axe murderer.

She started her engine and inadvertently attracted Audrey's attention. Damn! What was she going to say? She lowered the driver's window as Audrey peered in.

'Hello, Tina. I hope you're well. Did you want to see me?'

'No,' Tina said. 'Well, yes, in a way. I just wanted to check that you were all right.'

Audrey looked at the remains of the side mirror hanging by its wires. 'I'm fine, but I see that your car has had a bit of a mishap.'

'Your gentleman friend and I had a coming together last night. We slapped mirrors. Nobody's fault.'

'Well, it's very good of you to call by,' Audrey said. 'I'm off to the library to do a little research.'

'On your house? On the ghost boy?' She looked up at Audrey but could not maintain eye contact and stared at her hands in shame. 'I shouldn't have sold you the house.'

'You had no choice. I was determined to buy it.'

'Would you like a lift to the library? The pavement's a bit slippery.'

'Thank you. I think I'll walk. I need to blow away the cobwebs.'

'Let me put the house back on the market. Something bad lurks in there. I've seen him. It should be torn down. Destroyed. Please, don't go back in there. Not alone.'

'Thank you for your concern, Tina, but the only bad thing I've seen lurking around here is the company you keep.' She strode off, leaving Tina feeling even more wretched.

CHAPTER TWENTY-THREE

Since arriving in Hawksmead, Audrey had visited the town's Victorian library building several times, not for anything in particular but because she loved the smell of old books. She could also use the library's computers if she needed to do anything that was too fiddly for her phone; and there was the convenience of an ATM for withdrawing cash in warmth and safety.

Audrey went up to the front desk and was greeted by Shirley, a woman of similar age to her.

'I would like to look at newspapers from fifty years ago. Do you have old copies filed away in a vault by any slim chance?'

'In those days, newspapers were photographed on film,' Shirley said, clearly delighted to see Audrey again. 'We've an old viewer, somewhere.'

Audrey moistened her lips, doing her best to rein in her excitement. 'What level of bribery would it take for me to have access to the films and the viewer?'

'A cup of tea in the Olde Tea Shoppe would be nice,' Shirley said, smiling.

'You're on, and I'll throw in an Eccles cake.'

'Black Forest gateau is my cake of choice. But, before we get too excited, let's check that the bulb hasn't blown in the viewer.'

Audrey followed hot on Shirley's heels to a storeroom at the back of the library. The viewer was bolted to its own table which, conveniently, was on castors. Together, the two women wheeled it out and, despite its awkward, supermarket-trolley-like movement, they managed to push it to a spot where there was both an electrical plug socket and a table for the rolls of film.

Shirley plugged in the viewer, and Audrey turned on the switch. The light bulb came on.

'Leave it on. I'll go and get the rolls of film for…?'

'September to Christmas 1965,' Audrey answered.

A few minutes later, Shirley returned with a heavy cardboard box with *David Greig the Grocer* stamped in fading black ink on the side.

'I hope you've got plenty of time. Is there anything in particular you're wanting to read?'

'Some boys died who attended the old school. One of them was killed in my house.'

'I see. Well, I must get on with some work. Don't shout if you need anything.' Shirley smiled and walked away.

Audrey searched through the rolls that had been marked in blue ink; red copper showing through the faded script. She decided to start with the town's local newspaper, *The Hawksmead Chronicle*, and quickly figured out how to thread the film into the viewer. She picked up a roll marked September 1965.

Audrey was impressed with the old technology. If a story caught her eye she could zoom in and read the text in large type. Strangely, the roll of film started in August rather than September, so she scrolled, as fast as the machine would allow, through stories that made the headlines in what the press call the silly season.

That Magnificent Young Man in His Flying Machine was a headline she could not resist and very quickly she was reading about Ashley Ward, an eleven-year-old schoolboy, who flew his father's Cessna at Biggin Hill and was called the youngest trainee pilot in England. To see over the controls, he had to sit on two cushions.

Audrey scrolled on with a smile and thought back to when she first took to the road and had no licence and no brakes worthy of the name. Her father had brought home plans for a soapbox cart, drawn up by one of his designers in his construction company. A carpenter had cut pieces of wood to length so that she could nail them together and build a cart big enough to take both her and her young brother. She received five shillings out of her mother's housekeeping to buy pram wheels.

She and her brother loved their soapbox. They lived at the southern end of Sevenoaks on a residential hill called Brattle Wood, where the family had moved when Audrey was seven. The first time she and her brother rode the cart together, they had crashed into the kerb, flipped into the air and landed on the loose gravel road with both suffering badly scraped knees, hands and elbows. It didn't put Audrey off. She persuaded her father to bring home more wood, and for two shillings she managed to buy another set of pram wheels. Now, she and her brother could race. Very few families owned a car, so the road was mostly clear for the young drivers. Her brother was fearless, but Audrey was heavier, so her cart went faster, sometimes too fast, and she had to take quick action to avoid serious injury.

Audrey continued scrolling on through the film roll until a headline jumped out at her together with a picture of Robert Oakes in his school uniform. She read the article as quickly as possible but took her time when it came to the coroner's summation:

The schoolboy was the last to leave the boarding house and so no one saw what happened. It is assumed that in his haste not to be late for chapel, he tripped on the stairs and, in the resultant fall, broke his neck. His body was discovered in the hallway by his English master, who had called in at the boarding house to congratulate the boy on his performance in the school play.

The deaths of four boys, in one school, in one term, is highly regrettable and the school is urged to reconsider its duty of care to the pupils in its charge.

Audrey pushed her chair away from the viewer, ignoring the tears filling her eyes and pouring down her cheeks. What had happened? The last entry in the hidden diary had been: *Someone is coming up. I can hear the stairs creaking. Time to hide you, my friend.*

Who was that person, and did he or she have anything to do with the boy's death? Audrey mopped her face dry and dug deeper into the article.

Crown Courts in England and Wales, are giving parents the choice of paying for their miscreant sons to undergo rigorous correctional training at Hawksmead College, an independent outward-bound institution, in order to spare their little darlings from attending a government reform school such as Borstal. The physically rigorous regime that is part of the curriculum at Hawksmead College is considered by the courts to be sufficiently tough and preferable to the curriculum of crime that is the norm in approved Borstal detention centres.

However, the secret agreement between Prime Minister Wilson's Labour administration and Hawksmead College was exposed, not just through the unfortunate deaths of four innocent pupils, but by the savage injuries inflicted on fellow pupils by young thugs who should be wearing suits with arrows rather than open-necked shirts and corduroy shorts. Once the cosy arrangement between the courts and a school struggling to make up its numbers came to light, many parents removed their children and the school governors were forced, in certain instances, to refund the parents' deposits.

Audrey scrolled on to see if there were any further articles about the school and found a short piece recording that Neville Gibbs, the headmaster of Hawksmead College, was to take early retirement. He planned to return to Nepal where he had lost his fingers and toes attempting to be the first to climb Mount Everest.

Audrey pushed her chair away from the viewer and sighed. So that was it. The deaths of four boys, in one school term, were simply a footnote in history – if that.

A cup of coffee with a digestive biscuit nestling in its saucer was placed on the battered viewing trolley in front of Audrey.

'You look like you need it,' Shirley said.

Audrey smiled. 'Thank you. May I ask how long you have

lived in Hawksmead?'

Shirley looked around the library. An elderly man, seated at a long table littered with newspapers, appeared to be asleep. On the far side, in the young people's reading area, a primary school teacher was holding the attention of a group of children.

She turned back to Audrey. 'I was born here. Quite a few years before you were even a glint in your father's eye.'

'Not so many years. What can you tell me about the big school?'

'It was bad news for the town when the last pupils left the college. Many businesses closed down. The shop that sold the school uniform and games kits closed immediately.'

'How long ago was that?'

'It happened right in the middle of the banking crisis and it's been empty ever since.'

'What about the deaths of four boys in one school term? Do you remember anything about that?'

Shirley looked uncomfortable. 'No one in their right mind in that cold autumn will ever forget what happened. The weather was freezing, but those poor boys in their corduroy shorts still had to camp out on the moor. Two boys drowned in the river. Why they were in the river, canoeing, was never explained. But it was in full flood and dangerous. Another boy died on the bridge on his way to the school. That seems to have been a tragic accident, although it turns out that the driver of the car was a master at the school.'

'What was his name?'

'It was never released. I don't know why,' Shirley said with a shrug. 'Anyway, he'll be dead by now.'

There was a pause. Neither spoke.

'Well, I'd better get back to work,' Shirley said. 'We volunteers cannot stand around chatting all day!' She turned to go.

'The fourth boy,' Audrey stated. 'What do you know about the fourth boy who died? The one who fell down the stairs.'

Shirley looked even more uncomfortable. 'You're happy in your new home, aren't you?'

'Very.'

'Best leave it at that.'

'I know a boy died in my house.'

'If only it had been just one boy.'

Audrey thought about the ghost of a boy that Robert wrote about in his diary. 'Was there another boy who died?'

Shirley nodded. Tears welled up in her eyes and she slumped down in a chair sobbing quietly. She searched her sleeves for a handkerchief or tissue. Audrey came to the rescue, offering a perfectly ironed lace-trimmed hanky.

'I'm sorry,' Audrey said.

Shirley shook her head and took the hanky. 'You weren't to know. His name was Edward Holden. One morning, during his first term, we met on our bikes. I was twelve at the time, and he was thirteen. It was frosty cold, but it was a Sunday, so we were both just filling time. It sounds silly now, but we fell in love and promised each other that we would marry as soon as we were aged twenty-one – the age of consent back then. We met every Sunday, and Eddie told me about the school, the harsh physical regime, the bullying and… and…' Shirley trailed off.

'What happened?' Audrey took Shirley's hand.

'Eddie told me that he was having trouble with an older boy. He'd tried to kiss Eddie. One day, while Eddie was taking a shower, the older boy interfered with him. I didn't really understand what Eddie was telling me, but I could see his distress. The following Sunday, I rode on my bike to our meeting place by the bridge, but Eddie didn't show up. I was nervous about cycling to the boarding house as our meetings were secret. I thought that maybe he'd been punished for meeting me. The next day, at my school, a girl I didn't like came up to me and told me that my boyfriend was dead. When the boys woke up on the Sunday morning to go to chapel, Eddie was found hanging by his bed sheet in the hallway.' She sank her face in her hands. 'I loved him.'

Audrey watched as memories from fifty-five years ago came back with full intensity.

It took Shirley a couple of minutes to find herself again and, after wiping her face with Audrey's sodden handkerchief, she managed to rally a smile. 'That's not what I expected when I awoke this morning. You're the first person I've told. Not even my dear husband, God rest his soul, knew about Eddie and me. They say it's haunted, the boarding house, your new home. That Eddie still walks the stairs. If you see him – tell him, Shirley sends her love.'

She got up from the chair and looked at Audrey's handkerchief. 'I'll wash this.'

'I don't remember seeing you at my housewarming party.'

'I thought about leaving Hawksmead and did for a while. But I always wanted to be close to Eddie's spirit. I didn't want to leave him alone in that house – but I could never go in – never.'

CHAPTER TWENTY-FOUR

It was late morning when Audrey left the heat of the library and stepped out into the cold air. She embraced the icy prickles, keen to shake off the deep sadness that had enveloped her. Not just the death of Robert Oakes, but the suicide of Edward Holden. Thankfully, Malcolm was available to meet for lunch, and the thought was already lifting her spirits.

Every now and then, as she walked through the small town, a guest from her tea party would say hello, and Audrey rejoiced in the friendly conversations. She approached her home from the far side of the street and took a few moments to look at it. Her eyes drifted up to the top window where Tina believed she had seen the face of a schoolboy.

Come on. Show yourself. Don't leave me out. Audrey shook her head and crossed the road. She walked up her short drive, unlocked the heavy front door, and curled down her mouth when she spotted the deep gouge caused by the axe blade. She entered the hall and closed the door securely behind her. She wanted to freshen up, to make sure she looked her best for Malcolm.

Facing the closed door, with her back to the hall she felt a cold chill of fear, like bony fingers crawling up her spine. Behind her, she heard a creak. What would she see? Would it be the ghost of a boy Shirley still loved, fifty-five years after his death? Heart pounding, she turned and looked into her hallway. It was as it should be, just a hallway, large and gloomy; the weak autumnal sunlight filtering through the rippled Victorian window panes.

She breathed out and walked to the base of the stairs.

'Eddie. I met Shirley this morning, and she asked me to send you her love. She thinks about you every day and misses you very much.'

She cocked her head as if waiting for a reply. 'Look at me. I'm talking to myself, now.'

She placed her hand on the wooden handrail and a foot on the bottom step. She looked up to the half-landing and climbed the stairs, accompanied by their usual creaks and squeaks. At the top of the first flight, she turned and looked down into the hallway. She now understood why people in the town were so reluctant to enter her house. Too much had happened within its solid walls.

She felt the vibrations before she heard the faint ring of her mobile phone. She opened her bag and dug deep to retrieve it. The screen displayed the name *Malcolm,* and her heart skipped a beat.

'Hello handsome,' Audrey said, with a teenage smile.

'Well, that's the best answer to a phone call I've received in a very long while,' Malcolm laughed. 'In fact, according to my excellent long-term memory – ever! I should be with you in about twenty minutes. I've booked us a table at the… well, I'll leave it as a surprise. Suffice it to say, I have my own tankard hanging on a hook over the bar.'

Audrey slipped her phone away and, warmed by thoughts of lunch with Malcolm, walked up the stairs to change into something just a little more inviting than her thick trousers. They kept out the cold chill that would emanate off the dark waters of the River Hawk, but as Malcolm was picking her up in his car, she thought a dress was more appropriate. She got to the top floor landing and crossed over to the window. She looked down into the High Street and spotted Malcolm's Honda. What a gentleman; so considerate of him to give her a bit of time to smarten up.

She turned away from the window and entered the top dormitory room. Relief flooded through her – it was as messy as when she had left it. She quickly peeled off her clothes and selected a favourite daytime dress she'd picked up in the local Oxfam charity shop. She put it on, felt for the zip, smoothed the skirt, grabbed her bag, had a quick look around, and headed out of the room.

Thank you are two words that can mean a lot in the right context, but written in the dust that lay on the window pane across the top landing, they scared Audrey more than she thought possible. It was nearly lunchtime, not midnight, and yet she was petrified; almost too fearful to walk down the stairs.

'Get a grip, girl,' she murmured. She took a deep breath and could feel her heart pounding. She licked her dry lips and tried to swallow her fear.

'You're welcome, Eddie. You're very welcome.'

She hurried to the top of the stairs and ran down faster than she knew was safe. She reached the half-landing and looked down the wide stairs leading into the hallway. Malcolm was outside waiting for her. She was tempted to run into his arms, but she knew she had to keep a lid on it or she, too, would be too frightened to live in the old school boarding house.

She took another deep, calming breath and headed for the washroom. She switched on the lights and popped into her favourite cubicle. She didn't much like the long chain with its old porcelain handle, but the rush of water was certainly powerful and the natural action calmed her nerves. She came out of the cubicle and washed her hands.

Audrey knew she had not written *thank you* on the window pane and there was nobody, to her knowledge, in the house. So how had it got there? What rational explanation could there be?

She brushed her teeth – her hair, still thick and enhanced by colour, she gave a light flick with a hairbrush.

'I think that's as good as it gets,' she said to her reflection and hurried across the washroom. She opened the door, switched off the lights, and entered the dark corridor. Spurred by fear, she ran to the half-landing and almost skipped down the stairs. In the hallway, she lifted her coat from the wooden stand and was about to turn the door latch when she heard a loud creak coming from the staircase behind her.

She froze. 'Eddie… Shirley told me what happened. You can

rest, now.'

There was another loud creak. She had to hold her nerve. She took a deep breath and turned to face the hallway.

Standing on the half-landing was a powerfully built man. In his hand was the axe. Audrey glanced down at the spot where she had placed it after Malcolm had removed it from her door.

'I Kirill Dryomov – Spartak's brother. I come for axe and take look round.'

Audrey could feel her heart rate increasing, but she was determined to stay calm. 'You're becoming a nuisance.'

'No!' His response was loud and echoed in the almost unfurnished hall. 'You are the nuisance. We want you out of here. Gone. Do you understand, lady?'

'I understand that you have damaged my front door, broken into my house and are now threatening me. I suggest you get out before I call the police.'

Kirill laughed and walked down the stairs. 'Sell the house, lady.' He sauntered up to her, the axe loosely held in his left hand.

'Why do you want it so much?' She looked into his rough face and searched for some of the good looks that imbued his older brother. 'Is there buried treasure, is that it?'

'You steal it from us – like you steal axe.'

'Nonsense. Your Russian pride is hurt. No more than that. Move on to another project.'

'Are you not frightened? Just a little bit?'

She saw the corners of his mouth quivering.

The doorbell reverberated around the hall.

Audrey twisted the latch and pulled open the front door. Malcolm was standing on the step. His smile froze on seeing Kirill, who eased his way past Audrey. 'Thank you for axe. It was stolen from van.'

Audrey did not respond. Kirill looked at Malcolm. He gave him a brief nod, turned, and walked down the drive, the axe swinging at the end of his sinewed arm.

'You must call the police,' Malcolm urged as he helped Audrey put on her coat.

'It's good to see you.' She held his face in her hands, partly to stop them shaking, and kissed him on the lips. 'I have big plans for you and me.' She locked her front door and took his arm. 'I'll tell you over lunch. Where are we going?'

'I've booked a table at the Rorty Crankle Inn.' They walked to his car, which was still parked across the High Street. 'It offers the most amazing views of the moor, and the food is home cooking at its very best.'

Audrey looked at the smashed side mirror, held together with copious strips of sticky tape.

A massive beam spread across Malcolm's face. 'A slight mis-judgement on my part.'

Audrey laughed, relieved to be out of her house and in the company of such a charming man.

The Honda, with its two happy occupants, headed towards the River Hawk. Malcolm slowed as they approached the bridge; fifty years on, it was still only wide enough for one vehicle.

'My heart races every time I drive over this bridge,' he said, accelerating to climb up the sharp incline.

Audrey thought about Robert's friend, Mini, falling off his bike and being crushed by a car.

'In the morning, it can be very icy,' Malcolm continued. 'I think it's the refrigerating effect of the water below. I try to avoid it as much as possible.'

Audrey breathed a quiet sigh of relief when they came down the north side.

The Honda roared along the Old Military Road, past the turn-ing to Hawksmead College and up a gentle gradient towards the high ridge. Malcolm pulled over by a sign with an image of a camera. They got out, and the air whipped around Audrey's thin dress.

'A little of this can go a long way,' she laughed, hugging her coat to her.

'This beautiful expanse has been like this all my life. I hope it never changes. Of course it will. But for now, for the time I have left, I hope that we can come to this spot and share its wondrous beauty.'

Holding her coat closed with one hand, she slipped the other into Malcolm's. He gave it a gentle squeeze and looked down at her. She was fifteen again, and he was twenty-five. She hadn't wanted to wait when she was fifteen and in love with Paul McCartney, and she most certainly was not interested in wasting any time now.

'Warm hands, warm heart.' Malcolm smiled. 'If your husband was half as happy as you make me, he was a very lucky man.'

CHAPTER TWENTY-FIVE

There were quite a few vehicles in the seventeenth-century coaching inn car park but still plenty of spaces for Malcolm's Honda.

'Wait there.' He opened his door and the wind almost snatched it out of his hand. Bent against the razor-sharp air, he went around to the passenger door and used both hands to hold it open.

The wind was so strong, Audrey and Malcolm were almost propelled through the inn's battered door. Harry, the landlord, gave Malcolm a cheery welcome. His handsome ruddy face was topped off with a head of dark curls.

'Could you point me in the right direction?' Audrey asked, as she tried to recover her hair.

While she headed for the ladies, Harry gave Malcolm a double thumbs-up. 'You've landed on your feet there, mate. She's an absolute corker.' He escorted Malcolm to the dining section of the pub.

'I'm not sure I'm even awake.' Malcolm slapped his own cheek. 'This could be an amazing dream. If it is, don't wake me up.'

'You'd better hope she doesn't fall for *my* charms. I'll do my best to keep my natural charisma in check.'

'I am here!' called out Cathy, holding open the swing door to the kitchen.

Malcolm smiled at the comfortably plump, blue-eyed beauty, armed with a spatula and wearing a food-spattered striped apron. 'Hello, Cathy. I'm like a teenager on a first date. I want to demonstrate my feelings, but I'm scared of blowing out the flame.'

'Have you bought her anything special?' Cathy asked. 'A brooch? A necklace? A bracelet?'

'Er, no, not yet.'

'What about flowers?'

'I meant to. It slipped my mind.'

'Any romantic gesture at all?'

'I saved her from a madman with an axe. Does that count as romantic?'

Harry laughed. 'Halloween has a lot to answer for!'

'Apart from a "brief encounter" on the train,' Malcolm continued, 'I've only known her since her housewarming party last Saturday. I'm trying to keep real but it's no good!'

'I don't blame you, mate,' Harry said. 'She's gorgeous.'

'Harry, you're on very dangerous ground.' Cathy waved her spatula, threateningly, as Audrey emerged from the ladies.

'I know it's crazy, but it feels so wonderful,' Malcolm said. 'Why would she be interested in me? You should have seen the men at her tea party – their tongues were hanging out, even though most were at least twenty years younger than her. She simply emanates perfection. Or am I completely deluded?'

'I hope so,' Audrey said, poking Malcolm gently in the ribs.

'Audrey,' Harry said. 'This is my wife, Cathy. She's your chef for the day.'

'I hear you've moved into the old school boarding house,' Cathy said, shaking Audrey's hand. 'Was there nothing smaller for sale?'

Audrey laughed. 'I have plans.'

'Well, so do I, and it's to cook you and your handsome friend the best meal you'll ever eat this side of the moor!' They all laughed as Cathy retreated to the kitchen.

Harry showed them to their table. 'We're open all the way through until eleven tonight, so take your time.'

Audrey and Malcolm declined Harry's menu and said they wanted Cathy to surprise them.

'Ooh, she'll love that.' A few moments later, Harry returned with two crystal-glass flutes sparkling with champagne. 'On the house,' he said.

Malcolm and Audrey toasted Harry and Cathy and then they were left alone. For a moment, quite a long moment, they looked at each other.

Audrey broke the silence. 'The Rorty Crankle. Odd name. What does it mean?'

'I don't have the least idea. I think it's joke words, made up to mean something long forgotten. Probably very rude.' He smiled. 'How was your morning before that thug arrived?'

'I was in the library with a lovely person called Shirley. Do you know her?'

'What sort of age?'

'My sort of age. Well, a few years older. She's lived in Hawksmead almost all her life.'

'Although Hawksmead is my home town, for many years, I lived in Manchester.'

'Was that where you met your wife?'

'No, my wife was from Hawksmead too, but we had to move because of my work.'

'You were in marketing?'

'Yes. I've always had the gift of the pen. Coming up with marketing concepts and pithy copy was my stock in trade. I'm lucky. I got out before the internet took over. Words are cheap these days. Everyone's a blogger or writing acerbic comments on Facebook or Twitter – I'm sure they're having fun, but it's hard to monetise. In the 1970s, 80s and 90s, it was possible to make a very good living looking out of the window, opening my mind and allowing a brilliant idea to take root. Of course, not every seed that flew in was a rose; occasionally, what seemed promising would turn out to be Japanese knotweed!'

Audrey laughed as Harry arrived with their starter – beetroot and gin-cured salmon with freshly baked soda bread. For a few moments, they ate in silence.

'Why did you not have children?'

Malcolm paused his chewing and thought about the best way to answer Audrey's direct question.

'Of course, you can tell me to mind my own business.' She popped a piece of toast in her mouth.

'We tried. We tried everything. Unfortunately, IVF came too late for us. I think it wrecked our marriage. We didn't divorce, but we were divorced in every other way. They couldn't put their finger on it. She had the eggs, and I had plenty of little guys, but the chemistry wasn't there. We thought about adopting but we were getting on and the adoption agency put us near the bottom of the list. I expect we could have adopted a troublesome child, but neither of us wanted that. It was a baby we wanted. We had money, not to burn, but I was making a good living; we had lovely friends who all had children; but what she and I didn't have was love. Neither of us said it out loud but, deep down, she blamed me and I blamed her. We muddled through until she died. You and your husband were a bit luckier.' He took a sip of champagne.

Audrey steepled her fingers. 'I have been very lucky. Two boys, two lovely daughters-in-law, two grandchildren; it doesn't get any better, save for the fact that my keep-fit fanatic of a husband had repeated heart attacks until, finally, the one that killed him. He quit smoking when he was young; didn't drink much; was careful about what he ate...' Malcolm watched her blink back her sudden tears. 'Sixty-five – ' Her voice caught in her throat. 'Not even three score and ten.' She took a deep breath. 'Fortunately, touching wood, a weak heart is a gene my sons appear to have ducked.'

Malcolm caught the smell of beef wafting through from the kitchen and abandoned the remainder of his salmon. 'I'm sorry you've had to suffer such grief. How have your sons coped with the loss?'

'They miss him, but not quite as much as I'm sure he would like. Growing up, they had to live with a father for whom winning was in his DNA.' She smiled. 'Beating fellow highfliers, whether it was at squash, tennis or sailing that boat of his, gave him way too much pleasure. Of course, it's why he earned the big bucks. But, ultimately, the boys suffered issues with confidence, self-esteem. It's tough being the son of a successful go-getter. Still, his death has enabled me to help them buy bigger homes and to invest in the old school boarding house.'

'Invest?' Malcolm queried, raising his eyebrows.

'That's what I want to talk to you about, but something scrumptious is about to arrive.'

Two plates of steaming beef Wellington replaced the salmon starters. 'That looks magnificent, Harry,' Malcolm said, admiring the puff pastry wrapped fillet. 'Be sure to compliment the chef.'

'Nothing gives my misses greater pleasure than sweating over a hot stove for you, Malcolm. It annoys the hell out of me watching her cook for you with so much enthusiasm! By the way, when are we going cycling, again?' Harry looked at Audrey. 'Malcolm was quite the athlete in his youth. I've seen more of his padded cycling shorts than is healthy for any man.'

Harry walked off without waiting for a response.

'He's a good mate,' Malcolm said. 'He's seen me through a few rocky times.'

Audrey picked up her knife and fork. 'I am so pleased I changed into a dress. I don't think my slacks could have withstood the pressure. Bon appétit.'

'And here is the perfect accompaniment,' Harry said, proffering a wine bottle to Malcolm. 'A Cabernet Sauvignon with a rich oak flavour.'

'Pour away, but just give me a drop,' Malcolm said. 'I'm the one at the wheel, although my car is insured for anyone to drive should we both be incapacitated!'

Harry poured one and a quarter glasses. He placed the bottle on the table and, with a bow, he dramatically backed away.

'I like it here,' Audrey said, as she reached across the table to squeeze Malcolm's hand. 'If I had my own tankard, I would hang it above the bar, too.'

Malcolm laughed. 'Even Harry doesn't really know why he chose to buy the Rorty Crankle when he could have bought a pub in Hawksmead or Undermere. He said it was the moorland air and the total peace that did it for him, rather than any business sense.'

For a few moments they ate in silence. Malcolm was more than happy to accept Audrey at face value, but there was one question he knew he had to ask. He put down his knife and fork and looked across the table. 'What brought you to Hawksmead, Audrey? Why did you really buy the boarding house?'

Audrey put down her knife and fork and took a sip of wine. She picked up her napkin and dabbed her lips. 'I'm on the run – I robbed a bank and used the cash to buy the first building I could afford.' She said it with such gravitas that for a moment Malcolm was almost taken in.

'That was a line from a play I was in for an amateur theatre group,' Audrey continued. 'I got rave reviews.'

Malcolm laughed with relief. 'I'm not surprised.'

'By my being a bank robber or by my acting?'

'Hawksmead has an amateur group. You should join.' He took a forkful of food as Audrey took another sip of wine.

'The truth is,' she said, 'I've experienced life in Broadstairs, by the grey sea with its high cliffs; and I've experienced life in Sevenoaks with its money and commuting bankers. My generation, retired stockbrokers and their partners, are living smug, contented lives on the golf course, until someone like me becomes a widow. At first, my friends gathered round; I was invited everywhere, but then I began to notice that their husbands were absent. Frankly, it became clear that I was only on the guest list when the wives were grass widows, but not for the important events. Even though I was in my sixties, I was seen as competition, which I most certainly was not. So, I had a choice – be a lonely widow in Sevenoaks and wait for my friends to become widows too, or start a new, exciting life in a place far away from everything familiar. I looked at a map of England, stuck a pin in Hawksmead and searched online for properties for sale. I saw the old school boarding house and simply made a derisory offer, sight unseen. Nobody was more surprised than me when the offer was accepted. I think the charitable trust that owned it was fed up with paying council tax and other maintenance costs.'

'Where does the man with the axe fit in?'

'It was a petty tantrum, although I am going to change the back-door lock.' Audrey lifted her wine glass. 'It's so good not being the driver!' She took a deep glug.

'What about your children, your sons? They must be disappointed that you're not on hand for free babysitting?'

'Probably. But, as happy as I am to be a grandmother, I want to be me too. And, though my sons and their wives may protest, I know that weeks would go by without my seeing any of them. That's normal. Anyway, I shall still see them and, when I do, I'll have something to talk about.'

Harry approached the table and looked at the clean plates. 'Cathy will be very pleased.'

Audrey looked up at Harry. 'It was absolutely delicious.'

Malcolm added his high praise and caught Harry's eye and winked.

'Don't think I didn't see that!' Audrey laughed, stretching across the table to squeeze Malcolm's hand.

'I'll bring the dessert menu,' Harry said, taking away the plates. Audrey picked up her wine glass and looked at Malcolm.

'To you… the handsome marketeer.'

Malcolm picked up his glass, barely touched. 'To you, beautiful in every way.' They both took a sip.

'Are you up for a challenge?' Audrey asked.

'Of course. Always.'

'Help me turn the old school boarding house into a sanctuary full of warmth, laughter and great food for visitors to the moor.'

Malcolm withdrew his hand from Audrey's and used his napkin to dab his brow.

'It's a house that needs love,' she continued. 'It has seen tragedy and loneliness and fear, and I want to imbue it with joy.'

Malcolm replaced the napkin on his lap and looked into Audrey's sparkling eyes. 'I am honoured that you should ask me to share such an important venture, although I'm not sure how many useful years I've got in the tank.'

Before Audrey could respond, Harry came up to their table. 'And what would you two lovebirds like for dessert?'

'Just the bill, please Harry,' Audrey said.

They fought over the bill and then agreed to split it fifty-

fifty. They said their goodbyes, put on their coats, and stepped out into the chilly late-afternoon air as the soft autumnal sun began to slip down towards the horizon.

'This is just the beginning,' Audrey said.

It was fully dark and bitingly cold when Malcolm turned into Audrey's short drive and came to a halt. For a moment, they sat in silence and then Audrey reached out for his face and turned it to her, looking into his eyes.

Malcolm slid his arm under Audrey's and their mouths met. Old instincts took over, and soon they were kissing like teenagers at the end of a first date.

'Let's go in,' she whispered.

'I have a nice, big, comfy bed in my cottage.'

'We can push two beds together. Anyway, we only need one.'

They broke apart and got out of the car. She took Malcolm's arm and led him to her front door.

'My cottage is very cosy and warm,' shivered Malcolm.

Audrey laughed. 'The heating is on. We can always go to your cottage later.'

'Is there a reason why you have not moved in your furniture?'

'I'm renting out my home in Sevenoaks, furnished – anyway, I'm here to start again. Together we can turn this old house into the Hostel on the Moor.'

'Hostel on the Moor; I think I saw the film. It didn't end well.'

Audrey laughed as she turned the key in the lock and pushed open the heavy oak door. She switched on the light and the flickering strip lit the gloomy hall. 'Lighting is the first thing we need to get right.'

Malcolm stood on the threshold while Audrey slipped off her coat and hung it on the old clothes stand. 'I'm going upstairs to the top dormitory. You can go home and watch *Countdown* on TV and fantasise about Rachel Riley, or you can come upstairs with me.'

Malcolm stepped into the hallway. He turned to close the door, but the draught caught it and the slam echoed loudly through the building. Audrey helped him out of his coat and hung it next to hers. She reached for his hand and led him across the hall and up the first flight of stairs. Malcolm looked at the old school sign pointing to the lavatories.

'I may just have to take a detour,' he said.

'I'll be waiting.'

'Would you come with me? This house is distinctly creepy.'

Audrey took Malcolm's hand again and led him along the dark corridor to the washroom. She opened the door and switched on the lights, revealing the rows of washbasins and lavatory cubicles.

'All mod cons,' she said. 'But I think future walkers on the moor will draw the line at sharing a shower with a stranger.' She pointed at the cubicles. 'Take your pick. The one closest is my personal preference.'

'Thank you,' Malcolm said.

'I'll wait outside.' She turned and left him alone in the washroom.

Malcolm entered a cubicle and looked at the various messages scrawled on the wall. Being tall, he could see one that was high up by the cistern. As he leaned across the toilet bowl to read it, the door opened and closed in the cubicle next to his.

'Interesting writing on the wall,' Malcolm said. '*Matron's watching but it's Gibbs who's feeling.*' He smiled. 'Three apostrophes and all used correctly.'

There was no response from the neighbouring cubicle.

'Audrey? Are you there?'

Silence.

Malcolm carefully aimed for the bowl and was pleased to see that there was soft tissue and not old school Bronco non-absorbent lavatory paper. He pulled the chain, and water rushed down from the old metal cistern into the porcelain bowl. He opened his door and saw that the door to the neighbouring cubicle was closed. He pushed it, but it appeared bolted.

He crossed to the washbasin and looked at his ageing, handsome face as he soaped his hands. The main door to the washroom opened and Audrey put her head around. 'This girl's getting impatient,' she said with a big smile.

Malcolm looked at Audrey then at the cubicle next to the one he'd just used.

'Everything all right?'

'Yes,' he said. 'I was... I was just admiring some of the writing on your lavatory wall. Excellent grammar.'

Audrey took Malcolm's hand and led him along the corridor to the half-landing where he stopped and looked down into the hallway. Draped across the handrail were some fresh sheets which she put over her arm. He followed her up the short flight of stairs to the long corridor, and up the next two flights. Every step they took was accompanied by creaks and groans from the aged oak floorboards.

When they reached the top landing, Audrey flicked the light switch and glanced across to the window. 'Thank you' could just be discerned, written in the dust.

'Your ghost?' panted Malcolm.

'My Russian, I think. Done with his fat forefinger.'

'Perhaps I'm not quite as fit as I thought I was,' Malcolm said, as he sucked in a lungful of air.

'You will be after a few weeks.' She opened her bedroom door and turned on the feeble light.

Malcolm shivered. 'There's a definite chill.'

'I'll soon warm you up.' Audrey took his hand and gave it a squeeze. 'Wait there. I'll just be a jiffy.' He watched her throw the clean sheets onto a spare bed and swap around the thin and stained mattresses.

'Do you need any help?'

'Room service is not what it used to be.'

Malcolm laughed. 'Of course, back at my lovely, warm cottage, I have a very comfy mattress on my *double* bed, and one of those modern duvet thingies.'

Audrey chuckled as she tucked in the sheets and blankets. She crossed to the window and pulled the worn scrap of curtain material. 'Only the owls can see us up here, but...'

She looked across the dingy dormitory to Malcolm, and opened her arms. 'Welcome to my boudoir.' She came up to him and tilted her head back. For a moment, they stood facing each other – then the light bulb on the landing blew.

Audrey laughed. 'Good idea.' She turned off the dormitory light.

Later, lying wrapped in each other's arms, Audrey whispered: 'I knew I didn't need contraception but I thought you might need Viagra – how wrong was I?'

'It's been a long time.' He kissed her gently.

'I wasted too many years planning for a future that was snatched from me. Now, I don't want to think beyond tonight.'

CHAPTER TWENTY-SIX

Malcolm stirred, and he felt Audrey wake in his arms.

'Are you okay?' she whispered.

'I have to go.' He kissed her.

'Don't leave. I want to see the sunrise with you.'

'I have to go to the bogs.'

'Bogs?'

'The little boys' room.'

'Bogs. I've not heard you call it that before.'

'Ah, well, there's a reason for that – it's this house.'

'I don't understand.'

'After I graduated from Oxford, I taught English and drama for a short while up at the old school. It was an interim job before I got into marketing.' He leant in to kiss her again but couldn't locate her lips. 'I won't be long. Don't go anywhere!'

Malcolm eased his way off the narrow bed and slipped on his boxer shorts and T-shirt. He felt his way along the wall to the door and turned the knob. Pale light spilled across the landing from the window. He reached for the handrail, and although he had no desire to go down two flights of stairs to the bogs all on his own, his call of nature was getting more urgent.

Barefoot, he walked carefully down the stairs to the usual accompanying creaks. He arrived at the half-landing and looked down the long flight into the dark hallway. For a fleeting moment, he thought he saw a boy lying on the tiled floor but it was only a shadow caused by a balustrade. He shivered and was enveloped by overwhelming sadness. In the top dormitory room, he had just experienced the happiest moments of his seventy-five years, but now, standing on the half-landing, looking down into the gloom of the large hallway, he knew there was no escape from the past. He was held in the grip of a misery that had cursed his marriage to Mary and clouded every waking moment of his life since.

'Malcolm?'

He swung round and stared at Audrey, the contours of her slim frame encased within a sheer nightdress.

'What happened to Robert Oakes?'

It was fifty years since he'd last heard that name. His head throbbed as adrenaline powered his pumping heart.

'It was an accident.' His voice cracked, and he closed his eyes as the memory of a beautiful young woman flooded his mind. 'He was Roxane in my production of *Cyrano de Bergerac*. Exquisite. Fragile. Vulnerable. She touched something deep inside me. I wanted to protect her. I wanted to protect him.'

He felt a tongue of freezing air wrap around him.

'What happened?' Her voice came from the far end of a long tunnel.

'It was a Sunday morning. I found him alone, in the top dormitory room.'

'What did you do?'

'Nothing! I did nothing. But, he misunderstood me.' Malcolm turned his back on Audrey and gripped the handrail. 'I told him Roxane would live in my heart, forever.'

Silence.

Not a breath.

Not a creak.

He had to explain. 'I reached out for him. I wanted to protect him, but he ran away.'

'And you caught him here, on the landing?' Her voice sounded as cold as metal.

He nodded, roughly wiping away an escaping tear. 'I needed him to understand. I grabbed his arm, but he pulled free and tripped on a raised floorboard.' He felt Audrey's eyes boring into him. 'Why are you asking me about Robert Oakes?'

'He was my little brother.'

Despair filled his veins.

'I came here to find the truth,' he heard her say. 'But the truth has found me.'

Head bowed, Malcolm listened as her bare feet padded down the stairs into the hallway.

Icy tendrils of air made him turn. In the gloom was a boy. A boy he'd not seen for many years.

CHAPTER TWENTY-SEVEN

Audrey's hand shook as she poured boiling water into a teapot. She put the kettle down and sobbed for a little brother she hardly knew. She had come to Hawksmead to try and discover the truth but had betrayed her family by making love to the man responsible for her brother's death.

How she despised herself.

From the hallway, she heard Malcolm cry and then the sound of his body, thudding down the wooden staircase.

'Malcolm!' She hurried out of the kitchen, along the corridor and into the hallway. Near the base of the stairs lay Malcolm, broken and twisted. She whimpered, and her knees buckled under her.

He groaned. Her hand flew to her mouth. His eyes opened, and he looked up at her. She slid her hand under his head, so it was no longer resting on the cold, tiled floor, and strained to hear his words.

'I saw him. I saw Bobby. He spoke to me. He said… he said…' His eyes flickered and shut.

Audrey gently laid his head back on the hard floor. She hurried upstairs, her bare feet taking two steps at a time. She had to get her phone.

'Emergency. Which service do you require?'

'Ambulance. As fast as possible.' Audrey gasped as she tried to control her breathing.

'What is the nature of the emergency?'

Phone in hand, Audrey almost flew down the stairs. She reached the half-landing and looked down at Malcolm, lying on the floor in the hallway. 'My friend has fallen down the stairs,' she panted. 'He's seventy-five and is badly injured.'

'Is he breathing? Is he conscious?'

'He's breathing but not conscious.' She rattled off her name and address. 'Please send an ambulance.'

'An ambulance has been dispatched and will take approximately ten minutes. Please check the airway and confirm to me that he's breathing normally.'

Audrey ran downstairs and put her phone on loudspeaker. She rested her hand on Malcolm's chest. 'Yes, he's breathing but it's not good. He's badly hurt.'

'Is he in any immediate danger?'

'No.'

'Can the paramedics gain access to the location?'

'I'll open the front door. We're just in the hall.' Audrey got up and ran across to the front door which she pulled open. A cold draught flicked her flimsy nightdress. She hurried back to Malcolm and carefully slid her hand under his head.

'Can you tell me what happened?' asked the operator through the phone.

Before Audrey could respond, Malcolm stirred. 'He wants us to be happy.'

'Could you please state exactly what happened?' asked the operator, her voice strident on the phone's loudspeaker.

'I was so pleased to see him,' Malcolm continued. 'I rushed to tell you and stupidly tripped on the stairs, the way Robert tripped all those years ago. What an old fool.'

'The ambulance is outside,' said the operator. 'Good luck.'

Audrey heard the ambulance arrive in her drive.

'He was a gifted actor,' Malcolm rasped. 'Something magical happened when he walked on stage. There's not a day gone by when I have not thought about his Roxane.' Malcolm's eyes closed as a paramedic entered the hallway, carrying a heavy medical bag followed by an emergency ambulance driver wheeling a bright yellow stretcher.

'Malcolm!' Audrey said trying to shake him awake.

The paramedic eased Audrey out of her way and set about examining Malcolm.

'What's his name?' she asked Audrey.

'Malcolm. Malcolm Cadwallader.' And quietly, to herself, 'Mr C'.

'Malcolm, my name's Sandra and I'm going to examine you. Are you having any trouble breathing?'

'My ribs hurt, but I can manage all right.'

She placed her fingers over his right wrist and looked at her watch. After what seemed an eternity, she looked up at her colleague then spoke to Malcolm. 'I'm going to give you a little examination. Let me know where it hurts.'

She started with his head and slowly moved her hands down his arms. Malcolm emitted a dry, piercing cry.

'He has a dislocated left shoulder and fractured radius.' She continued down. 'Fractured ribs.' She reached his hips and Malcolm cried out again. 'Fractured pelvis.' She felt down both his legs.

'Malcolm,' Sandra said to him, 'we're going to get you off the floor and onto the stretcher, but before we do that, my friend, Toby, is going to give you something to ease the pain.'

Audrey watched as, with surprising speed, the paramedics set up a drip which they inserted into Malcolm's right arm.

'Ma'am,' began Toby.

'My name's Audrey. Audrey Willatt.'

'Mrs Willatt, could you tell us what led to Malcolm's fall?'

'Mr Cadwallader, Malcolm, was standing at the top of the stairs when I left him to go to the kitchen and make a pot of tea.'

'Did you see what happened?'

'No, but I heard his cry from the kitchen and ran back here.'

'Did he tell you how he fell?'

'He said he tripped on a raised board at the top of the stairs. I've only just bought the house and not had time to fix it.'

'And there's nobody else in the house?' Toby helped Sandra fit a neck brace.

'No. There's nobody else here. Just Malcolm and me.'

'No family members?'

'No.'

'No children?'

'No. There's no one else here.'

'No dogs?'

'No.'

Toby turned to Malcolm. His eyes were closed, and he was breathing more easily. 'Malcolm, Mr Cadwallader. Can you hear me?'

Malcolm opened his eyes.

'Were you pushed? Did somebody push you?'

Malcolm tried to shake his head. 'It was a silly accident.' He whimpered as he was eased onto the low-lying stretcher and strapped into place. Audrey slipped her bare feet into a pair of walking shoes and grabbed her coat off the stand. She followed the crew out of the house, into the freezing rain, leaving the front door open. She hurried past Malcolm's car to the ambulance parked at the end of her drive.

'Aren't you going to lock your house?' Sandra asked as she and Toby raised the trolley and slid Malcolm into the ambulance.

Audrey looked back at her open front door, as rain turned to luminescent hailstones in the weak light from the hallway. 'I won't come with you,' she said. 'I'll follow on shortly. Where are you taking him?'

'Undermere General Hospital. Are you sure you don't want to come with us?'

'We'll wait for you to lock up,' Toby said.

'No, I'll get dressed and make my own way to the hospital. Thank you for taking care of him.'

Shivering uncontrollably, Audrey re-entered the hall and pushed the door shut. She ran upstairs, dressed quickly and then picked up Malcolm's jacket. She searched his pockets and found his house and car keys, his wallet and phone, and shoved them in her handbag. She hurried back down to the hallway. On the floor was her own phone, which she retrieved.

Slamming the front door, she ran to Malcolm's car, slipped into the driver's seat, slid it forward and fired up the engine. She took a few seconds to find the switch for the lights and the stalk for the wipers. She had no idea where the hospital was but decided she would follow the road signs to Undermere and then use her phone to direct her to the exact location.

The car was an automatic so finding reverse was easy. She backed out of her drive and stopped in the road. What was she doing? Why was she rushing to the hospital? For a moment, she considered what had just happened, then turned back into her drive and switched off the engine.

She closed the car door and entered her hallway. The old school boarding house was quiet. There were no squeaks or creaks, just still, cold air. She stood in the dimly lit hall and a conversation that had changed her life when she was aged twenty came back as though it were yesterday. She was in the drawing room of a large Victorian house, watching her Aunt Margot pour tea into fine porcelain cups.

'I don't know what to do, Auntie. I'm completely torn,' said the young Audrey. Her aunt handed her a cup of tea and picked up a sharp knife to cut a slice of homemade Dundee cake.

'Well,' said her aunt. 'Let me see if I can help you. On the one hand you have Joey, who is rich, successful and has bought you a car; and on the other hand you have Duncan, who is young, penniless but full of potential.'

'That's about it. They both have their qualities.'

'However, I can assure you that you do not love them both equally.' Her aunt skilfully placed a slice of cake on a porcelain plate and handed it to Audrey. 'I'm going to ask you two questions and I want you to give me your first response to each. Question one: imagine that you will never ever see Joey again – how does that make you feel?'

Young Audrey shrugged. 'Not good. I love him.'

Her aunt pressed on. 'Second question: think about Duncan. Imagine never, ever, seeing him again. You have seen him for the last time. He is out of your life. How does that make you feel?'

Audrey snapped back to the present and looked about the hallway. She was alone. Her wonderful aunt who had helped to change the course of her life was gone. She was totally bereft.

Totally alone. Her life had lost all meaning. Was she simply a loose end counting down to her own demise? She felt for the wedding ring on her left hand and that, too, was gone.

'Duncan! I miss you. I bloody miss you!' She fell to her knees as tears flooded her eyes.

It did not take long for the cold floor to bite and for her whole body to be convulsed with shivers.

'I love you, Ordy.'

What was that? Who had spoken? She used the heel of her hands to push the tears from her eyes. All she could see were blurred objects and dark shadows. Was that a shape on the half-landing?

Her coat sleeve was a poor sponge as she attempted to clear her eyes. She looked up again and tried to focus.

CHAPTER TWENTY-EIGHT

It was still night when Audrey was permitted to enter the intensive care unit at Undermere General Hospital. She stared at Malcolm lying in the mechanised hospital bed, his face covered by an oxygen mask. A bag on a hook was attached to an intravenous line that disappeared into his arm. A cardiac monitor relayed the peaks and troughs of his beating heart, and a drainage bag attached to the bed was collecting his urine. On a trolley was a defibrillator.

Gavin, a nurse, placed an upright chair near the bed. 'He's sedated. He has a broken hip, a fractured left arm, and a dislocated shoulder, which we will relocate under general anaesthetic. He will be in hospital for some while. I'll be back, shortly.'

Audrey nodded and Gavin left.

Joshua, Audrey's miracle son, shouted from the living room. 'Mum, it's dad. I think we should call an ambulance.'

Duncan was slumped in his usual chair. His right hand was clamped to his left arm and his shirt collar, soaked with sweat, was tight around his swollen throat. He looked up at Audrey, his face contorted with pain as his tongue – grotesquely long – lolled out of his mouth.

The door to the ICU opened and two orderlies entered together with Nurse Jablonski and Dr Ryder, a registrar in her thirties who looked as though she had been working all night.

Nurse Jablonski gave Audrey's shoulder a gentle shake and Audrey's dilated eyes looked up at the pretty blonde nurse. 'Is he still alive?' She gripped the nurse's arm as she got to her feet. 'Tell me the truth.'

Dr Ryder turned to Audrey. 'We're taking him for a scan. We believe he may have a subdural haematoma caused by the bang to his head. If he has, he will be operated on immediately to remove the blood and stop the bleed.'

'What about his heart?' Audrey asked.

'For a man of his age and with his injuries from the fall, his heart is holding up pretty well. We've just got to put the broken bits back together.'

Audrey watched as the bed was wheeled out.

What fall?

Duncan had had a heart attack – he didn't fall. Perplexed, she looked out of the window and saw the sun rising over the hospital car park.

She heard a familiar ring tone and, instinctively, picked up her handbag from the floor and opened it. She took out her phone. Green *Answer* pulsed and she swiped the screen.

'Mrs Willatt, Audrey. It's Tony, Tony Blake.'

'Tony Blake?'

'I'm the photographer from *The Chronicle*.'

'The Chronicle?'

'You saved our baby.'

'Your baby?'

'You recognised the symptoms of meningitis.'

'Sorry, I'm a bit muddled.'

'I took your photograph and wrote the story about your haunted house. I came to your tea party.'

'I don't understand.'

Following Duncan's first heart attack more than twenty years ago, Audrey had suffered repeated nightmares. After his death, lack of sleep brought on by grief and stress had turned her nightmares, from which she could shake herself awake, into sleep terrors from which opening her eyes, walking around, even talking, did not free her from the images projected in her mind.

'Mrs Willatt? Is everything all right? My dad had a call this morning from a friend who saw an ambulance outside your house last night.'

Audrey looked at the empty space where the bed had been. 'I think something terrible has happened.' She furrowed her brow. 'Malcolm. Yes! Malcolm Cadwallader. I remember. He fell down the stairs. He's badly hurt.'

'Where are you now?'

'I'm at the hospital.' The hand holding her phone dropped to her side. She had to think. She had to clear her mind.

She picked up her bag and opened it to replace her phone and saw Malcolm's wallet, phone, and house and car keys. He had told her he had seen her brother – but that was impossible. What other lies had he told her?

'Excuse me,' Audrey said to the receptionist at the front desk in the intensive care unit. 'I have Malcolm Cadwallader's wallet and phone. Could you keep them safe for him?' She placed them on the counter.

'We prefer valuable items to be kept by family members,' replied the receptionist.

'I'm not family.'

'But you're his wife?'

'No.'

The receptionist frowned. 'His partner?'

'No.'

'But you're his friend?'

'No. I'm not his friend. I will not see him again.'

CHAPTER TWENTY-NINE

Tony Blake was excited. He couldn't help it. The newshound within him smelled a story. He scrolled down the names in his phone.

'Dad, hold the front page. I think I have something.' He gave his father an account of his brief conversation with Audrey.

He kissed his baby son goodbye, gave his wife a quick peck and almost leapt into his family-sized Skoda Octavia with its two child seats in the rear. The roads were particularly icy, and rush hour was building, so it took at least half an hour to get to Undermere General Hospital.

Tony hated paying for parking, but he knew that the hospital's out-sourced contractor operated a ruthless system of fines. He also knew the layout of the hospital well, having spent quite a bit of time wandering around when his son had been ill. He found his way to the intensive care unit and was about to try and blag his way past the receptionist when he saw Malcolm Cadwallader being wheeled back into his room.

'Granddad!'

He followed the orderlies into the side ward, ignoring repeated requests for him to return to reception. Malcolm was awake and looked at Tony, his mouth covered by an oxygen mask.

'Audrey rang me, Granddad. She told me what happened.'

The orderlies secured the wheels on the bed while Gavin, the nurse, checked that all the readings were in order. Once he was happy, he looked at Tony.

'Your grandfather has had a lucky escape. There's bruising but no bleed to the brain. We've just got to sort out the various broken bones and nasty dislocation of the shoulder and he'll be fit as a fiddle again.' He turned to Malcolm. 'I'll be back shortly with some more painkillers.' He smiled at Tony and followed the orderlies out of the room.

Tony looked at the monitor with its multi-coloured numbers and lines and at the bag supported on the side of the bed, about a third full of urine. He leaned in towards Malcolm. 'Would you like a drink?'

Malcolm removed his oxygen mask with his good arm and placed it below his chin. 'Thank you. My mouth is very dry.'

Tony picked up a plastic jug with a lid from the bedside trolley and poured a small quantity of water into a plastic cup. He held it whilst Malcolm took a few sips. He returned the cup to the trolley.

'I'm a friend of Audrey's. She told me what happened last night. I came over to see her.'

'She was here? At the hospital?'

'Yes,' Tony said.

'Please give her a message. It's very important.'

'You can tell me. I'll make sure she gets it.'

'I... I...' The words caught in his throat, confirming to Tony that there was definitely more to this story than simply falling down the stairs.

CHAPTER THIRTY

Audrey followed the road signs back to Hawksmead and parked Malcolm's car in her driveway. The morning air was bitingly cold and, as she entered her cavernous hall, her house did not feel much warmer.

She closed the front door and its bang echoed briefly. On the floor, near the base of the stairs, were remnants of medical packaging left by the paramedics last night. She looked up the stairs to the half-landing. What happened? Did Malcolm really see Bobby? Or was that the lie of a guilty man?

'Bobby! It's Audrey. I'm here. I've come to say goodbye.'

She stood and waited.

'I will always love you. You were never forgotten – not by Mummy, not by Daddy, not by me.'

The house replied with a heavy silence.

Audrey, her whole body weary, trudged up the stairs to the half-landing. She was desperate for a shower. She walked along the narrow corridor to the washroom and used her usual cubicle. She pulled the chain and peeled off her clothes, dropping them on the old terracotta tiled floor. In the large communal shower area, she turned on her usual tap. Icy water cascaded over her face and down her drawn, thin body. She didn't care. She soaped herself as best she could, but the cold water prevented her from making much lather.

Shivering almost uncontrollably, she towelled her skin dry, rubbing herself fiercely as she walked back to the main washroom area. She looked at her naked form in the mirror. She had achieved what she set out to do when she first decided to buy the old school boarding house, but she hadn't factored in the possibility of falling in love with the man responsible for her little brother's tragic death.

'I've failed, you, Mummy. I've failed you.'

Leaving her clothes and wet towel on the floor, she picked up her handbag and opened the washroom door. She would leave Hawksmead today. She looked back at the long row of toilet cubicles, complemented by the long row of washbasins. For a moment, she thought she heard Bobby's voice, but she knew it was in her head.

She let the washroom door close and, barefoot and naked, she trudged along the corridor to the half-landing. She looked down the stairs into the hallway.

'The Russians can have it.'

Her skin almost tinged with blue, she climbed up to the top landing and entered the dormitory. She looked at the dishevelled bedding from the night before and expected to be consumed with shame, but all she felt was overwhelming sadness. She shivered, and hastily dressed in the warmest clothes she had.

Still shivering, she pulled the two suitcases out from under her bed and placed them on top. She opened the lids and wasted no time folding clothes as she stuffed in as many as she could, leaving a rejected jumble of trousers and sweaters amongst the bedding.

Across the room, Audrey saw the encyclopaedia lying on the floor. She lifted it up and placed it on a bed. In the cut-out section she expected to see Robert's diary.

Where was it?

For a moment she felt sickening panic, but then she remembered it was in her handbag. She took it out, sat on her bed, and looked at the diary's fly leaf with its handwritten inscription:

This is the secret diary of Robert Oakes.
DO NOT READ UNTIL 2065

She turned to the first page; her brother's record of that autumn term sparking so many childhood memories for her. She read the short diary through to the last line, now knowing that the footsteps Bobby heard coming up the stairs were Malcolm's. She kissed the leather cover and placed the diary in her handbag.

It took some effort to close the two suitcases and carried the heaviest down into the hall. She went back upstairs into the washroom and packed as many toiletries as she could into her wash and make-up bags. Leaving them on the half-landing, she trudged up to her bedroom to collect the second suitcase. She hauled it off the bed and looked around the room. She thought about her little brother and his love for Mini, and she thought about her misplaced love for Malcolm.

She picked up her handbag and lugged the second suitcase down the two flights to the half-landing.

Something was wrong. She was sure she had left her wash and make-up bags at the top of the stairs – they were gone. She carried her suitcase down into the hallway and was shocked to see her toiletries and numerous items of make-up scattered across the tiled floor. It looked like an angry statement by somebody – or some*thing.*

She picked her way to the front entrance, put down her suitcase and opened the door. A great gust of wind snatched the latch from between her fingers and the heavy oak door slammed shut. She tried to open it again, but it wouldn't budge. An icy chill caused her to give an involuntary shiver.

Was some spectral presence in the hallway with her? She focused on the hardened woodgrain in the old timber door, too scared to turn around and take a look. She had loved her brother, but the thought of seeing him in ghostly form terrified her.

'I'm leaving, Bobby, and it is time for you to leave too.' She spoke without turning to look.

A sharp crack sent a jolt through her and Audrey felt her knees buckle. She screwed her eyes shut and blocked her ears against the creaking sound. She shook almost uncontrollably. Taking deep breaths, she turned around and opened her eyes.

Hanging at the end of bed sheets, twisted around his neck and tied to a newel post on the half-landing, was a young boy, his head at an impossible angle. She did not recognise his face, which was distorted and livid, with eyes bulging from their sockets; but she knew it was Eddie Holden, the boy Shirley had talked about with such deep sorrow when Audrey had visited the library.

She tried the front door again and it opened. She reached for her suitcase, but the door slammed shut. She turned the latch and pulled, but it wouldn't budge. Screwing up her courage a second time, Audrey turned around and looked back into the hall. Standing at the top of the stairs, wearing corduroy shorts, was her little brother.

'Bobby!'

The name came out in little more than a whispered croak as she dropped her handbag and ran to the base of the stairs.

Something pulled the boy from behind and his arms flailed at an unseen foe.

'*NO!*' Audrey screamed.

The boy stopped and looked down at her.

'Please don't!' She looked up into his sweet, sad face, big sister and little brother staring at each other for the first time in more than fifty years. 'I can't bear to see you fall.'

He smiled, touched his fingertips to his lips and blew her a kiss. Audrey felt embraced by a great warmth as he walked silently down the stairs and came towards her.

The front door blew open.

Bobby smiled, and she watched him walk across the hallway and out of the house to a place Audrey could not imagine.

She sank to her knees and wept, as fifty years of grief poured out. She thought about her dear mother breaking the devastating news to her. How her mother had fought to keep calm as she relayed to Audrey what had happened to Bobby.

The Oakes family had been solid and strong, but within ten years of Bobby's death, she saw her family disintegrate. Her father felt the loss of his only son every bit as keenly as her mother and dealt with the pain by distraction: distraction work; distraction sailing; distraction dating; anything that would occupy his mind. But her mother could not find any solace, despite throwing herself into her local amateur dramatic plays, meeting smart friends for bridge, entertaining frequently, and swimming at the local country club. It didn't work. Ten years on, Audrey saw the pain of loss in all its rawness when her mother told her she had breast cancer. Of course, everything was done to cure her of the disease, but in the mid-1970s, the technology was crude and the results more miss than hit. The cancer spread, and Audrey saw it was a blessed release. She knew that her mother loved her every bit as much as she had loved Robert, but now that Audrey was set-tled in her own home with her lovely Duncan, it was time for her mother to slip away into painless oblivion.

But how would her mother respond if she knew that Au-drey had slept with the man who was responsible for Robert's death? How would her father react at the age of eighty-nine? He was happily married to his favourite sailing companion and still in very good health. If she told him what had really hap-pened, if she showed him Bobby's diary, it could tip him over the edge and into his grave.

Roughly wiping away her tears, she knew she had to get out of the house. There would be no Hostel on the Moor. Despite its Grade II status, she hoped the old building would be destroyed.

Audrey picked up her handbag and opened it. She removed the front door keys and threw them onto the floor, amongst all her discarded make-up and toiletries, and hurried out of the house, leaving the door wide open.

Seeing Malcolm's Honda in her driveway sent ripples through her body.

What now? Had all hope of a future together been shattered by the truth?

Audrey walked past the Honda to the end of her driveway. Across the road, she saw a parked transit van and spotted Kir-ill Dryomov sitting at the wheel with the engine running. She may as well tell him now that the house was up for sale.

Checking for traffic, she stepped into the road and walked across to the van. Kirill looked in her direction and pulled away before she could speak to him.

She watched him go. No matter. The estate agency could arrange the sale.

She crossed back to her drive and looked at Malcolm's car. She would drop the keys off at *The Chronicle* and send a message to Tina, in case the car had to be moved before Malcolm was well enough to drive it – if he survived.

She was about to walk down the High Street when she changed her mind and headed towards the Old Military Road. She pulled the strap of her handbag over her shoulder and dug her bare hands deep into her pockets as moisture from her breath crystallised in the biting chill.

She could not remember ever feeling this wretched. Her head was a jumble of conflicting emotions laced with overwhelming guilt. Had she really seen Bobby? Had he really smiled or had it all been in her troubled mind? Shoulders hunched against the freezing air blowing off the moor, she paid no attention to the white transit van, following her some way behind.

Lost in so many thoughts, Audrey approached the humpback bridge over the River Hawk. The narrow strip of road glistened like a black silk ribbon. Her shoes were for walking and had good rubber grips, but she was not prepared for the slipperiness of the ice that coated the road, and she had to grab the stone wall at the side of the bridge to stop falling over.

She took a few calming breaths and steadied herself. She would be gone from Hawksmead soon, but she'd had to make this final pilgrimage to such a significant place in her brother's short life. The sun was up and the trees were almost entirely shorn of leaves, so Audrey could see across the moor to the Ridgeway and the forbidding sight of the former outward-bound boarding school. She thought about Bobby with his terrible stutter, trying to survive in such an austere environment; and his friend, Mini, being crushed on the bridge fifty years ago, exactly where she was standing now. She looked down at the river, awash with churning water, and thought about the two boys Bobby had written about, who had drowned trying to claw their way out of the swirling torrent.

Who remembered them now?

Who remembered Bobby?

CHAPTER THIRTY-ONE

Kirill didn't know what to do. He had driven to his brother's house that morning, as usual, and in no uncertain terms had been told to piss off. Spartak's skank of a girlfriend had recognised Kirill as the man with the axe and had decided to end the brief affair. Girls like that were dirt cheap in Russia, but his brother appeared to have fallen for her and blamed Kirill for the break-up. Why was it his fault? If the widow had not been so objectionable, he would not have been standing in her drive with an axe when Tina saw him.

The whole town knew that the Dryomov brothers had wanted the boarding house but when Audrey stole it from under their noses, people had lost their fear and openly laughed. The humiliation he felt was driving all reason from his mind. But it wasn't just losing the house that annoyed him, it was Audrey herself – her lack of fear, her scrawny frame, her very existence.

And now there she was, standing all alone on the bridge. To his surprise and horror he felt a surge in his pants. What was he thinking? She was twice his age. The blast of cannons from his phone blew apart his fantasies and his brother's name on the screen deflated his lust. He lifted his right hand and his grubby fat thumb hovered over the green *'Answer'* before swiping it.

'Zdravstvuj,' he said, reluctantly.

~

The torrent of water rushing between the bridge's three stone arches frightened Audrey. Her mother had loved swimming and would go in the grey-green sea even when it was freezing.

But it wasn't the cold that bothered Audrey; it was water's merciless power to kill.

She was six and in charge of looking after her four-year-old brother as they ran down the road with buckets and spades gripped in their little hands.

'You can play on the beach but you're not to swim.' Audrey had begged her mother to let them go on their own. 'If you want water for a sandcastle, you can fill your buckets from one of the rock pools.'

In the 1950s, there were few cars and crossing the road to the broad steps that led down to the beach was easy and safe. Audrey was mature for her six years and always took great care of her little brother.

The tide was out and there were plenty of rock pools for Bobby to explore. It was a sunny afternoon and lots of little children were on the beach having fun including a coach load of boys being minded by Roman Catholic nuns, looking hot in their flowing black habits. Audrey remembered seeing her brother playing with some boys by a shallow rock pool. They had a little boat and were building a harbour.

Her mother had given Audrey a shilling – easily enough to buy two ice creams. There was quite a queue leading up to the white-painted beach hut, and she waited patiently to be served, completely unaware that her little brother was in the process of being rounded up by one of the nuns. She did not see him being told by a pinched face to hold hands with another little boy. She did not see him being marched up the beach towards the waiting coach. She did not hear his protests or the nun ordering him to be quiet. She could only imagine the fear her little brother must have felt as every step took him further away from his big sister. Ice filled her veins as she thought about the nuns pushing her little brother up the coach's steps and with a hand on his back guiding him down the bus to one of the rear seats. She could almost hear, sixty years on, his scream when a nun slammed the door shut and the coach's engine rattled into life.

~

Kirill terminated the connection to Spartak. He would go and pick his brother up in his own good time. He licked his cracked lips as he contemplated the thin female form leaning against the side of the stone bridge. It wouldn't take much to grab her, tie her up in the back of his van and later, much later, dump her body out on the moor. What was it about this old woman that was driving him so crazy?

He opened the van door and felt the icy blast coming from the east. He liked the cold. He liked the bleakness of winter, the stark branches on the trees, the hard ground and the biting air. He smiled. He was downwind. She wouldn't hear him coming.

CHAPTER THIRTY-TWO

Tony had been moved by Malcolm's story and was keen to meet up with Audrey to get the complete picture. He contemplated phoning but decided to go straight to her house instead. The morning rush hour clogged the main roads, so he had taken the longer but less busy route across the moor along the Old Military Road. As he drove, he could feel his Skoda being buffeted by the easterly wind; snow was starting to fall, and soon his wipers were battling blizzard conditions. Although confident that his car was sufficiently reliable, he did feel vulnerable and began to regret his choice of route.

~

Kirill's phone buzzed in his pocket and the cannons boomed. He hurried back to the warmth of his van before he answered his brother's call.

'Do her no harm.' Spartak's voice through the phone's speaker bounced off the van's metal interior. 'You hear me? If anything happens to that woman – *anything* – I will go straight to the police and report this conversation.'

Kirill was shocked by Spartak's intuition. How had he known what Kirill was contemplating?

~

Snow blew into Audrey's face and prickled her skin but she could not lift her mind out of the despair into which she was sinking. She should be thinking of her sons and those that loved her today, not suffering the misery of her family's past. But the past had come around full circle and she could see no future for herself. She looked up from the fast-flowing river

175

and through the sparse trees to the moor now carpeted in white. She could just make out the soulless edifice of the old school. Her parents had wanted nothing but the best for her and her brother; her sweet brother who stuttered but dreamed of being an actor. Audrey's childhood had been very happy – ballet lessons, piano lessons, bike rides and roller skating. No knee pads or wrist guards in those days – just pure fun and the occasional scrape.

~

Was it Bobby's scream that made Audrey look towards the beach or a cry from a seagull? She saw that the tide was coming in and the waves were building, crashing fiercely onto the sandy shore. Although she couldn't see her brother, she didn't want to lose her place in the ice cream queue. Normally, she wore glasses, so the children building sandcastles on the beach were all a bit of a blur. Bobby was a good boy and knew not to go in the sea without his big sister. But Audrey's sense of responsibility got the better of her, and she broke away from the queue. She ran towards the rock pool where she had last seen her little brother as the rising tide hurled massive rollers onto the beach. With water swirling and sucking at her ankles, she saw that a section of beach was now cut off by the sea. Was Bobby playing behind the rocks?

She waded into the foamy water to get a better view of the dwindling beach, her focus entirely taken with scanning the shoreline and not the mighty rollers building behind her.

~

Kirill started the transit van and turned on the wipers to clear the snow from the screen. The woman was still standing on the bridge. Why? Was she insane? Even Kirill, who liked the cold and snow, would not stand exposed to the elements without a hat and gloves. An idea sparked in his mind.

~

Tony had his lights dipped and his wipers working hard as

he tore along the Old Military Road. He passed the turning to Hawksmead College and continued on, slowing as he approached the bridge. As a precaution, he hooted his horn.

~

Kirill's van was almost at the bridge when he saw Audrey turn her head. She must have heard something. Perhaps a car was coming in the opposite direction? He touched his brakes, but it was as though he didn't have any. His wheels locked, but the van continued in a straight line, heading directly towards Audrey who was standing with her back to him. She was about to be the cushion between his van's large bumper and the bridge's stone wall. In desperation, he blasted his horn and pumped his brakes. His brother would never believe that he had not intended to kill the woman, but that was exactly what he was about to do.

~

Tony crested the bridge and saw the white van, and then, to his perplexed horror, Audrey's lone figure standing in peril. He overreacted and slammed on his brakes, but his car's anti-locking system had no effect on his speed as he slid on ice towards the van and the woman who was now trapped in a pincer with nowhere to go.

~

Above the roar of water flowing under the bridge, Audrey had picked up a sound and turned her head. The message conveyed by her eyes that two vehicles were about to crash into her, triggered neurons in her brain to send an urgent message to her ballet-trained legs. Her muscles contracted, propelling her body up and back over the top of the low stone wall.

~

Tony could not look. He was a passenger at the wheel of his car and was shocked by the loudness of the bang as he and the van smashed into each other and then bounced into the stone wall. The ancient construction gave under the combined force, and the noses of both the Skoda and the van protruded over the fast-flowing river.

Convinced that Audrey had to be dead, Tony opened his door and snow immediately blew in. He pushed against the wind and stepped out of his car. His foot shot out from under him, and he crashed onto his back.

~

Kirill sat at his wheel, not comprehending what had just happened. He'd not been going fast but his van wouldn't stop. The woman, as if connected to a spring, had risen into the air and disappeared. He thought about her thin body and old age and allowed himself a smile. He had changed his mind about killing her, and he had a witness who would back him up that he hadn't, but she would still be out of the way.

The witness! He must talk to him. His brother may think he was lying and still report him to the police. Kirill climbed down from the transit van and felt his heavy boots slide out from under him. He hung onto his door until he regained his balance. Taking baby steps, he walked around the rear of his van and saw the driver of the car lying prostrate. He moved as quickly as the snow and black ice would permit and helped Tony get back on his feet.

'I couldn't stop,' Tony said.

'It is your fault. You were not driving carefully enough for condition. You pay for van.'

'Where is Audrey? The woman? We've got to call an ambulance.'

'She in river. Downstream somewhere.' Kirill tried to keep the elation he felt out of his voice. 'Probably dead, drowned.'

CHAPTER THIRTY-THREE

Following an early viewing, Tina approached Audrey's house and swung into the short driveway. She was surprised to see Malcolm's car with its taped-up side mirror and decided today was not the time to give Audrey her news. She was about to reverse her VW out when she noticed the front door was wide open with snow blowing in.

Debating what to do, she sat with her engine running. Finally, she switched it off and opened the driver's door. She walked past Malcolm's car, through the settling snow, to the open entrance and looked into the house.

'Audrey! It's Tina.'

She stepped into the hallway and searched for the light switch. It was morning, but the sun had not penetrated the thick layer of cloud. She flicked on the light and was immediately disturbed to see Audrey's two suitcases and toiletries scattered across the hall, partially covered by wind-blown snow. She spotted the door keys, picked them up and put them in her pocket then looked up the stairs into the gloom.

'Audrey! It's Tina. The front door's open.'

She listened for an answer. She looked back at the open door and then noticed the torn bits of medical packaging blown to the base of the stairs.

~

Tony moved as quickly as the black ice would allow to the downstream side of the bridge and stared at the rush of water funnelled between its three arches. Audrey's handbag swept past, tossed in the raging flow. Then he saw a head bob up

and hands scrape the stone bridge support, seeking purchase –
nails clawing at the joins.

'*AUDREY!*'

He hurried as fast as he could on the black ice to the Hawksmead side of the bridge and shouted to Kirill.

'Call the police. Call them *NOW.*'

Kirill took out his phone and followed Tony, who slid down
the snow-covered bank to the river's edge.

'Don't do it. You cannot save her!' Kirill yelled.

~

Audrey lost all sense of direction as she was spun uncontrollably. She could not tell which way was up or down. She
breathed in water and felt a great stabbing pain in her thin
chest. For a brief moment, her toes touched the bottom, and
she tried to push up, but the power enveloping her was too
great. She saw Bobby sitting in the back of the coach. She heard
his scream when the old engine roared. She saw his little friend
hold up his hand and speak to the nun. She saw the driver open
the door and the nun usher Bobby off the coach. She felt his
little arms squeeze her neck as they hugged and hugged. She
heard her mother calling them in for tea …and she felt great
contentment. She could stop fighting. She was home.

~

Tony did not have a plan. For a moment, he thought a log
was floating downstream and then he realised it was Audrey.
He knew if he gave it a second's thought he wouldn't have the
courage – so he threw himself into the freezing water – and immediately regretted it.

~

Resting her hand on the banister, Tina walked up the wide
wooden stairs to the half-landing. The thought of seeing the
pale face again terrified her. She hurried down the long corridor and climbed the stairs to the second floor and on up to the
top-floor landing. The faint *thank you* written by a fat forefin-

ger on the window pane was still discernible. To her right was the closed door to Audrey's bedroom. She reached for the old brass knob, pushed the door open and peered into the room. Through the window, snow was coating the bare boughs of the oak tree, casting the dormitory in a colourless glow. She flicked on the centre light.

On the beds and floor were untidy sheets and blankets and discarded clothing. But neatly folded on a far bed were Malcolm's jacket, shirt, tie and trousers.

She walked back onto the landing and was about to go downstairs when a siren caught her attention. She hurried to the window and looked down into the High Street just in time to see a police car, with blue lights flashing, race past.

Out of the corner of her eye she saw something move.

She spun round.

Across the landing was a slim figure.

'Audrey! I was so worried. Is everything okay? I've broken it off with Spartak. I'm so sorry they caused you trouble.' Another siren attracted Tina's attention. She looked down as an ambulance tore up the High Street.

She turned back to Audrey ...but she was gone.

~

Audrey's coat snagged a heavy branch that lay half on the bank and half in the water. It gave Tony the chance to save himself. With one hand he grabbed the branch, and with his other hand he grabbed the collar of Audrey's coat. The force of the current was phenomenal and he knew that he could not hold onto her for long.

'You. Take my hand.'

Tony looked at the great hulk sitting astride the branch. He inched his fingers towards Kirill and felt a wave of relief as the man's great paw clamped around his wrist.

'Let the woman go. She is done for,' Kirill shouted above the roar of the fast-flowing water.

'No!' Tony's lips were so numb he could hardly speak.

Kirill pulled Tony's arm and hauled him onto the slippery

riverbank.

'Help me,' Tony gasped, and together they pulled Audrey's body fully out of the river. Tony laid her on her back and could see she wasn't breathing. Hands shaking, he undid the zipper on her coat and tilted her head back.

'She's dead,' Kirill said.

'Go up to the street and tell the ambulance where we are.'

'Don't order me!'

'GO!'

Kirill stomped off, slipping on the snow-covered riverbank.

Tony did not have any medical training but he'd written an article about cardiopulmonary resuscitation, for his father's newspaper, so he sort of knew what he had to do.

Adrenaline sharpened his mind as he knelt astride Audrey's lifeless body and placed one hand on top of the other on her chest. He locked his elbows and pushed down. He remembered that he was supposed to sing the Bee Gees' hit *Stayin' Alive,* but he couldn't remember quite how it went. He pressed and pressed, and after thirty seconds he gripped Audrey's nose, clamped his mouth over hers and breathed air into her lungs. He saw her chest rise and blew again even harder. He went back to pumping her breastbone and, after about thirty compressions, he gripped her nose again and blew hard into her lungs.

The first person to arrive was a police officer who said he would take over, but Tony refused to stop. He pumped for thirty seconds, blew two big puffs into Audrey's lungs and pumped again.

What seemed like an eternity later, two paramedics slid down the snow-covered bank, dragging medical boxes. 'We'll take it from here, sir.'

~

Tina checked she had the house keys and left the old school boarding house, carefully locking the door behind her. She had definitely seen Audrey. She had spoken to her. And yet, and yet...

She teetered on her high heels through the snow to the end of the drive where she saw Kirill walking past, looking wet and muddy.

'What you do to my brother?' he called.

Tina was unsure how to respond or what to do. The massive man didn't seem to notice the biting cold or that his clothes were soaking wet.

'House up for sale,' he continued. 'She die.'

Tina approached him, warily.

'I pull her out of river, but she not look good. Not breathing. She go to hospital.' A giant hook of a hand grabbed Tina's arm and he hauled her close to him. 'Why you break up with Spartak?'

I broke up with him because his brother is a nutter with an axe, was what she wanted to say. What she did say was, 'I'm very fond of Spartak, but our cultures, our backgrounds are too different.'

Kirill looked into her eyes and let go of her arm. 'He miss you. You give it another try, yes?'

'I'll think about it.'

'Call him. Tell him you think about it.'

Tina watched Kirill walk off down the High Street then hurried as best she could to her VW Golf with its new side mirror. She had moved heaven and earth to get it fixed, but now, her perfect car was nothing more to her than a means of transport. She slid into the driver's seat and started the engine. The nearest accident and emergency unit was in Undermere General Hospital. It was still snowing, but her Golf had good tyres and front-wheel drive, so went well in slippery conditions. If the traffic wasn't too bad, she could get there and back before her next viewing appointment.

~

Tony had no choice but to go in the ambulance with Audrey. He knew he was suffering from hypothermia; his clothes were soaked and had been taken off him, and he had no means of getting home as his car was wrecked. Wrapped in a blanket and shivering almost uncontrollably, he didn't know whether he had saved Audrey's life or simply delayed her death. The small section of her skin he could see had the look of alabaster tinged with blue.

He'd asked Kirill to visit *The Chronicle* newspaper and let his father know what had happened. His phone lay dead amongst his wet clothes and no amount of drying in a bag of rice was likely to bring it back to life. But what about the heating pads distributed around Audrey's inert body? Could they bring her back to life?

CHAPTER THIRTY-FOUR

Audrey had been rushed through Accident & Emergency and was now in the Intensive Care Unit. Although her heart had a weak beat and she was breathing, her core temperature was still extremely low. The consultant physician had requested a haemodialysis machine, usually reserved for people with no kidney function. It was not easy getting the needles into Audrey's thin veins, but after a few worrying minutes her blood started to pump through the machine where it was gently warmed.

~

'She had nowhere to go apart from the river,' Tony said to Andy, who was looking down at his son.

Tony was lying in bed in a bay in Accident & Emergency, also surrounded by warming pads.

'The chilblains are driving me mad. I feel like my skin is on fire. The doctor said it will pass, but it's bloomin' agony.'

Andy lent his phone to Tony so he could call his wife. It took about twenty minutes to assure Eden that his life was not in danger and another twenty minutes listening to her berating him for putting himself at risk in the first place.

'Audrey would rather be dead than have your children grow up without a father,' Eden said, finally pausing to draw breath.

Tony heard Charlie crying in the background so, mercifully, the call was ended. He gave the phone back to his father.

'You scared her,' Andy said, 'but she's also immensely proud of you, as am I. I could not have a more wonderful son.' He turned his back and appeared to examine the *In Case of Fire* notice pinned to the wall.

~

In the hospital car park, Tina stuck the pay-and-display ticket on her windscreen and pressed the fob to lock her Golf. Fortunately, it had stopped snowing but it was still bitterly cold. She walked to the main entrance and went up to the reception desk. A few minutes later, she found herself sitting alone in the intensive care unit visitor area, thinking about Audrey. How could someone so full of life and vigour now be dying or dead?

'Have you come to see Audrey?'

Tina looked up, perplexed.

'My name's Tony Blake. This is my dad, Andy. We're with *The Chronicle*. We did a feature on your agency last year.'

'What's happened? Why are you wearing a bathrobe?'

'My son pulled Audrey out of the river,' Andy interjected.

Tina could not remember when she had last felt this confused. 'The Russian property developer told me *he* pulled her out.'

Andy emitted an ugly grunt.

'Let's say it was a joint effort,' Tony responded.

'If my son hadn't jumped into the river,' Andy said, 'Audrey would now be in the morgue.'

'We'd probably both be there if the Russian hadn't helped me.'

'Shouldn't you be in bed?' Tina asked. 'You're shivering.'

'I'm fine. I was in A&E, but I was brought over here so the same consultant could keep an eye on both Audrey and me. She may still not make it.' He swallowed hard. 'Fortunately, Malcolm's going to be okay.'

'Malcolm?' Now Tina's confusion was off the scale.

Tony told her about the fall and Malcolm's injuries.

'It's that house. It's cursed.' She looked at Andy. 'Are you going to put all this in your newspaper?'

'Yes. But at the moment, I don't know how the story is going to end.'

~

There was nothing else for Tina to do but go to work. She drove back to Hawksmead and tried to keep her mind focused on the viewings listed for that day, but her thoughts kept returning to Audrey and the old school boarding house.

Following a lacklustre viewing of a flat situated above Merlin's Hardware Store, she entered the estate agency. Without a word to her colleagues, she flopped down at her desk and put her head in her hands, exhausted, bereft of her usual vibrancy.

After a few moments, a mug of coffee was placed in front of her.

'Freshly brewed.'

Tina looked up at Trevor. 'You never make me coffee.'

'Yes I do. I made you coffee when you came for your interview.'

'That was three years ago. I was still in my final term at school.'

'Then I'm sure you're ready for another cup.'

She looked at the steam rising from the brown surface and did something she never allowed herself to do in front of her boss – she wept.

CHAPTER THIRTY-FIVE

Tony was in a quandary: should he tell Malcolm that Audrey was unconscious in the room next door and that she may not survive? Or was it better for Malcolm not to know?

He had been hailed a hero by his father, but he didn't feel one. Yes, there had been black ice and snow was falling but, whichever way he looked at it, his car had blocked Audrey's escape and forced her to jump into the river. And now he had to tell this kindly old man news that would probably kill him.

'Are you ill?' Malcolm asked, as he attempted to rally his hair.

Tony looked down at his towelling dressing gown and smiled. 'I'm fine, thank you, but I do have something to tell you.' He pulled up a chair and explained to Malcolm exactly what had happened earlier that morning. The old man listened, not interrupting at any point. It was only when Tony revealed that Audrey was in the room next door that Malcolm reacted.

~

'Show some spunk.' Her mother's words always inspired her and would invariably galvanise her into action.

'I'm too tired, Mummy.' Audrey opened her eyes and saw a blurred figure standing by her bed. She had no idea where she was or how she'd got into this room. She thought back and the last thing she remembered was Malcolm. She smiled. They had made love and it had felt so right. But how had she ended up here, surrounded by medical equipment? She tried to move but couldn't. Lead flowed through her veins.

'It's Tony, Mrs Willatt. You saved our baby.'

The cogs in her brain ground as she thought back to the Olde

Tea Shoppe. 'How is he?'

'He's perfect. Thanks to you. But how are you feeling?'

'What am I doing here?' She heard her voice, and it sounded little better than a death-rattle. She tried to take a deep breath, but her lungs hurt too much.

'You were on the bridge and jumped into the river to avoid being killed by a van …and a car.'

'I don't remember.'

'You don't remember being in the river?'

'Malcolm. I was with Malcolm. Where is he?'

'He was in your house.'

'Yes. We were together.' Audrey felt her lips rise in a smile.

'Do you remember him falling down the stairs?'

Her mouth opened, and a spasm rippled through her body. 'Is he all right? Is he hurt?' She saw Tony swallow as she searched his face.

'Malcolm has broken a few bones but he's all right and will make a full recovery.'

Audrey fought to sit up, but her muscles would not respond. It was as though her nerve connections had been broken.

'I want to see him.'

'I'm sure when you've recovered a bit more, they'll take you to him.'

Audrey took a few pained breaths. 'How did I get out of the river?' She looked at his dressing gown. 'Was it you?'

'Me and one of the Russian property developers pulled you out, but it was the medical staff who saved your life.'

Audrey reached for his hand and squeezed it. 'Thank you.'

'You know, I think Malcolm loves you.'

Audrey smiled. 'And I think, I love him.' She closed her eyes.

'Audrey, Mrs Willatt, why were you standing on the bridge in the freezing cold?'

For a moment, she saw her little brother reaching out for her.

'Audrey?'

'I don't know.' She took a painful breath and felt herself drifting away.

CHAPTER THIRTY-SIX

Eden watched her husband button up his shirt. She could see a slight tremor in his fingertips.

'It's very cold outside. Why not take the doctor's advice and stay a night? For observation. Just to be sure,' she said.

'I'm coming home.'

Eden held onto Tony's arm as they left the hospital, determined never to let him go again. Their car was in the police pound following the accident on the bridge, so she had borrowed her father-in-law's beaten-up Audi. By the time she had driven home to their new-build town house, it was almost eight p.m.

Tony's mother, Maggie, crept down the carpeted stairs in her stockinged feet. Comfortably plump, her chocolate-box smile hid the protective nature of a tigress, which Eden understood and admired.

Maggie had given Eden a hard time when she and Tony first started dating, but it didn't bother her. Eden knew she was clever but she was also proud of her rich, auburn locks and D-cup boobs which attracted much male attention. When she worked as a barmaid in the Falcon pub, as her mother kept reminding her, she had the pick of go-ahead young guys and more than one proposal of marriage – including Tony, who almost popped the question before she'd pulled his second pint.

'Believe it or not Mrs Blake, it's not every woman's ambition to earn squillions of bucks simply to pay for a nanny. I want to care for my future husband, my future home and my future children, should we be so blessed.'

'But Tony told me how well you did at school,' said Maggie.

'For Christ's sake, you got offered a place at Cambridge. I would have given anything to have received that honour.'

'I let somebody else who wanted it more have the privilege.'

'But Newnham College – how could you turn it down?'

'God has given me a great brain, and I'm wasting it. It's like having a Ferrari and using it for the school run.'

'I couldn't have put it better myself.'

The marriage went ahead. Nine months after the honeymoon, exhausted from giving birth to Georgiana, Eden still had enough strength to grip her mother-in-law's hand. The two women, who loved the same young man, locked eyes.

'Maggie,' Eden said. 'This little baby has a mother who is fiercely ambitious. Her mother is going to be the very best mum this world has ever seen. Your beautiful granddaughter is going to have her mummy nurturing her from the moment she wakes to the moment she falls asleep.' She let go of Maggie's hand and reached for a plastic cup of water. She took a sip then fixed her eyes on her mother-in-law. 'I'll read her stories, we'll join other mums at playgroups, we'll go to the park, we'll play games, we'll sing songs, we'll...'

'I get it,' Maggie said. 'I have one child because I was too busy building my pension pot to give Tony a brother or sister. I get it, and I love you for it.'

'I'll pop up and give them a kiss.' Tony peeled off his coat and handed it to Eden.

'They've just gone down.' Maggie kissed her son. 'I told Georgiana you'd see her when she wakes in the morning.'

'I'll be quiet as a mouse.' Tony crept upstairs, and Maggie headed off to the kitchen.

Eden hung their coats in the understairs cupboard and waited in the hall. She could hear her mother-in-law clattering about and Sky News blaring from the sitting room. She sat on the stairs and tears of relief coursed down her freckly cheeks. Their baby son had escaped unscathed from meningitis and now her husband from a watery grave. She knew she should feel blessed, relieved, but her confidence was gone, and all she felt was fear.

She heard Tony coming down the stairs and got up to make way. Immediately, she could see something was wrong. Just as he reached the bottom tread, his knees buckled, and he collapsed into her arms, causing them both to fall in a heap on the carpeted floor.

'Mags, we need you,' Eden shouted as she tried to prevent Tony's head from hitting the newel post at the base of the stairs.

'What's going on?' Andy called from the sitting room.

Maggie was the first to appear and helped Eden place Tony on his side with his face angled towards the floor.

'What happened?' Andy shouted, coming to help.

'Not so loud,' Maggie responded. 'You'll wake the little ones.'

'He's breathing, all right.' Eden tried to appear calm. 'I think he fainted.'

Maggie reached for the landline phone. 'I'll get an ambulance.'

'No,' Tony mumbled. 'I'm all right.'

'You don't look it, son,' Andy said. He turned to Maggie. 'I'll drive him. It'll be quicker.'

Tony struggled in Eden's arms. 'No, I'm fine.' He tried to push himself off the floor. 'I'm all right. Just a bit tired.'

They all helped Tony get off the floor and onto his feet.

'Right, let's get you to a comfy seat.' Andy took the brunt of his son's weight and guided him to an armchair in the sitting room. Eden found a footstool, and Andy placed his son's feet on it. Maggie grabbed the TV remote and turned off the news. For a moment there was silence – then a child-like wail from deep within burst through Tony's shivering lips, and his whole body convulsed in sobs as his hands clawed the air for purchase on an imaginary river bank.

'It's shock – pure and simple,' Andy said. 'I'll make us some tea.'

Eden hugged her husband and made gentle noises to try and soothe him. From upstairs she heard her baby's high-pitched cry and turned to her mother-in-law for help. She saw Maggie was weeping. But another, closer cry, grabbed her attention.

Standing in a nightie holding her bunny was Georgiana, tears coursing down her pink cheeks.

Andy emerged from the kitchen and swiped away his tears. He scooped up his granddaughter.

'We're all playing a game, darling,' Andy explained. 'We're seeing who can cry the loudest. And I think your baby brother is the winner.'

He carried Georgiana out of the sitting room and away from Tony's child-like sobs.

Several minutes passed before Eden was able to calm her husband down. Maggie emerged from the kitchen with a tray of tea which she placed on a side table. She poured a half cup, tipped in some milk and reached for the sugar bowl.

'He doesn't take sugar,' Eden said.

'It will help with the shock.'

Eden held the cup for Tony, and he took a few sips.

'Thank you,' he said, and he closed his eyes.

Maggie poured two more cups and handed one to Eden. She looked at Tony. 'He's exhausted. He'll feel better in the morning.'

'We all will.'

'You know, Eden, there's something about Audrey I find bothersome. She's here on a mission. I can feel it.'

Andy entered from the hallway. 'They're settled – thank God. Any tea left?'

'Mum,' Tony said in a quiet voice. 'Charlie is asleep upstairs thanks to Audrey coming here. Her mission, whatever it is, doesn't matter.'

CHAPTER THIRTY-SEVEN

It took several days before sensation fully returned to Audrey's hands and feet. She felt as though she'd slept for more hours than there were in each day, but she understood from her consultant physician that her body had had to shut down conscious brain activity to martial all its resources to repair damage to nerves caused by hypothermia.

When awake, her thoughts invariably returned to Malcolm.

'We're just keeping an eye on him,' Audrey was told. 'He's had a nasty shock to the system, and we want to monitor him closely for at least a couple of weeks.'

'It may seem odd,' Audrey later explained to Tina, 'but I don't want Malcolm to see me looking like this, like an old lady.'

'Tony says he's completely smitten and worships the ground you walk on. And he's not looking his best, either.'

Audrey had never felt so weak. She could move all her limbs but still needed to rest on an arm to walk to the lavatory.

'What about you?' Audrey asked. 'Who is your beau these days?'

Tina looked shamefaced. 'I don't have one. Spartak keeps bombarding me with messages and Sean doesn't want "soiled goods".' She forced a smile. 'But I like your doctor, Mr Bisterzo.'

Audrey chuckled. 'So do I.'

~

Every day, Tony came to check on Malcolm and, every day, Tina came to check on Audrey.

'Well, fancy meeting you,' Tony said, spotting Tina waiting by reception in the intensive care unit. 'Have you been in to see her, yet?'

'She's with the doctor.'

A door opened and a tall, good-looking Italian emerged. Mr Bisterzo smiled as he approached them. 'She's doing well.' He turned to Tony. 'And how are you feeling?'

Tony looked a bit sheepish. 'I'm fine. Although I don't think I could beat you at tennis yet.'

'What about golf?'

'You're on! There's crazy golf by the kiddies' playground in Solefield Park.'

Mr Bisterzo laughed. 'Not exactly what I had in mind, but I'll be there. To be serious; your actions in the river, and after you pulled Mrs Willatt out, saved her life. No bones about it.'

'It was the least I could do.'

The consultant nodded. 'Well, as testament to how brave you are, Mrs Willatt will be released to a general ward tomorrow.'

'Great news,' Tony and Tina said in tandem.

Mr Bisterzo turned to go then looked back at Tony. 'Pound a hole? Or we could make it ten pounds if you want more excitement.'

'Bring it on. Ten pounds it is.'

Mr Bisterzo laughed again and walked away.

Tony turned to Tina. 'How many holes are there at the crazy golf?'

'Eighteen, I think.'

'Shit. I'd better get practising.'

CHAPTER THIRTY-EIGHT

Audrey was reluctant to let her sons know what had happened to her, but she was worried that they would try and call her mobile phone, which she no longer had.

'I saw your handbag in the river,' Tony said, sitting by Tina on one of their daily visits.

'What a nuisance – I liked that bag!' She smiled. 'I also liked my phone, purse and debit card.'

'We have a spare iPhone at the office,' Tina said. 'I'll bring it in so you can take your time going through emails. Can you remember your password?'

'I think so. Fortunately, not everything got washed away.'

What are you going to do about your house?'

Audrey looked at Tina, a bit puzzled. 'Malcolm and I are going to turn it into a hostel. Of course, it needs loads of renovation, new plumbing and wiring, but I have the financial resources. Since the school closed, the town has fewer visitors, so I'm hoping that the hostel will encourage people to return.'

'I think it's a brilliant idea,' Tony said. 'If we don't keep refreshing Hawksmead, all the enterprising people will leave.' He kissed Audrey on her cheek. 'I can tell you're definitely on the mend.'

Audrey smiled and looked up at her handsome saviour. 'How is Charlie?'

'Up to his usual tricks and fit as a fiddle, thanks to you. I'll see you again soon.' Tony smiled and left the unit.

Tina turned a serious-looking face to Audrey. 'I saw you.'

'You saw me – when?'

'On the morning you nearly drowned. I was up on the top landing in your house, and you were there. I spoke to you.'

Audrey stared at Tina as the wisp of a memory floated into her mind. 'I thought it was a dream. You were looking out of the window.'

'Let me sell the house.' Tina grasped Audrey's hand. 'Too many bad things have happened there.'

Audrey felt herself smiling. 'I found love in that house. I found a man with whom I want to share the rest of how many days, months, years, we have together.'

'But he fell down the stairs,' pressed Tina.

'He probably tripped on the same raised board that I tripped on when I first arrived. A hammer and a few nails should sort it out.'

CHAPTER THIRTY-NINE

Spartak Dryomov hesitated for a moment. So far, he had a clean record in England, and although human rights legislation would make it hard for the British authorities to deport him and his brother back to Russia, and even harder to prevent them returning to England, he did not want the inconvenience of being arrested. He switched on his heavy, long-handled Mag-Lite torch and pointed the beam at the door so that his brother could see where to place the jemmy. In summer, at this time of the early morning, it would be daylight, and more people would be about, but the cold and wind and impenetrable darkness would keep snooping eyes away.

He smiled when he saw the lock had not been changed since Kirill broke in to retrieve the axe, so the jemmy was redundant. They stepped across the threshold into the laundry room. In Spartak's left hand was a 1950s' electric fire he'd seen tossed into a skip and had kept for just such an occasion as this. Around his waist was his tool belt with an assorted selection of screwdrivers and pliers, a short extension cord and socket with a programmable timer, and a coil of copper wiring.

Spartak had begun his working life as an electrician and his brother as a bricklayer and plasterer. They had come to England to get rich but had found the English unpredictable and difficult to bribe. Even physical threats had proved to be of limited value, which was why their plan for the old school boarding house was the simple, smart solution, especially as the owner was safely tucked up in a hospital bed. They'd locate the main electrical fuse box and swap the thin circuit-breaking copper wires with much thicker eighteen-gauge wire that would not easily break with a power surge. He hoped the old house did not have modern trip switches; if it did, he would have to resort to Kirill's plan and splash around the petrol they had in cans sitting in the back of their van. Either way, the house would be destroyed and the land put up for sale. The old widow owed her life to Kirill so, with a bit of pressure, he was sure she would sell to them.

They found the electrical circuit board in the understairs cupboard and, as expected, it had the old style ceramic fuses with thin copper wiring. But what really caught Spartak's attention, behind an assortment of old Hoover upright vacuum cleaners, was a pile of at least a dozen electric fires, similar to the one he'd brought.

'Christmas has come early,' Spartak said.

'You have brought coals to Newcastle,' Kirill responded, laughing at his own joke.

Spartak turned off the main power supply and pulled out all the ceramic fuses. Kirill held the torch while he cut the thin copper wires and replaced them with the thick wire. He then selected five of the old electric fires.

Carrying their booty, they wandered around the old school boarding house, deciding where to place the fires. Spartak was particularly pleased to see that each room had the small old-fashioned Bakelite sockets that were specifically designed to power table lamps. He cut off the plugs from the fires and inserted the wires into the sockets, which would become live when the room light was switched on. To keep the wires in place, he rammed nails into the sockets. If there was a cupboard nearby, he hid the fire inside, facing it towards the dusty, dry wood panelling. If there wasn't a cupboard, he hid the fire behind an item of old furniture or curtains.

They reached the top dormitory room, and Spartak looked for the small-sized lighting socket. He tore off the plug from the end of the extension cord and pushed in the wires, securing them with two nails. Next, he cut the coiled filaments within the electric fire and made a new connection with the eighteen-gauge thick copper wire.

'Just to make sure,' Spartak said to himself more than to his brother. 'This will definitely cause a ring of fire throughout the whole lighting circuit.' He used a screwdriver to force the old copper wires into the timer socket, secured them with two nails, then hid the fire and extension cord under one of the un-used beds.

Through the window, they saw the first signs of dawn. Spartak loosened the bulb from the centre light and flicked on the light switch.

'For how many hours have you set the timer?' Kirill asked.

'Relax. We'll be drinking Moskovskaya in the Falcon long before this place goes up.'

Back in the understairs cupboard, Spartak turned on the mains power.

CHAPTER FORTY

Jessica Bassett had been in the police service for twenty-five years and was still surprised by how often people... well, surprised her. Audrey was a legend in Hawksmead and so Jessica had expected to see quite a few get-well cards but not the bundles that were stacked up on the windowsill by Audrey's bed, one of four in the side ward. Two of the other beds were occupied – one old patient in her nineties looked asleep and the other, a young woman who'd crashed on the Old Military Road whilst talking on her phone, had earbuds in and, from the jangly noise leaking out, was listening to Tinie Tempah.

'We've taken statements from Anthony Blake and Kirill Dryomov with regard to what happened on the bridge, but we would very much like to hear your thoughts. Are you still having problems remembering?'

'I've slept on it for quite a few nights. All I can remember is being with Malcolm Cadwallader, following a lovely day out, and then waking up in this hospital. I do recall a few dreams, mostly childhood memories, but nothing that will confirm exactly what happened. I have no idea why I was on the bridge and absolutely no memory of being in the river. All I can say is, without Tony Blake's brave actions, I wouldn't be here.'

'He feels partly responsible.'

'Really? I don't even blame that wretched Russian,' Audrey laughed. 'I know about black ice; my brother wrote about it in his...'

'You've remembered something?'

'No, it's nothing.'

'It might be something. Don't force it. There's no hurry.'

'No, it's gone. Thank you for coming. You have a perfect bedside manner, and if anyone could tease out the truth, I'm sure you could.'

'You mentioned your brother. Could you give me his contact details? He may be able to fill in the blanks.'

Audrey closed her eyes, and Jessica saw tears trickle from the corners.

She leant across and gently squeezed Audrey's arm. 'I am so sorry to have caused you distress.'

'Tissue, please.'

Jessica reached across for a box on the bedside unit and pulled out a couple. Audrey mopped her eyes.

'I'm sorry. Fifty years ago, my brother attended Hawksmead College. He didn't return home.'

Jessica stiffened.

'I'm very tired,' Audrey whispered.

There were a dozen questions Jessica wanted to ask. She waited for Audrey to open her eyes, but Audrey appeared to be asleep. Her questions would have to wait for another day.

Audrey heard the door open and close. She had to get back to the house and retrieve the diary. The door opened again, and she felt the kiss of an angel on her forehead.

She opened her eyes.

Tina lurched back.

'Tina!'

'It's good to see you looking better.'

'It's lovely to see you. I didn't mean to frighten you.'

'I thought you were asleep.'

'I've done enough sleeping. What I need now is a shower, some clothes, and some money. I managed to persuade my bank to deliver a new debit card here, and not to my home in Sevenoaks, but until I get it, I do not have a brass farthing.'

Although she felt weak, the shower made Audrey feel good. She could see she was skinny but, as she smiled to herself, her former model agency would probably say she still had more to lose.

CHAPTER FORTY-ONE

The planned meeting with Audrey meant a great deal to the old, broken man. He had undergone an operation to relocate his shoulder and to screw a plate to secure his fractured hip. He also had a plaster cast to set his arm and wrist.

'You know, I have it on good authority that Audrey Willatt really cares about you,' Tony said. 'She wants you two to be together and to turn the old school boarding house into a hostel for ramblers.'

'Are you sure?' Malcolm asked. 'When did she tell you that?'

'She's been chatting to Tina whilst I've been here with you. Tina's been filling me in.'

'But I don't understand. After what happened, I felt sure she'd want to be shot of the place. She has no reason to stay.'

'Perhaps it's fortunate she has no memory of your fall. Her time in the river seems to have washed it away.'

'She can't remember ...anything?'

'Nothing bad. According to Tina, her last memory is of a very happy time with you.'

Malcolm nodded. *What about my confession? Did that get washed away too? What if she regains her memory in the coming days?*

~

Tina stopped her car behind Malcolm's, which was still parked in Audrey's drive. She took a deep breath and forced herself to open the door. She climbed out and pushed back her hair as she walked up to the front entrance. She removed Audrey's house keys from her shoulder bag and, feeling more than a little trepidatious, unlocked the heavy oak door.

Fortunately, Audrey had abandoned her suitcases in the hall-way, so she wouldn't have to climb the creaking stairs up to the top of the house. The hallway appeared as she had last seen it, although some of the toiletry containers looked cracked and crushed. She switched on the feeble light and opened one of the suitcases. Audrey had given her explicit instructions, but find-ing the right clothes and underwear took a bit of time.

As quickly as she could, she put together three outfits and hoped that Audrey would approve. Despite leaving the front door open and switching on the hall light, she still had to use the torch in her phone to help her select items of make-up scat-tered across the floor that were still usable.

Clothes draped over her arm, and a pair of shoes in her hand, Tina switched off the light, locked the door and rejoiced in get-ting out of the house and back into her car.

~

Tony held a mirror for Malcolm as he used his right hand to comb his hair and smarten up his pyjamas. He got Tony to place his dressing gown on the side of the bed so that when it hung down, it hid the yellow urine collecting in a plastic bag.

The spring in the door handle squeaked. Tony hurried away from the bed and stood by the window.

Malcolm, tense, excited, nervous, watched the door open and was momentarily disappointed to see Tina enter the room.

'Mr Cadwallader. There is somebody here to see you.' She held the door open and Malcolm saw Audrey standing in the corridor wearing a patterned turtle-neck sweater, and a plain-coloured woollen skirt that came to just below her knee. His first impression was how thin she looked, but he was thrilled to see the amazing sparkle in her eyes.

'May I come in?' Audrey asked. Her voice was weaker than he remembered. He beckoned with his good arm.

Audrey smiled and walked in. She leaned over the bed and kissed his cheek. 'I've missed you.'

'We'll leave you to it,' Tony said. 'Tina's got houses to sell, and

I've got a ninetieth birthday party to photograph.'

Audrey blew them a kiss. When the door was closed, she pulled up a chair and sat as close to the bedside as her chair would allow. Malcolm clasped her hand in his. Fortunately, he was the only patient currently residing in the small side ward.

'I have something to tell you,' Malcolm said, trying to instil some youth into his gravelly voice. 'It's a confession which you've heard before but don't remember.'

'What I do remember was absolutely lovely.'

'It was. It was.' Malcolm's resolve began to waiver.

She squeezed his hand. 'We're together. That's all that matters.'

Malcolm licked his dry lips. He had to get this right. 'When I came down from Oxford, I was twenty-one; the first generation not to have to put on a uniform and fight a war, or do national service. It was before The Beatles; Cliff Richard was the young star at the time. I had a first in English and no job and no idea of what I wanted to do. I heard that Hawksmead College was looking for an English master, and I applied. It was easy for someone like me to get a job teaching – educated and from a respectable family. I quite enjoyed my time at the school, although the boys were often challenging. They mostly came from troubled backgrounds, sent to be physically educated in the hope that it would improve their minds. The school had almost no admissions criteria apart from being able to afford the fees. Unfortunately, some boys destined for reform school could elect to come to us, if the courts approved and their parents could afford it. We provided a tough environment, designed to straighten out the troublemakers, but it didn't work. There were fights, and serious physical injury often resulted. For the more sensitive boys, there were the arts; a place of safety away from violence, but there was no drama group. I wanted to change that, and although Mr Gibbs, the headmaster, was not at all cultured, he was persuaded to allow me to form a dramatic society.'

He felt Audrey stiffen but kept a firm grip on her hand. 'In September, fifty years ago, your brother arrived. He was brilliant at English; he could write an essay on any subject and give it a unique viewpoint, and he was kind to other boys. He had a dreadful stutter, not helped by the harsh regime and the brutal violence. I didn't think he'd last a term. But then he walked on stage to audition for Roxane in *Cyrano de Bergerac*, and I saw something magical.'

Audrey pulled her hand away.

'May I have a drink of water?' Malcolm asked.

She looked at the side table and poured a small quantity of water into a plastic cup.

He took a few sips and handed the cup back to her. 'Do you remember when we were in bed together?'

She nodded.

'Do you remember what I told you prior to my falling down the stairs?'

'Lying with you in my narrow bed is the last thing I remember, until I woke up here, in hospital.'

He should quit now, he thought. Even telling this wonderful woman half the truth would probably drive her away.

'You were his English master?'

'Yes.'

'You were the Mr C in his diary?'

Malcolm's stomach heaved. Diary? This was the first he'd heard of a diary. What had the boy said? He took a breath and continued. 'The Sunday morning, after the final performance of *Cyrano*, I drove to the boarding house to congratulate Bobby on his mesmerising Roxane. We chatted, and I offered him a lift in my motorcar to avoid him being late for Sunday chapel. He ran down the stairs ahead of me, full of youthful exuberance. I tried to keep up and arrived at the top of the stairs in the hallway in time to see him tumbling down, head over heels.'

He could not look at her.

'Why did you lie to the police?'

Malcolm was shocked by her question. 'How do you mean?'

'I read a newspaper article in which it stated that when you arrived at the boarding house you found Bobby lying on the floor in the hallway.'

'I... I was foolish. I thought that if I told the police I'd gone up to the dormitory, it could imply that I had acted inappropriately in some way and was responsible for him rushing down the stairs.'

'But you were responsible. You had already acted inappropriately when you took him back to your cottage.'

The knife blade slipped between his ribs and found his heart. He felt her eyes on him. He took a moment to breathe. He could still smell the shampoo in Bobby's blond hair when he'd wrapped his arms around the boy. To this day, he did not know what he had wanted to do other than hold Roxane.

'Did he run down the stairs in youthful exuberance, or was he desperate to get away from you?'

'I did nothing. Nothing to harm him. I would never have harmed him.' Malcolm knew he had to look her in the eyes. 'Perhaps it was the wrong time, the wrong place, but I told Bobby he was so good in the role of Roxane, he could become a professional actor. He was excited by his achievement after suffering so much from other boys. Despite his stammer, he knew he had the skill, the talent, to make an audience believe. Full of confidence, he rushed ahead of me down the stairs and must have tripped when he reached the half-landing. It was an accident. A terrible, terrible, tragic accident.'

He waited for her to say something.

'Did you touch him?'

Malcolm was shocked by the directness of her question. 'Good God no!'

'But he ran away from you?'

'I told you, he was excited about the play and was looking forward to having a ride in my car.'

'He had a bicycle.'

'It was cold. Bitterly cold that morning. Icy.' He closed his eyes and tried to erase the memory of what happened. He heard Audrey draw a deep breath and get up from the chair.

Malcolm opened his eyes and looked up at her.

'Is that it?' Audrey asked.

He felt himself shrivel before her eyes. 'Earlier that dreadful term, I had driven into a boy on the bridge and killed him.'

Audrey's hand shot up to her mouth.

'There was black ice,' he continued. 'I couldn't stop.'

'You were the schoolmaster driving the car?'

Malcolm nodded. 'I lost control and crushed a young life. I nearly killed Bobby, too. The shock of the accident affected me badly, and from then on I was desperate to protect your brother.'

He felt the heat of Audrey's penetrating gaze. A few seconds later, she left without saying another word.

Malcolm looked at the ceiling in his side ward. For a few brief moments, he had believed it possible that he could spend his final days in the company of the most wonderful woman he'd ever met. He had been drawn to Audrey as soon as he saw her. Why had he not connected her to Robert Oakes? Now he knew the relationship, the similarity between Bobby's Roxane and Audrey was undeniable.

CHAPTER FORTY-TWO

Audrey returned to her ward and retrieved five twenty-pound notes that Tina had withdrawn from an ATM and Audrey had hidden in her pillow slip. In the bedside cabinet, she found her house keys. Why they had been discarded on the floor in her hallway she had not the least idea, but the fact that Tina had also found her suitcases packed and in the hallway told their own story. She knew she was not yet strong enough to be officially discharged from hospital, but she had to get Bobby's diary. That was all that mattered to her now; that – and leaving Hawksmead for good.

Audrey paid the taxi driver and walked to the front entrance of the old school boarding house, past Malcolm's Honda with its battered side mirror. It was one of those bleak days when it never really gets light, and the coat she'd borrowed from a receptionist she'd befriended in the intensive care unit was not really up to the job.

She pushed open the heavy door, flicked on the hall light, and looked at her two suitcases lying on the floor. Stepping around them, she walked to the base of the stairs, kicking aside various toiletry items. She was too weak to hurry, so took her time climbing to the half-landing. At the top, she took a few deep breaths into her weakened lungs and headed up the short flight to the first floor corridor. She switched on the light, walked to the end and headed up to the second floor, flicking more old light switches as she went.

By the time Audrey reached the top floor landing she was exhausted, and slumped down on the wooden floorboards to catch her breath. She looked across to the dormitory that had been her bedroom for what seemed an eternity, and could not help but think of lying in bed with Malcolm. Something about the man was still alight within her. She hoped, once she had left Hawksmead, her feelings for him would fade.

Audrey struggled to her feet. She pushed open the dormitory door and looked at the mess of sheets and blankets and discarded clothing, including Malcolm's jacket and trousers. Out of pride she felt she should tidy up, but she simply wanted to retrieve Bobby's diary and get on the train, south.

She looked at the rotted shelf then spotted the encyclopaedia lying on a bed, and opened it. The cut-out section was empty – no diary.

Had someone been in the house and stolen it?

No, she must have hidden it somewhere else; probably under her pillow.

She went to switch the light on and saw the switch was already down. She looked at the bulb, took a pained breath, and in the dim daylight searched her bed, throwing all her bed clothes on the floor.

Hot and emotionally exhausted, realisation finally dawned. She had lost her handbag when she fell in the river, and together with her wallet and phone must have been Bobby's diary.

She sat on her bed and wept. She had lost her only thread to Bobby and betrayed his memory. How she wished the river had swept her away, too. Her brother was dead; her mother was dead; her husband was dead and… her heart yearned for Malcolm. How could she ever confess to her father, aged eighty-nine, that she was in love with the man responsible for killing his only son, even if it had been a tragic accident?

'Audrey, get up, wash your face and show some spunk. Stop feeling sorry for yourself.'

She smiled as she remembered her mother's stern words. She pushed herself back onto her feet and walked out of the dormitory and down the creaking stairs to the half-landing. She looked into the hall and continued on, along the dark corridor to the washroom. She pushed open the door and switched on the lights.

There was an almighty bang as one of the bulbs blew. For a moment, Audrey was taken aback – shocked.

Then she smiled. 'Yes. You're right – time to go.'

She entered a cubicle and slumped down on the old wooden seat. She didn't bother to flush and went to one of the many washbasins. She splashed water on her face, looked in the mirror, grimaced and took a deep, resigned, breath – and coughed.

She coughed again.

CHAPTER FORTY-THREE

The electrical lighting circuit had heated up as Spartak Dryomov planned. Within the walls, hot wires burned through insulating sleeves, causing wood panelling, baked dry over one hundred and fifty years, to catch fire. Helped by paraffin firelighters stacked around the fuse box, the cupboard under the stairs was soon ablaze and the main hallway thick with smoke.

In the washroom, Audrey coughed every time she took a breath.

She opened the door to the corridor and was engulfed by hot, acrid smoke. She slammed the door shut and hurried to a washbasin to flush out her mouth. She was in trouble; five minutes earlier she had wanted to curl up and die, but now, she absolutely did not.

She looked across at the windows on the far side of the washroom. They were more like high-level vents, horizontally hinged with opaque glass, and way too high to reach. Even if she had a stepladder and could open them or break the reinforced glass, the gap was too small for her to crawl through.

There only one way out and that was through the main entrance hallway. What were her choices? She could stay where she was, keep the door shut and wait for help, or she could make a dash for it.

Audrey leant over the washbasin, full of indecision. The tiles through her shoes were heating up. It was only a matter of minutes before the washroom would succumb to the fire. She was trapped without a phone and nobody knew she was in the house. How ironic that she should nearly die by drowning and now was about to die by fire.

Water. The one thing she had was water. Audrey grabbed the

towels and her bathrobe hanging on a hook and rushed to the shower area. She hoped the fire had not yet destroyed the water flow. She turned on the cold tap and allowed the increasingly hot water to drench her clothes, towels and bathrobe.

She put the soaking robe over her borrowed coat and the wet towels over her head and hurried to the closed door.

The remaining lights went out.

The floor almost glowed with heat. To protect her feet, she had to jump from one foot to the other.

She was frightened, very frightened, but she had no choice. She took a few deep breaths, filtered through a wet towel, and opened the door, hiding behind it as scorching, caustic smoke roared into the washroom. She hurried through the doorway and was immediately engulfed by the noxious killer.

Her head covered, Audrey edged her way along the corridor to the top of the stairs. She could feel flames scorching her legs as the wet towels rapidly dried.

The crackle of the flames consuming the wooden staircase that led down to the hall was truly terrifying, and she was tempted to rush back to the temporary respite of the washroom.

'Show some spunk, girl,' she said to herself as she launched into the flames that were burning up the tinder-like stairs. The old oak planks, their life's work done, held her weight, but flames licked with gusto through the gaps in the joins, barbecuing her calves. She knew that taking a breath could be fatal, but she was desperate for air. It was a relief to reach the tiles in the hallway, and she aimed for where she knew was the front door and salvation. But her foot caught one of her suitcases lying open on the floor and she lost her balance, landing hard. She heard a bone break and felt stabbing pain in her right forearm. How easy it would be to give up and slip away into blessed oblivion.

Ten feet, girl. She could only be ten feet from the door. With her good arm, she dragged herself along the floor and came to the base of the front door. She reached up for the latch, but it was too high. She had to get to her feet, but her legs were screaming with pain and refused to respond to the command from her neurons. She was inches from cool, fresh air but couldn't move. Even with layers of towel over her mouth, every breath she took was thick with burning smoke. Her head felt as though it was about to burst, and her eyes, though screwed shut, were being stabbed with a thousand skewers. Worst of all was the sound – the incessant roar of a furnace as flames consumed the wood panelling.

Audrey almost laughed. She had told her sons that when it was her time, she was to be cremated.

'Well, be careful what you wish for, girl,' said her inner scared voice.

CHAPTER FORTY-FOUR

'Audrey's house is on fire!'

Tina heard Tony's voice on her hands-free speaker as she drove along the Old Military Road. She was on her way to a viewing of a modern townhouse at the southern end of Hawksmead, and had decided to avoid the inevitable traffic by taking the longer route across the moor.

'Did you notice anything wrong when you went to collect her clothes?' Tony continued.

'I didn't smell any smoke, or burning. Have you called the fire brigade?'

'Someone rushed into *The Chronicle* to tell my dad, and Dad called me as he wants me to take pictures. I'm on my way there now but the traffic is terrible. I presume the emergency services have been called. At least we know Audrey and Malcolm are safely tucked up together in hospital.'

~

But Audrey wasn't safely tucked up in hospital. She was a skinny little ballerina in a tutu who had attempted an arabesque by raising a straight leg behind her and had toppled over onto the floor.

"Get up girl!" said Miss Bush. The headmistress in Audrey's ballet school was never to be disobeyed. Even the girls' parents followed her instructions to the letter.

Audrey forced her agonised body to move and stretched up for the door latch. The metal seared her hand and her skin fused to the hot surface. Whimpering with pain, she protected her fingers with her towel, reached up again and managed to pull the door open. Wind off the moor blew ice cold air into her face and she staggered through the open gap.

Burned and broken-boned, she stumbled down her drive, bumping into Malcolm's car, as oxygen, sucked in through the front door, fed the fire. Victorian panes shattered throughout the boarding house, hurling molten glass and debris into the air as voracious tongues licked up the sides of the building.

~

Tina blasted her horn to clear a way through onlookers who were blocking the end of the short drive. Through her windscreen she spotted Audrey's frail figure hobbling towards her; bare skin showing through burnt clothes and black soot around her mouth and nose. Leaving her door open and her treasured car unlocked, Tina rushed to help Audrey and was astounded by the blast of heat from the roaring flames.

'Audrey, it's Tina.' She placed her arm carefully around Audrey's shoulder and guided her to the Golf. She opened the passenger door and eased Audrey in, not bothering with the seat belt, anxious not to inflict further pain.

Tina slipped into the driver's seat and grimaced at the smell of Audrey's scorched skin. She fired up the engine, tooted her horn several times to clear a path and reversed into the High Street, expertly spinning her steering wheel so her car was pointed in the right direction.

Headlights on full beam, despite the sun not yet setting, Tina hared south through Hawksmead, her manicured thumb stabbing the horn on her steering wheel whenever another vehicle looked likely to block her route.

'Call Tony Blake,' she barked at her hands-free phone, and within two rings Tony answered.

'I'm on the way to Undermere Hospital with Audrey. She's badly hurt. Can you call and let them know? I should be there within ten minutes. Tell them she has burns, smoke inhalation and is in a critical condition.'

Tina drove with great precision and as fast as she dared, oblivious to flashing speed cameras. Red traffic lights she used simply as a guide. Even a Ford Fiesta's sharp-blue roof lights reflecting into her eyes from her rear-view mirror did not cause her foot to lift from the accelerator.

The Ford Fiesta police patrol car kept pace with the Golf and added the wail of its siren to the flashing roof lights and full-beam headlights.

'Shit!' Tina felt the natural fear of authority stir her gut. She stole a glance at Audrey, who was either unconscious or asleep.

A Range Rover Sport pulled out of a side turning ahead of the Golf and Tina was forced to slam her foot on the brake. Audrey slid forward and hit the dashboard. The police car behind swerved and took the opportunity to accelerate and pull up alongside Tina's door. She mouthed, *'Help'* at the police officer in the passenger seat and pointed at Audrey who had slumped back at an angle.

The police car pulled in front of her and forced Tina to slow to jogging speed. Ahead was a lay-by with a bus stop and the Ford Fiesta's rear light signalled left, indicating for her to follow.

Tina looked at Audrey and couldn't tell whether she was asleep, unconscious or dead. All she knew was that wasting time talking to the police was not going to help. She saw the officers open their car doors, glanced into her recently replaced side mirror, saw that it was sort of clear behind and pumped her accelerator. The turbocharged stratified injection VW Golf engine spun the front wheels, and she shot off, almost hitting the police car's open door. The driver of a Lexus Hybrid braked hard behind and blasted his horn. Tina gave him an apologetic wave before indicating she was turning right. Ahead was the entrance to the hospital.

NO ENTRY

AUTHORISED VEHICLES ONLY

Tina took a chance and swerved across the on-coming traffic, ignoring the horn and flashing lights of a silver Mercedes C-Class Coupé, a car she normally would have taken time to admire. Ahead was a curved drive, lined with conifer trees, which she fervently hoped was one-way only as she injected copious quantities of fuel into her engine. A quick glance in her rear-view mirror reminded her that the police were hot on her rear bumper so now was not the moment to falter. She rounded the next bend, saw the ambulance entrance for Accident & Emergency, pressed her thumb down on the horn button and slid to an untidy halt. The tailgating police car almost rear-ended her as Tina leapt out and ran around the nose to open Audrey's door. A male doctor and two female nurses, all wearing green scrubs, came through the main entrance, wheeling a stretcher.

'She's badly burned!' Tina shouted, standing back to let the doctor lean into the car to examine Audrey slumped in the passenger seat.

'Hello, my name is Dr Chaudri – can you hear me?'

Audrey nodded. 'I think my right arm is broken.' The doctor had to lean in to hear her raspy words. 'My lungs are painful. And I think I'm a bit burnt – my legs hurt like hell.'

'We need to get you out of the car and onto the stretcher,' Dr Chaudri said, his tone gentle.

Tina watched anxiously. Every time the doctor touched Audrey she whimpered in pain. 'Let me try myself,' Audrey croaked.

Tina, the doctor and the nurses watched as Audrey eased her blackened clothes and roasted body out of the VW. She staggered like a child taking its first steps to the wheeled stretcher and screamed as she eased herself onto it.

Tina wanted to stay with Audrey but was persuaded by the police officer driving the patrol car to move her Golf first.

'Nice driving by the way.'

She smiled at the compliment.

'With luck, you should only get a six-month ban.'

'What?' Tina was shocked.

'It's all the cameras. Here's my card,' he said. 'I'm PC Gary Burton. Let me know when your case is heard, and I'll put in a good word. And if you want a chat or fancy a meal out, you've got my number.'

He winked and headed back to his patrol car.

Tina called after him. 'A little unprofessional under the circumstances, don't you think?'

'I wish your grandma all the best,' he called back as he opened his car door.

Tina got into her Golf and negotiated her way past various No Entry signs to the hospital's extortionate pay-and-display public car park. She was standing by the machine, waiting for her ticket to be printed when she saw Tony pulling in, driving his father's Audi. Ticket in hand, she went over to him.

'The fire has all but destroyed the house,' Tony said, using the electronic key fob to lock his car. 'It went up like a tinderbox. Another Grade II building destroyed.' He looked at Tina. 'How is she?'

'Not good.'

After sticking the parking tickets to their windscreens, Tina accompanied Tony to the hospital's main entrance.

In Accident & Emergency, they saw Audrey on the trolley, breathing with an oxygen mask, and a woman wearing a white coat over her green scrubs, taking her pulse.

As they approached, Tina heard her say, 'Mrs Willatt. I am Miss Caringi, a consultant physician. You have first and second-degree burns, which are exceedingly painful, but they will heal. The treatment involves bandaging to prevent infection. At this stage, I don't think you need skin grafts, but it may become necessary in coming days. Our main concern is the damage to your trachea and lungs. We'll do a blood test to determine how much oxygen your lungs are currently able to absorb.'

~

After much discussion, Tina and Tony agreed that Malcolm should be told about Audrey's fire and subsequent injuries. They entered his side ward and Tony approached the bed. Tina waited near the door.

'When she's up to visitors, would you like us to arrange a wheelchair for you to go and see her?' Tony asked.

Malcolm looked up at him and took a deep breath. 'No. It's

over between us. I'm the last person she wants to see, but I think her sons should be told. She won't want to worry them, but they ought to know. Tell me the truth. Please. How serious is it?'

'Well, Tina drove like the clappers to get her here as quickly as possible. She gave no quarter. Even outran the police.'

'I can believe that.' Malcolm looked at Tina. 'Thank you.'

'She is hurt,' Tony continued, 'but they've told us she will heal. It's bad, but it could have been a lot worse.'

Tina walked a few paces towards the bed. 'Her lungs have suffered a bit.'

'Do you know what caused the fire?' Malcolm asked.

Tony looked at Tina. 'Any ideas?'

She blew out her cheeks and shrugged. 'I expect there'll be an investigation.'

'And it's destroyed the whole house?' Malcolm wrinkled his brow.

'It can be rebuilt, of course,' Tony said. 'I'm sure Audrey was insured.'

Tina turned to Tony. 'What about Malcolm's car? It's parked in the drive.'

He looked puzzled. 'The drive was blocked by fallen rubble. I'm sorry, Malcolm, I didn't see your car.'

'Alas poor, Honda, I knew it well.' Malcolm shook his head and offered a wintry smile. 'At least it saves me the bother of getting the side mirror fixed.'

CHAPTER FORTY-FIVE

Audrey did not want any fanfare. As soon as her consultant told her that she could leave hospital and go home to plenty of rest, she sought out the clothes that Tina had brought weeks ago, before the fire, and carefully put on a lightweight dress. Her skin still felt tender, but she was healing well, and her broken arm was now in a supportive bandage.

She went to the hospital shop and bought a pack of envelopes, using a second replacement debit card delivered by the bank a few days earlier. On her way back to the side ward, she removed her maximum daily allowance from the hospital ATM. In her room, she wrote the names of nursing staff and junior doctors on the envelopes, and enclosed several twenty-pound notes in each. Her writing arm still felt weak, but the broken bone had fused well, and she was confident that some gentle tennis, when summer came, would strengthen her muscles.

Hoping she had left no one out, she went to the unit reception and gave the envelopes to Amy, one of the receptionists.

'Your hospital, your colleagues have saved my life, twice. This is a small thank-you to you all.'

'Why have you included me? You've already replaced my coat with a much more expensive one.'

'It's for you to spend on your little ones this Christmas.'

Amy came out from behind the reception area and gave Audrey a gentle hug.

~

Wearing a dark blue raincoat Tina had picked up for her from Marks & Spencer in Undermere, Audrey took it easy as she walked down the corridor to the main entrance. She saw a taxi waiting and a man leaning against the front passenger door.

'Mrs Willatt?'

Audrey smiled. 'Is it that obvious?'

'You're a celebrity!'

For several weeks, *The Hawksmead Chronicle* had run stories about Audrey and her little brother. The mix of tragedy, ghostly sightings, and a conflagration linked to rumours of arson, kept readers hooked from week to week.

Online, fake news abounded, with superimposed images of spooky schoolboys turning old photos of the boarding house into MSN clickbait.

Producers from reality TV shows had zoomed in on Tina's beauty and youth, and offered her increasing sums of money to appear on *Love Island,* or fly to Australia to join the cast of *I'm A Celebrity… Get Me Out of Here!*

'As tempted as I am by the money,' Tina had told Audrey, 'I am a home-girl, and I do not want a brief moment of fame to come between me and my plans to build a business empire.'

CHAPTER FORTY-SIX

The train pulled out of Undermere railway station, and Audrey sat back in the first class carriage. She had chosen a table seat as she didn't want people to see her sitting with her legs not quite touching. Tender skin rubbing against tender skin was still painful, so keeping cool air circulating was essential.

As the train headed south, the view through the window of the bleak and beautiful moorland countryside brought tears to her eyes, which surprised her. She leaned back against the seat, resting her head, and tried to clear her mind. Instinctively, she went to feel for her wedding ring and remembered it had come off and dropped between the floorboards in the boarding house – now gone for good.

The gentle movement of the high-speed train lulled her into the twilight zone between being awake and asleep. It had been when she was dummy at a bridge tea with her lady friends that the idea to investigate her brother's death had first taken hold. She was still amazed that the old school boarding house had actually been up for sale, and how quickly it had given up its tragic secret. What surprised her most of all was how much she had fallen for Hawksmead and its wonderful residents. She loved Tina – during her weeks of recovery, she had become the daughter Audrey never had; and she thought of Tony as a favourite nephew, with a lovely wife and two beautiful children.

Malcolm's face entered her mind uninvited, and she snapped her eyes open to wipe the image. A tall man was standing by her table.

'Good morning, ma'am. May I take your order for lunch?' asked the liveried waiter.

'I'll have the salmon, please.'

'Anything to drink?'

Audrey looked at the menu and selected a quarter bottle of Sauvignon Blanc. Whilst waiting for her food, she tried not to think about Malcolm and their wonderful meal at the Rorty Crankle. But when a gentleman walked past her seat who looked like him from behind, her heart skipped a beat and she hastily turned away. She was not wearing a scrap of make-up; her hair was long over-due for a colour and her exposed upper chest was decidedly blotchy. Not a pretty sight, for sure.

Why was she even thinking about Malcolm? It was over. Finished. Every mile, she was excising him a bit more from her life.

She arrived at Euston Station and took the Circle Line to Liverpool Street Station. Joshua, Audrey's elder son, had wanted to meet her, but she had kept quiet about when she would be arriving as she wanted more time for her body to heal and, more importantly, to regain her equilibrium.

She bought a rail ticket to Wivenhoe, a village situated on the River Colne, near the old Roman city of Colchester. Sitting at a table, she tried to read the free London Evening Standard newspaper but her thoughts kept wandering back to the people she had left behind. Audrey had always made friends easily, but the friends she had made in Hawksmead were completely different to her friends in Sevenoaks. Perhaps it was their youth she loved, but there was more to it than that. Both Tony and Tina had gone way beyond what most good people would do to help an older person. Why had she left them without saying goodbye? Of course, she knew why.

Audrey looked out at the River Colne as her train approached Wivenhoe Railway Station. Once a ship building and fishing village, it still retained its industrial charm despite the prolific growth of new housing. Stepping onto the platform, it felt odd not having a handbag; she carried a supermarket plastic bag containing a couple of items of clothing, a toothbrush, toothpaste, bits of make-up and an almost empty bottle of mineral water. In her coat pockets were her return ticket to London, her bank card, and a small packet of tissues.

The air was damp and cold, and the light was fading fast as Audrey made her way to the water's edge. She took a few moments to breathe in the fresh, salty air and to martial her thoughts. She walked up Quay Street and knocked on the blue stable-style front door to a small two up, two down cottage. Within a few seconds, a bolt was drawn and the door opened. It was quite a while since she'd last seen Richard Oakes and her father, at the age of eighty-nine, did look a bit older.

'Hi, Daddy. Sorry to arrive unannounced. May I come in for a cup of tea?'

She saw his brow furrow with surprise and then his eyebrows almost join as concern, laced with anger, took precedence.

CHAPTER FORTY-SEVEN

Tina had three more days before her appearance in the magistrates' court to face a charge of speeding and driving without due care and attention, and the inevitable loss of her licence. She decided to take a couple of hours off and drove in her VW to the hospital. She liked Malcolm and had hoped that he and Audrey would get back together.

Malcolm leant on Tina's arm, looking frail, bent and old. A metal walking stick, supplied by the hospital, and a profound limp had removed the last vestiges of his youth.

She looked at his baggy clothes. 'I should have bought you a size smaller.'

'Marks & Spencer usually fit me like a glove, a glove that fits of course, but I've lost a bit of weight. Oh, I nearly forgot. I must pick up my wallet and mobile phone from reception. They've been keeping them safe for me.'

'What about your keys?'

'My car is no longer with us, of course, but my house keys would have been handy. Best guess, they were consumed by the fire, along with my favourite suit.'

'Forgive me for asking the obvious, but how are we going to get in? I'm already up on one charge for speeding, I don't want to add breaking and entering.'

Malcolm laughed. 'Perfect Locks should be at the property when we get home. Tony organised it for me.'

'Heating? It's been really cold.'

'The boiler is on a timer, so the cottage should've remained warm.'

'It's funny,' Tina said. 'We've had many chats over the last few weeks, but I've never thought to ask you about your boiler.'

Malcolm laughed. 'I'm grateful for all you've done. Your visits gave me great comfort. I'm a lucky man.'

'Who needs to build up his strength.'

'Food,' Malcolm said. 'Would it be possible... ?'

'I've bought a few essentials to tide you over for a couple of days. If you text me a list, I'll do a much bigger shop.'

'I would very much appreciate your company for tea rather than waste your time in a supermarket. I can order goods on-line and have them delivered.'

Tina, who liked to go everywhere fast, found Malcolm's walking pace painfully slow. It was a great relief to leave the hospital's recycled air and head to her car.

'When are you up before the beak?' Malcolm asked.

For a moment, Tina was completely puzzled. 'The beak? Oh, you mean, when do I go to court?'

'Yes. I'm going to speak to the magistrate. Let the court know how your driving saved Audrey's life.'

~

At that very moment, in the county of Essex, Audrey's father looked at her with a mix of love and disapproval. 'Where is the diary now?'

She examined the scarred skin on the backs of her hands. 'I lost it when I fell in the river. That is what I presume happened. All I remember is lying in bed in the old school boarding house and then waking up in hospital.'

'That was the first time you were in hospital?' Rosemary asked, a slim, attractive, dark-haired woman, far removed from the fair looks of Audrey's mother, her father's late first wife. 'You were admitted again, after the fire?'

Audrey took a long breath. Her lungs felt better, thanks to the damp river air, but were nowhere near as good as new. She was very fond of her stepmother and realised that Rosemary and her father would be celebrating their fortieth wedding an-niversary in a few months. Following the death of Audrey's mother, her father had been bereft of company until, through correspondence initiated by a letter he wrote to a sailing magazine, he met and fell in love with Rosemary.

'Yes,' Audrey replied. 'I was in the house when it caught fire and became trapped.'

'What are you going to do now?' her father asked.

'I plan to give the property to the people of Hawksmead.'

He nodded. 'And with your life?'

She looked at her father and her stepmother. The bond of love, forged over forty years, was evident in every aspect of their life together.

'I don't know,' Audrey answered. She really didn't know. Her life felt empty.

'When did you last see Freddie and Belle?'

Audrey looked at her father and smiled. 'I hope to see them very soon.'

'Joshua brought them to see us,' her father added. 'He was very worried about you.'

Audrey had been so wrapped up in another world, she knew she had neglected her living family. She had achieved what she set out to do and must now get on with being a good grandmother, a good mother and a good daughter.

'Have you made plans for Christmas?' Rosemary asked. 'You know, you're always welcome here.'

Audrey smiled. Her family needed her. She had to accept that she was no longer a wife, a partner …a lover.

CHAPTER FORTY-EIGHT

Audrey booked a room at the Royal Oak Hotel at the southern end of Sevenoaks. Within a day, she had selected a furnished cottage to rent in Bosville Road, a short walk from the railway station and near the town's former cattle market. She didn't want to disrupt the family renting her home so close to Christmas and, in truth, she didn't even want to visit the house her husband's firm had built.

She kept her eyes closed and allowed the taxi to lull her into a soporific state. Memories of happy years raising her boys, sharing school runs, meeting friends, hosting dinners and helping her husband deal with local authorities and investment bankers crowded her thoughts. Duncan always said that she was his secret weapon. She didn't want today's reality to supplant so many happy memories.

They turned left into her drive and she marvelled, as she always did, at the way her husband had created the effect of a winding road blasted out of a stone quarry, now shaded by mature deciduous trees. She remembered the day when the giant rocks were delivered and positioned, and the saplings first planted. The next day, she had given birth to her younger son, Benjamin.

In a spacious, three-car garage, she saw her Skoda Estate and was surprised to see how the paintwork shone. She paid the taxi driver and turned to approach the front door when it was opened by a slim, stylish woman, mid-thirties, whose figure belied the fact she had given birth to three boys over four years. Quite a production line, smiled Audrey to herself.

Lucy held out a long, slim arm that was complemented by fine-boned fingers.

'You cleaned my car,' Audrey said, shaking Lucy's hand.

'Mike insisted on giving it a thorough going over,' Lucy replied, standing aside to let Audrey into her home.

Did she want to go in? It would be rude not to. Audrey crossed the threshold and was hit by a massive surprise. Where Louis van Staaten paintings of Dutch barges had once hung, there were now beautiful painted portraits, signed by Lucy, of her husband and their three sons.

Audrey felt overwhelming relief. This was not her home. Yes, it was her house, but it was Lucy's family home, and Audrey felt nothing more than a welcome visitor. There were no ghosts from the past; just bricks and mortar, for which Lucy and Mike were paying a substantial rent. Her life in this house was locked away in her albums and in her memories. People make a home, and without those she loved, this big house with its picture windows was just a building to be let for other families to enjoy.

For the first time since returning to Sevenoaks, she felt confident she could find a new kind of contentment living in the old market town.

CHAPTER FORTY-NINE

A Widow's Retreat

Following the death of her husband, long-time Sevenoaks resident Audrey Willatt wished to start afresh in a new town, with new people and in an old school boarding house with a reputation for being haunted.

'I wasn't rejecting Sevenoaks,' explained Audrey to *The Chronicle*. 'I simply couldn't live with all the memories. Everywhere I looked, I was reminded of my dear husband, Duncan, and the wonderful times we shared with our sons. I suppose you could say I needed a rest from grieving.'

That rest involved moving to Hawksmead – a small town on the edge of a vast moor – crossing swords with the Russian mafia, nearly drowning in a flooded river and just escaping with her life when her haunted house was destroyed by fire.

We caught up with Mrs Willatt on her return to Sevenoaks and asked her how she feels about our town after all she has been through.

'I can now move on. I needed to make a break with the past, but my life was, and is, and always will be in the beautiful town of Sevenoaks. And the weather's much warmer down here!'

Scars clearly evident on her hands and legs, we ventured to ask the wanderer returned one last question. Did she see any ghosts in the old school boarding house?

'Not that I recall,' said Mrs Willatt, although her smile conveyed to our reporter a different story.

~

After getting through a second Christmas without her darling Duncan, but with the joyous company of her grandchildren, Audrey settled back into life in Sevenoaks. She occupied her days as best she could with bridge, long walks with fellow ramblers, and visits with girlfriends to West End musicals but, no matter how hard she worked to live in the present, the recent past still woke her in the small hours.

When summer finally arrived, the weather was mixed including heavy downpours and a heatwave in mid-July. She was pleased she'd kept up her membership of the local country club as she started almost every day with an early morning swim in the open-air swimming pool. Often on Saturdays, her elder son would give his wife a break and bring her grandchildren to visit for picnics and swimming.

Her younger son would ring for a long chat most weeks, but there were too many hours for her to fill to keep the deep pain of loneliness at bay.

It was late summer when the invitation came via email as the sender did not know her current postal address. For several minutes, Audrey stared at the screen on her new tablet. On the one hand, she was settled in her cottage and didn't want the upheaval; on the other hand, how could she say no?

CHAPTER FIFTY

Audrey sat back in her first-class train seat and watched England's lush countryside pass her window. There were a few marks on her legs from the fire, but they were no longer tender.

The train pulled into Undermere Station, and she took a taxi to the White Hart Hotel. She had arrived a day early as she wanted time to rest, unpack, and to let the creases drop out of her dress and coat. In truth, she was nervous and wished to look her best for the people who had once meant, for a short while, a great deal to her.

She ate a light supper in the hotel and woke up to a beautiful September morning, feeling rested. She went down for breakfast and was surprised by the butterflies she felt in her stomach. Back up in her room, a local hairdresser washed, dried and styled her hair. She would have liked a professional make-up artist to sort out her face, but a light base, a little rouge on the lips and a few flicks with a mascara brush would have to do.

'I've seen you looking worse,' she said to her reflection in the dressing table mirror.

The bedroom phone rang and the hotel's reception informed Audrey that her taxi was waiting. She took a last look in a full-length mirror, grabbed her handbag, bought especially for the event, and took the lift to the ground floor. Normally she would have walked, but she didn't want to risk tripping on the stairs in her heels.

~

It had not been a great year for the Dryomov brothers. Both had been summoned to the crown court charged with VAT fraud and the misappropriation of council subsidies. Bribery

233

had secured the original contract to build new homes to the south of Hawksmead but they had been caught in a police sting handing over dirty money to the director of planning when tendering to extend the housing development. There was a risk they could be deported, although their solicitor had told them that deportation orders are rarely carried out. Despite the threat, they continued their lucrative sideline dealing in smuggled caviar, vodka, cigarettes, counterfeit icons, forged paintings and fake Fabergé eggs.

You can't always get what you want – Mick Jagger's voice blared from the white transit van's radio as Spartak pulled over at the top of Hawksmead High Street. How ironic, he thought, turning up the volume. Even he, with his handsome face, lean body, charisma and cash could not get what he wanted more than anything in the world. His brother had offered to kill the competition, but he knew that would not work. There had to be a smarter way.

CHAPTER FIFTY-ONE

Audrey paid the taxi driver and got out at the southern end of Hawksmead High Street. More than eight months had passed since she had last stood in the former mill town and almost a year since she had arrived at the old school boarding house, hoping to discover more about the circumstances surrounding her brother's death. Of course, it was impossible to think about Bobby without thinking about Malcolm. She hoped he was well, that his bones had healed and that he could look forward to a few happy years. She adjusted her coat and placed her purse in her matching handbag.

The weather had held, and Audrey grew warm as she walked up the High Street. She came to the Olde Tea Shoppe and was surprised to see the Closed sign on the door. Below, stuck to the glass, was a handwritten note which brought a smile to her face.

Audrey continued on up the High Street. The library came into view, and she thought about Shirley and her young love for Edward Holden. She checked the time on her watch and crossed the road to the library on the off-chance that Shirley may be working. She pushed the door but it was locked. In the window was a neatly printed note. Audrey read it and laughed out loud. There was clearly a pattern forming. She walked past the Falcon pub and tested the door. Surprisingly, it opened, and she looked into the gloom.

'Sorry love, just about to close,' Ted said, wearing a smart suit and tie, complemented by a yellow rose in his button hole.

'I'll see you there,' Audrey replied letting the door close behind her. She continued on. The Methodist Church, both plain and imposing, came into sight and beyond it was an uncluttered view, through trees still in leaf, across the river to the moor.

Where was her house? She had expected to see something, but there was just the garden wall and an empty space where the old school boarding house had once stood. She didn't know what to feel, but as she walked towards the entrance to her driveway she could never have imagined the incredible sight that graced her eyes. Spilling out onto the pavement from her drive was a great crowd of people dressed in their Sunday best.

'Audrey!'

She tried to locate the source of the voice.

'Audrey! Audrey Willatt!'

Finally, she clapped eyes on Heather wearing a beautiful, simple dress, far removed from the utilitarian attire she invariably wore in the Falcon.

'Look! It's Audrey Willatt,' came another voice.

She could hear a hum of voices speaking her name as dozens of pairs of eyes turned towards her.

Audrey smiled – she was home. She was with the people she had come to know and love.

'How wonderful to see you,' Maggie said, kissing Audrey on each cheek, taking care not to clash their wide-brimmed hats.

'Andy's borrowed Tony's camera and is taking the pictures,' Maggie continued. 'Needless to say, the wedding of the year is going to make *The Chronicle*'s front page.'

'Mrs Willatt!'

Audrey recognised Colin Turner, a local councillor, who was with his wife, Penny. 'How lovely that you're here on this special day. As you can see, they took a leaf out of your book.'

'Really?' Audrey wondered what leaf that could be.

'They invited the whole town to their wedding – as you did for your housewarming.'

Several others came up to welcome Audrey back to Hawksmead, telling her how much she had been missed and how they wished she would make the little town her home again.

'I'm coming to the end of my time,' Vivian said, the September sun reflecting in her mayoral chain. 'Next month, I have to pass on the chain of office to Malcolm Cadwallader. He's our new mayor. After what he's done here, we persuaded him to stand and then couldn't get anyone to stand against him.'

Audrey's heart flipped. 'Malcolm?'

'Follow me.' Vivian took Audrey's arm and led her down the short drive, past wedding guests who applauded or held out their hands to shake Audrey's. People parted to make way for her, and she was able to see what had happened to her former home. Where there had once been an imposing oak door and a giant red-brick edifice, only the stone foundations remained. Amongst the ruins were newly planted shrubs, trees in tubs, and wild flowers. Beyond was a vision of breathtaking beauty.

'I call it the Garden of Eden,' Amy said, 'as I love to come here and sit while my children play.' Audrey recognised her as one of the receptionists in Undermere's intensive care unit whose coat she had borrowed and replaced.

Audrey walked on, shaking hands and kissing, with a growing following of wedding guests and excited children running around.

'Malcolm came to the council and we agreed his plan,' Colin Turner said. 'This is entirely his vision and his money. For years people had crossed the road to avoid the old school boarding house but Malcolm wanted to change that by creating a memorial garden. The council helped sort out the removal of all the rubble and make the ruin safe for visitors.'

'Audrey!' She turned as Andy Blake came up to her, smartly dressed in a suit and tie, with a white rose in his lapel, and gripping his son's long lens camera. 'Have you seen the memorial? Follow me.'

He took Audrey's arm and, joined by Maggie, and more than a dozen wedding guests, he led her to where the oil-fired boiler had once stood. In its place was a large memorial stone.

This garden is dedicated to the memory of five
schoolboys who were taken from their families:
Edward Holden, Christopher Wilkins,
David Turnbull, Mark Small and Robert Oakes.

Please relax, enjoy and love each other
in their memory.

'Malcolm planned for the garden to be dedicated to your brother and Mark Small, a boy he knew from when he was a teacher up at the school,' Andy explained. 'And to two boys who drowned in the River Hawk by the bridge as you nearly did. When news of the memorial spread, he was told about the suicide of Edward Holden a few years earlier.'

Audrey read and reread the names carved into the memorial stone and then looked at the garden, resplendent with colour.

'Malcolm did all this?' Her voice cracked as she spoke.

'He got professionals in to help him and loads of volunteers – me included,' Andy said.

'It's beautiful,' Audrey whispered.

'Audrey.' Andy spoke as close to her ear as her hat would allow. 'Malcolm told me what happened to your brother and his involvement; and also the incident on the bridge with black ice. My son nearly killed you in the same way.'

Audrey gave Andy a little nod and called out to Colin Turner. 'Does the council intend to rebuild the house?'

'The insurance money you kindly donated,' Colin called back, 'we are using to help finance genuinely affordable homes for young people who have grown up in Hawksmead. We have no plans to rebuild the boarding house.'

'Perfect.' She gave him a thumbs-up, much to the councillor's evident pleasure.

Beyond him was Malcolm, standing tall and looking very dapper in his formal suit. He was chatting to Maureen, an elegant widow and bridge fanatic whom Audrey had met at her housewarming party.

'Everything all right?' Andy asked.

She looked up at him and smiled. 'Yes, thank you. And thank you for helping to create this wonderful garden. I am so grateful for what you and others have done.'

She walked away as casually as she could and pretended to enjoy the gentle majesty of the garden. Every now and then, she stole a look in Malcolm's direction and was not sure whether she was relieved to see him still chatting to Maureen or annoyed. She felt her pulse quickening and knew her cheeks were flushed. She understood why Malcolm as a young man had fallen for her brother. Bobby had the kind of adorable looks that made people want to hug him. He and Audrey had always looked very much alike when they were children. As Roxane, standing centre stage in the *Cyrano de Bergerac* cast photograph hanging in the Falcon pub, Robert looked beautiful. Malcolm, as a young, inexperienced man, had confused emotions. He had fallen in love with Roxane and, fifty years on, Audrey had rekindled those buried emotions. But what about now? Was she looking old? Did the scars on her legs show? He looked wonderful. She loved his posture, his slim physique, his fine cheekbones and defined jaw. His work, producing this magical experience, had clearly rejuvenated him, and she wished she'd been here to help.

Eleanor sidled up beside Audrey. 'Maureen has had the hots for Malcolm long before she became a very merry widow.'

Audrey looked at Eleanor, and the two women hugged as best their two hats would allow.

'What a wonderful day, and what glorious weather,' Eleanor continued. 'The whole town will never forget this wedding.'

'I'm so looking forward to seeing Tina. I know she'll look stunning. Have you seen the lucky groom?'

'I think he's hiding behind the wall, practising his speech, together with his best man, Tony Blake. Over the last few months, the two couples have been almost inseparable. Tina is an honorary aunt to Georgiana and Charlie.'

'Where is Charlie?'

'He's being looked after by Shirley – you know, from the library. On Saturday afternoons, she often meets up with the two couples and the little ones at my tea shop, and they usually stay long after I put up the closed sign. Malcolm often joins them, following a hard day working here in the garden.'

Audrey blinked back tears. 'I don't know what to do.'

Holding Audrey's hand between both of hers, Eleanor looked

squarely into Audrey's eyes. 'I regret one thing in my life. I had a chance to fulfil a dream, but I convinced myself that it wasn't the right thing to do. You know what? Sometimes the right thing is the wrong thing and vice-versa, if that makes any sense.'

Audrey laughed and licked her dry lips. She was on the fast track to old age. But standing twenty metres away was a man who complemented all that she was and loved. For the first time in her life, she felt a tsunami of heat spread throughout her entire body, and her breathing became short, almost painful, as her damaged lungs sucked in the warm air.

'Are you all right?' Eleanor asked.

Black sheets flapped in front of Audrey's eyes as she fell backwards down a long tunnel... fainting like a teenager at her first Beatles concert.

CHAPTER FIFTY-TWO

Malcolm had been aware of Audrey from the moment she had arrived in the garden. When he saw her faint, he wanted to rush to her side. Now he was acutely aware that she was back on her feet and coming closer. Every sinew in his body stiffened. She was almost upon him before he could politely interrupt Maureen's flow. She smiled encouragingly and stepped away.

The gabble of chat and laughter quietened as the two people who were responsible for giving the memorial garden to the townsfolk of Hawksmead came to meet again for the first time since the old school boarding house had been consumed by flames.

Malcolm looked into Audrey's eyes. He felt his knees go and wished he still had his hospital walking stick.

Silence.

His heart was pounding.

What was she going to say to him?

Audrey wrapped her arms around Malcolm's neck and kissed him gently on the lips. A cheer went up, accompanied by spontaneous applause.

Hawksmead's Brass Band blasted out Mendelssohn's *The Wedding March* and the guests, almost as one, stretched their necks to see Tina and her father, John Small, riding in the rear of an open-top vintage Rolls-Royce Silver Ghost.

A black Daimler came to a halt behind the Rolls, and the liveried chauffeur got out before the car had fully stopped. He opened the rear passenger door and Eden, Tina's chief bridesmaid, dressed in pale peach, stepped out of the car, followed by Georgiana, in a mini version of the same dress. Taking her daughter's hand, Eden walked towards the rear of the Rolls and stood back as the chauffeur opened the tiny side door and offered his gloved hand to the bride.

Eden straightened out Tina's ivory wedding dress and veil. The bride's father, resplendent in a dove-grey morning suit, came to offer his arm. Eden and Georgiana picked up Tina's train as the stunning bride was escorted down the red-carpeted driveway.

The music played on. The splendour of the setting, the warmth of the September sun and the natural scents from the memorial garden were intoxicating, and many guests, before a vow had been spoken, reached for lace-trimmed handkerchiefs, or used the tip of a finger to wipe away an escaping tear. Even tough old journo Andy blinked back tears as he looked upon his daughter, Eden, and his little granddaughter, Georgiana, undertaking bridesmaid duties.

Tina walked slowly with her father down the carpeted path to a flower entwined pergola. Waiting to greet her, with the Holy Book open in his hand, was the tall figure of William Longden, the Methodist minister. Standing before him, watching his beautiful bride approach, was her husband-to-be, PC Gary Burton, supported by his Best Man, Tony Blake.

Audrey kept a firm grip on Malcolm's arm. 'Where would you like us to be married?'

He looked into her eyes. 'It's the bride's right to choose.'

'Welcome,' Reverend Longden announced, 'to a very special day in the history of Hawksmead. We are here in this beautiful memorial garden to bear witness and to celebrate the marriage of Christina Louise Small to Gary Simon Burton.'

Audrey heard the eighty-six-year-old minister's words as her mind swam in a sea of happiness. She looked at Tina and a great wave of love washed over her. For a few seconds, she had felt guilty for abandoning her friends in Sevenoaks – it had been a wonderful summer catching up whilst her body healed, but Hawksmead felt like home.

'The ceremony was to be in the Methodist church,' Malcolm

said, quietly. 'But as the weather was so good, Reverend Long-den was more than happy to agree to officiate in the garden so the whole town could come. I think our lovely mayoress sorted out the licence.'

Following the ceremony, champagne corks popped every few seconds. Trestle tables, adorned with white tablecloths, were resplendent with finger food on silver-effect platters, together with a three-tiered, iced wedding cake with two figures standing on top. The atmosphere of joy and love, bathed in a sun that was dipping to the horizon way too quickly, was like nothing Audrey had ever experienced.

Tina and Gary were honoured by a speech from her proud and emotional father. 'Finally, I would like to thank Malcolm Cadwallader whose concept it was to create this memorial garden and for including the name of my big brother, Mark Small, who was killed on the bridge, aged thirteen, when a car skidded on black ice.'

Audrey whispered to Malcolm. 'Does he know?'

Malcolm shook his head. 'I confessed all to Andy Blake. I thought he would print it in his paper, but he said that it served no purpose.'

A voice shouted from the back of the crowd, 'I know who was driving that car!' It was Vincent, whom Audrey had met in the Falcon on her first evening in Hawksmead. The garden went quiet. 'It was the same person who killed my beautiful Roxane,' declaimed the former Cyrano de Bergerac.

Everyone looked at Vincent who was wearing a smart suit and appeared stone cold sober.

From within the throng, Ted shouted, 'Vincent! Keep your mouth shut.'

Audrey squeezed Malcolm's arm then stepped forward to the dais. 'May I speak?'

John Small nodded and offered her the microphone, which Audrey accepted.

'Almost a year ago, I came to Hawksmead in the hope that I would uncover the truth behind my brother's death in the old school boarding house fifty-one years ago. I discovered that in one term, two boys drowned in the river and that one boy was killed on the bridge by a car skidding on black ice. Those three deaths traumatised a young teacher who reached out to protect my brother. That same teacher subsequently suffered a further agony when my brother died falling down the boarding house stairs.'

'He killed my Roxane,' Vincent shouted.

'No he didn't,' responded Audrey, her voice soft but firm. 'He was a young man who witnessed a tragic accident that affected his entire life.'

Silence.

Audrey stepped off the dais and handed the microphone to PC Gary Burton.

'You're looking a bit better than when I last saw you, Mrs Willatt.'

'Many congratulations.' She kissed him on the cheek.

John Small, Tina's father and Mark Small's younger brother, walked up to Malcolm. Audrey hurried to be by his side.

'My mother received a letter from Robert Oakes,' John Small said. 'The boy wrote in precise detail what happened on the bridge. He made it clear, you were not to blame.' He offered his hand to Malcolm.

Gary Burton cleared his throat into the microphone.

'Ladies and gentlemen, I would like to thank you all for your generous gifts but, more importantly, for your presence on this, our very special day. My wife and I...'

He was interrupted by cheers of approval.

'My wife and I would like to propose a toast to two people whose kindness and generosity have given our wonderful town this memorial garden. Ladies and gentlemen – I present the arresting...' He paused for the inevitable laugh. 'I present... the amazing Audrey Willatt and Malcolm Cadwallader.'

The guests repeated the names and John Small was the first to applaud the couple.

'Finally,' Gary continued, 'I would like to propose a toast to my wife's beautiful bridesmaids.'

As the sun lost its brilliance, torches planted around the garden were lit by Malcolm. The cake was cut and Tony, who had relieved his father of the camera, took lots of photos.

Audrey and Malcolm were chatting to Eleanor when Tina, accompanied by her new husband, came to say goodbye. Audrey hugged the young estate agent. As the two women, more than forty years apart in age, looked upon each other, Audrey knew that she would spend the rest of her days in Hawksmead.

Tina and Gary headed for the Rolls Royce as copious quantities of confetti petals were thrown from all angles. The chauffeur opened the rear door and Tina slipped onto the Silver Ghost's soft leather seat. Eden and Georgiana made great play of ensuring that her wedding dress did not get trapped in the door. Gary got in the far side and slid across the seat to his beaming bride.

The chauffeur backed the car out into the High Street as guests, tears streaming down their faces, waved goodbye.

'Gary! Be warned,' Tony bellowed. 'This is the last time Tina will not be in the driving seat!'

With smiles as broad as Hawksmead High Street, the happy couple waved goodbye and blew countless kisses as their luxury carriage pulled away, escorted by two BMW police motorcycles, with blue and yellow livery and flashing blue lights.

Most of the wedding guests had departed when the Reverend William Longden walked, in the growing darkness, along the carpeted pathway to where Audrey and Malcolm were chatting to Andy and Maggie. Staff from the catering company were clearing up the last of the debris, and folding away trestle tables and chairs.

'I've married a lot of young couples,' the reverend said, 'but I am hard pushed to recall a happier wedding or one in a more beautiful setting. You have absolutely worked wonders, Malcolm.'

'It was a labour of love and, of course, I had a lot of help,' Malcolm replied.

Reverend Longden turned his keen eyes to Audrey. 'The

town has missed you Mrs Willatt. We all hope that we can persuade you to linger a little longer this time.'

'I intend to linger for the rest of my days.' Audrey gently squeezed Malcolm's arm.

She heard a whisper in the mighty oak tree and looked up to see the leaves rustling in the late summer breeze.

CHAPTER FIFTY-THREE

'Mum, listen to me... It's too quick... We don't know him... We've not even met him... Don't do this to us... You belong here... With your family... We've lost Dad, we nearly lost you, and now you're forsaking us for some old man who's probably just desperate to have you cook and wash for him.'

Audrey listened as her elder son tried his best to reason with her. Although she was disappointed that both her boys had declined the wedding invitation, in some respects she was relieved.

~

Undermere Town Hall provided a classic Victorian setting for the smartly dressed couple. Accompanied by their witnesses – Andy from *The Chronicle* and his wife, Maggie – and Ted and Heather from *The Falcon* – Audrey and Malcolm celebrated their marriage on another glorious September day followed by a wedding reception at the Rorty Crankle Inn overlooking the Ridgeway. Harry and Cathy had taken on extra staff so they, too, could join in the celebrations.

'It's unusual for a former pupil to be friends with a teacher once school days are over,' Audrey commented to Ted.

'You know I played Christian in *Cyrano de Bergerac* up at the old school? Your brother played Roxane. Well, the boys that drowned in the river were two of my best friends. They weren't in the play, so they had to go out camping on the moor for three days with the rest of the school – outward-bound training in its rawest form. For some reason, they were allowed to canoe on the river when it was in full flood without life jackets, and that's how they came to drown. My parents were abroad in the

Far East, and I had no way of expressing my grief. Malcolm recognised how I felt and helped me through a very difficult time. A few years later, we ran into each other and became firm friends.' Ted paused. 'He told me what happened to your brother. I did my best to help him, but the burden he's carried all these years is considerable. Today is the first time I have seen him looking genuinely happy.'

~

Audrey was surprised by how quickly she settled into married life with Malcolm. His cottage was small but she came with nothing apart from her favourite van Staaten painting, transported from her house in Sevenoaks. Looking for a place to hang it, Malcolm removed the photograph of his first wife, Mary.

'No, Malcolm,' protested Audrey. 'This is still her home.'

'Mary's niece, Rosie, has always loved this photo of her aunt and asked me to leave it for her when I shuffle off this mortal coil. I think she would be thrilled to have it now.'

~

It was a Sunday morning, and Audrey and Malcolm were sitting in bed listening to *Love Songs* on Radio 2. Malcolm was reading the latest Peter James' thriller and Audrey was trying to learn lines. She'd joined Hawksmead Amateur Dramatic Society, and their last play before the Christmas pantomime was a supernatural thriller called *The Widow*. Audrey had been cast as an American, determined to go to any lengths to save the life of her sickly son.

'Any good?' Malcolm asked.

'Ssshh.' Audrey sighed and put the play down. 'You're going to have to help me. At the moment, my memory is like Teflon.'

'Nothing sticking? Ha-ha... I know what will help. Let's go out on the moor and tackle the Ridgeway while the weather is still fine.'

'Great idea. We could park your shiny new motor by the memorial garden, walk over the bridge and set off for the moor.

We could take a picnic.'

'I have a better idea. Why don't we drive, not walk, over the bridge and park the car in the grounds of the old school? There's a public path that leads to the Ridgeway.'

'On the other hand, we could drive to the Rorty Crankle Inn, have a drink and walk from there.'

Malcolm laughed. 'That's a stroll, not a walk!'

Hawksmead was quiet, apart from the cheerful calling to prayer of church bells. Malcolm parked his snazzy-looking, silver Honda Civic hatchback across the road from the memorial garden.

'Why are we stopping?' Audrey asked.

'I want to take a quick look at the garden – make sure that the gardeners are doing a good job.'

They both got out of the car, and Malcolm retrieved a beechwood walking stick from the boot.

'Alarm?'

He pressed the car fob and saw the hazard lights flash as he and Audrey crossed the High Street.

'What a glorious wedding,' she said. 'Tina looked so happy.'

Audrey's phone beeped and she opened her bag to take it out. She swiped the screen and read a text message. 'It's Tina! What timing. She's asked if we're free for Sunday lunch.'

'What about our picnic?' Malcolm's eyebrows, knitted.

'What about my clothes? I'm dressed for walking, not a smart lunch.'

'Tell you what, let's invite Tina and Gary to lunch up at the Rorty Crankle, then we can see them and also have our walk.'

Audrey tapped out their reply and was thrilled to receive a thumbs-up and a smiley face. She slipped her arm through Malcolm's, and they walked down the drive to the place where Audrey's oak front door had opened and closed for more than one hundred and fifty years.

'Who's that?' Malcolm pointed with his free arm through the trees to a figure.

Audrey put her finger to her lips and then gestured to

Malcolm. Even without her spectacles and despite the person's back being towards them, Audrey recognised who it was, kneeling by the memorial stone.

Treading carefully, they walked around the foundations of the destroyed building and along the perimeter wall.

After almost a minute, the person got to her feet and turned towards them. She waited for Audrey and Malcolm to approach her.

'Thank you,' Shirley said to Malcolm. 'His parents must be dead by now but Eddie has a sister, somewhere.'

'I'll call by at the library in the morning,' Audrey said, 'and we'll work out a plan of action to find her.'

'It's beautiful, Malcolm.' Tears sparkled Shirley's eyes. 'I must go.' She headed towards the entrance to the drive.

Audrey called after her. 'Shirley. I still owe you tea and cake.'

'I've not forgotten!' She blew Audrey a kiss.

They watched Shirley walk through the young trees and then, as one, turned and looked at the five engraved names on the memorial stone. For a moment, neither spoke.

Audrey stepped away from Malcolm and touched her fingers to her lips and rested her hand on top of the memorial. 'Be at peace, my love.'

For a moment, she allowed memories of her brother to course through her mind.

'Come on,' Audrey said, resolutely. 'Let's conquer the heights of the Ridgeway.' She turned, but Malcolm was nowhere to be seen. Rising panic set in as her eyes scanned the garden.

'Over here!' he called.

Looking through the trees, she saw Malcolm standing in the driveway. She hurried over to him, surprised by her stressed reaction. In his hand was a bunch of white and pink dahlias.

'For the love of my life.'

Audrey took the flowers and put the blooms to her nose. 'I have an idea,' she said.

CHAPTER FIFTY-FOUR

'Tina's policeman is becoming nuisance,' growled Kirill. 'Because of you, he's destroying our business, our lives. If he tries trick again, leave him to me.' Kirill was at the wheel of the van as they raced down the Old Military Road. It was Sunday morning so there weren't many cars around. 'We have bad smell since arrest. He think he can screw us.'

'At least the road is clear,' Spartak observed from the passenger seat. But even a clear road could not lift his gloom since all hope was lost, following Tina's marriage. Perhaps he should go online and find a Russian bride? He gave the thought a hollow laugh.

~

'They've done a good job repairing it,' Audrey said as she and Malcolm walked towards the humpback bridge, with its three arches and gently flowing river.

'I understand they managed to retrieve the lost stones from the river bed,' he replied. 'It's not quite invisible mending but it's pretty good.'

'I still think the council could do something about making the bridge safer.'

'Hm, yes. Traffic lights to make it single file and a separate footbridge would be a start. Perhaps I could put my new mayoral status to good use?'

She squeezed his arm.

~

Spartak saw they were exceeding sixty miles per hour. 'Slow down.'

'Don't tell me how to drive.' Kirill spat phlegm out of his side window. They passed the end of the road that led to Hawk-smead College. 'We should buy old school.'

'And set it on fire, too?' Spartak shook his head. 'All we did was make the whole town happy.'

~

'Please can we not live dangerously?' Malcolm strived to see over the brow of the humpback bridge.

Audrey took a deep smell of the dahlias and threw them over the stone parapet into the river. She watched as they fluttered down to the rippling water and disappeared under the arch. 'Sleep well, my angels.'

~

Kirill heard the blast of cannons from Tchaikovsky's 1812 Overture and he reached into his top pocket. The text was in Russian and he took his eyes off the road for a few seconds to read it, despite the van's high speed. He grunted and handed the phone to his brother.

Spartak read the message and looked up. Ahead was the humpback bridge. 'You're going too fast.'

There was another blast of cannon fire and both men took their eyes off the road to look at the phone's screen:

A warrant has been executed to search your properties, currently being enforced. See you in court. Regards, Gary Burton.

'Watch out!' Spartak jabbed his finger at the windscreen.

Kirill could not believe what he was seeing. A few seconds ago the road leading to the bridge had been clear, but now two people were standing in the middle of the road, holding hands. It was too late to brake. He had no choice but to drive into them. Time seemed to slow as the van bore down. Why were they not leaping out of the way? Why were they making no attempt to save themselves?

Spartak dropped the phone and grabbed the wheel with his

right hand. He jerked it down and the van swerved away from the mouth of the bridge.

But it was too late.

The two boys, wearing corduroy shorts, were doomed. Kirill braced himself for the thud. But there was no impact. No thud.

The van veered off the road and shot like an arrow through the beech hedgerow.

~

From the apex of the bridge, Audrey and Malcolm watched as the van hit a low, dry-stone wall and flipped into the air. It landed with a metal crunching *humph* and rolled and rolled again, slamming into the base of a mature oak tree.

~

William Longden shook hands with each member of his congregation, which had swelled since he had officiated at Tina and Gary's wedding. There was a sudden change in air pressure before he heard a mighty *whoomp* carried on the breeze.

Everyone stopped to look.

They waited.

A second even louder explosion was accompanied by a warm glow in the sky.

CHAPTER FIFTY-FIVE

'Next spring,' Audrey said, as she and Malcolm shared a pot of tea the following Wednesday. They were with Eden, who had popped into the Olde Tea Shoppe with her children.

Eleanor entered from the kitchen with a tiered display stand bedecked with cakes.

'Next spring, I promise,' Audrey repeated, placing her hand on Malcolm's arm.

'Wee-wee, Mummy,' Georgiana announced.

'I'll take her.' Eleanor lifted the former bridesmaid off her chair, and held her little hand as they hurried to the rear of the tea room.

'Next spring – what?' Eden asked as she offered a forkful of sponge cake to her son.

'Next spring, Malcolm and I are going to walk the Ridgeway.'

Eden looked at Malcolm.

'God willing,' he said, with a smile creasing his handsome face. 'Please excuse me.' He eased out of his chair and winced. 'My hip, my joints, my muscles seize up if I sit around too long, especially if they know I'm enjoying myself. They like to remind me of my great age.' He headed for the lavatory, holding the door for Eleanor, who emerged with Georgiana.

Shirley entered the Olde Tea Shoppe and smiled at Audrey. 'A very happy newly-married gentleman popped by the library this morning and told me you would be here.'

Audrey got up from her chair and kissed Shirley on the cheek. 'Black Forest gateau?'

The toot-toot of a car's horn attracted their attention. Audrey looked out of the window and saw a white VW Golf reverse into a parking space.

'It's Tina!' She hurried out to greet the young estate agent, but it was a man who got out of the similar-looking car.

Embarrassed by her mistake, Audrey turned and did a quick check of her hair in the tea shop's window. But the face that looked back wasn't hers. In the reflection, she saw a young woman – a woman she'd only seen in a photograph hanging in Malcolm's cottage.

Audrey re-entered the tea shop, slightly disturbed by what she thought she had just seen.

Eden spotted Audrey's puzzled expression as she sat back down at the table. 'Are you all right?'

'For a moment, I thought I saw Mary, Malcolm's first wife. She was smiling. It's given me quite a shock.'

'I knew her a little,' Shirley said. 'Very sad. But in her final days, I think she and Malcolm found the love for each other that was missing for so much of their marriage.'

'She had a very kind face. I would like to have met her.'

'Perhaps you just have.' Shirley rested her hand on Audrey's. 'She's buried in the Methodist churchyard, next to your memorial garden.'

Audrey's phone beeped and she took it out of her bag. 'It's a text from my son, Joshua. He's booked a family room in the Falcon pub for half term.' She heard another beep coming from the rear of the tea shop and glowed with pride as her new husband weaved his way between the chairs towards her.

'I've received a text. It's from your younger son,' Malcolm said. 'He was wondering whether it's okay for him and his wife to stay for a couple of nights at the cottage. I hope you don't mind but I've texted back a smiley face and a thumbs up.'

Audrey's smile turned into a big grin.

~

Bridge to Eternity ends in the autumn of 2016.

Breaking through the Shadows begins on
September 29, 2019 - Tina's birthday.

BREAKING THROUGH THE SHADOWS

Hawksmead Book 2

Romola Farr

WILDMOOR
PRESS

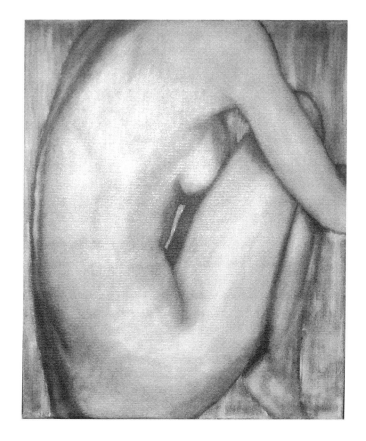

Breaking through the shadows
takes more than raw courage.

1

It was her birthday. 29th September, 2019. Libra. When she was a child she celebrated it with pretty dresses, pretty friends, pretty cakes. Aged fifteen, she giggled through her first kiss. Aged twenty-five, she woke up alone as she had done for nearly two years.

Waiting.

Waiting.

Waiting.

Her mother had persuaded her to return to the family home in Hawksmead. She had new friends in London. She had a good job. But there was a gap, a chasm, that no amount of birthday cards and presents could ever bridge.

Tina laughed as she flicked her blonde hair and ran beautifully manicured fingers down her long, slim calf. It was her twenty-third birthday and she was ready for her present.

The door to the rented flat banged shut and her whole body stiffened. She listened. There was movement in the hallway.

'Police. Anyone home? Come out, come out, wherever you are.' It was a young man's voice.

She waited, not moving. The handle to the bedroom door squeaked and it swung open. Almost filling the frame stood a police officer. He wore a white shirt, black tie, stab vest with pouches, radio, camera, and a utility belt with handcuffs, extendable baton, CS spray, medical kit, and torch.

'Good evening, officer. How may I be of service?'

'Is dinner in the oven?'

'No.'

'Is beer in the fridge?'

'All gone.'

'Do you have anything to confess?'

'Oh yes.'

He smiled and removed his heavy vest, dropping it on the carpet. He unclipped his belt and it fell around his feet.

'Boots,' she said.

'If you insist, madam.' He bent down and swiftly loosened both laces and pulled off his heavy footwear.

'Now go and wash your hands.'

He laughed. 'It was all going so well.' He left the bedroom and returned in no more than a minute drying his hands on a small towel and stripped down to a T-shirt and boxer shorts. 'You look beautiful, sweetheart.'

'You look pretty buff yourself, Detective Sergeant Burton.' She loved her police officer; he was tall, toned, determined to achieve more than the target, to go the extra mile, and some. Of course, she had gone more than the extra mile for him by leaving her great job, her childhood friends, and her parents, to travel hundreds of miles to London.

'It's the Met. The big one. The dream.'

'The next station stop is Hawksmead,' announced a man's voice through the carriage speakers.

She hadn't checked her Facebook page or Instagram. She couldn't focus on her novel. Her eyes stared out of the carriage window but she had been oblivious to London's ugly suburbs giving way to England's green and golden, late-summer hues. Her mind was far away on the District Line as the tube came into Southfields station, decked out with flowers and tennis paraphernalia to celebrate Wimbledon fortnight. She'd got off early from work to give her time to prepare dinner for her handsome husband. She had suggested inviting the couple who lived in the flat below to make it more of a party, but Gary was suspicious of them.

'The problem is, I cannot get any info on the guy.'

'You mean you've Googled him?'

'More than that, a lot more, but there's nothing. I like to know

who I'm dealing with before I break bread.'

'His parents brought him here from Serbia in the late nineties to escape the Balkan war. He went to UCL to study Russian where he met Sofie, whose parents are from Albania. He works for the Foreign Office and she is in some sort of security job.'

'How do you know all this?'

'I was showing a flat to a would-be purchaser near St James's and bumped into Sofie. We went for coffee and she asked me to forget what I'd seen.'

'What had you seen?'

'She was kissing an older man. Very handsome.'

'They're having an affair?'

'I'm not sure. She told me, he saved her life.'

'Saved her life, how?'

'She wouldn't say.'

'So, both Miroslav and Sofie work for our Government?'

'They are both British and speak several lingos.'

'Well done, sweetheart. I'm impressed. Invite them to dinner. I've a few questions I'd like to ask. Give them a little interrogation.'

'And that's why you and I will always dine alone.'

2

Audrey Cadwallader glanced at her watch and compared the time with the Honda's clock.

'Can you put your foot down a bit, darling?'

'I'm in my eightieth year and they would like nothing more than to rob me of my licence. But for you, my sweet, it is a piddling sacrifice.'

Audrey felt a surge of power as her husband roared down Hawksmead High Street, surprisingly busy for a Sunday.

'We should've gone to Undermere,' Malcolm said, crossing the centre line. 'If you miss it, make sure you blame me. It will take the sting out of your father's rebuke.'

'I should never have agreed to travel on the weekend,' Audrey replied. 'The train service is always so unreliable.'

'Well, let's hope it's reliably late this morning.' Malcolm indicated left and swung the little car into Hawksmead station forecourt.

'I've something to tell you.'

Tina sat up in bed and saw Gary's eyes drop down to her boobs. 'What is it?' Her heart thumped. Every day she feared bad news until he walked back through the door.

'I've been asked to...' He hesitated.

'If we have to move, we have to move. It's just rented.'

He took a breath. 'They've offered me a job. I can turn it down, of course.'

'You want to do it, otherwise you would've turned it down already.'

'It's a challenge. There'll be training. But, it could have its risks.'

She felt her mouth go dry. He reached for her but she was too quick. Her lithe limbs slipped out from under the duvet and she stood by the bed, naked and afraid. 'Tell me what it is.'

'They want me to…'

'No!' She held up her hand. 'Don't tell me. I don't want to know. It's bad enough praying every day that you come home, safe.' She gave him a hard look. 'I'm going to take a shower.'

'Tina. Wait. Please. You have to know one thing.'

She stood with her hands resting lightly on her slender hips.

'I'll be assuming a new identity and going undercover.'

'What happens if we're seen together? Won't your cover be blown?'

'The operation is outside the capital and… and I won't be coming home for three months, possibly six.'

'Six months!'

'It might only be six days. I need time to earn their trust.'

'Whose trust?' She stared at him.

No response.

She reached for her dressing gown hanging on the back of the bedroom door. 'When do you leave?'

'In about ten days.'

'Then I'd better make the most of you while you're here.' She dropped the gown and flung her light frame on top of him.

The train squeaked and clanked to a grinding halt as Tina hauled her yellow suitcase off the rack. She extended the handle and wheeled it to the carriage door.

'Why yellow?' she had asked her policeman husband.

'It's easy to spot on airport conveyor belts, people won't take it by mistake, and it's a very unattractive colour to thieves.' Gary's wise words echoed around her head as tears flooded her eyes. She had to clear them with the heel of her hand to locate the illuminated button. The door hissed as it sprang into life and slid open.

She stepped down from the carriage. The first difference she noticed was the air. How she had missed its earthy smell. The second, after the train had pulled out of the station and she was standing alone on the platform, was the silence.

The quiet.

The loneliness.

She sank to her knees and wept.

'Are you okay?' spoke the voice of an elderly woman. She felt an arm slide around her shoulder.

'I'm all right. Leave me alone, please.'

'It's Audrey, Tina.'

She looked into the kindly face of the woman squatting down bedside her. 'Audrey?'

'I'm here for you. We all are.'

'I look a mess.' She roughly wiped away her tears and stood.

Audrey held out her hand. 'Can you help me up? It's my knees. Too much ballet in my youth.'

Tina managed a small smile and gripped the woman's hand. More than forty years apart in age, they looked at each other, then hugged.

'*The next train to arrive at platform one is the twelve forty-five for London King's Cross.*'

A long intercity train ground to a noisy halt. Tina pulled apart from Audrey and saw a blue wheeled suitcase abandoned a few feet away. 'Your train! You'll miss it.' She heard the guard's strident whistle.

Audrey brushed aside her concern with a small backwards wave of her hand. 'I'll call Malcolm and he can join us for a coffee at the Olde Tea Shoppe.'

'Isn't it closed on Sundays?'

'Not anymore. Eleanor says it's one of her busiest days.'

Tina opened her mouth to speak but the air was filled with sharp blasts from the guard's whistle, followed by the carriage wheels gathering speed as the long train pulled out of the station.

She was flicking through the latest offerings on Netflix when her phone buzzed. Most evenings sitting alone in their London flat, Tina binged her way through big dramas. Her favourite was a Spanish series set in the late 1950s called Velvet. She liked seeing haute couture mixed with high drama and romance. Her phone had buzzed just as Alberto had swept Ana off her feet and carried her to their luxury bed. When was Gary going to ever do that? She pressed pause. A few moments later, Sofie was in her flat. The two couples shared a terraced, Edwardian house, split in two on South-fields grid. It was a popular area for families with good transport links, good schools, and a great park where children could play. Tina wanted a baby, but that was definitely on hold until Gary was home.

She looked at Sofie who was a little above average height, ath-letic, with brown hair and eyes, and a Slavic nose above a generous mouth. When not smiling she could look very serious. She was not smiling now.

'Is everything all right?' Tina asked.

'No.'

'What is it? Tell me.'

'Have you heard from Gary?'

'I told you, he's away on a job. He should be back soon.' Tina did her best to disguise her true emotion.

'But, have you heard from him?'

'No.'

'Gary and I work together. At the Met.'

Tina stared at her friend. 'You're a police officer?' That explained why her clothes were always so practical.

'Sort of.'

'Why didn't you tell me?'

Sofie smiled. 'Need to know... I hope you understand.'

Tina unscrewed the metal cap from a bottle of red wine and poured it into a tumbler. She took a long pull and threw the glass into the sink where it shattered. 'Well? What have you got to say, my lying friend?'

'We've lost contact with Gary.'

Tina stopped breathing.

'There are many ways he could let us know he's okay, but he's made no sign for over a month.'

'What are you going to do?' Tina could barely mouth the words.

'Monitor, as best we can. But, I think we must prepare for the worst.'

'The worst! What are you saying?'

'We will not give up searching for him, but he was mixing with dangerous people.'

'How could you let him, Sofie? How could you? I thought you were my friend.'

Towing their wheeled suitcases side-by-side, the old and the young strolled up Hawksmead High Street.

'It all looks the same,' Tina said, as they passed bow-fronted shops, some closed, some open.

'What time are your parents expecting you?' Audrey asked.

'They've given up on me. They want me to move on, but I can't. I can only move back.'

'They miss you. We all do.'

'I know. I've had so many cards, emails, texts. I'm sorry. I couldn't reply. I had nothing to say.'

'What about your job?'

'They were great. Everyone's been lovely. I was sad to say goodbye.'

Audrey stopped pulling her case and looked at the young woman who had married the man of her dreams in Hawksmead's memorial garden attended by what had felt like the whole town.

Tears filled Tina's eyes. 'They've given up looking. It's been almost two years but they still won't tell me what the job was or who he was spying on. They've abandoned Gary and just want me to go away. And now I have abandoned him, too.'

Audrey gripped Tina's arms. 'You saved me when I needed your help the most. Now it's my turn.'

3

Malcolm had heard his phone ring whilst driving home and then heard it buzz as a text came through. It would be Audrey letting him know that she was safely on the train bound for the big smoke. Since their marriage three years ago, every day had been one of pure pleasure. Both had been widowed and both had nearly died in accidents before realising they had a second chance of happiness, if they would only grasp it.

As he walked up the path to Mint Cottage, he pulled a few brown leaves off the rose bushes and stopped to breathe in the petals' heady scent. He had a quick look at his bedding plants and saw that his choice of fuchsias, petunias and geraniums were still competing to offer bees brightly coloured blooms, before the weather changed.

His phone buzzed again as he slid a key into the front door. He was looking forward to settling down to the preamble before the next round in the Formula One racing calendar. The text message cancelled his plan and within a minute the sole of his shoe was pressing down on the Honda's accelerator pedal.

Eleanor placed two buck rarebits on the table in front of Tina and Audrey, beside two glasses of orange juice and two cappuccinos. The Olde Tea Shoppe was her livelihood but music was in her bones. Despite being a non-believer, she enjoyed playing the pipe organ in the Methodist church every other Sunday and at various recitals. A professional opera singer, now retired, and a divorcee with no children, she'd given up all hope of finding a man to accompany her through her dotage.

'I hope I've got the egg right,' she said. 'Perhaps I should take it off the menu and just cook Welsh rarebit – a lot easier.'

'But you could lose your buck rarebit clientele,' Audrey

smiled.

'True, but every time I cook a poached egg I'm walking on egg shells – literally!' Eleanor turned to Audrey's companion whose face was hidden behind her lank blonde hair. 'It's lovely to see you, Tina. I am so sorry.'

Tina scooped her hair behind her ear and looked at Eleanor. 'It's why I've come back. I need...' Fat tears filled her eyes and spilled down her cheeks. She roughly wiped them away. 'He's missing, presumed dead, but he's not dead to me. I know Gary. He would never leave me without a fight.'

'What's the latest from the police?' Eleanor glanced at Audrey who gave an almost imperceptible shake of her head.

'They think he's dead,' Tina said. 'But until they find his body I won't give up.' She picked up her knife and fork and stabbed the poached egg, spilling yolk over melted cheese and toast.

In the halcyon days of the 1950s when Malcolm had learned to drive and owners of cars were but few, it was possible to simply pull up and park almost anywhere at any time. Hawksmead had so far resisted the march of traffic wardens and the scourge of yellow lines, but following the Sunday service exodus from St. Michael's Church, parking spaces near the Olde Tea Shoppe were as rare as a vegetarian with a shotgun on a grouse moor.

Malcolm parked his Honda in the short drive leading to the memorial garden. Through the windscreen he could see the remaining low, uneven walls of the former school boarding house, now home to a variety of young trees, shrubs and late summer blooms. He opened the car door and eased his way out. Although still sprightly at seventy-nine, if seated too long in one position his pinned bones gave him jip. He yearned to walk around the high perimeter wall encircling the garden and to say a little prayer in front of the memorial, but he was anxious about Audrey and, especially, Tina. He owed that beautiful young woman more than he could ever repay, and it saddened him greatly to think of the cruel blow that had robbed her of happiness. Her husband was dead, of that he was sure. But, without a body, it was impossible for the young widow to start the grieving process.

Tina looked at her plate and was surprised to see that she had eaten all the buck rarebit. The quaint tea shop was full of happy chatty people and Eleanor was busy sliding her ample hips between wooden chairs as she dealt with the Sunday rush. Three years ago when Tina and her newlywed husband, Gary, had departed for London, Eleanor had worked alone, but word of mouth had clearly increased footfall and she now had a young waitress to help her, and a trainee chef in the kitchen.

Slim fingers picked up the dirty plate. 'Would you like to see menu?'

Tina looked into a pretty but unsmiling face. 'Are you Polish?'

'Yes.'

'My name's Tina. Have you worked here long?'

'I bring you bill.' She turned away, snaked through the chairs, and pushed open the swing door into the kitchen. Audrey emerged from the lavatory and worked her way back to the table.

'Thank you for bringing me here,' Tina said. 'I wish we'd never left Hawksmead. This is home.'

Audrey placed her hand over Tina's. 'Let Hawksmead help you build a new life. We can't turn the clock back but we can help you make your days more bearable. Four years ago I came here as a widow looking for an answer to a question that had all but destroyed my family. I found more than an answer. I found friendship and love. The internet brought me here, it brought you and me together – not in a swipe right sort of way, of course.'

Tina couldn't help but smile.

'But, without the internet,' Audrey continued, 'I would never have made the leap from Sevenoaks to Hawksmead, and changed my life from that of an aging widow to a happy and fulfilled aging wife.'

'You think I should try a dating app?'

'Hawksmead is teeming with people who really care about

you, especially your dear parents, but until you find that some-one who tightens your stomach, who makes your heart pound with excitement, it's going to be almost impossible for friends and work ever to be enough for you to build a new, happy life.'

Tina looked around at the people filling up tables in the tea shop. There were a few men, but they were clearly all taken, al-though at least a couple kept casting their eyes in her direction.

'That's my point.' Audrey squeezed her hand. 'You can't fish in this pond. Gary is too tough an act for the young bucks of Hawksmead to follow.'

Tina picked up her glass of orange juice. 'I know you're right.' She took a sip and put it down. 'I started drinking too much. It was the only way to dull the pain.' She looked down at her left hand. Could she really take off her engagement and wedding rings, given to her by the man she loved, and would continue to love to her dying breath? She looked at Audrey. 'You were on your way to London. I've spoiled your plans.'

'I called my father when I was in the loo and as soon as I explained, he was absolutely categorical that I should not con-sider visiting him until you were sorted out. His words.'

'Do you really think dating again will sort me out?'

'Gary wouldn't want you to pine your life away.'

Breakfast in the big man's impressive home was invariably excel-lent. The house was set in fifty acres of lush countryside northeast of London. The grounds were patrolled twenty-four hours a day by a private security firm mostly made-up of ex-army and so-called reformed criminals. The perimeter fence was razor wire fitted with sensors to alert security if there was a breach, and was patrolled by dogs on running leads. The house itself was tastefully designed with a mock-Tudor facade, but with large bullet-proof picture win-dows instead of classic, single-glazed leaded lights. The entrance was grand and equally impregnable with two black-steel doors set in a secured metal frame. In effect, the house was a charming fortress built to withstand attacks from burglars and, more import-antly, the police.

'If the bastards ever do get in,' Frank Cottee snarled to Gary,

'there's a secret room where we can hole up for days, weeks if necessary.'

Gary digested that fact. 'The police always get architect plans before making a raid.'

'That's why the architect knows nothing about it. What kind of fool do you take me for?' Frank was a charming host but the criminal in him regularly bubbled to the surface.

'May I take your order, sir?'

Gary looked up at the plump, middle-aged Spanish maid, decked out in full livery with an embroidered FC. Showing-off was Frank's Achilles heel. Every summer, he hosted a charity fete in his fifty-acre garden and would often hold extravagant balls, peopled by local dignitaries and politicians. He wanted everyone to see what his power and money had bought him and few would've been unimpressed by the Italian marble floors, the vast interior reception rooms and bedroom-suites, many with triple aspect views; the sumptuous spa, steam room and gym by a magnificent indoor swimming pool; and an underground garage with turntable and car lift.

'Mr Gary? What would you like?'

He was dragged back from his thoughts. 'The Full Monty, please, Marta.'

'Thank you, sir.' Marta looked at Frank's strikingly beautiful daughter. 'And for you, Miss Stacy?'

'Coffee and pomegranate juice.' Stacy was still in riding gear from an early morning gallop around the estate. Her father had built an equestrian centre for his only child and, for a short while, she had entertained the idea of becoming an Olympic three-day eventer. Her usual day clothes were high-end designer and mostly chic, although the flash-Essex in her would occasionally break through the careful facade.

Gary was always wary, especially in her father's presence, but Stacy, when she smiled, totally disarmed him. The night before he had slipped-up in her company and called her Tina. He feared he'd wrecked the whole undercover operation, but the conversation over breakfast was light and free-flowing so he felt confident that he'd got away with his error. He hoped so. Criminals such as Frank

Cottee did not get rich by playing nice. He got rich by smelting smuggled gold, distributing cocaine, money laundering, internet scams, protection, a few legitimate property deals, and bumping-off anyone who got in his way. Gary's cover job was that of a luxury car dealer and fixer. He and Frank had hit it off, immediately, but Stacy was a different story.

Frank's driver and minder, Keith Hardman, was seated at the far end of the dining table. He rarely spoke unless directly addressed.

'Keith,' Gary called. 'Stacy told me that you used to box. I don't believe her – you're way too handsome.' He hoped his joke would help him get back in the fold.

Keith stopped eating his scrambled eggs and put down his knife and fork. He looked at Gary. 'Thank you. You're too kind.'

'By the way, I love your name.' Gary felt encouraged.

'What's special about Keith?' He picked up his knife and fork and shovelled a large slab of toast, egg and bacon into his mouth.

'Hardman. It's a perfect name for a minder. It's the same as a vicar being called Shepherd.'

'Or someone being called Large when they're little,' interjected Stacy. 'Or Small when they're tall, as in Tina Small.'

The thud in Gary's gut was like a punch from Keith Hardman. He fought to remain calm, normal, to not panic. He forced a smile and looked into Stacy's flint-hard eyes.

'All I had to do,' Stacy continued, 'was Google Gary and Tina and up popped a photo on the Hawksmead Chronicle website celebrating the marriage of Police Constable Gary Burton to Tina Small, estate agent. Does your wife know what her policeman husband has been doing of late?'

The game was up. He shook his head. 'She knows nothing.'

Frank sat back in his chair and spoke from the end of the long table. 'Ignorance ain't always bliss 'cause she's gonna know nothin' of what's about to happen to you. It will be her punishment for making the wrong choice of husband. But, one day, she will fully appreciate your betrayal.'

Gary tried to control his breathing, but his heart was a sledge-hammer under his ribs. 'My superiors know I am investigating you. If I don't check-in, they'll tear this place apart. You can't make me *disappear.'*

'I assure you, son, I can. I'm a very creative wizard.' He picked up a glass of freshly squeezed orange juice and swilled it around his mouth.

'Daddy, I don't want him to disappear.' Stacy's voice cracked on the last word. She took a breath. 'I want to see him suffer, every day. I need to know he is suffering.'

Hardman got up from the table.

Rise House was a detached, double-fronted, 1920s' property in Woodland Rise, a secluded and select leafy lane off Hawksmead High Street. To the left was a short drive and double garage. To the centre were solid oak gates and a wide York-stone path leading to a terracotta tiled step and an open porch. Curtains were drawn across a first-floor bedroom window.

Malcolm enveloped Tina within his long arms. 'Dinner, lunch… anytime, anywhere. Or we could walk the high ridge before winter sets in.'

She prised herself free and looked into his faded blue eyes, framed by crinkled skin. 'Thank you.' She kissed him on his cheek.

Audrey held Tina at arms' length. 'Whenever it gets too much – and it will – don't be a martyr. You have to give yourself a break.'

She nodded and reached for her wheeled suitcase.

'Are your parents expecting you?' Malcolm asked.

'I sent them messages but I've not heard back. It's not a problem, I have a key. I just hope they haven't changed the alarm code.'

'If there's any problem,' Audrey said, 'come and stay with us.'

'Any problem,' echoed Malcolm.

'And, I know it can't be,' Audrey paused, 'but happy birthday.'

Tina smiled. 'Thank you for my card. You never forget.' She blew a kiss to them both and they watched the forlorn young woman wheel her suitcase down the path towards the porch and front door.

'Come on,' Audrey said. 'I think we need to stretch our legs.'

Malcolm offered his left arm and gripped the extended handle of her suitcase. With the wheels clattering behind them, they shared the pleasure of a gentle stroll on the warm, late September day.

'Where is everyone?' Malcolm asked.

'They've fallen asleep on the sofa whilst watching Formula One.' She squeezed his arm.

'Tina worries me.'

'Yes, but all we can do is be there for her.'

4

Tina rang the bell instead of searching the depths of her handbag for the door key. Her mother had once let slip that she and her father were still sexually active. She sincerely hoped this was not one of their more energetic moments. She rang the bell again and waited.

Nothing.

She dug deep for the door keys and slid a solid brass key into the mortise lock. It was unlocked. She pulled it out and slid the Yale key into the top lock and turned. The door opened. She pushed it back and saw a pile of mail, leaflets and a copy of the local Hawksmead Chronicle newspaper, strewn on the floor.

'Mum! Dad!' She wrinkled her nose and closed the door. 'It's me. There's a terrible smell coming from somewhere.' She walked through the hallway into the large reception room. The first thing to strike her was the elaborately framed, wall-mounted portrait of Tina and Gary on their wedding day. She closed her eyes and took a few deep breaths to steady herself. But it had the opposite effect and dizziness forced her to seek out the sofa. She sat down and put her head between her knees to try and stop it from spinning. Hot, she peeled off her jacket.

'Mum!' she called. Exhausted, she closed her eyes and was quickly asleep.

Audrey was deep in thought as she and Malcolm wandered along Woodland Rise, her case clattering behind them.

'There's still plenty of daylight,' he said. 'We could drive up to the Rorty Crankle, have a brisk walk on the moor and earn ourselves a light late lunch, courtesy of Harry and Cathy.'

She squeezed her husband's arm. 'Mr Cadwallader, you are full of very good ideas.'

He stopped and looked down at his wife. 'What's that mosquito buzzing in your ear telling you?'

'Her parents might be away and I hate to think of her all alone in that big house. She needs to be with people. She's had more than enough loneliness waiting for Gary to return.' Audrey dipped her long fingers into her handbag and removed her phone. She swiped the screen, scrolled down her contacts and put the phone to her ear. 'It's ringing. Damn. Voicemail.' She cut the connection and slipped her arm through Malcolm's. 'I'll try again later.'

Tina stirred. Her head, pulsed. She took a few deep breaths and pushed herself onto her feet. She swayed and staggered as she made her way back into the hallway. Grabbing the handrail she placed a foot on the bottom step of the carpeted tread and lurched her way up to the first floor. Sweating from heat, she saw that her parents' bedroom door was shut. She sucked more air into her heaving lungs as she zigzagged her way across the landing, knocking over a Chinese vase precariously positioned on top of a pine, Doric column. It fell on the carpet and broke in two.

'Oh no!' She almost fell to her knees and reached for the broken pieces. Could they be glued? Her head was pounding as she forced herself back on her feet and banged with her palm on her parents' closed bedroom door.

'Mummy.'

Her knees buckled, her elbow caught the handle and the door sprung open. She could just make out her parents lying on the king-sized bed before she vomited on the thick-pile carpet.

Arm in arm, Audrey and Malcolm strolled along the leafy lane towards Hawksmead High Street, their unspoken thoughts accompanied by the rattling suitcase wheels.

'What about your father?' Malcolm asked. 'Are you going to set another date to visit?'

'Hang on. I'll try Tina again.' She stopped and retrieved her phone from her handbag. She tapped the screen and put it to her ear. She sighed. 'Tina, it's Audrey. Please call me back ASAP.' She dropped the phone into her bag and continued walking. 'Come on.'

Malcolm looked at his wife. 'You're going the wrong way.'

'I have to know her parents are home.'

'You want me to drag this suitcase all the way back to Rise House?'

'If you would be so kind.'

'I tell you what. I'll drag this heavy weight back to the motor and I'll pick you up from the house.'

'Perfect. See you shortly.' Audrey marched off down Woodland Rise and almost broke into a jog. But, aged nearly seventy, power-walking was the best she could do. Anyway, there was no hurry. She just had to be sure that Tina was safely restored to her parents' care.

Twenty minutes later, she stood at the end of the short drive leading to Rise House and liked what she saw. In Sevenoaks, the house she'd shared with her late husband, Duncan, and where their two sons had grown-up, was rented out. Although she loved Malcolm's two-up, two-down cottage, there were times when she missed the space. The double-fronted house owned by Tina's parents met with her approval. The tended beds with their shrubs and flowers were still vibrant and although the lawn could do with a bit of a trim, it was uniformly green without any dead patches or moss. She particularly liked the symmetry of the bow windows to the left and right of the portico entrance. She and Malcolm had run into Tina's parents a few times since her marriage to Gary and although Audrey would not class them as close friends, they had a mutual love for Tina and a shared history going back decades.

She took a deep breath and strode down the path to the front door. To the right was a porcelain bell push with the word PRESS. She obliged and heard the answering ring.

Someone was at the front door. Tina had to get help. She had to save her parents. She gripped the bedroom door frame to try and lever herself up but her head would not stop spinning.

Using her last reserves of grit and determination, she dragged her body across the wool carpet to the top of the stairs, ignoring the shards of broken vase and the vomit on her hand. She tried to push herself up, but the handrail was too high for her to reach. Floral wallpaper turned grey and she tumbled down the carpeted stairs to the half-landing.

Audrey was puzzled. Tina had not answered her phone and now nobody was answering the front door. She was not naturally nosey but something was not right. She looked back to the road. There were no passers-by and no Malcolm. She bent down and lifted the flap to the letterbox. There was another flap on the inside of the door so she couldn't see in. But she didn't need to. The smell of death told her all she needed to know. She reached for her phone and dialled 999.

'Emergency. Which service?'

'Police, oh and ambulance. Actually, fire service, too.'

'What is the nature of the problem?'

'I'm standing outside a friend's house and I think something bad has happened. Very bad.'

A few more questions and responses were concluded with Audrey giving the call handler the address.

'A police vehicle has been dispatched. Please wait until it arrives.'

Audrey terminated the call and checked the windows to left and right of the front door, but they were all sealed shut. Worse, they were leaded and double-glazed with fifteen small panes per window. Great for keeping out burglars. To the far left was an up-and-over double garage door and to the far right a solid wooden gate which Audrey presumed led around the side of the house to the rear garden. She tried it but, of course, it was locked and had sharp spikes at the top, designed to keep out the most gymnastic of burglar. Even if she got around the back, it was sure to be equally tough to break in.

'Have you rung the doorbell?'

Audrey looked at Malcolm.

'I didn't hear you come. I've called the police.'

'Why?'

'Put your nose to the letterbox. There's a terrible smell.'

'Have you tried calling Tina again?'

Audrey reached for her phone as Malcolm bent down and pushed open the letterbox flap. 'Good God!' He recoiled and let the flap snap down.

'Lift the flap again. I think I heard her phone.'

Malcolm did as she suggested. 'Yes. I can hear it ringing. She's definitely in the house.'

'Malcolm. We have to get in.'

'The police may have one of those battering rams. It's not the kind of door you can simply shoulder open.'

'We cannot wait for the police. By the time they arrive it could be too late. Do you have anything in your car we could use?'

'You mean like a jemmy?'

'Yes! That would be perfect.'

Audrey watched Malcolm hurry as best he could up the path and with growing frustration, observed him painstakingly hook back each wooden gate to a short wooden post.

'What are you doing?' called Audrey.

Malcolm acknowledged her entreaty with a brief wave and hurried around the nose of the Honda to the driver's door. The car was almost four years old but it still looked shiny and new. One of the great joys being married to Malcolm was that he rarely lazed around. He was always busy, always looking for another job to do – in the house, in the garden or sprucing up the car. It seemed his sole aim was to try and make Audrey's world as perfect as possible.

The Honda's engine sparked into life. Much to Audrey's surprise, Malcolm mounted the pavement and drove slowly down the footpath leading to the front door. He lowered the driver's window.

'What on earth…?' Audrey asked.

'I don't have a jemmy, but I have a battering ram.'

'Your car?'

'Stand back. Stand right away.' Malcolm did up his seat belt.

Audrey watched as he eased the Honda's front wheels up the step until the nose of the car was under the porch. 'It's a pity it's an automatic,' he shouted. 'But I'll do what I can. We may have to cancel our trip to Florida to pay for the damage.' He raised the window.

Audrey held her breath. The engine roared and she smelt the burning clutch as Malcolm held the car on the brake. Suddenly, the front wheels spun on the terracotta tiles and the car lurched forward, smashing into the front door and frame.

It held.

He reversed and rammed again.

The side window lowered.

Audrey bent down. 'What's the problem?'

'I can't get enough momentum.'

'Keep trying.'

The *whoop-whoop* of a police siren attracted both their attentions as a marked patrol car came to a halt. Its doors opened and two young police officers hurried down the path towards them.

'Don't speak. Listen,' Audrey commanded. 'There's a young woman in the house not answering her phone or the door, accompanied by a stench that can only mean one thing. We have to get in.'

The two policemen looked at each other. 'Get the big red,' said the older man. The younger police officer hurried back to the patrol car.

'Sir. Would you mind backing up?'

Malcolm nodded and reversed the Honda. The front of the car banged down on the edge of the step and broken glass from the headlights fell onto the path. He turned off the engine and got out. 'I think we'll need a taxi home,' he said to Audrey.

The younger policeman arrived carrying in two gloved hands a heavy red tube with a handle at the top and another at the rear.

'That should do it,' commented Malcolm.

'It weighs sixteen kilos,' said the older policeman, 'and if my young colleague here operates it right, it can exert an impact equivalent to three tonnes.'

'Shall I get on?' asked the younger man.

'One moment.' The older policemen rang the doorbell then banged on the door. He squatted and opened the flap to the letterbox, recoiled, and almost staggered as he stepped back. 'Get it open.'

The young police officer carefully targeted the head of the ram and swung it back like a mediaeval log hanging from a trapeze. The door opened immediately.

'Geeezus!' said the young policeman.

The senior officer turned to Audrey and Malcolm. 'Wait here.'

He entered the hallway, followed closely by Audrey.

'I said wait outside, madam!'

'Tina!' Audrey shouted.

'She's on the stairs,' said the senior officer.

Audrey rushed to the half landing and put her face close to Tina's head, which was lying on the carpet.

Malcolm sidled past the two police officers and entered the sitting room.

'Sir!' shouted the senior officer. 'I order you to get out of the house.'

'We need to open windows at the rear,' Malcolm called back.

The senior officer spoke into his radio by his left lapel. 'We're attending Rise House, Woodland Rise. We require ambulance assistance. Lights and siren.' He turned to his colleague. 'Check upstairs.'

'I don't know about you, boss, but I feel a bit woozy.'

Malcolm re-entered the hallway. 'Carbon monoxide, I'm sure of it.'

'Audrey?' Tina's eyes blinked several times.

Audrey smiled. 'You're going to be okay.'

'My parents.'

'I'll check on them.' She turned to her husband. 'Malcolm?'

He climbed the first short flight of stairs and eased his tall frame down. He put his arm around Tina as Audrey stepped up to the landing.

'Madam. Don't touch anything,' ordered the senior officer. 'Do you hear me?'

Audrey felt sick as she stood at the top of the stairs. The stink of death was overwhelming. She forced herself to cross the landing, avoiding the pieces of broken vase, and stopped by the pool of vomit. She peered into the master bedroom. The stench was beyond any smell she had ever experienced. As her eyes adjusted to the dim light seeping through the closed curtains, she saw two semi-naked bloated bodies entwined on the bed.

5

'Did you see the ANPR camera?' Malcolm asked as he pulled on the handbrake and turned off the engine. 'They really are determined to squeeze us dry.'

Audrey released her seat belt.

'I like this Daewoo,' continued Malcolm. 'I feel unfaithful to my beloved Honda, but this little beauty has a lot to offer.'

Audrey opened her door and looked at the grey hospital edifice. 'I had hoped I'd never darken those corridors again. I feel breathless just thinking about it.'

'The last time I walked or rather limped out of there was when Tina came to collect me after my accident.'

'I've not given this place a moment's thought for four years and now it feels like I never left.'

'They did a good job for us – let's hope they're still on their game.'

Tina was awake. The air she was breathing tasted strangely good. She was comfortable apart from the mask covering her nose and mouth. Nothing hurt. But she was frightened of opening her eyes. She didn't know why she was scared but she knew that something bad had happened. She just didn't know what.

'Hello, I'm Dr Manson. Are you a relative?' The young woman was talking quietly and Tina had to strain to hear her voice.

'I owe her my life, so we are more than connected.' Tina recognised the refined voice of the older woman, but couldn't place it.

'We knew her late parents,' said another voice. This time a man and quite elderly. Late parents? What was he saying? She strained to hear their conversation.

'Her brother lives in New Zealand,' the older woman said. 'I understand that the police are getting in touch. But, that's all by the by. Our sole concern is Tina. Please tell us how she is.'

Tina tried to move her arm but her whole body felt paralysed. All she could do was lie there and listen.

'As I am sure you are aware, carbon monoxide is lethal. We are giving her oxygen to try and flush it out of her system.' The doctor was talking quietly and Tina couldn't be sure she was hearing her right. 'Even if CO poisoning doesn't kill a patient, the damage it can do is often irreversible.'

'What kind of damage?' interjected the elderly man.

'We need to do tests to determine the extent but, from what we know, Tina was exposed to a high level of carbon monoxide. The effect can be tremors, stiffness in the joints and, generally, slowness in thought and movement. In extreme cases, impaired vision and hearing.'

She can't be talking about me? I can hear, perfectly.

'How long before you know?' the older woman, asked.

Audrey?

'The length of time it takes to recover from carbon monoxide poisoning varies with the individual. Is Tina a smoker?'

'Would that have an effect?' Of course – dear Malcolm.

'Smokers often have higher than normal carboxyhaemoglobin in their blood, which makes it hard for us to determine what the level would have been prior to the CO poisoning.'

'I'm sure she wasn't a smoker,' Audrey said.

'I see. Well, the level of carboxyhaemoglobin in Tina's blood was very high. The lack of oxygen will, most likely, have caused some damage, especially to the nervous system and brain, how much we can only tell when she wakes.'

'I think losing both parents will have the greater effect,' Audrey said.

Tina forced her eyes to open. Her hand flopped onto the oxygen mask and she dragged it clear of her mouth. 'What are you saying?' She didn't recognise her own hoarse voice.

Audrey was the first to react and went to the side of the bed. 'Tina, it's Audrey.'

'Long time no see.'

'You've had an accident, but you're going to be okay. Malcolm and I are here to help you get well.'

'I feel fine. Just a bit groggy.'

From the other side of the bed, Dr Manson carefully replaced the oxygen mask. 'Hello Tina. You're suffering from the effects of carbon monoxide poisoning. Oxygen will help flush it out of your bloodstream. So no talking. Rest and give your body a chance to get better.' She looked at Audrey. 'Would you come and find me before you go?'

'Of course.'

Tina watched the doctor leave the side ward.

'Shall I get us a cup of tea?' Malcolm asked. His voice sounded far, far away as Tina slipped back into blissful oblivion.

Dr Manson was finishing a phone conversation when Audrey and Malcolm approached. She handed the receiver back to the receptionist and looked with tired eyes at the elderly couple.

'Leaving already?'

Audrey smiled. 'She's fallen asleep. We'll come back tomorrow. Hopefully, you'll be able to tell us a bit more by then.'

'She very nearly died,' Dr Manson said. 'I've spoken to a senior consultant and in his opinion, Tina will inevitably suffer memory loss, problems with her balance, and there could be a change to her character, her personality.'

'Will the effects be permanent?' Malcolm asked. 'Or will she get better over time?'

Audrey made a half-step towards the young doctor. 'Or could she get worse, like people who've had a stroke?'

Malcolm touched his wife's arm. 'That's a bit gloomy, darling.'

Dr Manson looked from one pair of ageing eyes to the other, and took a tired breath. 'CO poisoning is not like a stroke where the symptoms in severe cases can get worse, but carbon monoxide deprives the blood of oxygen, and lack of oxygen for a prolonged period does cause damage. How much, we don't know yet.'

6

Tina pressed the red Help button she hoped would summon a nurse. It was morning, the early October sun was nearly up and there was already a bustle around the side ward.

Nobody answered her call.

She pulled off her oxygen mask and gently eased her legs out of bed and planted her feet on the cold floor. She looked down and saw a tube coming out from under her gown that was plugged into a plastic bottle hanging on the side of her bed. She unhooked it and shuffled in bare feet out of the side ward.

Amy, one of the receptionists, looked up from her screen and got to her feet. 'Please go back to bed. A nurse will be along, soon.'

'I need the loo, *now*.'

'Okay, let me help you.' Amy came out from behind the curved reception desk and took Tina's arm.

'Your face looks familiar,' Tina said.

'You and your friend... was it Tony? ...were almost permanent fixtures here when that lovely elderly couple were guests in this establishment a few years ago.'

Tina almost laughed but it hurt too much.

'I went to your wedding,' Amy said. 'I am so sorry about Gary.'

'I have to go to the loo, *now*,' responded Tina.

'It's just along here. If you have any problem, there's a red string pull. I'll come straightaway.'

Tina entered the loo, parted her gown at the back and sat down.

Amy had forgotten all about her one-time friend and current patient when Tina suddenly appeared in front of the reception desk holding her gown closed at the rear. In her free hand was the bottle of urine.

'Can someone please remove this? I'd like to take a shower.'

'When the doctor sees you later this morning, you can ask her.'

'Do you know where my things are?'

'The clothes you came in are stored in your bedside cabinet. They've been laundered. I have a key.'

'What about my phone?'

'All you had were your clothes. You can use this phone.' Amy pushed a landline phone towards her.

'I don't know the number.'

Amy moved her mouse and looked at the computer screen. 'We do have a contact number for you. I'll write it down.' She copied the number onto a small pad with *Undermere General Hospital* printed at the top and peeled off the sheet.

'Thank you.' Tina stared at the piece of paper. 'Could you dial it for me? My eyes are a bit blurred.'

'Of course.' Amy stood and pulled the phone's base towards her. She looked at the number she'd just written and tapped the keypad.

'Mum, it's me,' Tina said. 'I'm in hospital. I don't know what's happened but can you come and get me?' She listened. 'Audrey?' She listened some more and then looked at Amy. 'When can I see the doctor?'

'She does her round at about eleven.'

Tina spoke into the phone. 'Can you come late morning?' She listened. 'Thank you. Bye.' She placed the receiver back on its base and focused her eyes on Amy. 'What's going on? Please tell me.'

'I wish I could. I'm sorry.'

'Why won't anyone tell me?' It was more of a wail than a question.

'We really would like you to stay for another day,' Dr Manson said. 'Especially as you're still a bit foggy.'

Tina stood by the bed in the side ward, trying her best to keep her mind focused on what the petite doctor was saying. The door was open and many noises were coming from the communal acute wards.

'I want to see my parents. I don't understand why they've not visited.'

'When the police came, you were asleep. Let me call them and they can explain what happened to you. It's not for me.'

'I want this out.' She pointed to the bottle half-full of urine hooked to the side of the bed.

'Okay.'

'Thank you for what you have done for me, Dr Manson. I am really grateful.' She admired the young woman, who conveyed confidence, knowledge and authority with such ease.

'Is anyone coming to collect you?'

'My friend, Audrey.'

'Do not hesitate to come back if you feel unwell.'

'I will. I promise.'

'Okay, lie down.' Dr Manson snatched a couple of latex gloves from a wall-mounted dispenser and closed the door.

Malcolm was going to make chicken Elizabeth. He didn't know how long Audrey would be, so had decided to prepare a meal that was not time sensitive and could be eaten hot or cold. Before Audrey left for the hospital, they had prepared the spare bedroom. The days ahead were going to be even tougher for Tina than they had been since Gary went missing. But, he and Audrey were determined to do all they could to support the beautiful young woman, especially through the inevitable post mortem and double funeral.

Tina sat down on an upright chair by her hospital bed and waited. She was wearing the clothes she'd had on when she was brought into hospital by the ambulance, freshly laundered but creased. She had nothing else. No phone, no purse, no keys.

A face appeared around the door.

'Audrey!' She leapt to her feet, lost her balance, and had to use the bed to recover. 'Still a bit shaky.' She gave Audrey a hug. 'Have you spoken to my parents?'

'Let's get out of here. We can talk in the car.'

'Yes of course. '

'Do you have everything?'

'Yes, apart from my parents. I don't understand what's going on. It's most unlike them.'

Audrey walked with Tina across the hospital car park and tapped her debit card on the machine reader to validate her ticket.

'The cost has almost doubled in four years,' Tina observed as they approached the Daewoo. 'New car?'

'Rental. The Honda is in for a bit of surgery.'

Tina laughed. 'Malcolm's heavy right foot?'

'He's really looking forward to seeing you.'

'I'm sorry for being such a poor friend. I'm not myself, these days.'

Audrey drove Tina straight to the cottage. The young woman was very tense and, at times, it had been difficult to deflect questions about her parents. Audrey's aim was to get her safely inside before breaking the devastating news. She parked and switched off the engine.

'Audrey, may I ask you a question?'

'Why don't we have a nice cup of tea, first?' Audrey released her seatbelt. 'Malcolm's always got cake.'

'Wait. Please. It's about Malcolm and you.'

'Malcolm?'

'Are you happy?'

'Happy?'

'Is it possible to find true love… as a widow?'

Audrey took Tina's hand in hers. 'This is a very, very tough time for you. But, you will meet another man and you will fall in love. Every relationship is unique. I have found a man in Malcolm who makes me laugh and feel loved every day. I treasure the many happy memories I have of my life with Duncan but, as a friend of my mother often said, we're a long time dead. So, we need to live in the present, smell the crumpets and eat Malcolm's homemade jam.'

He heard the front door open and hurried through to the narrow hallway. Two days ago, Tina had looked thin and strained but Malcolm was still surprised by her emaciated appearance and lack of vivacity.

'Darling Malcolm,' Tina said. 'I'm just popping in for a quick cuppa and then I must go to my parents. They'll be wondering what's happening.'

His heart flipped. 'Is there time for a hug?' For a brief second as her face brightened, he saw the Tina who had helped save Audrey's life, and helped him recover after a bone-shattering fall.

'I'm a bit smelly,' she laughed. 'I've not had a shower for goodness knows how long.'

He wrapped his arms around the young woman who felt as frail as she looked.

8

Tina was puzzled. She was sitting on the sofa in Malcolm's front room sipping a cup of tea but there was no chit-chat. Sunday was the first time she had seen Audrey and Malcolm since Gary had disappeared. She hadn't even been back for Christmas or Easter. They both looked a bit older, a bit plumper and a whole lot more content than when estate agent Tina had first sold Audrey the old school boarding house at the north end of Hawksmead. Flames flickered through her mind as she remembered the fire that had destroyed the Victorian building and nearly killed Audrey. She thought about the high-speed car chase when she'd rushed Audrey to hospital pursued by flashing blue lights, driven by a police officer who continued to chase her all the way to the altar.

Gary. Such a cocky young man. How she missed him.

'Lovely tea, Malcolm. I like the blend.' Tina smiled as she returned the cup to its saucer. 'Your cottage looks lovely, too. It's quite a while since I was last here, but I hope you know how much you two mean to me. Whatever is on your mind, whatever you have to say, won't change that.'

She watched the elderly couple look at each other and felt a lump of lead drop into her stomach.

Audrey got up and sat beside her on the sofa. She took Tina's hand in hers. 'Darling.' She swallowed. 'Your parents have died. It was a terrible accident which the authorities are investigating. We are so sorry.'

Tina pulled her hand away. 'No. You're wrong. I saw them. They were in bed, having a nap. They're fine.' She pushed herself up onto her feet. 'I have to talk to them. I have to go home.' She looked at Malcolm. 'Will you drive me?'

'We'll all go,' Audrey said.

The elderly couple's cottage was on a quiet road about half-way between the bustling centre of Undermere and the former mill town of Hawksmead, where Tina's parents lived. Malcolm took the Old Military Road across the moor, driving cautiously. If Tina were at the wheel she would've really put her foot down, but she had to be patient. It would only be a few more minutes before she saw her folks.

'Slow down for the bridge,' Audrey ordered from the rear seat.

'As if I wouldn't,' responded Malcolm. They approached an old stone humpback bridge which was only wide enough for a single vehicle. He tooted his horn and Tina felt her stomach flip as the car came down on the town side.

'Watch the speed camera,' she warned. 'I got done a few years ago.'

They all looked to their left as they passed the entrance to the memorial garden where the old school boarding house had once stood.

'You must visit the garden, Tina,' Audrey said. 'It's looking glorious.'

'I would like that.'

Malcolm turned off the High Street and into Woodland Rise. He drove the Daewoo slowly along the winding, tree-lined road and came to a gentle stop by Rise House.

Something wasn't right. Tina released her seat belt and opened the passenger door. She hurried down the pathway and came to a wooden box that had been constructed around the entrance. Stapled to the plywood was a laminated sheet.

POLICE NOTICE
Do Not Enter
This building is deemed unsafe for persons and animals
owing to toxic air.
By Order of the Magistrate's Court, Undermere, entrance is
prohibited until work is completed to obviate the danger.

There was more but Tina couldn't read it as her vision was blurred by tears. She felt Audrey's arm around her shoulders as she sank to her knees and sobbed. Everyone she loved was spinning down a never-ending tunnel as the pain of loss enveloped her. She thought her heart would seize and her brain would melt. Her stomach retched and she vomited a pathetic stream of tea and cake. Tears poured down her cheeks as her whole body convulsed in grief.

'Everything all right?'

Kneeling on the path with her arm around Tina, Audrey looked up at a man wearing blue overalls, a white hard hat and carrying a grey case. Hanging around his neck was a gas mask designed to cover his whole face, with a black tube over his shoulder to a bright orange tank strapped to his back.

'This is her parents' house.'

The man nodded. 'I have written instructions from the coroner to determine the source of poisoning.'

'Could she go into the house? It might help.'

'I'm afraid not.'

'I brought her here three days ago. When she got taken to hospital, her handbag and bright yellow suitcase were left in the sitting room. Could I pop in and retrieve them?'

'I'll get them. Please do not follow me in.'

'I won't.'

The engineer unlocked the narrow door fitted at the front of the temporary construction and pulled on his mask. He turned on a tap, checked that Audrey was not about to follow him, and entered the building.

Audrey looked up the path to Malcolm who was standing by the Daewoo. Parked behind was a white van with blue wording on the side panel, but Audrey needed her glasses to read it.

'Madam.' The gas engineer put down Tina's suitcase and placed her handbag on top.

'Is there gas?'

'There's quite a process to go through before I can declare the house safe. I'd better get on.' He re-entered the temporary structure and made sure that the door was closed and locked.

Malcolm picked up Tina's handbag and pulled her case along the path to the Daewoo.

Audrey kept her arm tight around Tina's shoulders as she tried to absorb every twitch and spasm of overwhelming loss and grief.

9

He hated the heat, he hated the sickly smell. The Heath Robinson network of air conditioning units and pipes, cobbled together to disguise the growing of marijuana on the floor below, was impressive. Dermot O'Hanlon, the apparent leader of the travelling family, seemed inordinately proud of their illegal achievements and, when Gary had first arrived, insisted on demonstrating to him every aspect of his ingenuity.

'Yer see, Gary, we may be stupid spud pickers to Britain but, given a chance, we rule the world. It amuses the hell out of me that we are farming this wonderful cash crop right under the noses of the boys in blue.' He laughed, but Gary did not see the joke. 'I know this game inside out. It's in my DNA. You reckon your police helicopters will stumble across this cannabis farm because we're thick Irish itinerants. Dream on. There are no telltale heat sources for their infrared cameras to detect, even in winter.'

The ground floor was taken up with a large refectory, changing and shower rooms, and staff accommodation and offices. The first floor was untouched by the travellers and was all classrooms, the top floor was given over to dormitories and shower rooms where Gary and the migrants slept, but the second floor was where all the illegal activity took place. Windows were blacked out by original wooden shutters and men, mostly young of East Asian origin, worked silently tending the plants.

'Heat from all these lamps,' Dermot insisted on explaining, 'usually give the game away but this middle floor is cocooned. Of course, heat has to go somewhere and the dormitories above would get so hot, no frost or snow would settle on the school roof. One of your police whirlybirds would be sure to take a closer look.'

Dermot took him up to the top floor and proudly showed how the air conditioning units in the dormitories, which Gary would discover hummed and squeaked day and night, extracted the hot air.

'We're Irish, Gary, and we're smart. Hot air is expelled along these flexible pipes, via the back stairs. Now, I know what you're thinking. You think we're so simple as to release hot, pungent, cannabis vapour into the air around the school, for visitors to inhale.' Dermot tapped his head. 'But God gave me the solution. Five hundred years ago, monks from the monastery redirected the brook to turn a water wheel for grinding their corn.' He laughed and once again Gary could not see the joke. 'Yer see, the hot, stinking air is pumped into the fast-flowing brook and although it bubbles to the surface, it is cold and the stink is dissipated.' He slapped Gary's back. 'Clever eh? You've gotta admit it.'

'Thank you for the tour. Very illuminating.' Gary had witnessed much low level criminal activity since being held captive in various locations, but this cannabis farm was a major leap.

'We're not done, yet,' Dermot insisted. 'Power needed for the UVA and LED lamps that speed the growth of our marijuana plants, and turn the fans in the air-conditioning units, draws high levels of electricity from the grid.'

That was the straw Gary was grasping. He had hoped the excessive demand of power, even if cables were diverted around an electricity meter, would attract the attention of the authorities.

'I can see your wheels turning.' Dermot almost winked conspiratorially. 'In the early 1970s, Gary, power workers and coal miners were on strike and caused frequent power cuts.' He guided Gary down to the top of the back stairs that led to the basement, the chains linking his hand and ankle cuffs clinking as they walked.

Dermot pulled open the door and Gary could hear a slight hum coming from somewhere in the darkness below. 'To solve the problem of power being cut off,' Dermot said, continuing his lecture, 'this remote school out on the moor installed its own electricity generator and, if you listen carefully, you can hear it still works. But how is it fuelled, I hear you ask. I agree with you, buying diesel in cans to run the generator could attract unwelcome interest. Rather than fill cans with diesel at the nearest service station, we fill our vans and trucks in the usual way and then the fuel is simply siphoned off. Nobody is any the wiser.' Dermot slapped Gary on the back again. 'And that, my friend, concludes our tour.'

Gary smiled to himself. Hawksmead College really was a seat of learning, an education. It was a pity he was chained to it.

'She's asleep,' Audrey said in a quiet voice as Malcolm poured boiling water into a floral teapot. She looked through the kitchen window, not appreciating the brightly-coloured blooms, trimmed verges, and perfectly shaped bushes, all benefitting from the early autumn's warm weather.

'I have never witnessed such pain,' Malcolm said as he put the lid on the pot and placed it on a tray.

'No.'

He looked at Audrey. 'What can we do?'

'You can make sure she eats.'

He nodded and briefly smiled. 'We should contact her brother.'

'His number will be in her phone, I presume. I'll put it on charge.'

'We'll have to figure out the pass code.'

'It'll be the date of her wedding,' Audrey said. 'I know Tina.'

'Gary's parents? Did you meet them at the wedding?'

'His mother was there. His father died a long while ago.'

'She must be so wretched.'

Audrey took in a deep breath. Her wheeze, since being trapped by fire, would always be with her. 'She ended her life.'

Malcolm stared at her. 'I didn't know.'

'I ran into Tina's father in the memorial garden. We spent a little while sitting and talking. He told me the sad news.'

'Why didn't you tell me?'

Audrey took another wheezy breath. 'Okay. John and I often meet – or rather met – in your beautiful memorial garden. Sometimes we talked about the loss of his brother and some-times we talked about mine. Sometimes, we just talked. And, sometimes, we just sat on the bench and looked at their names carved in the memorial stone.'

Malcolm nodded. 'I didn't know.'

'I was John's connection to a brother he barely knew. I never met Mark but you know how close he and my brother were.'

Malcolm swiped away an escaping tear.

She touched his arm. 'Not for one second did John blame you for what happened. You know that.'

'Black ice... not my fault but I'll never forgive myself.'

'I know. Do you understand why I didn't tell you?'

Malcolm nodded.

She kissed his cheek.

'Thank you.' He pulled back his shoulders. 'Cake?'

Audrey nodded and smiled.

Malcolm reached for a tin and pulled the roof off Buck-ingham Palace. 'Shop-bought Battenberg or home-made jam sponge?'

'I think I need a slice of your homemade jam sponge more than ever.'

Tina opened her eyes. The room was dark. Not even weak rays from a streetlight. For a moment, she had no idea where she was. But, she needed the lavatory and she needed it fast. She got out of the comfortable single bed and ricocheted off a chest of drawers into a side table which fell over onto the thick car-pet, which she could feel under her bare feet.

She really needed a pee. Her knees pressed against the side of the bed as she eased her way around the base and headed for what she thought was the window. She felt fabric in her hand and pulled a curtain back along its track. Weak, yellow rays from a sodium street light brought a little definition to the furniture and she was able to locate the door. She turned the porcelain knob and pulled.

Darkness.

Where was she?

That could wait. She had to find a loo or she'd wet her pyjamas. How did *they* get on? She felt along the wall and found a switch. A hanging light with a floral shade lit a narrow landing. She tip-toed across to an open door and the cool linoleum told her feet she was in the right place. She arced her hand and it came into contact with a string pull. At the end was a large ceramic toggle. She pulled and was almost blinded by ceiling lights. She didn't mind as she could see well enough the object of her desire. Leaving the door open, she hurried to the lavatory, pulled down her pyjamas and let go almost before she felt the cold plastic of the seat.

Once the pressure was off, her estate-agent eye was able to take in her surroundings. The bathroom was pretty and well-appointed with a period-style enamelled bath that looked very tempting.

Audrey was on a beach, a massive wave crashed over her and she spun round and round as if in her mother's Bendix washing machine. She didn't know which way was up. She clawed the water but it held her in its suffocating embrace. She opened her mouth to scream.

'Audrey! Audrey!' whispered a man's voice.

She was being shaken and gradually she surfaced. A shaft of dawn light found a gap in the curtains.

Her lungs hurt.

'I was drowning.'

'You were dreaming, my darling.'

'Water. There's water! I can hear it.'

Malcolm hugged her to him. 'It's Tina. She's running a bath.'

'I was on a beach, searching for my little brother. I couldn't find him. And then I was drowning.'

'You're safe, now.'

'Yes.' Audrey kissed her husband. 'We have a special someone to take care of. How are we going to do that?'

'Perhaps a cup of tea will help.' He eased away from her.

'Or coffee. Better for joining the dots.'

Tina lay in the bath, cocooned in the comforting warmth and bubbles. She tried to quell the voices in her head but one came through, as he always did.

'Mrs Burton... we cannot find him. As you know, he was working undercover to expose a criminal family. We lost contact and despite all our efforts he's disappeared. We are doing what we can, Mrs Burton. We will never give up looking for Gary.'

She closed her eyes and submerged her head in the water. They did give up. When the Detective Chief Inspector retired his words were seared in her memory. *'It's time for you to start living again. It's been more than two years. If Gary were still alive, he would have found a way to make contact.'*

Only her parents' positivity had kept her hopes alive. Her parents...

The Irishman yanked his chain and the policeman was immediately awake. Not that Gary ever slept well in the hand and ankle cuffs he had to wear, whether he was working outside, nurturing marijuana plants, eating, washing or sleeping.

It was always hard to tell whether it was day or night in the long dormitory as the windowpanes were blacked out and the shutters closed. There were thirty metal beds with thin mattresses, of which about half were occupied. He was the only one chained.

On a metal tray was a bowl of porridge and a cup of tea. He could not fault the quality of the food. It was nutritious if basic, but not nearly enough for the work he was forced to do, by day picking potatoes and at night tending marijuana plants.

'Breakfast in bed, Dermot,' Gary said. 'You're clearly going for a Michelin star.'

'We have a visitor, later.'

'Who?'

'Don't get excited. Just some old geezer to do with the building's trustees. He's not about to break you free.'

Despite his youth and training, the opportunities to escape his captors had been few. Frankly, Gary was impressed. At times, he felt crushed by his situation despite being assured by the Irishman that there would come a time when he and his co-workers would be released.

He didn't believe him. He knew that the former outward-bound school had its own cesspit. But he played along, waiting, watching... hoping for an opportunity. But, after more than two years being moved around the country and almost suffo-cating more than once in the confines of a lorry trailer, now being so near to where he grew up was acutely painful. He missed his wife. He missed his life. He went over and over how he got it so badly wrong. How he'd managed to make a massive rookie mistake. He was the only one to blame. But the price he had to pay was pretty damned high.

The October weather was good, and the thought of another twelve-hour shift in the tropical heat of the enclosed building, lit with LED lamps, sickened him. But the Vietnamese workers seemed to thrive in the heavy, dense air. Many had travelled from the poorest regions of Vietnam, at great financial cost, only to find that the promised land was forced labour growing grass. Born in the tropics, they preferred the pungent smell of marijuana to the mud of the potato field. Marijuana was the gang's staple crop but the home-grown potatoes were a use-ful cover and helped to feed the twenty-five or so Vietnamese workers.

Gary was impressed by the travellers' simple and yet effect-ive working practices. Mostly, the migrants were passive – everyone loved someone and that someone's continued good health relied on the migrants co-operating. Gary knew that the danger to Tina from Frank Cottee was all too real. There were times when he could have tried to escape, but that would have put her life at risk.

10

Malcolm showered and shaved in the small cloakroom off the hallway on the ground floor. He didn't much like the face with its white stubble staring back at him but he was approaching eighty so he knew he had to be grateful.

Since marrying Audrey three years ago, he had enjoyed life more than he had thought possible. His remarkable wife had come to Hawksmead as a new widow on a quest to learn the truth behind her little brother's tragic death. And now Tina, who had been his friend and saviour during the dark days when it looked as though he and Audrey would be apart for good, was suffering the loss of her young husband, compounded by the sudden deaths of her parents. Somehow, he and Audrey had to help her build a new life.

'Not easy,' he said as he lathered his chin. 'Not easy at all.'

Audrey heard Tina leave the bathroom and hurried in to have a quick wash. She hoped the smell of crispy bacon wafting up from the kitchen would lure Tina to have some breakfast. The young woman was underweight whereas Audrey, examining her naked form in a full-length mirror fixed to the wall, was definitely looking a little rounded. She blamed Malcolm and smiled. His homemade scones and damson jam, topped by Cornish clotted cream, were pure heaven. Throw in Sunday lunches at the Rorty Crankle out on the moor and her 1970s' frame, once Twiggy-like when she was a photographic model, was now, as Malcolm put it, perfectly plump and a comfortable cushion. She laughed and immediately felt guilty. It would be a long time before their guest would laugh again.

Tina lifted the lid of her suitcase and looked at her neatly folded clothes. The Oxfam shop in Southfields had done very well. She'd had to be brutal; not just about clothes she couldn't fit in her case but about personal knick-knacks and gifts... and all Gary's clothes.

'If you return to London,' said Iain, her team leader, 'do not think about working anywhere else but here.'

She would not return. For all its charms, London would never be home. Where was home? She thought it was with her parents... she screwed her eyes shut and slammed the door on her grief. 'Breathe in to one and out to three,' she said to herself. It took a few deep breaths to restore her composure.

Almost exhausted by the effort, she riffled through her case. What should she put on? The early October weather was still quite warm so she slipped on a pair of comfortable joggers with a drawstring waist, blue socks, a white camisole and a casual shirt. She looked in the mirror. Her eyes were red, her cheeks hollow and her blonde hair needed shaping. She was a pale shadow of the young estate agent who had had such big dreams when she first worked for Harper Dennis, aged eighteen. Now, she had no dreams, no hope, no future. There was nothing left. Just a brother who had chosen to live on the other side of the world.

No!

She had more than that. She had friends who cared for her, and she had Audrey and Malcolm. They had written to her both jointly and individually. Although she had rarely replied, they had never given up on her. She felt the tears coming and quickly wiped them away.

The aroma of cooked bacon wafting up the stairs made her tummy rumble and for the first time since Gary had disappeared, she felt real hunger. She grabbed a brush and quickly pulled it through her hair. For a short while she was determined to take a break from the tsunami of grief. She still felt a bit odd – there were blanks in her mind – it was hard to think straight – images would appear uninvited.

She pulled open the bedroom door. All the times she had visited Malcolm's home when he and Audrey were apart, she had never been up to the first floor. She tiptoed in her socks across the landing and quietly walked down the steep stairs. From the hallway, she entered the sitting room and looked at its gilt-framed paintings, antique furniture, chintz covered sofa, and assorted *objets* on the mantelpiece. It was as if she were seeing them for the first time. Double doors were open to the dining room where the rosewood table was laid for breakfast with decorative place mats, strawberry patterned china, matching pots for jam and marmalade, silver cutlery and an incongruous bottle of HP brown sauce.

Audrey carried a matching strawberry-patterned pot of coffee into the dining room and placed it on a heat-proof coaster. She looked at her.

'It's the smell of bacon,' Tina said.

Audrey nodded and smiled. 'Malcolm likes to bake it in the oven so that it's extra crispy. He's also cooked tomatoes from his garden, and scrambled eggs in his own special way. Secret recipe.'

'Thank you.'

'Tea or coffee?'

'The coffee pot winked at me.'

Audrey laughed. 'A lot of things wink at you in Malcolm's cottage, hence my larger dress size. Come and sit down.' She pulled out a rosewood chair with a woven padded seat. Tina sat down facing the French windows and the neat garden with its raised beds and wooden pergola.

Malcolm entered from the kitchen carrying a rack of carefully balanced toast.

'Your garden looks so pretty, Malcolm.'

'It's been a good summer.'

'You should see the memorial garden,' Audrey said. 'It's truly beautiful. There are benches now, so visitors can sit and have a picnic, or read, or do what I do.'

Tina waited for her to expand. She saw Audrey and Malcolm exchange looks. 'Please don't walk on egg shells. It's lovely to see you. To be here.'

'Let's get down to business,' Malcolm said. 'The full works,

Tina?'

She smiled. 'The full works.'

He slipped away into the kitchen and Audrey poured coffee into Tina's cup.

'We want you to stay here,' Audrey said. 'I mean, live with us. Use this as your base. No ties. Just, until you want to move on.'

Tina took a few deep breaths. 'I may not be that easy to live with. I'm a bit of a basket case. I'm not the person I was.'

'Life changes us all.' Audrey put her hand on Tina's. 'We are here for when you need us.' They both looked up as Malcolm placed a plate with crispy bacon rashers, grilled tomatoes, mushrooms and scrambled eggs in front of Tina.

'The Mint Cottage special,' he said, and hurried back to the kitchen.

Audrey stage-whispered towards Tina's ear. 'The old man's a great cook but he always caters for the five thousand. There are only so many times one wants to eat leftovers.'

Malcolm returned with two more steaming plates. He placed one in front of Audrey and one at a place set opposite Tina. 'Toast?' He indicated the toast rack.

Tina's head began to spin; she gripped the table edge and took several deep breaths to steady herself. Once her vision had settled, she dared to turn her head and look at Audrey. 'Thank you for welcoming me into your home. You have both been incredibly kind.' She looked up at Malcolm who was still standing. 'And thank you for your more than generous offer.' Tears filled her eyes and she had to blink several times to push them back. 'I accept.'

'Excellent,' Malcolm said and he pulled out his chair. 'But it is only toast, albeit from a home-baked loaf.'

Tina grinned and used her linen napkin to wipe away an escapee.

11

The uniformed police officer escorted Tina to the double garage situated to the side of Rise House.

'Do you have the remote?'

She looked at the policeman. 'I have a key for the house. The car keys will be in a metal dish on a side table in the hallway.'

'I'm very sorry, miss, but the house is still under investigation. It's not been released yet. It's why I'm here. You can't go in.'

'How long have you been with the Undermere force?'

'About six years. I've been offered promotion but I like being in uniform, out on the road.'

'Did you ever work with Gary Burton?'

'Gary!' He looked intently at the young woman. 'I am so sorry. It's Tina, isn't it?'

She nodded.

'We are all devastated about Gary. And then to have this on top. We all feel for you down at the station. Gary was very popular. There's a framed photo of your wedding in the gents' toilet.'

Tina gasped.

'I mean, it's there because it's the only place the brass would permit us to hang it.' He paused. When he spoke again his voice was thick with emotion. 'They will find him, Tina. They will bring him home. They will.'

'Thank you.' She turned and walked up the drive away from the house.

'Don't you want your car?' called the copper.

Tina looked back at him. 'I don't have the garage fob or car key.'

'Then, I'd better get them.'

She watched as he used a key to open the door in the temporary wooden structure.

'Hold your breath!' she shouted. 'I mean it.'

'It's all been shut off; should be okay.' He vanished from view and a few seconds later he emerged with an electronic garage door fob attached to a VW Golf key. He pressed the fob and the garage door lifted and slid over two parked cars – a teal blue Mercedes 220 SE two-door, and a white VW Golf, four-door.

'That is a beauty.' The police officer approached the Mercedes. 'A true classic. It has to be mid 1960s.'

'1965. Dad bought it in honour of his brother who died that year. Uncle Mark had a die-cast model he and my dad used to play with together.'

The policeman touched the metal with his fingertips. 'Phenomenal condition.'

'Yes. Dad kept it polished. It's almost too precious to drive.'

'And the Golf is yours?'

'It was mine. Dad bought it off me for an inflated price when Gary and I moved to London. Gary said I shouldn't drive in the city as there were too many ways for me to get a ticket – yellow junction boxes, bus lanes, speed cameras. In reality, I sold it because we needed the money. Mum uses it as a runaround.' She paused. 'At least she did.'

'Here's the key.' He handed the VW key and fob to her. 'Insurance?'

She nodded. 'Thank you, yes. What's your name?'

'Hett. PC Hett. Matthew.'

Tina leaned forward and kissed him on the cheek. 'Thank you, Matthew.'

She opened the driver's door and slipped into the familiar seat of the white VW Golf. The interior had a comforting aroma – a mix of leather and cleaning spray.

She smiled.

She was home.

12

Trevor Harper rubbed his eyes. His estate agency business was ticking over but increasing levels of regulation were complicating both sales and lettings. His main problem was the turnover of staff. As soon as negotiators got any good, they left him for one of the chains. Or, got married and moved down south. He heard the door open and Max, a negotiator who he wouldn't mind getting rid of, leapt to his feet.

'What are you doing here?' Max almost shouted. 'You're not coming back?'

Trevor looked at the person standing by the door. 'Tina?' His beautiful and talented young negotiator was now a gaunt figure. He pushed back his chair and wrapped his arms around her. He didn't know what to say. He turned to Max. 'Brew us some coffee, then pop out for pain au raisin and pain au chocolat.'

'What? Why? She's not a client?'

Trevor pulled apart from Tina and removed his wallet from his jacket pocket. 'Here's some cash.' He handed Max a note. 'The prodigal has returned.'

'The what?'

'Go get the pastries. I'll make the coffee.'

Max snatched the money and Tina held the door open for him. He stomped out.

'You're his nemesis,' Trevor said with a big grin.

Tina closed the door. 'I'm surprised he's still here.'

'Do you know how hard it is to get rid of dead wood?'

She laughed. Trevor saw her face light up, but not like it used to. 'Come and sit down.' He gestured to a sitting area.

'Can we sit at your desk?'

'Yes. Of course. I'll grab you a seat.' He pulled over a chair on castors from another desk and Tina sat down. 'It's so good to see you, Tina. We've missed you. I heard about your husband. Terrible.'

'My parents' house will be for sale, soon. I'll make sure you get the business.'

'Are they moving? Downsizing?'

She told him in sparse words what had happened.

Silence.

Trevor looked at his former negotiator. At one time the world was at her feet, now it was crushing her. The door opened and Max sauntered in carrying a paper bag. 'Thank you Max. Get a couple of plates, make the coffee then take an early lunch – on me.'

'What's going on?' Max looked both pleased at the free lunch but annoyed at being ordered around.

'Tell you what, Max. Forget the coffee. Go now.'

Max examined the cash in his hand. 'Don't expect any change.' He threw the bag of pastries on Trevor's desk, pulled the door open and banged it shut behind him.

'Where is everyone?' Tina asked, looking around the agency.

'One is on maternity leave. One has a dental appointment. One is on holiday in Morocco. That leaves Max and me. I would get rid of him but he's been here too long and can be useful.' He swallowed and stood. 'Tina, I'm so sorry.'

She half-smiled and shrugged. 'It never rains but it pours?'

He picked up the bag of pastries. 'I'll make us some coffee.'

She followed him into the tiny kitchen where he put a pod in the Nespresso machine and a cup under the spout. Without thinking, she opened a cupboard and removed a couple of plates. 'How's the family?' she asked.

'Olivia kicked me out. I'm in rental accommodation above Merlin's hardware store on Hawksmead High Street.'

'Trevor, I remember that flat. It's a dump. There's mould on the walls and last time I looked it was infested with moths.'

'Yes it is a dump, but it's a cheap dump.'

'What happened?'

He put another pod in the machine. 'I made a stupid decision.'

'We all have history.'

They waited for the coffee to finish then Trevor placed both cups and plates on a tray together with a small jug of milk.

'I had access to a chunk of cash. A friend of mine who had made quite a bit out of property advised me to buy some cheap houses in Hull.' He carried the tray to his desk.

Tina picked up the bag of pastries and followed. 'Hull?'

'Kingston upon Hull.'

'Why there?'

'There was supposedly a lot of investment and regeneration. I stupidly listened to my friend. In the three years since I bought the houses they've halved in value. I can't even sell them. They're rented out to the local authority who use them as temporary housing. At least once a month there's a police raid – usually for drugs or to recover stolen goods.'

'But why did you and Olivia break up?'

'I used her inheritance to buy the houses. Bad decision.'

'She'll come round, I'm sure.'

'Tina. I mucked up my family and I mucked up my business. I should've made you a partner. If I had, you might not have left for London.' Immediately, he regretted his words. 'How can I help?' He placed a cup of coffee in front of her and slid across the milk jug. 'Is there anything I can do for you?'

Tina stood and wandered around the empty agency. 'I presume your online presence is better than your kerb appeal?'

Trevor forced a laugh. 'It's not bad. Max is in charge of that. With everything that's going on, I've not given it the attention I should. Pain au raisin or pain au chocolat?'

'Au raisin, thank you.'

'Come back.'

Tina looked momentarily confused.

Trevor pushed on. 'It's why you're here, isn't it?'

She slumped down on the wheeled chair. 'For a few minutes I wanted to wind back the clock.'

'To when you sold the old school boarding house?'

She smiled. 'That changed a lot of lives. At the moment I'm staying with Audrey and Malcolm Cadwallader. They've been really good to me.'

'They owe you a lot.'

She looked down at her hands.

'Do you have any plans?' he asked.

'My parents' funeral. Clearing the house. Selling it.'

'Don't you have a brother?'

She nodded. 'As soon as he can get away from work, he'll fly back to help with the funeral and stuff. He's married, now.'

'I thought he was gay.'

'He is. New Zealand was one of the first countries to allow gay weddings.'

Trevor took a bite of pain au chocolat followed by a sip of coffee. 'The school on the moor could do with your magic touch.'

'Has it not sold?'

'Who would buy it? The old monastery is Grade I, the land is designated National Park and the school buildings look like Dartmoor Prison... not a lot of charm. Although it's not all doom and gloom. We did manage to let it out to a charity that finds work for migrant labour. The rent is minimal but the trustees are happy as it covers a few costs. In an ideal world, they would like to be shot of it.'

'You could sell it to Disney and turn it into a medieval theme park.'

'You know, if it sold, I think some aspects of planning would be relaxed.'

Tina looked at her Swatch.

'Have you somewhere to be?' Trevor asked.

'I came here because I have nowhere to go apart from back to Malcolm's cottage.'

'You have friends, Tina. Many friends.'

'Friends I have neglected.'

'Nobody blames you for keeping vigil for Gary. And now with your parents... let your friends be your friends.'

'It's good to see you, Trevor.' She stood to leave.

'Commission only. You don't even need to come in, unless you want to.' He looked up at his former star negotiator. 'I need your help, Tina.'

'I can't come back.'

'No. I understand. How about just this one special project? Use your skills to find a buyer.'

'But it's let.'

'One month's notice. No problem.'

'Commission?'

'Ten percent.'

'Wow.'

'I can still negotiate.'

'What will I get?'

'I should've made you a partner years ago. Fifty-fifty. Five per cent.'

'Where do I begin?'

'I have no idea.'

'I'm not a miracle worker.'

'Yes you are. Get in your car. Go see the place and spin your gold.'

'Keys?'

'All out. You'll have to knock.'

13

Industrial potato picking is usually undertaken by two machines that harvest the crop in tandem. No such luxury for Gary. He squatted down in the mud and picked each tuber individually and then chucked it into an old plastic bucket. It was a warm, clear day out in the potato field and for a few moments he imagined being a free man, despite being chained hand and foot. The school was remote, set in a beautiful but forbidding landscape. His captors had two drones with cameras they used to survey the area for uninvited attention. He had to admit, it was a neat set up from which all manner of crimes were probably being committed, including the growing of marijuana, exploiting illegal migrants, and no doubt much more yet to be discovered.

One day, soon, bad weather would prevent the flying of drones and he would make his escape. But he had to be patient and choose his moment, carefully. He would not buy his freedom at Tina's expense.

Hawksmead High Street looked little changed from when Tina had last driven her pride and joy. Every bow-fronted shop window triggered memories of a time when she thought she was sophisticated, but now realised she'd been ignorant and naive.

She was a twenty-one-year-old estate agent when she had sold the old school boarding house at the top of Hawksmead High Street to Audrey. More than forty years apart in age, the two women had immediately clicked, pricking Tina's conscience for selling the gloomy house with a sad history to such a lovely and vibrant woman. But it was the history of the house that had brought Audrey and Malcolm together, and its later destruction by fire that introduced Tina to her policeman.

Over the following spring months and through much of the summer, Malcolm and friends had created a beautiful garden with a memorial stone engraved with the names of five boys who had attended Hawksmead College in the 1960s and who had all tragically died. On a glorious September afternoon in the memorial garden, Reverend William Longden had married Christina Louise Small to Gary Simon Burton. It was the happiest day of her life. Three years later, the October sun was shining but there was a deep ache in her heart.

She focused on the road and came to the humpback bridge spanning the River Hawk. Through tear-filled eyes she negotiated the stone-built bridge with its single-lane and felt her stomach flip as the VW Golf thumped down on the north side. She used the heel of her hand to try and clear her eyes but she was going too fast. Fortunately, the Old Military Road was clear of traffic and she got away with her erratic driving.

A rusting sign pointed to the right and she turned into the school's mile-long drive. Bordered by hawthorn hedges and deep ditches, the winding road could be hazardous, especially in the wet at night, but it invited Tina to open up her carburettor and stretch the rubber on her tyres. In a little over a minute, she rounded a final bend and swept onto the oval apron in front of the former boarding school. She skidded to a halt on the loose gravel, turned off her engine, released her seatbelt and climbed out. Several vehicles were parked near the main entrance towards one end of the long building; big old cars whose glory days were far behind, and classic white tradesmen's vans, rust showing through muddy wheel arches.

Ivy grew unchecked up the mighty Victorian facade, blocking out most of the windows. To the far left were the ruins of an old monastery, torn down by King Henry VIII in the mid sixteenth century. Across the fields to the right, were ramshackle barns and sheds. Much work needed to be done if she had any hope of finding a buyer. A tiny buzz attracted her attention, she looked up at the sky and spotted the small dot of a drone flying high overhead.

The crunch of large feet on gravel startled her but she stood

her ground as a tall man approached. In his hand was a con-
troller with a screen, two stubby aerials and two joysticks. He
stopped about ten feet from her.

'And who might you be?'

His few words told her he was from the Republic of Ireland,
endorsed by his dark wavy hair, deep blue eyes, and white
teeth that almost shone from his tanned face. He had to be
late thirties but his clothes were out of an old movie. He wore
battered suede boots, heavy cotton trousers that looked like
buckskin, a check shirt, floral waistcoat and an almost matching neckerchief.

'I'm a consultant for the estate agency selling this property,'
Tina said.

'Well, you're not doing a very good job. If it wasn't for us, this
place would be overrun with rats.'

'That's why I'm here, to see what needs to be done.'

'Forget it. There's no market for a place like this.'

She smiled as she flexed her selling muscles. 'There's always
a market if sold in the right way.'

'Look, sweetheart, we're helping people here. We're making
a bit of money so can pay more rent, if that's what it's all
about.' He moved closer to her, touching distance. 'We're here
to help people. Not just those seeking to make England their
new home, but the local community. Perhaps we could help
you, too?'

She felt a strange conflict inside her. The man was handsome, goddamned sexy, and was cocooning her with his silky
Irish lilt. It was intoxicating.

'Mr O'Hanlon?'

'Dermot. And who might you be?'

'Tina. Tina Small.' Why hadn't she used her married name?
She waited for him to offer his hand but he reached for a pocket
in his waistcoat and offered her his phone.

'Put your number in here, please.'

'Why?'

'Do it.'

She took his phone and thumbed in her number.

'Now call it,' he ordered.

It took a few seconds before they heard her phone ringing in the car.

'Next time, Tina…' He came right up to her so she could feel the warmth of his breath. '…make an appointment.'

She reached out her hand and gently pushed him away. 'Next time, I'll come with a team.'

'A team? A team of what?'

She handed back the phone and opened her car door. 'I'm serious about selling this place. But, before I can do that, it has to be spruced up.' She got in the car.

O'Hanlon held the top of the door. 'Look. I have people scraping around picking potatoes. Let me get them to clear the weeds and the ivy. As you say, spruce the place up and, if you're happy, you pay a fair price for their effort.'

She looked up at him and was infuriated by the hot feeling creeping up her chest and neck. 'If you do the job well, I'm sure the trustees would be happy to forego the rent for a week or two.'

'A month… at the very least.'

'Well let's see the result first. I must go.'

He continued to hold the door. 'I take it you're married, Tina?'

She was momentarily flustered and looked at the rings on her left hand. 'Yes. No. I'm not sure.'

'Perhaps we could discuss your marital status over a drink? What are you doing this evening?' His direct approach and un-blinking eyes fringed by dark lashes, rekindled her dormant desires. He pushed on. 'Do you know the Falcon pub?'

'Yes.'

'I'll be there at seven. It would be grand to see you.' He stepped away from the car and closed the door.

She felt him watching her through the side window as she clicked-in her seatbelt and started the engine. From the corner of her eye she saw him give a little wave. Heat burned her cheeks. She pushed the gear lever into first and released the clutch. The Golf lurched forward but was held by the handbrake. The engine stalled. She took a breath, restarted the engine and swiftly pulled away. As she swung around the large oval apron she sneaked a peek.

He waved again.

Gary looked up from his muddy furrow and caught a glimpse of a white car.

Another dealer picking up his stash. In broad daylight. When was somebody going to get suspicious?

In the pale blue sky, he saw a hawk circling above, its beautiful wings and wide tail perfectly designed for swooping to the ground and catching an unwary rabbit in its talons.

The black dot of a drone attracted his attention. It was also perfectly designed to survey the landscape through its high-definition camera lens. For the price of a few quid on Amazon, it was easy for his captors to keep watch.

Roll on winter. Roll on freezing fog.

14

Tina decided to take the scenic route back to Malcolm's cottage along the Old Military Road. She wouldn't go that way at night. Even in daylight the road carved a dangerously curved route through a beautiful but bleak rolling landscape with treacherous bogs, deep gorges, sharp-edged escarpments, and rapid water courses in a vast area where mobile phone coverage was patchy at best.

Dermot O'Hanlon's handsome, smiling face flashed before her eyes. Her friend, Audrey, had come to Hawksmead, newly widowed, and had found love in a truly unexpected way. Could the same happen to Tina? Or was it simply a sexual awakening after more than two years sleeping in a lonely bed?

Please forgive me, Gary.

She looked at the car clock and planned her afternoon.

Malcolm heard the front door open and smiled. He'd insisted on giving Tina a key, so she could come and go as she pleased. It was part of his strategy to help her settle in and feel at home rather than a guest.

'Is that you, Tina?'

'Yes. I thought I'd pop back for a while before going out again.'

'There's a little lunch if you're feeling peckish.'

'I am, thank you. I'll just wash my hands.'

Malcolm heard her enter the cloakroom off the hallway as his wife came down the stairs.

'Did you mention lunch?' Audrey asked, as she approached the kitchen. 'Not that I've earned it and we did have a very good breakfast.'

'It's only a few bits and pieces from the farmers' market,

aided and abetted by Waitrose.'

'Sounds delicious.'

'I'll be back in a minute.' Malcolm went into the hallway and took his time climbing the stairs.

Tina opened the cloakroom door and stood in the entrance to the kitchen.

'I see you've been reacquainted with your car,' Audrey said.

Tina smiled. 'Yes. I met a kindly policeman who knew Gary. The house is still sealed.'

'They have to be sure. It must've been horrible for you.'

Tina paused. 'I went to Harper Dennis.'

'I didn't expect that.'

'Nor I. The car took me there. I've been offered a job, or rather a project.'

'Are you sure that's a good idea?'

'I have to do something.'

'If you're worried about money, it's not a problem. We can help.'

Tina felt the resurgence of her tears. 'That is so kind. The Met is still paying Gary's salary, so I'm fine. I'm just not fine in my head. I have to do something or else I'll go mad.'

'Yes. You're right to keep busy. Malcolm often says that doing nothing is the fast track to dementia. Although, I quite enjoy doing nothing.'

Audrey removed a bottle of sparkling elderflower from the fridge and took three glasses out of a cupboard. 'It's just a light lunch before an afternoon snooze.' She carried the bottle and glasses to the dining table.

Tina heard Malcolm come down the stairs and smiled when he entered the kitchen. 'I've been to your old haunt,' she said.

He looked a bit puzzled. 'Not Paddy Power the bookie on Hawksmead High Street?'

She laughed. 'Almost. Well he is Irish. I drove up to the old school and met a guy who runs a charity helping migrants.'

'That'll be O'Hanlon.' Malcolm ushered Tina into the dining room.

'You know him?' she asked.

'We have met. His name is on the contract. I'm one of the school's trustees. When I was Mayor of Hawksmead they invited me onto the board.' He turned to the dining table. 'You sit there, Tina, facing the garden.'

She pulled out her chair and admired the lovely spread. 'A light lunch?'

'What were you doing up at the old school?' Audrey asked as she sat down.

'I've been tasked with finding a buyer.'

'For the school?'

'I'm delighted,' Malcolm interjected. 'Once it's sold, it will free up cash to provide a myriad of activities for young people. At the moment, it's of no use to anyone.'

'Apart from helping migrants.'

Malcolm looked intently at Tina. 'What do you make of O'Hanlon?'

'He's clearly a bit of a rogue but seems okay.'

'I hope you're right. I was against him taking over the old school building. I felt, and still do, that he's up to no good, and that getting him and his travelling companions out could be a problem. But, my fellow trustees were keen to take any money going, so I was out-voted.'

'I'll let you know more after my meeting tonight,' Tina said.

Malcolm exchanged a glance with Audrey seated at the end of the table.

'It's just a drink,' she explained, emphatically.

'You *should* go out,' Audrey said placing her napkin on her lap. 'Just take care.'

'Don't worry. I learned my lesson after the Russian.' She thought back to another encounter four years ago with a crooked property developer whose sculpted features and rough charm had more than turned her head.

'Yes, he was also a bit of a rogue,' Audrey responded, 'but very handsome.'

Malcolm cleared his throat. 'Why do women always go for bad boys?'

'Because, Malcolm,' Audrey said, 'I find you impossible to resist!'

He burst out laughing.

Tina smiled. 'I promise it won't happen again.'

15

Magdalena Jablonski was an opportunist. She was barely out of her teens when Britain opened its doors to new members of the European Union. She was tall, handsome, athletic, and used her physical might to good effect as a professional cleaner, eventually running her own company, specialising in end of tenancy cleans for lettings agencies, including Harper Dennis.

She had decided not to live in London and chose the town of Undermere as it was big enough to find work but not so big that she would feel like an ant. Almost fifteen years later, she had married a fellow Pole but divorced him within a year for sleeping with Paulina, her prettiest cleaner. It was the jolt she had needed. She sold her cleaning business and used the money to train as a beautician. It didn't take long before she was visiting homes providing manicures and pedicures, facials, make-up tips, eyebrow threading, and all forms of waxing.

'I am aesthetician,' she would say. 'I go where hairs should fear to grow.' Her big problem had been managing all her clients. Her solution was to open a salon and train staff the way she had trained her cleaners. A newsagents had recently closed in Hawksmead High Street and although the rent was quite high, compounded by rates, she felt that a salon was the only way to make real money. But what to call it? She spoke to her English clients but none of their ideas worked for her.

'I think I have name for salon,' she said to Maureen, a woman in the autumn of her life who was always perfectly groomed and liked everything just so.

'I hope it's not one of those dreadful puns that hairdressers love so much like Curl-up and Dye.'

'No pun. Straight to point. Can you guess?' She guided Maureen's hand under a curved LED lamp to harden the nail gel.

'Let me see. File Away?'

'File Away? No. It should be File *Here* not File *Away*.'

Maureen laughed. 'Let's try again. House of Nails?'

'You make me sound like hardware store.'

'It's not just nails, is it?'

'I give total package, but not cut hair on head.'

'Oh, this is a good pun.' Maureen looked very excited.

'You said no puns.'

'Ignore what I said. This is so good… Mag Wax.'

'Mag Wax?' Magdalena was totally perplexed. 'What pun is that?'

'Mag Wax as in Mad Max! You know, the 1980s film with Mel Gibson.'

'I not heard of such thing. Customer think I crazy, mad woman. No I have name. Change hand.'

'*Change hand*? That's terrible.'

'Put left hand under lamp.'

Maureen laughed and changed hands. 'Tell me. What's it going to be?'

'Wax Polish.'

Maureen burst out laughing. 'That's the best pun yet.'

'No pun. I wax and I Polish.' Magdalena watched Maureen as she tried to contain her giggles.

Without fail, every time Magdalena said *Wax Polish* her clients fell about laughing but all thought the name, brilliant.

'Why it funny? Why you laugh?' But what did please her was that every client promised to visit her salon.

A new business is always a risk but Magdalena had thought it through and was confident that the salon would be a success. She wanted to still supply a personal service, but she knew she couldn't handle all the work on her own. She'd heard that her ex-husband and Paulina had broken up and so she contacted the young woman.

They spoke in Polish and it was to the point. 'You finish with husband?'

'He no good,' Paulina retorted. 'Why you marry him?'

'He ask me. Big mistake. You come back. Work for me.'

'I am happy in job.'

'Nobody is happy as cleaner. Only boss happy. I train you to be beautician. Plenty money.'

A few doors down from the salon was the office for The Hawksmead Chronicle. The bell pinged when Magdalena entered and she was met by a tall man, late fifties, with sandy greying hair and a welcoming smile revealing crossed front teeth. 'You are the famous Magdalena,' he said.

Magdalena was not usually lost for words but this charming man had taken the wind out of her sails. 'Yes. Are you psychic?'

He held out his hand. 'Andy Blake. My daughter-in-law told me she's delighted you're opening a beauty salon in Hawksmead. It saves her driving to Undermere. With three children, nothing's easy.'

She shook his hand. 'Thank you. I have opening in two weeks. I want to put in advertisement.'

'There'll be no charge if you agree to my son, Tony, taking photographs of the event. Perhaps he could also write a feature story about you, your history and your hopes for the future?'

'He is good photographer. I see his photos.' She held out her hand. 'We have deal.'

Andy shook her hand again. 'How about an Ad that the reader can cut out to get a discount on treatment, say for a month after opening? Just to get you going.'

A tall, gangly young man entered the office from the street. Over his shoulder was a large bag Magdalena knew contained his photographic equipment.

'Hi Dad.'

'Tony, I would like you to meet Magdalena, she owns the new beauty salon up the road.'

'Magdalena!' Tony's face broke into a big smile. 'How wonderful to see you. It's been way too long.'

'Not since Tina's wedding, I think.'

'Eden is thrilled you're opening a salon in Hawksmead.'

'I should have called her. Given home visit.'

'In truth, she likes to go out and get her beauty treatments, to have a rest away from the little ones.'

'Tony.'

Andy's son turned to his father.

'Magdalena's agreed to our coverage of her grand opening.'

'Brilliant!' Tony smiled at Magdalena. 'I'm sure Wax Polish is going to be a big success.'

'Thank you. It's Wax *Polish*.'

'That's what I said!'

'It's his northern accent,' Andy laughed.

16

Magdalena had enjoyed a busy morning that had gone through lunch into mid afternoon. Paulina had worked for eight hours straight so the young assistant had left for home when Magdalena heard the bell tinkle above the door. She looked up from her work station and her mouth fell open. She leapt to her feet. The young woman standing by the open door had excellent posture, and blonde hair that shone with conditioner. But her clothes looked a size too big for a frame that was short of her famed, natural curves. More than anything, her eyes lacked their former spirit.

'Tina!'

The young woman looked directly at Magdalena and her smile lit up her face, the way Magdalena remembered when she had first started to clean for Harper Dennis.

'Hello Mags.'

A great wave of emotion washed over Magdalena. She knew Tina had lost her husband and the news that her parents had died in tragic circumstances had spread throughout the little town. Without another word, she walked over to Tina and wrapped her arms around her, feeling her bones as they hugged. 'We have missed you so much.' She cupped Tina's chin in her large hands and kissed each cheek twice.

'It is wonderful to see you, Mags.'

'I won't ask how you are. I imagine.' She released Tina's face. 'Would you like tea or something stronger? I still have drink from grand opening.'

'I wish I hadn't waited so long to come home.'

'You had to wait. You had to be sure he no come back.'

'I'll never be sure.' Tina walked into the salon and Magdalena shut the door.

'No. That is truth. But Gary would not want you to waste precious life.'

'Wow, Mags, I cannot believe this was the old newsagent. Look at it.' She continued in a deliberately seductive sales voice. 'Bright yet soft lighting, delicate decor with floating shelves displaying gorgeous-looking products, vibrantly coloured abstract art, all-white workstations, easy-clean padded chairs, a sofa and coffee table in the waiting area, and a chevron-patterned tiled floor that is pure drama.'

Magdalena laughed. 'I didn't know it was so good 'til you tell me!'

Tina gripped her arms. 'Mags, it's fantastic. You've got everything here. I'm so impressed.'

'I'm now impressed with self, too.'

They both laughed.

'You want treatment?' Magdalena looked Tina up and down. 'What you really need is good meal. You are too thin, my darling.'

'I don't think I can put on weight between now and seven this evening. I have a date.'

Magdalena felt a twinge of disappointment. 'A date?'

'Well, sort of. He's Irish. He runs a charity helping migrants. They're based up at the old school.'

Magdalena took Tina's hands in hers. 'Be careful, my sweet. They are travelling people. I don't trust them.'

'It's just a drink. I managed to get my hair shaped but I am worried about the rest of me.'

'I give facial, do make-up. You look like movie star.'

Tina laughed. 'If only. But I would love to have my legs waxed. I have neglected my personal grooming.'

'You blondes don't know what hair is.'

'I want to feel good. He won't know, of course, but I will.'

Magdalena put the closed sign up and locked the door.

'You mustn't turn away customers,' Tina said.

'End of day. No customers. Come into my house of wax.' She guided Tina to a secluded section of the salon and pulled a curtain around a padded treatment table, with a headrest at one end and a roll of paper at the base 'You like music? Lady Gaga?'

'I love her.'

Magdalena fiddled with her phone and Lady Gaga's distinctive voice filled the air through white Sonos speakers. She placed the phone on a white plastic treatment station with sections and shelves for wooden spatulas, talcum powder, pots of wax, assorted creams and lotions, and a wax heater.

'Take off trouser and lie down. Have you had wax before?'

'A few times. But never with Lady Gaga for company.' Tina unlaced her trainers and peeled off her jeans. She draped them over a chair.

Magadalena pulled the paper from the roll over the entire length of the table and smoothed it flat. 'Hop on.' She slipped on a pair of ultra thin silicone gloves whilst Tina made herself comfortable. 'You, lucky. I strip off hairs in next to no time.' She ran her hands up Tina's legs. 'Bikini?'

'I was thinking of having the Full Monty.'

'What's that?'

'You know… smooth all over.'

'It's very fashionable. Take brief off.'

Tina rolled down her briefs and Magdalena placed them on the chair. She felt her mouth go dry and didn't trust herself to speak. From the moment they first met at Harper Dennis, she had fallen for Tina, who was eighteen and just out of school at the time, but did her best to always hide it.

'You've gone very quiet,' Tina said.

Magdalena looked into her eyes and swallowed. 'Would you like legs or bun first?'

Tina laughed. 'Bun! That's a new one on me.'

'If I do privates first, you have longer recovery time before drink with gypsy.'

'I think *traveller* is what they prefer.'

'Yes. You right. I no like Polack so I understand. Right. Let's get going. The wax is warm not hot and I will quickly strip your bun bare, my pretty. First I sprinkle powder to absorb body lotion.'

Magdalena worked fast to make the process as comfortable as possible. She used a wooden spatula to paste on narrow strips of thick green wax, before ripping each one off. As soon as she did, she pressed her free hand against the tender bare skin to ease the painful shock.

'Usually, it takes three times as long to clear foliage but God kind to you.'

Tina did not respond.

Magdalena looked up from her task and saw a tear trickle from the corner of her eye.

'I don't think God's been that kind to me,' Tina said, in little more than a whisper.

Magdalena was angry with herself. 'No. He has not.' She reached for a tub of cream that was ultra expensive and saved for special clients. 'This will wipe away pain of wax.' She unscrewed the lid and felt overwhelming desire for the exceptionally pretty but vulnerable young woman lying on the couch. 'It's a bit cool,' she said as she scooped up a wad of cream and smoothed it over Tina's pink skin in gentle, circling motions.

'That feels nice.'

Magdalena glanced at Tina's face and saw that her eyes were closed. 'You have beautiful shape.'

'Shame I can't show it off!'

'Shame I can't put photo in window like barber shop.'

Tina burst out laughing.

Magdalena continued to work the cream with her fingertips.

'Mmm, that feels really good. You have a magic touch. No wonder your clients love you.'

Magdalena pulled her hand away as her eyes filled. 'Tina, I am not good person.'

'What do you mean?' She sat up on her elbows.

Magdalena took a deep breath. 'I like you wrong way. I always have. I so sorry.' Tears coursed down her cheeks.

'I don't understand. You're married. Were married.'

'Yes. I Catholic. My thoughts are a sin. I never confess to priest. Please don't hate me.'

Tina lay back down on the padded table. 'Mags... finish what you started. Legs please.'

Later, they shared the white faux-leather sofa in the waiting area as they worked their way through a bottle of Sauvignon Blanc. Magdalena was back to her old self, the self she projected when Tina was starting out as an estate agent.

'My husband seduced Paulina who worked for me in cleaning company. I break with him 'cause I like *her* …and I jealous. She now works here, as beautician.' Her eyes sparkled as a bright smile lit up her face.

'Has she had the wax treatment?'

Magdalena choked on her wine and some splashed on the sofa.

17

It was gone seven in the evening when Tina left Wax Polish and headed down to The Falcon. She felt good and slightly shocked by how much she had enjoyed the delicate touch of Magdalena's fingers.

She pulled open the door to The Falcon and walked up to the bar. It was a traditional, old-style pub with dark wood tables and chairs, padded benches in wood-panelled booths, and rosewood-framed black and white photographs of school plays, cricket matches, fetes and picnics.

'Hello Ted.'

The once-handsome barman, now stout and florid but with a massive smile of welcome looked at her through the row of metal tankards hanging above the darkly-stained counter. 'Good grief. Heather!' he boomed. 'Kill the fatted calf.'

A petite, pretty, blonde popped up from behind the bar. 'I wouldn't call you a calf, Ted, more of an old bull.'

'Look who's here.'

Heather stared at Tina open-mouthed. 'Ted. Gin, tonic, zest of lemon. I'll make the pork sandwiches. She looks half-starved.'

'May I have a hug first?' Tina asked.

Ted leaned across the bar and gave Tina an all embracing hug.

Heather opened the bar door and came into the public area to greet her. 'We're so happy to see you… and so sorry.'

'I thought I'd be forgotten.' She gave Heather a hug.

'Never. Never my darling.'

'I wanted to come home. But I couldn't face returning without Gary.'

'There's no news?'

Tina shook her head.

'Take a seat. Ted'll bring you your drink and I'll be back in a few mins.'

'Hello.' The voice had an enticing come-hither tone.

Tina looked behind her into smiling Irish eyes. All her dark and depressing thoughts evaporated.

'My name's Dermot,' he continued in his gorgeous accent. 'In case you had forgotten.'

'I hadn't forgotten.' She held out her hand.

His smile cocooned her in a teenage world of fantasy. 'These two lovely people got a hug.' He indicated Heather and Ted with his eyes.

'They've more than earned it.' She pulled her hand back but kept out of hugging range.

'I have a booth,' he said. 'Would you care to join me?'

Heather lightly touched Tina's arm. 'I'll bring your food over.'

'Food? Whatever you're making, could it be for two?' Dermot asked.

'Of course.'

Tina felt his hand gently rest on her upper arm as he guided her to a booth where there was a tall glass of black liquid. She slid onto a padded bench seat and he sat opposite her.

'I love these old pubs,' he said. 'Full of character. Reminds me of a nice little establishment in Mullingar.'

'Is that where you're from?'

'From there and everywhere. Travellers see the whole world as their home.'

'Well you can keep your thieving hands out of mine!' The voice was rough, intoxicated.

Tina and Dermot looked up at the red, bloated face of a man in his early seventies.

'I don't believe we've been introduced,' Dermot said, holding out his hand.

The man ignored the peace offering and looked down at Tina. 'Watch your step, girlie. He'll have those rings off your fingers to give to one of his gypsy tarts.' He laughed and took a swig from his tankard.

Tina glanced down at her wedding and engagement rings.

'Listen, old man,' Dermot said. 'You don't know me and I don't know you. So, be off.'

'Ten years ago your type broke into my home, but I got him with my old school cricket bat. I knocked him for six.'

Tina saw Dermot's face, flush. 'We've mended our ways since then.'

'Vincent,' called Ted from the bar. 'Leave the young couple alone.'

'Couple... I like the sound of that.' Dermot turned to Ted standing with his hands planted on the counter top. 'Another drink for my friend, kind sir.' He reached into a pocket and pulled out a wad of well-handled notes. He peeled one off. 'This should cover it.'

Vincent snatched the cash. 'It cost a lot more than that to fix my window.' He looked down at Tina. 'Gary forgotten, already?' He turned his back and meandered to the bar.

Dermot looked at Tina. 'I take it, Gary's your husband?'

She felt a large lump of guilt in her gut. 'Yes.'

'What time would he be expecting you back?'

She was pleased to see his disappointment. 'I'm...' She hesitated saying the words. 'I'm a widow.'

Relief, even joy swept over his handsome face. 'I'm sorry to hear that, and for one so young.'

Ted placed a gin and tonic on the table in front of Tina. 'My apologies for Vincent,' he said to Dermot. 'He's a troubled man. His head says one thing and his heart says another.'

Dermot watched Ted return to the bar then picked up his tall glass and looked into her eyes. 'To *your* good health.'

'I must go.' She slid across the booth.

Dermot put down his glass and reached for her wrist. 'Don't go, my darlin'. How does it help Gary for you to go now?'

The touch of his hand ignited a fizz, she knew would be hard to ignore, especially if it grew stronger. 'It's not just Gary. My parents died a few days ago. I should be wearing black, lighting candles, praying, wailing.'

'Jesus! I had no idea you were Roman Catholic.'

'Oh I'm not. But I *should* be doing all those things. Shouldn't I?'

'They will come later. Right now you're in shock. It's devastating what's happened to you.'

Heather placed two tempting plates of pork and apple sandwiches in front of them. 'There's napkins over there.' She indicated a paper napkin dispenser on the table.

Tina smiled. 'Thank you, Heather.'

The older woman rested her hand gently on Tina's shoulder. 'It's so lovely to see you.' She turned away and hurried back to the kitchen.

'They like you here,' Dermot said, picking up a sandwich quarter.

Tina relaxed. 'What is that dark brew? Guinness?'

'Guinness without a head? No, it's Cola. Guinness doesn't travel well to England.'

'I've never drunk Guinness.'

'It's a hard drink to like but an even harder drink to give up.' He bit into his sandwich.

She mirrored him and picked up a sandwich quarter.

'What's your story, Tina?' His Adam's apple bobbed as he swallowed. 'Putting aside the obvious, why are you the belle of the ball?'

She put down her sandwich and took a sip of her gin and tonic, intoxicated by his blue eyes which she could now see had flecks of green.

'Did something happen?' Dermot pressed. 'I think so. It's not just your natural charm that has made you so popular with these folks.'

She took another sip of her drink. 'Four years ago, Audrey, the woman I'm staying with, came to Hawksmead to find out what happened to her little brother in the 1960s. I had sold her the school boarding house which used to stand at the top of the High Street. It's now a memorial garden in memory of her brother, Robert, and his best friend, my Uncle Mark – both died in tragic accidents. Ted, the landlord, knew her brother as they had acted in the same school play along with our drunken friend, Vincent, who had fallen in love with Robert.'

'In love?'

'Vincent played Cyrano de Bergerac and Audrey's brother was Roxane.'

'I can see how the wires could get crossed.'

'There's a cast photo from the play over there.' She indicated a clutch of old framed photos hanging on a far wall. 'Anyway, you can see how we're all linked.'

'There's more than that,' he pushed.

She sipped her drink and fought to suppress her awakened desire. 'Audrey's house caught fire and she only just managed to escape. I drove her to hospital. It's how I met my husband. He was in the patrol car chasing me.'

She saw Dermot take a deep breath as he leaned back away from her. 'Your husband was a policeman?'

'Yes. Anyway, the remains of the boarding house were removed and Audrey's husband created a beautiful memorial garden to honour the memory of Audrey's brother, my Uncle Mark, and three other boys who died whilst attending the school. It's where Gary and I were married.'

Dermot picked up his glass and took a long pull of cola. He placed the glass gently on the old, stained table. 'I'm beginning to get a sense as to why you are held in such high esteem.'

She laughed. 'I don't know about that!'

'To be serious. What family do you have, Tina?'

'When the coroner releases my parents' bodies and we can lay them to rest, my brother will fly back.' She felt a tear trickle down her cheek and roughly swiped it away. 'He lives in New Zealand with his husband.'

'Husband? What a modern world it is.'

'Not everywhere.'

'True. In my community, certain things are acceptable and certain things are not.'

'Tell me about your community.'

'Honour. Code. Secrecy. They are what we live by. It protects us from outsiders.'

'People like me?'

'The police, the authorities, those who would hurt us.' A pint of Guinness was slopped down in front of him.

'Drink your poison then get out.'

'Please Vincent.' Tina touched the elderly man's hand and he immediately softened.

'You mean much to me, Tina,' Vincent slurred. 'I didn't know your Uncle Mark but I knew Roxane, Audrey's little brother.' He looked at Dermot. 'Have a care with this gentleman. "Traveller" is a catch-all phrase for tax dodger, sponger, fly-tipper, confidence trickster, burglar, and all-round nuisance.'

Dermot stiffened as Vincent lurched away.

'Thank you for not retaliating,' she said. 'He's led a sad life.'

'I couldn't argue with the guy. Travellers are all those things... and more.'

'More?'

'He forgot to mention loyalty and big loving hearts. I hope I can prove that to you in the coming weeks.'

She bit into her sandwich as the fizz got stronger.

18

Magdalena was overwhelmed with guilt and kept crying as she prepared her salon for the following morning's rush, ensuring that all implements were in their correct place and all surfaces clean. Her final job before going upstairs to her little flat was to mop the floor. A clean floor was a must in her eyes and often she would ask Paulina to give it another mop during quiet periods.

Her business really was booming. Customers were prepared to give up buying magazines and eating out, but they regarded personal grooming as a necessity, and word-of-mouth was bringing in new clients every week.

Why did I not have control of self? Why am I not normal?

She trudged upstairs to her flat and tried to answer her question. She had waxed so many legs and given some beautiful women the *Full Monty* but had never succumbed to touch anyone inappropriately. Was she really a lesbian? Did she really like women more than men?

She removed a bottle of white wine from the fridge and broke her own golden rule by drinking alone. Two easily-acquired habits affect women's skin – smoking and drinking. Many Poles smoked but Magdalena had resisted. She was big-boned with full breasts and a curvy figure so eating the right food was essential. And she was determined not to put on the kilos her dear mother had done, before a botched operation to clear a blood vessel had triggered a massive and fatal stroke.

She took a plate with smoked mackerel, tomatoes, cucumber, grated carrot and lettuce to her small pine dining table and considered turning on the television. Her thoughts were a complete jumble. She was Roman Catholic and sex outside marriage was a sin. Sex with a woman was inexcusable.

She had to get a grip on her emotions.

Was she straight or was she gay? She had been married and had enjoyed sleeping with her husband but she had thoughts about women that were not normal, as she put it. When she first met Tina, she had fought hard to quell the feelings she had for the young estate agent. Tina was blonde with a heart-shaped face, a straight nose and a generous mouth. Neither too tall nor too short, she had the kind of body that wore clothes to perfection. More than that, unlike many British girls who stomped, Tina walked with a natural grace that was a joy to watch. Paulina, her assistant, was similar in many ways to Tina although she had the annoying habit of regularly going outside for a smoke. When her husband walked out on Magdalena and started a relationship with Paulina, the jealousy she felt she knew was the wrong way round.

What was she? Google told her she may be bicurious. Or gynesexual – attracted to femininity. And yet, she wasn't turned on by men dressed in women's clothes. Yes, she was happy to go to a drag night at the Hope and Anchor pub in Undermere, but the men she had slept with, and there were only a few, had been, as far as she knew, happily straight. Why couldn't she be happily straight? She'd managed to keep a lid on her desires until Tina walked into her salon. Now, all she could think about was kissing every inch of her body.

That was the truth.

She could sleep with a man and enjoy making love but the person she wanted to share her bed, share her world, share her life with was Tina.

Magdalena took a slug of wine and laughed. 'Well, that ain't gonna happen!' She spoke in English as she thought about her-self as a young girl, who knew barely a word of English when she left Poland, so long ago.

Her phone buzzed. The clock told her it was nearly midnight. She swiped the screen and saw that it was a text from Tina.

I'm too drunk to drive to Audrey's cottage. May I stay with you?

Magdalena's heart went thump. The feeling that rippled

through her body would dictate her actions. She was out of control. Her hands shook as her thumbs moved quickly over the screen.

Of course, my sweet. Coming down.

She put her untouched plate of food in the fridge, grabbed her keys and hurried down the stairs to the salon flicking on lights as she went. She could see Tina's outline through the semi-opaque glass door. Consumed with excitement, she inserted a key in the lock and pulled it open.

'Come in. Come in.'

Tina entered the salon and Magdalena relocked the door. 'Come up to the flat and tell me how you got on.'

'It's late. I feel bad. I just need your sofa for a few hours.'

'You shall sleep in my bed and I will sleep on bed of nails to atone for my sins.'

Tina laughed and Magdalena followed her up the stairs into her flat.

'Wow. It's lovely, Mags. A real home. Not like I imagined at all. The decor is really pretty. I love it.'

'Wine or coffee?'

'Wine. I'm buzzing enough, already.'

Magdalena poured Tina a glass of wine and placed it on a coffee table in front of a two-seater sofa. She reached for her own glass on the dining table and managed to splash some of the wine. 'Look at me. I'm too excited to hear.' She grabbed a tea towel from the small kitchen, wiped the base of the glass and stared at Tina. 'To you, my sweet.'

Tina smiled and raised her glass. 'To the success of Wax Polish.'

'Sit down.' Magdalena indicated the sofa and sat down beside her. 'I can see you're all fired up. Tell all.'

'When I first met Gary, I wasn't completely bowled over until we met again for a drink and I saw the man not the uniform. This morning, when I first met Dermot, I was instantly attracted to him but wary of my reaction. This evening, when we met again, I felt the same churn in my gut I'd felt for Gary on our first date. Mags, he is so attractive; I can't even begin to describe how much he lights my fire.'

'He's a gypsy. A traveller.'

'I think that's part of it, but he's also incredibly handsome. Not in an obvious way but his soul seems to penetrate right through to my heart. The more we talked, the more I wanted to give my whole being to him. If he'd taken me round to the back alley, I would've happily gone.'

'But you resisted?'

'Only just. More than two years without sex has taken its toll.'

'What's next? Do you have any plans to see him again?'

'I said I'd be up at the old school tomorrow to have a proper look around. I need good photos so that I can create a decent prospectus.'

'And Gary?' It was cruel of her to mention him but her inner voice had lost control.

'He's gone, Mags. He's gone. I have to accept that, now.'

19

Gary couldn't sleep. Snoring, like a baton in a relay race, reverberated around the long dormitory room to a constant background of whirring from the air-conditioning units. He envied the unfortunate Vietnamese men and teenage boys who tossed and turned on thin, lumpy mattresses. At least they had each other, and could speak in a language that their jailers did not understand. They kept their distance from him as his hand and ankle cuffs marked him out as doomed. He was on his own, that was for sure, and had to dig very deep just to get through each day.

The aged wooden floorboards were warmed by heat rising from the grow lamps above the marijuana forest in the room directly below. Although the air in the dormitory was kept fairly cool, the air-conditioning units did not remove the ever-pungent smell that overwhelmed the natural odours of the former boarding school.

He had tried all the usual tricks to win round individual captors but, he had to admit, the travellers were too well-bonded for him to drive a wedge between them. There had been moments when violence may have enabled him to escape, but the threat to Tina's safety, he knew, was not an idle one. In more than two years held captive travelling around the country and for over six months at the old school, the only friend he'd managed to make was Hector, a bullmastiff. For some reason, the ugly hound liked him.

Why couldn't he get to sleep? He was exhausted but his brain refused to take him into another world. He loved dreaming. Sometimes Tina would appear and the glow would help him through another interminable day.

He squeezed his eyes shut and forced himself to relax. Just as he was nodding-off, a hand shook his shoulder. He opened his eyes and looked up at an annoyingly handsome face.

'I have news,' Dermot said.

His lilting, friendly tone reminded Gary of a famous TV presenter, but he'd learned early on that Dermot's surface charm betrayed a ruthless determination.

'Your in-laws. They're dead.'

Gary felt a sick thud in his gut.

'Faulty boiler, it would appear.' Dermot sat down on the side of the bed. 'CO poisoning – the silent killer. Deeply tragic, but wholly avoidable. It just goes to show how important it is to fit a modern carbon monoxide alarm.'

If Gary had been in any doubt about the risk to Tina if he escaped, the deaths of her parents, whether accidental or not, shattered all hope that he could break free and not endanger the person he loved more than anyone in the world.

'You'll be relieved to know Tina's okay. She was in hospital for a short time but is tickety-boo, now.'

The white car he saw… it must've been Tina's. He squeezed his eyes shut and fought the tears that came every time he thought about his sweet and courageous wife.

'Come to bed, Mags.'

Magdalena looked up from her prostrate position on the small sofa to the exquisite young woman, too small for her borrowed pyjamas.

'Are you sure?'

'One hundred per cent. Tonight of all nights, I do not want to sleep alone.'

Magdalena threw off the blanket and carried it into the bedroom.

'Which side do you usually sleep?' Tina asked.

Magdalena smiled. 'The left.' She placed the blanket on a chair.

Tina slipped into bed and folded the duvet back.

Magdalena switched off the bedside light and got in beside

her. 'I have done soul searching,' she said, 'and I have concluded that I am bad person. Very bad.'

'You are a beautiful person, Mags.'

'But, could you love me?'

'I love you already.'

'But, you're not… gay.'

'That's true. I don't want to live with a woman but I enjoy the company of women.'

Magdalena couldn't see Tina but she luxuriated in her warmth. Moments later, she pushed her away. 'Forgive me, my darling. I cannot be this close to you. I lose control. I sleep on sofa.'

'No, stay. I'll put my pillow between us.'

Magdalena tried to sleep, to think of her accounts, anything that could distract her from the little beauty lying so near. She whispered, 'I love you, my sweet. We all do in Hawksmead. Good night. Sleep tight.'

'Shall I lay the table for three?' Malcolm asked as he pulled open the cutlery drawer.

Audrey checked her phone. 'Yes. Depending on traffic, she should be back in a few minutes.'

'I don't remember ever meeting Magdalena.'

'She was at Tina's wedding. She's tall, very striking, even beautiful. And has a lovely way with words.'

'I'm so pleased Tina had the sense not to drink and drive.' He selected an assortment of knives, forks and spoons, and closed the sideboard drawer.

'That girl has a lot of sense,' Audrey responded as she placed mats on the dining table. 'But with all she's going through, don't be surprised if she's a little unbalanced at times.'

Malcolm nodded. He placed the cutlery in a bunch on the table and entered the kitchen.

Audrey heard the front door open. 'Tina?' She hurried to the hallway via the sitting room.

'I can smell bacon.' Tina hung up her jacket and kicked off her shoes. 'I missed you.' She gave Audrey a kiss and a hug.

'We missed you, too,' Malcolm declared from the kitchen.

Audrey followed Tina through the sitting room into the dining room as Malcolm carried in a plate with scrambled eggs on toast, grilled mushrooms, tomatoes and crispy bacon.

'Ooh that looks tasty. I'll be back in a minute.' Tina scooted off to the cloakroom.

Malcolm put the plate on a tablemat and returned to the kitchen. Audrey trailed after him. 'Isn't it delightful sharing your cottage with Tina?'

He picked up two more plates, piled with food. 'It's not *my* cottage, it's our home. And yes it is.'

She followed him back into the dining room.

'She was there for us,' he said, 'when we really needed her.' He put the plates on the table and returned to the kitchen.

The cloakroom door opened and a few seconds later Audrey delighted in seeing Tina's smiling face. 'You look surprisingly fresh,' Audrey said as she pulled out a chair for their special friend.

'I had a good evening and it was a treat to catch up with Magdalena again. Her beauty salon's doing really well.'

'I was sorry to hear her marriage broke down.'

'She took revenge on her husband by hiring the woman he ran off with. Needless to say, that relationship is over.'

Malcolm placed a pot of fresh coffee on a mat. 'Please sit.'

'I feel you're both waiting on me,' Tina said with a smile as she and Audrey sat down. She looked at the plate of food. 'You're a master chef, Malcolm. I can't tell you enough how much it means to me to stay with you.'

He leaned across the table and put his hand on hers. 'Tina, sweetheart. We would love you to treat this as your home for as long as you want. Without your courage and devotion, Audrey and I would have nothing like the life we relish each day.'

'But come and go as you please,' Audrey added resting her fingers on Tina's other hand. 'We don't want you to feel beholden.'

Tina looked from Audrey to Malcolm. 'Thank you. I do have one request.'

Audrey squeezed her hand.

'Would you mind releasing my hands so that we can all eat this lovely breakfast?'

21

Rain hammered down on Tina's VW Golf as she drove at a leisurely pace along the winding Old Military Road. She loved the moors but on a dull, wet day, with its subdued green and brown hues, forbidding ridges, and flash floods, the bright lights of London's West End were much more appealing. She saw the sign warning drivers that they were approaching a school, now bent and rusting, and turned left into the long, twisting drive, lined with hawthorn hedges and rather menacing-looking ditches. She pressed the accelerator and in little more than a minute was at the former outward-bound boarding school. As she circled the large gravelled apron in front of the ivy-clad edifice, the rain came down so hard she decided to sit it out in the comfort of her Golf, which she parked away from a large white van, and an assortment of trucks and cars.

She picked up her phone from its hands-free rest and checked her messages. There was one text. *Sweetie. Thank you for being so kind. I am here for you whenever you need wax or bed for night. I am your friend.*

Tina thumbed in a brief reply. *You are much more than my friend.*

Another text came through. *xx.*

ROFF! ROFF!

She jumped and looked through the rain-soaked side window at a snarling, tan, bullmastiff with a scarred pelt over solid muscle.

She lowered her window an inch and rain spattered her face as she looked up into a void, shrouded by a dripping waterproof hood.

'I'm here to take some photos, once the rain stops.'

'There'll be no photos done here.' He had an accent similar to Dermot's, but without the lyricism or charm.

'Kind sir, would you call your lord and master and tell him Tina's here?'

'Tina?'

'Yes. The one who had supper with him last night. He knows I'm coming today.'

'Okay, follow me, but no photos.'

'Not today, I fear. Of course, it might brighten up. It often does in these parts. Have you got a firm grip of your dog?'

'He won't harm you, unless I tell him to.' He pulled open the door and the rain lashed her.

She reached for a golf umbrella and climbed out, closing the car door behind her. She pressed a button and the large umbrella sprung open, startling the dog, who barked and snarled.

The man pulled on the lead and the heavy chain cinched the dog's neck. 'Don't you know it's dangerous to open an umbrella in an electric storm?' Below his dripping hood, she could just discern his ravaged face, deeply lined and furrowed with a patchy beard and bushy brows.

'What's your name?' Tina asked, deciding to ignore his advice. She was not going to look like a drowned rat when she saw Dermot again.

'My name's Eamonn. Follow me.'

A bolt of lightning was swiftly proceeded by a deafening crash of thunder. The dog cowered at the man's feet and was rewarded by a heavy kick in its ribs. It yelped in pain and lurched away from Eamonn, who lost grip of the wet leather lead.

Tina looked at the safety of her car. Maybe it wasn't a good idea to come to such a remote place alone.

'*Get back here!*' The ferocity of the man's command made her jump. But he was directing his ire towards the dog who stood his ground, baring his teeth. The rain continued to bucket down. 'Get back here.' He had real menace in his voice and Tina hoped the dog would teach him a lesson.

FLASH! CRASH! CRACK! FLASH! Rolling boulders of thunder... The terrified dog sank down onto his haunches as Tina, reluctantly, closed the umbrella. Within seconds her hair was soaked. The man went to grab the trailing lead but the dog jumped away and snarled. There was another flash and an immediate deep rumble of thunder. The dog cowed. Eamonn bent down again to pick up the trailing lead but the dog leapt back and galloped away across the gravelled apron towards the field and distant farm buildings.

'Are you coming?' His voice matched the dog's growl.

Tina duly followed the man to an entrance on the far side of the former school. She was surprised to see at least half a dozen grubby-looking caravans parked in an over-grown sports field, with rugby posts standing at precarious angles. An old sheep pen was home to a variety of large dogs, all tethered and all looking miserable in the torrential rain.

Gary was soaked. His worn boots were clogged with mud as he trudged through the downpour, made harder by the ankle cuffs linked by the steel chain. He entered a barn, a former milking parlour, and settled down on some rotting hessian sacks. The rain pounded the rusting metal roof and he was surrounded by pools of water. From his low position he had a perfect view of the former school. Through the downpour he could just make out the ruins of the old abbey tacked to the side of the Victorian hellhole. In a store room he had found a prospectus detailing the school's history. *Isolated on the moor, the former workhouse was once a residence for impoverished families, orphans, cripples, lunatics, fallen women, unmarried mothers, and the decrepit. In 1901, following the death of Queen Victoria, the workhouse closed and the building was converted into a hospital for infectious diseases. In the 1920s, it was sold to a philanthropist who saw it as a perfect fit for a new style of educational establishment. It had everything an outward-bound school required: kitchens, chapel, bakery, laundry, plenty of farmland to supply vegetables and milk, and wards that were converted into a refectory, dormitories, and classrooms. Troubled boys were sent to the school to be straightened-out through rigorous work, discipline and physical activities.*

Gary could easily imagine what those activities entailed; he was experiencing them for himself. Five boys did not make it home to their parents and their tragic deaths were commemorated in a beautiful, walled garden created by Malcolm Cadwallader from land donated by Audrey. The memorial garden had been an emotional setting for Gary's marriage to Tina three years back. What a glorious day that had been. He would never have met her if she hadn't driven like a racing driver to Undermere hospital with a badly burned Audrey.

Police Constable Gary Burton, fresh from a hot-pursuit training course, had given chase with his blue lights flashing and his siren wailing. When he had finally caught up with her outside Accident & Emergency, he was spellbound by the determined and beautiful young woman.

Grrrrr...

'Come here, Hector.' Gary watched as the bedraggled dog approached. He looked as cold, wet and miserable as Gary. 'Come here, boy.' The scarred and brutalised beast came within arm's length and Gary gently stroked his muzzle and ears. The dog came closer and Gary hugged the beast to him. 'Good boy. I'll get you out of here. I promise. One day, soon.'

The rain continued to pound the muddy potato field. There would be no drones flying today. Perhaps he and Hector should just make a run for it? The nearest help was in Hawksmead. If they managed to get across the boggy moor they would come to the River Hawk. At this time of year, especially after all the rain, it would be in full flood and way too powerful to swim across, especially with hand and ankle cuffs. But, if they followed the bank downstream they would eventually reach the humpback bridge – and freedom.

'Tina's here.'

Gary woke from his reverie and looked up at Dermot, dripping wet in his rain-proof windcheater with hood. He considered begging the handsome bastard not to hurt her but behind his Irish charm, he doubted there was a shred of empathy.

'She has many friends in Hawksmead.' Gary tried to shore up his weakened voice. 'Hurt her and they will come for you.'

Deep from within Hector came the low rumble of a growl. Gary hugged the dog closer to him.

Dermot squatted. 'No harm will come to her, of that I give you my word. Just as long as you are a good little boy.'

Tina was so near to him he could almost smell the beautiful scent of her hair. But, if she saw Gary and realised he was alive, Dermot would have no choice but to keep her quiet, one way or another. 'Why is she here?'

'She wants to sell the school, but that's not going to happen.'

If anyone could find a buyer for the school, Tina could, but Gary was not about to tell that to Dermot.

'Stay in here,' Dermot commanded. 'I'll let you know when she's safely gone.'

'I'm soaked through and cold. I have a fever coming on.'

Dermot reached for Hector's lead and stood up. 'The school has its own chapel and mortuary. We'd give you a good Irish send-off.'

Gary watched Dermot battle the rain as he and Hector trudged back across the field towards the pen where other dogs were huddled.

22

'Tina me darlin'!'

She looked up from her cup of coffee at Dermot. She was seated on a stool at a long refectory table in a large, antiquated kitchen. Through grubby window panes she could see the vast expanse of rain-soaked farmland and, beyond, the moor with its brutal beauty.

'Where is everyone?' There was a slight tremor in her voice. Eamonn and his big dog had unnerved her. She felt vulnerable.

Dermot poured a mug of coffee and sat down at the end of the table, a few feet from her. 'Our main site is on common land south of Undermere. That's where the children and women are. As for the migrants, some are resting up in the dorm or playing cards in a day room, but most are out working on construction sites in Undermere or attending private jobs – decorating or gardening.'

'Gardening? In this weather?'

'They're tough. Just travelling to the UK in the pitch black of a refrigerated lorry is pretty bad. Some don't make it. A little rain is nothing to them. I know they miss the warmth of Southeast Asia, but they would rather be here where they can earn a lot more money, which they send home to support their loved ones. To them, Britain is a land of bounty, but they came here illegally, some were trafficked, so it's not as straightforward as they expected. Most of my time is taken up fighting Government deportation orders.'

Tina nodded. It was funny seeing Dermot the day after their intimate chat the night before. She felt his rough hand on hers. 'Not good weather for photos, I fear.'

'I hoped it would clear, but it looks set in.'

'Another day.' He took a slurp of his coffee.

'I can still look around and see what's best to shoot.'

'And I'd be honoured to escort you. Some parts have been closed off by the trustees for being too dangerous, rotten floorboards and the like. Whoever buys this place will have to spend a fortune just to make it safe.'

'There are buyers out there. Not many, but I will find one. I'm sorry.'

'That's your job. But don't be too good at it. We like it here.' He smiled and she felt a surprising rush of heat.

Neon lights hummed into life revealing a long, dismal corridor, half wood panelled and half cracked and scarred yellowed plaster walls. The windows to the left were cloaked in ivy to the exterior and the doors to the right were all closed.

'This is a safe floor,' Dermot said. 'Although I've yet to explore it.'

Tina walked ahead of him along the corridor on cracked linoleum, and opened the first door. Weak daylight from windows at the back of the building exposed a traditional school science lab with aged wooden workbenches sporting an array of old equipment including microscopes, assorted glass bottles with rubber bungs, weighing scales, racks with test tubes, and Bunsen burners joined by rubber tubes to blue cylinders marked GAS.

They approached a schoolmaster's desk, standing on a raised plinth. Behind was a large blackboard with just discernible words written in chalk: *ARBEIT MACHT FREI.*

'Poor taste.' Dermot undid his neckerchief. 'About a million Jewish souls died in Auschwitz.' He used the cloth to rub away the words. 'And about twenty thousand Roma and Sinti. Gypsies.'

'It's probably just a schoolboy likening the college to a concentration camp. Not really understanding the insult. It would've been written long before you arrived.'

'I'm not surprised this place closed.' He stepped down from the plinth and came up close to her. 'It's like turning back the

351

clock.'

'I don't think they spent much time in classrooms. It was an outward-bound school. A regime of hard physical exercise. Sometimes, too hard.'

'Nothing much to photograph here.'

She heard a scraping sound above her. 'What was that?'

'Rats. As soon as we get rid of them they're back.'

She sighed. 'I think you're right. The interior isn't worth photographing. A developer will completely gut it, anyway. I'll focus on the exterior. I know I can get some great shots of the old abbey ruins.' She weaved her way past acid-stained workbenches to the rain-spattered windows on the far side of the classroom. Through a grimy pane she looked down on a muddy field and scattered barns, barely standing. Beyond was the vast expanse of moorland with its rolling hills, high ridges and scattered clumps of trees. 'I won't bother with the farm buildings as they're bound to be demolished. Most important of all is getting decent shots of this view. It must be even more amazing from the top floor. Yes, I think I can make it work for a buyer.' Her last few words were more to herself than to Dermot.

She looked round and saw that he was still standing near the desk. She smiled. Day or night, he looked good. 'Imagine this room,' she continued, 'converted into a hotel suite.' Her natural enthusiasm enriched her words as she turned back to the window. 'How wonderful it would be to wake up to this view. In summer, the setting sun must be beyond stunning.' She spotted a hunched figure emerging from the largest barn. 'There's a man out there getting soaked. Is he one of your migrants?'

Dermot came up behind her. 'No, he's one of my guys. Lazy bastard. The charity works damned hard to find employment for struggling migrants, and all my cousin can do is skive.'

Tina faced him and before she knew what she was doing, her hand was on his arm. 'Don't worry. It's not likely to be a quick sale and it could take another year before development begins.'

Dermot gently broke away as rain continued to hammer the window panes. 'I love this old school,' he said, 'surrounded by all this ancient moorland. It's uniquely beautiful. I don't want to see the potato field concreted over, or the bog turned into a housing estate with paved drives and box-like units.'

'They won't build houses on this land,' Tina said, standing close enough to feel the heat from his body. 'Maybe a golf course or two. Indoor tennis courts, a gym. Any construction would be in and around where there are buildings already.'

'I hope you're right.'

She looked up at Dermot and felt a ripple as their eyes connected. 'I would like to see the abbey ruins.' The husk in her voice brought a flush to her cheeks. She was sure Dermot had noticed. What was going on? She was in mourning.

'Why not come back when it's not raining? You'll get soaked out there.'

'I'm an estate agent. We go where others fear to tread.'

The entrance hall to the old school was enormous and dark. Its walls were part oak-panelled and part lath and plaster, deeply scuffed from decades of human traffic, as was the uneven stone floor. Dermot located a switch and old, stained lights flickered on.

'Follow me.' He led Tina down a long corridor to a door marked *Headmaster* in faded gold leaf. He pushed it open and reached for a switch. A neon strip, hanging in the centre, blinked on. 'This is my home.' He unhooked his still-wet windcheater from a freestanding coat and umbrella stand and slipped it on.

Tina looked around the study. To one side was a large oak desk and an old fashioned computer and monitor. Hung on a wall were black and white photographs of mountains and mountaineers from a bygone era, and lying scattered across the threadbare carpeted floor were yellowed newspapers and text books, and stained ordnance survey maps.

Discarded newspapers fluttered as she crossed the room to the window, where rain continued its assault. 'My uncle went to this school.'

'Your uncle? When was that?'

'In the 1960s. He didn't survive.' She looked through the blurred glass across a vegetable patch to dilapidated outbuildings.

'Oh, that's calamitous.' Dermot sounded sincere. 'What happened to him?' He came up behind her.

She glanced at him over her shoulder. 'Black ice on the humpback bridge leading to Hawksmead. He was riding his bike to school and a car, driven by a young schoolmaster, crushed him. Not the driver's fault.'

'I'm sorry to hear that.'

'That same term, two boys drowned in the river, also by the humpback bridge.'

'It seems that old stone bridge has a lot to answer for.'

She looked into his blue eyes, fringed by dark lashes and heavy brows. 'Do you believe in life after death?'

'That's a big question which deserves a considered answer.' He placed his hands at the tops of her arms. 'I've not known you long and you've suffered great personal loss. But, could you find it in your heart to join me for a late lunch? It's such a miserable day. I feel we need cheering up.'

Sheltering from the persistent rain under an old bicycle shelter, Gary kept himself concealed as he watched two figures cross the apron, sharing a golfing umbrella. He was sure it was Tina with Dermot but was still shocked when he saw Dermot get in the front passenger seat of her VW Golf.

Jealousy was quickly replaced with joy. Surely this was his chance to escape? It could be hours before Dermot discovered he was gone. By then, Gary should have alerted his mates in Undermere police and ensured Dermot was arrested. Tina could be secreted away to a safe house until Stacy and her father, Frank, were in custody.

He looked up at the sky and was thrilled to see that the rain did not look like letting up anytime soon. His ankle cuffs linked by the toughened steel chain to handcuffs would slow him down, but at least they weren't the kind of heavy irons that slaves in the colonies were forced to wear.

Forked lightning cut through the blackened clouds, followed by an almighty crack and a growling rumble of thunder. By road the school was about two miles from the humpback bridge that traversed the River Hawk, but the risk of being seen by one of the travellers coming or going was considerable.

He hobbled through the pounding rain away from the old school across the gravelled apron. When he was a police patrol officer, he knew the roads all around Hawksmead and Undermere but had totally ignored the countryside. On a day like today, the vast expanse looked formidable. His vision blurred by rain, he still managed to make out the peat bogs and hillocks he knew hid deep gullies. In the distance he could just see the famous Ridgeway – a high hill with a twisting ridge he'd been meaning to traverse but had never quite got round to tackling. Luckily, the Ridgeway was to the southeast and his trajectory was southwest. But, without the sun to guide him, there was a risk of walking around in circles and eventually dying from hypothermia.

He hobbled on. Not quite running but going faster than a walk, despite the ankle cuffs. He was cold and very wet but he hoped the rain would continue, preventing search by the dreaded drone. Tina, his gorgeous wife, would spin her natural web of charm around the Irishman and Gary was confident that he had at least two to three hours before anyone would come looking for him.

'If you ever try to escape, Tina's last thoughts will be of you and how much you betrayed her.' Stacy's threat echoed around his head as he scrambled over a dry stone wall. His old boots were clogged with mud as he drove himself forward, seeking firm ground.

This was it. He had gone beyond the bounds of the former boarding school.

23

It felt odd but quite nice to have a handsome stranger sitting in the front passenger seat of her Golf. His clothes had an old worldly smell that charmed her. She drove especially carefully along the country road as the surface was awash with torrents of water that filled the deep ditches to each side.

She glanced at Dermot. 'At least there won't be a problem getting a table. People are tough around here but this rain is too much.'

'Climate change. It's like watching a train wreck in slow motion.'

'I have to be honest. For the last couple of years, the climate has not been at the top of my worries.' She eased the car around a sharp bend and pressed the accelerator as they began to climb a long hill.

'I get that. It's hard to worry about the environment when you're worried sick about someone you love.'

She glanced at Dermot with his strong nose balanced by an equally strong chin. 'What's your story, Dermot?'

'Traveller. There's not much more to tell.'

'Any children?'

'None that I know of.'

They crested the brow of the hill and were presented with a vast landscape of soft green and brown hues, with peaks and ridges shrouded in rain and mist. Tina didn't bother to indicate left as she swerved into the walled car park of the Rorty Crankle – deserted, save for two cars that probably belonged to the owners of the seventeenth-century coaching inn. She pulled on her handbrake and cut the engine. Rain continued to pound the car's roof.

'I thought it would let up,' Dermot said, 'but it looks set in.' He released her seat belt and then his own.

Tina looked through the blurred windscreen. 'When I was growing up, I took this beautiful space for granted. Walking on the moor was for tourists, not me. I see it differently now. My parents loved to come up here for Sunday lunch, then walk off the excess before driving home.'

'But not on a day like today. The colours look soft but I know the landscape is treacherous. You wouldn't get me out there.' He turned to her, and smiled. 'Ready to run the gauntlet?'

Dermot did his best to shield them both from the rain as they ran to the pub's main entrance. They burst through the double doors and laughed with relief as water puddles formed on the aged wooden floor.

A deep voice boomed from the bar. 'Cathy! Look who's here.' He was a tall man, with a grey mop of curly hair and a ruddy complexion. He came out from behind the bar and approached them with open arms. He engulfed Tina and hugged her into his solid girth. 'It is beyond wonderful to see you, my darling. We are so sorry. So very sorry.' He kissed her damp hair.

Tina looked up at the big man, raindrops on her shiny cheeks. 'It's wonderful to see you, too, Harry. I should've come home much sooner.'

'We are all so sorry. And now your dear parents...' That was too much for Tina, and Dermot stood back as she buried her face in Harry's chest. Her shoulders convulsed as she sobbed. Harry held her while Dermot watched and waited, wishing that she were in his arms. She looked so beautiful, so fragile. The policeman's wife had tapped an emotion deep within his heart. He wanted her; unfortunately, there was someone else – the daughter of an Essex crime lord. What kind of revenge would she wreak if she found out his true feelings for Tina?

He knew.

He knew Stacy Cottee all too well.

The rain was biting. Gary was bone cold. The spongy earth seemed to suck at his feet with every stride. He was exhausted.

The stark outline of the former workhouse taunted him.

Was there no escape?

He forced himself to keep going, but two years of captivity had flayed the fat from his bones. The desire to crawl into a hole was almost overwhelming.

He had already lost one boot, stuck in the cloying mud. It didn't matter. His whole frame was soaked, his white skin tinged blue.

Keep going. Keep going.

Distant barking carried on the north-easterly wind.

He kept pushing.

More barking. Louder. Fiercer. This time he turned to look. There were at least five men, each holding back a dog, no more than one hundred metres behind him.

He found a stone path and although he was able to get a better purchase, the sharp stones tore at the sole of his bare foot. He tried running with his booted foot on the path and the other foot on softer ground.

The barking was much closer now. What would the dogs do to him? Was he a man, or red raw meat? He hobbled over another small brow, lost his balance and rolled down a short bank. He clawed at the sodden earth as he fell into the swollen torrent of the River Hawk. The bubbling, fast-flowing, freezing water took him into its fatal embrace. Ahead was the hump-back bridge with its stone arches. He had no strength. No fight. At least the love of his life would have his body to kiss goodbye.

Harry handed menus to Tina and Dermot. 'Everything is on the house. This is my treat.'

'Thank you, Harry,' Tina said. 'It's so lovely to see you, and a feast as well, but I insist we pay.'

'Let me tell you, my dear. Those old lovebirds you brought together have more than filled my coffers every week, and my heart with their joy and laughter. As for your dear parents...' He sniffed and hurried away.

'That is beyond generous.' Dermot opened his menu. 'People really respond to you.'

'There's a lot of shared history.'

'It's more than that. It's something within you that touches their souls.'

She laughed. 'I cannot imagine what that is.'

'I feel it too.'

She looked into his eyes and felt again the fizz of an electrical charge. She had no control over it and it often came when not wanted. But, at that moment, sitting in the pub's comforting warmth, opposite a man who was powerfully attractive, she didn't mind.

Gary.

Everyone said he had to be dead. But short of a body how could she be sure?

'What are you thinking? I can see those pretty cogs, turning.'

She smiled and picked up her glass of sparkling cranberry juice. 'I was thinking about... you.'

'Me?'

'Yes. I was thinking about your life and wondering what your big dream may be.'

'My dream? My dream is... sitting in front of me.'

Her vessels opened and hot blood pulsed into her cheeks. It happened so quickly, she didn't have a chance to fight the blushing by contracting her buttocks, her usual technique.

'I didn't mean to embarrass you.'

She picked up her napkin and placed it on her lap, resisting the desire to cover her face. 'It's a while since a man complimented me that way.'

'Words are cheap but I mean it. I like you Tina.' He reached across the table and took her hand. She didn't resist.

Gary hugged the stone bridge as the gushing, icy water tried to suck him away. His fingers were beyond numb. He had nothing left to give. He was shattered. His eyes closed and his grip relaxed. The torrent grabbed him and tossed him over and over. He was spun around until a metal eye for tying barges snagged the chain linking his handcuffs. He gasped and water filled his mouth as his head banged the stone arch. The broken branch of a tree tore him free and he was swept out from under the bridge into strong hands.

He felt himself being dragged out of the water onto the river bank. He tried to open his eyes but he was spinning round and round down a long tunnel.

'Coffee?'

Tina tore her eyes away from Dermot and looked up into Harry's jovial face.

'I'd love a mint tea if you have it.'

'Cathy loves a mint tea,' Harry replied. 'Even I sometimes drink it. We all have our moments of madness.' He looked at Dermot who laughed. 'And you, good sir. May I tempt you to an infusion?'

'There's nothing in this pub that I don't find tempting.'

'Even me?' Harry winked.

'You look tip-top from where I'm sitting,' Dermot declared.

Harry guffawed.

'If you have builder's tea,' Dermot continued, 'that would go down very well.'

The white VW Golf swerved around a Land Rover Discovery and roared straight through traffic lights on red. Gary gave chase, his siren wailing. He saw the Golf slide across oncoming traffic and skid to a halt outside Accident & Emergency. The driver's door opened and an angel emerged.

'*Tina!*'

He tried to reach her but he was sinking deeper and deeper into the sucking, swirling torrent…

Harry held the door open for Tina and Dermot and they stepped out into the dwindling light. The rain had let up. Dermot placed his arm around her shoulder and guided her back to the car park. She pressed her remote and the indicator lights on her beloved Golf flashed. They slipped into the front seats and she slotted the key into the ignition.

Dermot touched her arm. 'Don't start it yet.'

She turned to look at him and, once again, felt a rush of heat spread throughout her entire body. Something about the man rendered her helpless. She touched his face with her palm and he kissed it.

Heavy slaps pounded his numb cheeks as hands shook him. His whole body shivered and convulsed with spasms. He didn't try to open his eyes. He knew he was on the floor of a van, back on the road to hell.

Tina clicked-in her seatbelt and started the engine, switched on the lights and reversed the car out of its slot. They turned onto the Old Military Road and in the fading light of day, she drove with haste along the deserted, meandering scar.

They didn't speak. She focused on her driving, knowing she was going too fast for the conditions.

Ahead, pin pricks of light grew bigger and she slowed as they came to the junction for the former boarding school. Head-lights on full beam blinded her as a van cut across their path.

'That's odd,' Dermot said.

Tina accelerated up the mile-long drive and saw the white van coming to a halt on the far side of the gravelled apron.

'Stop here.' He held up his hand. 'Don't go near.'

She halted the Golf some way from the van. Lit by her head-lights, she saw two men get out and go to the rear doors. They stood by them, waiting, looking towards her car.

'I'd better see what they're up to.' He kissed her tenderly on the lips. 'Go home to your elderly friends. They are clearly good people.' He opened his door and almost ran to the van. She waited and watched as he talked to the men.

Surprisingly disappointed, she swung the car around the apron, her tyres spitting grit. But, something flashed in the corner of her eye and she slammed on her brakes. She thrust the gear lever into reverse and quickly backed up, flicking her headlights onto full beam.

What is that? A Porsche Spyder? Here?

She was tempted to get out of her car and take a closer look but the rain had returned. Could it be Dermot's? She hoped so and smiled at the prospect of giving it a spin, as she roared-off down the long drive.

Gary felt himself being hauled out of the back of the van and carried without due care into the school and down to the basement. He was numb with cold; his whole body shook with spasms. They dumped him onto a concrete floor and water cascaded over him, gradually getting warmer. He lost track of time as he relished the hot water pounding down until chilblains set in and his ankles and feet burned, and became excruciatingly itchy.

Rough hands pulled him out of the shower and he opened his eyes. Eamonn O'Hanlon, Dermot's less attractive older brother, shouted in his face. 'Take your clothes off.'

Gary saw that his ankle and handcuffs had been removed, exposing scarred and raw skin. It took massive effort to get to his feet in the former school changing room, and his hands shook as he peeled off his clothes, leaving them in a pile on the floor. His swollen feet looked a mess and were beyond itchy.

'You've a cut on your head,' Eamonn said. 'We've someone here to fix it. Dry yourself.' He handed Gary a used towel with baked-on mud stains.

Gary looked down at his intensely white skin. Two years in captivity had weakened his once muscular physique. He used the towel to dry his hair and noticed splashes of dark red blood. He walked over to a row of washbasins and cleared condensation from a wall mirror, heavily silvering at its edges. There was a large gash just below his hairline.

'You're a bit shrivelled for my taste,' spoke a voice from Essex.

He didn't bother to cover himself as hatred coursed through his veins.

'Sit down, Gary. I'll fix yer 'ead.'

He stared at Stacy and imagined wrapping his towel around her neck. Eamonn had gone so he could do it.

'Relax.' Stacy held out a first aid box with a red cross.

'Come near me, and I promise you'll regret it.'

'Oh come on Gary. Put aside your hard feelings. We had something, once.'

'We had nothing. It was all pretence.'

He had seen Stacy come and go over the summer as her romance with Dermot had blossomed, but this was the first time she'd spoken to him since that fatal breakfast in her father's house. He put the towel on a wooden bench and sat on it, picking up another towel to cover himself.

Stacy looked at his head. 'You want to be careful. This is nasty.' She put the box down beside him and opened a pack of gauze. 'It should be stitched properly,' she said dabbing his head. 'But I've got butterfly stitches. They'll bind the wound. It will leave a bit of a scar, though.'

He was surprised by how tenderly she administered the wound, pulling it together and using the narrow sticky strips to hold the skin in place.

'How've you been, Stacy?'

She continued to work. 'I've been fine, thank you, Gary.'

'And your dad?'

'All well. Tip top.'

'How's business?'

'Surprisingly good. And you? Are you enjoying your sabbatical from the Met?'

'Absolutely. It's wonderful. Thank you so much for the opportunity.'

'You're welcome.' She put the pack of strips back in the box and took out a small canister. Using her left hand to shield his eyes, she sprayed the wound. 'A bit of antiseptic.' She returned the canister to the box. 'Try to keep it clean.'

'How's your love life? Are you still open to all comers?'

'Don't push it Gary, or I'll rip the strips off.'

He paused before continuing. 'I didn't mean it to happen, Stacy. I apologise. I am genuinely sorry.'

'Are you doing anything tonight, Gary?'

He had found himself alone with Stacy in the small flat he was renting in Chigwell. She only had to look at him and he felt a stir-

ring in a part of his anatomy that should be entirely reserved for his wife. She was twenty-eight, brunette, crystal-blue eyes, straight nose, generous mouth, breasts worthy of attention, and legs that promised heaven.

"Remember, Gary. Sleeping with the enemy is not an option. Keep your night stick, zipped. It will cost us a conviction and we could end up paying compensation."

He knew it was not acceptable for an undercover police officer to form an intimate sexual relationship with a target, but Stacy was beyond beautiful. She was unbelievably alluring. She was also Frank Cottee's only daughter and should be entirely off limits; but the two men, thirty years or more apart in age, got along better than Gary had with his own late father.

In the written guidance he had received during training it stated: When a police officer deems it necessary and proportionate to achieve operational objectives, communications of a sexual nature may be authorised.

Gary had not been authorised and he could not claim an immediate and credible threat to himself or others, but surely this was a chance for him to break into the Cottee inner circle? To crack a criminal syndicate that was running rings around the authorities.

'What are you thinking?' Stacy asked.

He looked into her eyes and knew he was a goner. 'I was just running through all the women I've met…'

'You mean, slept with.'

'Not one, and I've dated some beauties, comes close to you.' *It was a lie. There was one and her name was Tina.*

'What are you gonna do about it?' *Her voice sounded breathy. Were they her pheromones at work – or his?*

She moved in close and he could feel the hardening tips of her breasts through his shirt. She was a criminal with a criminal gene running from head to toe through her sculpted body. Blood surged through his veins. Her head tilted up and he cushioned his lips against hers. Their tongues met and they kissed like teenagers.

Within seconds she had removed her top and bra and the promise of exquisite breasts was fulfilled. She kicked off her pleated, Victoria Beckham miniskirt and peeled off her tights and thong at a speed Gary felt sure had broken all records. Within moments, they were lying naked on the plush carpet and he was covering her slim, smooth, skin with butterfly kisses.

He and Stacy were more sexually compatible than any woman he'd ever slept with – including Tina. He really fancied her beyond the stuff of dreams, but he loved Tina, he loved his wife and knew he was doing wrong.

One night, following a great meal out in Southend, and after more than a few glasses of Prosecco, he and Stacy were in bed and building to yet another amazing crescendo. He could not believe how incredible she was. They were a perfect, physical fit and she drove all reason from his mind.

'Oh my God, Tina!' He could not hold himself back and the explosion blasted his mind. His whole body pulsed. Twenty seconds later and panting hard, he was finally able to look at Stacy and did not like the expression in her eyes.

'Are you cheatin' on me?'

'Of course not. I love you. When have I had the opportunity to cheat? We're together all the time. Did you not come?'

'So who is she, then?'

'Who? What are you talking about?'

'Tina.'

'Tina? I don't understand.'

'You shouted, Tina, when you blew your rocks.'

'No I didn't. I don't know anyone called Tina.'

'Well it either came out of your mouth or your dick, but I definitely heard it.'

Gary eased himself away from her and grabbed a fistful of tissues, which she reluctantly accepted.

'She's a girl I broke up with about a year ago. We were together for quite a long time.'

'Tina what?'

'What's it matter?'

'What the fuck's her name?'

'It's Turner.'

'Tina Turner? Don't take me for a fool.'

'Stacy. I'm not telling you her name because I don't want you to *hurt her.'*

'Now why would I do that?'

'Jealousy?'

'She does have a great singing voice, I grant you that.'

'Tina gave me the elbow which is why I moved to Essex. I had to get away. Make a change.'

'But you still love her. Wish she was here instead of me.' She threw back the bed covers and retrieved her clothes from the floor.

'Please Stacy, don't go. I've got something for you. I was waiting for the right moment but this may be my only moment.'

It was Gary's escape chute. "When all else fails, get down on your knees." Wise words from an old police hand with many years working undercover. He grabbed a pair of boxer shorts from the floor and pulled them on, opened his sock drawer and removed a small, velvet-covered box.

He looked at Stacy.

She stared back at him.

'Stacy, my darling.' He went down on one knee. 'Would you do me the great honour of becoming my wife?' He opened the box to reveal a gold band with a diamond centrepiece, surrounded by sapphires.

'Gary and Stacy. Sounds more like a comedy show than a married couple.' She took the ring out of the box and slipped it on her wedding finger. 'The band is too big.'

'I misjudged it.'

She took the box out of his hand and used her enamelled thumb nail to remove the recessed base. Inside was a folded receipt.

'Jewellers always hide them there just in case the proposal is rejected. Okay, let's see how much I am worth.' She unfolded the piece of paper and held it under the bedside light. 'Mmm, Hatton Garden. Quality assured. My dad considered getting involved in that bonkers raid – but he was too young.' She laughed at her own joke – all the raiders had been pensioners. 'Is this Tina's reject ring?'

'Of course not. I bought it to match your crystal-blue eyes.'

'Well you must have second sight. This receipt is dated before you even knew me.' The last few words were spat at him followed by the hurling of the velvet box. 'I'll keep the ring. It's gotta be

worth a few quid.'

Gary got to his feet. 'It's Gavin and Stacy, the comedy show. Yes, I bought it before I met you but not before I'd seen your photo. Of course, I wanted to work for your dad but it was you I fantasised about. It was you I fell in love with. And then I met you and I knew my feelings were for real.'

'Nice try. Good effort. I'll see you in the morning. Come for breakfast.'

Come for breakfast. He would always remember those fatal words.

Stacy packed up the first-aid box and replaced the lid.

'Wait here. I'll find you some clothes.'

He reached for her hand. 'I am sorry for hurting you. I mean it.'

'Save it.' She pulled her hand free.

He called after her. 'He doesn't love you.'

She turned and stared at him. 'What are you talking about?'

'Dermot. He has a wandering eye.'

She didn't have a ready response.

He decided to push the point. 'Ask him where he's been this afternoon. More importantly, who he's been with.' He was taking a calculated risk but he had to sow dissent and he was confident that Tina would be protected by Dermot.

'Piss off, Gary.' She marched out of the changing room.

Tina parked her car behind Malcolm's repaired Honda and took a few deep breaths. Sodium-coloured street lamps cast the world she now called home in a strange yellow light. A large pool of water from the recent heavy rain had gathered by a blocked drain.

What was she doing?

She took another breath and released her seatbelt.

Her phone buzzed in her handbag. It was a call via Whats-App.

'Sam! Where are you?'

'They won't let me in. Some tosser on the door said it's a

crime scene.'

'Samuel... be polite. The police are just doing their job.'

'Their job?'

'They have to make sure.'

'Of what? You said they were gassed.'

'Yes. Carbon monoxide poisoning.'

'Where am I going to stay?'

'Walk back to the High Street, turn right and a little way down on the left is the Falcon. They have rooms.'

'Is it still run by Heather and Ted?'

'Yes; remind them who you are.'

'When will I see you?'

'In a couple of hours. We can either eat at the pub or have a bite in The Old Forge.'

'Put 'em on.' Stacy threw a few items of clothing at Gary.

'Charity shop?'

'You know how much I care about the third world.'

'Developing world.'

'Get dressed.'

Gary looked at the clothes. 'Mmm... not bad.'

'So tell me, where was Dermot?'

He looked at her. 'Why not ask him yourself?'

'No. You tell me.'

He took a moment to deliberate his response. 'Listen Stacy. The police already assume I am buried in ready-mix concrete. My wife thinks she is a widow. I'm sure Dermot was one hundred per cent discrete when they went out.'

Her eyes turned to flint. 'When was that?'

'Last night and again today. He seems to like her.'

'Bollocks. You're full of it. I don't believe a word.'

'I saw them kiss.'

Had he blown it? Said too much? Her whole frame looked rigid.

'Stacy, I got involved with you despite orders not to. I couldn't help myself. You're beautiful. It's not Tina's fault. Her parents have just died and Dermot offered a shoulder.'

She stormed out.

He reached for the clothes she'd brought and as he put them on, wondered whether he'd been a complete and utter fool.

A minute later, the door opened and Dermot strode in. Following was Eamonn carrying the chains and cuffs, which he threw on the floor at Gary's feet.

He ignored them and looked at Dermot. 'Did you talk to her?'

'Who?'

'Stacy. She's going after Tina.'

Dermot was momentarily silent. 'What did you say to her?'

'The truth.'

'You fool!' He looked as though he was about to punch him.

Through high windows with their toughened glass came the faint throaty roar of a car engine sparking into life. Dermot almost ran from the room.

'Put the cuffs on,' Eamonn snarled.

Gary sat on the bench and picked up the cuffs. 'You'll have to help me.' He slumped into himself, keeping his eyes slightly open.

Eamonn knelt down on one knee in front of him and Gary took his chance. He whipped the chain joining the hand and ankle cuffs around the leathery man's throat and pulled with all his remaining strength.

24

Tina pushed open the door to the Falcon and looked around the pub. Ted was serving behind the bar.

'Tina!' he called.

She walked over to him.

'You'll be looking for your brother,' he smiled.

'Thank you for finding him a room.'

'We are here to help you both. It's a very tough time.'

'Thank you.'

'G & T?'

'Diet Coke, please.' She opened her bag.

'Put that away.'

'You can't keep giving me free drinks.'

'I can and I will.' He opened a bottle and poured the bubbling liquid into a tall, iced glass. 'Gavin's over there.' He indicated an alcove near the rear of the pub.

'He uses Samuel, his middle name, these days. Well, since he met his husband, Luke.'

'What's wrong with Gavin?'

'He says it's too common. Not classy enough.'

'But, it means white hawk, perfect for a man of Hawksmead. And don't forget Sir Gawain, he was one of King Arthur's Knights of the Round Table, and a mighty warrior. On the other hand there was St. Gavinus, a noble Christian, who ended up dying as a martyr.'

'Gavin was also the name of an ex of mine who my brother never liked.'

Ted laughed. 'Samuel, good choice. I'll try to remember.'

She blew him a kiss and picked up her coke. 'Thank you.'

Sam was thumbing a message on his phone as Tina approached.

'How's my big brother?' She put her drink on the stained and scarred oak table.

He stood and hugged her. 'You're thin. I need to fatten you up.'

'For the kill?'

He laughed and let her go. 'I've booked us a table at The Old Forge.'

'Thank you.' She slid onto the bench opposite him and they sat in silence for a few moments. 'It's just you and me, now,' she said.

'Don't make your big brother cry. I'm already a girl's blouse.'

'It's so stupid.'

'Dad was always cautious. It won't be his fault.'

'It doesn't matter. Whatever the cause – they're dead.'

Sam took a deep breath. 'Are you going to be okay?' He used his hand to wipe his eyes.

'Are you?'

'I don't know. It didn't feel real in New Zealand. It still doesn't.'

'How's Luke?'

Sam blew his nose into a paper napkin. 'He's well, thank you. But, I can't leave him on his own for too long. You know what men are like.'

Tina almost smiled. 'I've met someone.'

'Whilst all this is going on you've found time to meet someone?' Sam looked intently at his sister.

'He's been gone nearly two and a half years and missing for over two.'

'You've accepted... he's not coming back?'

She nodded.

'I'm so sorry.'

'It's not been easy. I've been like a robot. Working, drinking, sleeping.'

'Sex?' Sam cocked an eyebrow.

She looked at him sharply. 'No. Not yet.'

'Who's the guy?'

'His name's Dermot O'Hanlon.'

'Ah, the luck of the Irish.' He looked at his watch. 'We'd better head off. You can tell me all about him over a classic prawn cocktail, assuming it's still on The Old Forge menu.'

Below ground level it was very dark as Gary felt his way along a corridor. There were lights, but he didn't dare turn them on. He bashed into several abandoned tables, chairs and boxes as he hurried past open doors that led to a former bakery, laundry facility and various empty rooms.

What drove Gary crazy was the knowledge that he was so close to civilisation, to freedom. But the Irish travellers were canny. They were used to living outside society, taking what they needed to survive. He was surprised they'd risked attracting the attention of the police by linking up with a ruthless criminal family that had all but destroyed his life. He constantly thought about Tina and the danger he had put her in.

Had he been a fool telling Stacy about Dermot's interest in her?

Had he put her needlessly at risk?

He had seen in Dermot's eye that Tina was more than just another girl. Surely, that gave her some protection?

Eamonn's hands and ankles were chained to a cast-iron water pipe, and a soiled rugby sock had been stuffed in his mouth. He knew Gary could easily have throttled him, but he still had the principles of a police officer.

Fool.

He spat out the sock and continued to spit to get rid of the taste.

Sam leaned back in his chair in the Old Forge; a traditional, country restaurant with dying embers in an inglenook fireplace and low beams ready to catch the heads of tall diners of which there were only a few at the brandy and coffee stage. 'Do you plan to see her again?'

'Of course I plan to see her again.' Tina smiled. 'When I need another wax. And for the occasional drink or coffee. We're friends.'

'Friends? She wants to be your lesbian lover!'

Tina was aware of a couple at a neighbouring table turning their heads towards them. 'She knows I am *not* a lesbian,' she whispered.

'I think you're playing with fire, my darling.'

'She *knows* I like men. Dermot in particular.'

Sam leaned across the table and spoke like an investigating detective in a TV drama. 'Despite knowing Magdalena's proclivities, after seeing Dermot, you went back and stayed the night.'

'I couldn't drive. I'd had too much to drink.'

'You could have taken a taxi. Instead, you decided to share a bed with your lesbian friend.'

Tina licked her lips. 'I needed company.'

'You needed company,' he echoed. 'What about her feelings?' He dabbed his mouth with a napkin. 'It must've been torture for her.'

Tina blew out her cheeks and sighed. 'Yes, you're right. It was wrong of me.' Fat tears rolled down her cheeks. 'I don't know what I'm doing. I'm not myself.'

Sam reached across the table and squeezed her hand.

Gary came to a pantry off a scullery that had clearly not been used since the school closed nearly a decade earlier. Behind built-in shelving was a space, large enough to sit upright, with a vent Gary had been working to remove over the past few weeks. With a bit more chipping, he was sure he could push it out and crawl through the gap in the bricks. He'd checked its location from the outside and although there was a bit of a drop, the landing was on grass which, thanks to the rain, would be soft. He would hide for two or three days and then in the dead hours of night he would make a run for it, down the long drive rather than across the moor.

He risked switching on a light and the old bulb's yellowed glow revealed a disturbing handwritten sign: *To whom it may concern. We are aware of you squirreling away tins of food and have removed them. There is no escape.*

Gary checked his hideaway and saw that his tool for chipping at the bricks, and his stash of food had gone. Once again, he had underestimated the travellers. He turned off the light and slumped down on the floor, exhausted. Eamonn would be found soon and then they would come for him.

He heard a bark. A few seconds later, lights flickered on in the corridor and Hector ran into the pantry, all excited to see him.

'Don't lie to me, Dermot.'

They were standing in the Headmaster's study. He looked at Stacy and saw flecks of danger in her eyes. 'I admit. I like her but it's all part of the job. Keep your friends close and your enemies closer.'

'How close do you intend to keep her?'

Dermot risked touching her arms. 'Close enough to hear what's happenin' in Hawksmead, nothin' more than that.'

'We agreed that if Gary tried to escape, we'd take away his most prized possession.'

'All the while there is a threat to Tina, we can keep him in check. We hurt her, or worse, who knows what he might do.'

'I think we should do him now. It's too dangerous keeping him alive. Everyone thinks he's dead, anyway.'

'Kill him?'

'You know it's the right decision.'

'Murder a policeman?'

'Does it bother you?'

'Of course it bothers me! I don't kill people. I rob, I thieve, I extort, I exploit – but I don't murder.'

'Keep your scruples. I'll call daddy. He'll sort it out. Her too.'

Dermot gripped her arms. 'If he touches her I'll feckin' kill him!'

Stacy pulled herself free. 'That's all I needed to know.' There were tears in her eyes.

'I'm sorry. I can't help it. She means a lot to me.'

Stacy curled her lip. 'Well enjoy her while you can.'

Audrey heard the front door open and smiled. It was joyous to have Tina live with them. She missed her married sons in the south of England and, not having a daughter to dote on, Tina was a very special addition.

'Would you like a cup of cocoa?' Audrey called from the kitchen.

'Hot chocolate?'

'Of course.'

Tina appeared in the doorway. 'Where's Malcolm? I didn't see his car.'

'He's up at the Rorty Crankle. It's the board of trustees' annual general meeting. He couldn't wait to give them the good news.'

'What news?'

'That the same person who managed to sell the old boarding house is now on the case selling the main school.'

Tina's mouth dropped open. 'I think I feel a bit of a panic attack coming on. I may need something stronger than a hot chocolate.'

Audrey laughed. 'There's a lovely white in the fridge.' She opened the door and retrieved the bottle, unscrewed the cap and gave Tina a generous glass.

'Thank you. I hope the weather's better tomorrow.'

'I heard it's going to be sunny but with a biting easterly.'

'Good. I need decent light for the photographs. In the rain, the school looks really depressing, and not a little frightening.' She took a sip of wine. 'I want to get drunk, but I know it won't help.' She put her glass down on the worktop.

'What is it, Tina?'

'I can't get balanced. I can't think straight. I'm all over the place. Sometimes, I forget that my parents are even dead. I feel dislocated from reality.'

Audrey put her arms around her. 'That's how I felt when my husband died. I think I was still dislocated from reality when I first came up here.' She gently stroked Tina's hair. 'It takes time. Your emotions are going to be up and down for a while, not helped by the carbon monoxide poisoning. You must be kind to yourself. Just go with the flow unless, as my mother said, you're in the Niagara River.'

Tina pulled back and smiled. 'Or the River Hawk.'

'Too true.' Audrey poured herself a glass of wine and put the bottle back in the fridge. 'How's your brother?'

'He's holding it together – just. In truth, we're a bit of a pathetic pair.'

Audrey picked up her wine. 'You're there for each other. That's all that matters.'

'I've met someone I like.'

Audrey stared; the wine glass frozen, mid air.

'He's an Irish traveller in charge of the migrants up at the old school. Until I know what happened to Gary how could I even think about starting a new relationship? I feel guilty as hell. What sort of wife am I?'

'Until death do us part.'

'You think he's dead?'

'I didn't say that, but we marry to share our lives. When that is no longer possible it behoves us to move on. We have to.'

'Do you really believe that?'

'What I do believe is that love comes in many guises and from many directions. How could I fall for someone who was indirectly responsible for the death of my brother? I wasted eight precious months agonising and if it hadn't been for you inviting me to your wedding, I would never have met the real Malcolm. I would not have experienced three years – and counting, I hope – of love, of companionship, of joyous marriage. He's brought me a happiness I thought was gone for good.' She put down her glass and took Tina's hands in hers. 'Sweetheart, the past is the past. The real sin is to deprive our hearts of love out of a sense of pointless guilt, or duty.' She released Tina's hands and took a gulp of wine. 'Mmm, it *is* good.'

'What about my parents? What would they think?'

'All parents ever want, is for their child to be happy.'

'Despite everything, you think I should see him?'

'What's the alternative? Netflix?'

'You know what, I'm going to focus on selling that old school, and then see where my heart takes me.'

A voice spoke from the hallway. 'Now that's the kind of fighting talk I like to hear.'

Tina grinned as Malcolm hung up his coat.

25

Gary shuffled down the corridor to the headmaster's study. He was wearing his regular ankle and handcuffs. Since being discovered in his hideaway, he'd been escorted everywhere he went by at least two burly travellers, one he'd come to like.

'What happened to your face?' Gary asked Martin who had a fresh cut on his left cheek and jaw.

'I was in a pub and all I did was state a fact.'

'Very dangerous, especially for a man with your accent.'

'What is it with you people? Why are you so antagonistic to folks like us?'

'You don't pay tax. You fly tip. You break into homes. You do house renovations and extort additional payments. You park your caravans in beauty spots and when you're forced out, you leave all your crap.'

Martin slowly nodded his head. 'I take your point.'

'What was the fact you imparted?'

'I was sittin', havin' me pint, when some blokes were makin' thick Irish jokes. You know the sort of thing. *Which is the quickest way to Hawksmead?* Are you going by foot or car? *Car.* Then that's the quickest way.'

Gary smiled. 'I know a few more.'

'I bet you do.'

'What was your response?'

'I asked them a question. *What d'yer call the few good-looking girls in Undermere? The ones that aren't obese?*'

'What do you call them?'

'*Polish.*'

Gary laughed. 'I bet that went down well.'

'Can yer believe it? Some bloke with a fat bint of a girlfriend took exception to my observation. I won't be partin' with cash in that pub again.' Martin knocked on the headmaster's door and pushed it open. Gary sauntered in, as best he could. Sunlight brought the shabbiness of the decor into sharp focus.

Dermot lounged on the old sofa. 'Thank you, Martin. You can go.'

Martin nodded to his boss and closed the door behind him.

Dermot looked up at Gary. 'Why did you do it?'

'I'm a police officer. It's my duty to uphold the law.'

'Is it also your duty to put your wife in danger?'

'She was already in danger. At least now I know she's got you to protect her.'

'But for how long? If Tina finds a buyer and we get notice to quit, who knows what will happen?'

'You could give evidence in court against the Cottee family. That would earn you a reduced sentence. I'd speak on your behalf.'

Dermot gave a dry laugh. 'You really don't understand us at all, do you?'

26

The heavy rain lasted longer than usual for the time of year. Tina found it incredibly frustrating waiting for the clouds to break, but the rain did finally stop and the weather looked fine for at least a day or two. She parked her Golf away from the school's main entrance, and away from a clutch of vans, lorries and old German cars. The Porsche Spyder had either gone or was hidden from her view. She lifted a tripod and camera out of her car boot and, without announcing her arrival, moved around the grounds seeking out good angles from which to shoot. The photo she liked best was when she placed the old abbey ruins in the foreground with the autumnal sun giving the low stone walls long, dramatic shadows. In the background was the red-brick Victorian edifice, its sharp angles in stark contrast to the ancient moorland's gentle shapes and hues.

Pleased with her work, she carried the camera and tripod into the school via the main entrance and, from the hallway with its worn stone floor and panelled walls, she entered the refectory, the largest room in the building. At one end, was a stage with a classic proscenium arch, framed with sun-bleached, raggedy curtains. She considered the sunlight probing the exterior ivy and grubby windows and tried to find an angle that truly reflected the scale of the room. On the camera's LCD screen she saw a figure standing on the stage. Her heart thumped as she watched him jump down with an easy grace and manoeuvre his way towards her, around numerous oak dining tables and benches.

'What do you think of this room?' she asked.

Dermot stopped and smiled as he looked about him. 'I can almost smell the school dinners, can't you?'

'I smell chlorine.'

He sniffed. 'No, it's definitely boiled cabbage.'

She laughed. 'Now you come to mention it, I can smell it too.'

'Where did you get chlorine from?'

'I was imagining a swimming pool and spa. It's easily big enough and wouldn't need much digging as the basement is below.'

Dermot nodded then his face turned serious.

'What's up?' she asked, as the muscles in her gut clenched.

'When we first met, and in the Falcon, and the next day up at the Rorty Whatsit, you plucked a chord in my heart. I mean it. You can have no idea how much you mean to me.'

Her mouth went dry.

'And it's because of my feelings for you I have to snuff out what I had hoped would be something pretty special – pretty special, to me, anyway.'

She couldn't respond. All joy from the sunny day had evaporated.

He continued. 'I have this t'ing with another woman and, right now, I cannot afford to break off the relationship. I'm sorry. I genuinely am.'

It was a punch to the gut that forced her to find a resting place at the end of one of the long benches. She looked at him, all gossamer joy of a new romance gone. 'Are you married? Is that what you're telling me?'

'To Stacy?' He grinned and sat down on the bench a few feet from her. He reached for her hand but she pulled it away. 'If only it were that easy.'

Tina was surprised by how hurt she felt after such a brief acquaintance. She summoned all her resolve and stood. 'I must get on.'

He nodded. 'Of course.' He got to his feet and for a moment they looked into each other's eyes. As she watched him leave the room, a new sadness enveloped her.

Later, satisfied with her work but feeling totally deflated, she carried the camera and tripod back to her car and put it in the boot. Her mind kept wandering as she tried to run through the shots she had taken and whether she had enough to spark the imaginations of potential buyers. She slammed the lid and was shocked to see Dermot standing just a few feet away.

'Don't go yet. Please. I have a jar of instant coffee in my office and Barmbrack fresh from Ireland.'

'Barmbrack? What's that when it's at home?'

'It's a cake we eat in the month of Halloween, rich in fruit and spice, and with a dash of whiskey. Let me cut you a slice.'

It was enough to breach her resistance. They walked with unseemly haste to the main entrance, across the echoing hallway and down the long corridor to the headmaster's study. The door was barely closed before he cupped her face in his hands. Their lips came together and his tongue entered her mouth. He pressed his body against hers, pushing her up against the door. She wanted this man and pulled apart the popper at the top of her jeans, wishing she'd worn a skirt. But there were so many hazards in and around the old school it had made sense to protect her legs.

Dermot helped her peel off her jeans and she kicked them aside. His fingers stroked her hair, her breast and the thin fabric at the top of her thighs. In the small of her back she felt the door handle turn and it opened an inch.

'Private business,' he yelled, and slammed it shut with his hand. 'Come back later.'

'Let me in.' Tina recognised the woman's accent as typical Essex.

'I'll join you in a minute,' Dermot said. 'I'll see you in the staff kitchen.'

'Who've you got in there?'

Tina unravelled her jeans and pulled them on as fast as she could.

'It's the estate agent. She's a little upset. You know, what with what's happened to her parents.'

Tina took the cue and poked both her eyes. She sat down on the sofa and put her face in her hands. The door opened.

'I lost my mother when I was a child,' the woman said. 'She'll get over it.'

'I wasn't expecting you, today, Stacy me darlin'.'

'Daddy sent me. He's not 'appy about the current situation.'

Tina had poked her eyes a bit too hard and they were both watering profusely. She looked up at the blurred woman.

'Grief comes back to me in waves. Mr O'Hanlon was being very kind giving me some privacy.' She got up from the sofa and wiped away her tears. 'You're very beautiful.'

Stacy ignored the compliment and opened the door. 'Leave us,' she said.

Tina nodded and left the room. The door slammed behind her. For the second time that day she felt totally deflated. Somehow, she had to protect herself more. Her emotions were all over the place.

27

Tap. Tap.

The knock on the guest bedroom door told Tina who it was and she looked up from the screen of her borrowed laptop. For the last couple of days she'd been sitting at an escritoire trying to find the right words that would spark the interest in a certain type of investor.

'Come in.'

The door opened and Malcolm entered carrying a tray with a small cafetière, milk jug, cup and saucer, and a plate with a slice of Victoria sponge, cake fork and napkin. 'I thought you may be ready for elevenses.'

'Elevenses?'

'An old expression.' He placed the tray on a rosewood bureau. 'How are you getting on?'

'Struggling a bit. I'm trying to get into the brains of billionaires; trip their levers, but it's not easy.'

'They are a unique breed. Perhaps I can help.'

Tina was a bit slow responding. 'That's very kind of you.'

Malcolm smiled. 'I know what you're thinking. You're wondering whether an octogenarian can have any ideas that are relevant today.'

'Not at all, Malcolm. I just didn't want to take up your time with my problem.'

'Ah, but it's my problem too. The trustees are relying on you and me to get the school sold. Don't forget, after I gave up teaching I used to make my living writing advertising and marketing copy.'

'Of course! It had slipped my mind. I'd love to have your help.'

'Let me pour your coffee. Caffeine got me through many a tough brief. The worst jobs were producing brochures for the big insurance companies. They paid well but boy were they happy to peddle half-truths.'

He carried the cup and saucer over to her. She noticed a slight shake as he placed it next to the laptop. 'You are brilliant at selling, Tina, and my recommendation is that you should trust your first instincts. In my opinion, one's initial ideas are invariably the best.'

She laughed. 'I wish that were true.'

'Let's look at the market.'

'You sit down at the desk.' She got up from her chair. 'And I'll prop myself up on the bed.'

'Deal.'

Malcolm took over the upright chair and Tina plumped the pillows on one of the two single beds she'd been sleeping in.

'I'll create a new file,' Malcolm said, 'where I can type a few notes.' He clicked and tapped like an old pro, surprising her by how adept he was using the computer. Two-hands typing, not the usual single digit. He looked at her over his shoulder. 'Who are we targeting?'

'The big property developers – all the ones who have *"Homes"* in their company name.'

'Do we really want to replace the old school with an identikit housing estate?'

'No. But do we have a choice?'

'You tell me.'

Tina got off the bed and took a sip of coffee. 'Mmm, this is good.'

'Coffee connects the dots like nothing else.'

'You're right. I hate those big housing developers. They could build with style if they wanted to, with good materials, decent insulation, quality green spaces, but all they do is try to get around the regulations. They couldn't give a stuff about the natural environment, and nor do most councils. If developers had had their way, Audrey's old school boarding house would be a block of flats instead of a beautiful, tranquil memorial garden.'

'Unfortunately, the trustees cannot afford to donate the land, as Audrey did, and also follow through with their plans to build a youth centre with year-round sports facilities.'

'So, we have to approach the right kind of buyers. Problem is, I'm struggling to find an angle.'

'Have another sip of coffee.'

Tina did as instructed. 'The person we need to attract must be an entrepreneur who has courage in his DNA…'

'Or her DNA,' Malcolm interjected.

'Nice thought, but unlikely.'

'Forgive me. Go on my dear.'

'It has to be someone with the financial resources to capitalise on opportunities the typical, unimaginative, business majority simply cannot see.'

'Who do you have in mind?'

'Someone I once saw kissing a former friend.'

28

Abel Cornfield looked out of the side window of the helicopter as his pilot circled above Hawksmead College. He could see the ruins of the monastery overshadowed by the former Victorian workhouse. There were a few remote barns that may have to go, and assorted caravans parked on the rugby pitch – they would belong to the travellers.

'Drone,' said the pilot's voice through his headphones.

Abel looked at him. The pilot pointed to a small object tracking the helicopter.

'Interesting,' Abel said. 'It looks a bit bigger than a toy.'

'I think it's the Matrice – the go-to drone for aerial photography in Hollywood. Six rotors for a perfectly steady shot.'

'The estate agent's really on her game.'

'Where shall I put you down, sir?'

Abel looked at the gravelled area in front of the school. He saw a number of parked vehicles and a white car coming to a halt.

'As near to the front of the building as possible.'

The pilot swooped away from the drone and came to a gentle touchdown on a patch of level grass. Abel looked at the austere facade, parts exposed and parts almost entirely hidden by ivy, as he waited for the rotor to slow. In his late forties, tall, slim, with good posture, a strong handsome face, crowned with an excellent head of light brown hair, he always dressed well because he only had smart clothes. He turned to the pilot. 'Come with me. I'll see if I can get you a coffee.'

'Thank you, sir, but I have a flask and I don't like to leave the helicopter unattended until I know who's around.'

'I'll be an hour or so.' Abel saw a young woman emerge from

the white car. 'That's the agent.'

'She looks well turned-out,' the pilot stated.

Abel laughed. 'She is. We've had many face to face chats on-line. I'm impressed with her.' He opened the door and carefully stepped down to the ground. Keeping upright, confident that his head was well below the slowly turning rotor blades, he strode across the sodden grass towards the gravelled apron.

'Lord Cornfield. Welcome,' Tina said, offering her hand.

'Abel, please.' He felt her fine bones as they briefly shook hands. 'It's good to meet you in person, Christina.'

'Everyone calls me Tina.'

'I like Christina.'

She smiled. 'Let me show you around.'

An hour later, after showing the prospective purchaser the Victorian interior, but only the places where Dermot had told her it was safe to go, they were standing almost midway between the dilapidated barns and milking parlour, and the caravans belonging to the travellers.

'Let me get this straight,' Abel said. 'The school building is Grade II but the ruins are Grade I.'

'That's right,' Tina nodded. 'But I think you'll have plenty of latitude when it comes to planning, short of tearing the whole lot down, of course. The school was good for the town and the loss of its business is sorely missed. Any plan that will help to regenerate Hawksmead will be looked upon favourably, I'm sure. Are you thinking of an hotel?'

'More ambitious than that. I want to reinstate the farm, build tennis courts, squash courts, and a couple of golf courses, one to be PGA standard. We could have clay-pigeon shooting and guided tours on the moor. One of the barns could be converted into a luxury cinema showing the latest films. As for the school building itself, I've examined the floor plan and it will have to be completely gutted. Part will be set aside for re-covering addicts, rich ones of course, and the remainder will be a five-star hotel with indoor and outdoor swimming pools, his and her gyms and spas, and two or three fabulous restaurants, one open to locals.' He turned to Tina. 'What do you think? Can you see it?'

'Yes Abel. I think it's an excellent plan.'

He smiled. 'Christina, would you mind if I took you somewhere special to celebrate our deal? Purely business.'

The man's hazel eyes were fixed on her as heat spread to her extremities. She curled her toes, hoping that the concentration would stop her cheeks pulsing red. She was a far cry from the confident young woman who had married Gary. And her start-stop relationship with Dermot had driven all balance from her mind.

'Of course, Lord Cornfield. Where would you like to go? There's a lovely gastro-pub a few miles from here called The Rorty Crankle Inn.'

'I was thinking of a few days in the Eternal City. I take it, you do have a passport?'

'Should I accept?' Tina was enjoying a late lunch in the little cottage. 'We've only met once, although we've talked a lot via Zoom and on the phone.'

'How old did you say he was?' Malcolm asked, standing, as he poured her a glass of sparkling elderflower.

'According to Wiki he's forty-eight.'

'Nearly double your age,' Audrey observed. 'I cannot imagine why he wants to take you to Rome?'

'He wants to thank her, my dear,' Malcolm said. 'The way billionaires like to do.'

Audrey laughed and looked at Tina. 'Do you want to be thanked by him?'

'I haven't been thanked since Gary.' She looked at her half-eaten salmon. 'Anyway, he said it's purely business. He wants me to look at properties. I should probably say no.'

Audrey took Tina's hand in hers. 'You have many challenges ahead. Take this time out. Enjoy Rome... the paintings, the statues, the Coliseum.'

Malcolm interjected. 'The Basilica will feed your soul like no other place on earth.'

'He's right,' Audrey said. She squeezed her hand. 'Relish the opportunity.'

'But,' Malcolm stared down at her, glass jug slightly shaking. 'Remember, this a business trip to thank you for services already given.'

Audrey squeezed her hand again. 'You don't owe him anything.'

'You're not bait to be gobbled up.'

Tina looked from one concerned face to the other.

Audrey squeezed her hand, yet again. 'Trust your instincts but also listen to what your heart is telling you. If you like him, let him know. Don't waste time. Life really is too short.'

29

The AgustaWestland AW109 lifted off from in front of the old school. Tina watched her white VW Golf getting smaller and smaller as the spinning rotor above her head swept her away. She was seated to the left of the pilot wearing headphones that matched his.

'Would you mind circling over the school?' she said into the microphone.

'It'll run us a bit light on fuel,' the pilot replied. 'But, if I feather the rotor, we should just about make it.'

'No, no… that's fine. Don't waste fuel.'

He ignored her and swept low over the main school building. 'Don't worry, Mrs Burton. Fuel's not a problem.'

Tina kicked herself for being taken in by the handsome pilot with his perfect vowels and consonants. This was her first flight in a helicopter and she loved the view out of the window. From the air the school and surrounding land looked amazing.

The small figure of a man ran out of a side entrance. He waved at the helicopter with both hands, tripped and fell on the grass. She watched him scramble to his feet and wave frantically. Tina gave him a little wave back although she knew he wouldn't see it. She watched the man jumping around and was about to ask the pilot to go lower when he swept her high up into the sky, leaving her stomach somewhere below her seat.

Gary fell to the ground and wept. He had seen Tina's VW Golf and had kept out of sight. If she had seen him, Dermot would have taken her captive and made some excuse to the pilot. But once the helicopter was safely in the air, he hoped she would recognise his frantic waving and let him know that she was getting help.

A large, long, slobbering tongue washed his face, which cheered him up, just a bit. Hector, the scarred and brutalised bullmastiff, would always tug on his chain to be petted whenever he saw Gary, often receiving a kick from Eamonn for *going soft*.

Hands grabbed Gary and he was dragged along the ground, back into the school, accompanied by Hector's barking.

'Leave us.' Dermot ordered his brother and another who had helped him. He squatted down and looked at Gary, constrained by both hand and ankle cuffs. 'Did she see you?'

'The police will be on their way very soon.'

'What would you do in my position?'

'Go back to Ireland… disappear.'

Dermot smiled and shook his head. 'She didn't see you. I know Tina well enough to know she would never leave you. That girl's got courage. She would've got the pilot to land.' He stood up. 'Gary, you're forcing my hand.' He gripped the chain linking Gary's handcuffs and hauled him to his feet. 'I think you'd better make peace with your maker.'

'I didn't take you for a killer.'

Dermot shook his head. 'I'm not… unfortunately, I know someone who is.'

Tina loved the views out of the window but was keen not to distract the pilot who seemed to be focusing hard. She saw the meandering swathe of the River Thames and felt her stomach flip as the pilot swooped the helicopter above the grey river. They followed it downstream giving her an excellent view of the Houses of Parliament, Nelson's Column, St Paul's Cathedral, and the Tower of London. The pilot performed a u-turn and they flew back upstream past the glacial Shard towering above; and past the great wheel of the London Eye before setting down on a circle with an H at the heliport near Battersea Bridge.

'Stunning views. Thank you, Graham.'

'Lord Cornfield wanted me to give you a little tour of London.'

The pilot guided the aircraft along the ramp towards the heliport's futuristic reception building and parked it within a marked circle. She wanted to thank God for a safe landing but she and God had been distant since Gary's disappearance.

'I'll bring your bag,' Graham said.

The wind ruffled her hair as she carefully stepped down in her trainers to the deck. She was both incredibly excited and incredibly nervous. Graham carried her small, grey suitcase, borrowed from Audrey, and walked with her to a smart reception and waiting area.

Abel, wearing a lightweight suit and tie, and immaculate, soft-leather shoes, opened his arms. 'Welcome to London, Christina. Your car awaits.'

She sank back into the impossibly soft leather seat of a Bentley Mulsanne. The last time she'd been in the rear of a chauffeured car was on her wedding day. She pushed the memory to the back of her mind and determined to relish the luxury experience as much as possible. The exterior of the car had almost taken her breath away. She loved its nose with its wide, vertical grille below the sweeping Bentley marque. The car looked so solid, so sleek, so James Bond. The first thing she noticed about the interior was the phenomenal aroma of fine leather. She should have worn heels. The unbelievably soft mat in the foot well was too good even for her almost new trainers. In front of her was a touch-screen tablet for her personal use. The cream-leather interior and seats, monogrammed with the striking Bentley logo, were beyond any luxury she had ever experienced. She peeked between the front seats and saw a futuristic dashboard set in traditional, highly-polished wood.

The driver glanced over his shoulder. 'All good, sir?'

Abel turned to Tina. She smiled and clicked her seatbelt.

'Thank you, Gary,' Abel replied. 'All good.'

Damn. Why did the chauffeur have to be called Gary?

'It's Sebastian, sir. Gary's not well, today.'

Phew.

'I must pay more attention. Thank you Sebastian.'

'Heathrow Terminal Three, sir?'

'Yes.'

She felt the beating thud of her heart. What was it telling her? She'd only known this handsome, powerful man for such a short while. She turned to him and put on her brightest smile. 'Thank you for meeting me.'

'I would've come in the helicopter but I was arranging funds for the purchase of the school.'

'You don't have it sitting in your current account?'

'I don't have it sitting in the UK.'

30

'That's a Ford Galaxy,' Malcolm said from the kitchen.

Audrey was sitting at the rosewood dining table with her tablet propped up by *The Mill on the Floss* by George Eliot and held from slipping by an embossed, leather-bound edition of *Romola*. On the tablet's screen was a YouTube video demonstrating how to use a Singer sewing machine for beginners.

'My mother used to run-up little tops and skirts for me all the time,' Audrey responded. 'I'm not sure I'm going to master this. To think I've gone through the majority of my life not really knowing what a bobbin actually is. I thought it was called a cotton reel. How wrong was I?'

'It's probably a taxi, one of the older ones,' Malcolm pressed on. 'My hands are covered in flour. Could you do me the honour and open the door, my darling?'

'The bell's not gone, yet.'

'It won't be Tina, so it's bound to ring.'

'Ours isn't the only cottage.'

'The taxi's going. Could you see who it is?'

Audrey paused the video on her tablet. 'Perhaps I'll just keep my mother's sewing machine in the front room as a curiosity, a talking point, and let another generation learn how to use it.'

'I don't understand why they've not rung the doorbell yet.'

Audrey got up from her chair. 'I'll see who it is.' She walked through the sitting room into the hall and pulled open the front door. Kneeling on the flagstone path was a young man Audrey immediately recognised but had never met. She hurried to him and took her time to squat down. Tentatively, she rested a hand on his shoulder.

'Sam?'

He roughly wiped away his tears. 'Yes, I'm sorry. Please forgive me. I get overwhelmed.'

'Come inside.'

'I don't want to bother you.'

'I live near an old mill town once renowned for its textiles and am struggling to sew in a straight line. I can assure you you're not bothering me, as long as you help me up.'

Sam got to his feet and she took his hand.

'I've been trying to get in touch with Tina,' he said, 'but her phone's off.'

'She's gone to Rome.'

'Alone?'

'Not exactly.'

'With the Irish traveller? I know she liked him.'

'Come inside and I'll tell you all about it.'

'I don't understand why she didn't let me know she was going.'

'It was all a bit rushed. Last minute. She said you were away in London.' Audrey guided Sam into the hallway and through to a seat on the sofa.

'I was seeing old mates. I grew up in Hawksmead but I only truly felt accepted in London. I needed a break.' He paused. 'Audrey, my mother told me about my Uncle Mark and how he and your little brother had a special relationship. It meant a lot to me to know that.'

Malcolm closed the front door and stood in the entrance to the hallway. 'Would you care for some Dundee?'

Audrey and Sam looked up at the slim, elegant man with white flour decorating his blue-striped apron.

'Malcolm?' asked Sam.

'At your service.'

'Tina has told me so much about you.' He turned to Audrey. 'Thank you both for taking care of her.'

'You're more than welcome to stay with us,' Malcolm said. 'There are twin beds in your sister's room.'

Sam chuckled. 'Thank you. I don't think Tina and I have ever shared a bedroom. It's so kind of you to offer, but the Falcon is a friendly place and it's near my parents' home.' He searched his rain jacket and found a handy-sized pack of tissues. 'The police have confirmed it was an accident. The boiler was old and the battery in the carbon monoxide alarm had run out.' He blew his nose.

'An easy oversight,' Malcolm said. 'I must test our smoke alarms.'

Sam looked at Audrey. 'I heard about your fire.'

Malcolm untied his apron. 'Tina drove like the clappers to get Audrey to hospital. Gary was the policeman in hot pursuit.'

Sam smiled. 'She told me more than once how she fought the law but the law won!'

'It was a beautiful wedding,' Audrey said.

'I am so sorry I missed it. I've seen photos, of course, but I never met Gary, except online.' He looked up at Malcolm. 'You created a wonderful memorial garden. I'll go there to pay my respects before I return to New Zealand.'

'Next door is the Methodist church,' Audrey said. 'It has a charming graveyard.'

Sam looked at her. 'You think my parents could be buried there?'

'Reverend Longden married your sister.'

'Believe you me,' interjected Malcolm. 'William Longden admired your parents so much he would pick up a shovel himself.'

Audrey looked at her husband. 'I'm not sure about that, Malcolm. Not everyone is as sprightly as you. And he is eighty-nine.'

31

Tina watched the chauffeur remove Audrey's loaned suitcase from the boot of the Bentley and place it next to Abel's. He extended the handle.

'Would you like me to wheel the bags in for you, sir?'

'Thank you, Sebastian,' Abel replied, 'but we can manage from here.'

'Have a lovely trip, sir.'

'I'm sure we will.'

Sebastian nodded to Tina and got back in the car. She watched it glide away.

Abel smiled at her. 'Are you all right pulling your bag?'

She gripped the handle. 'Nobody drives it but me.'

He laughed, the automatic doors opened and she followed him into the most futuristic airport terminal she'd ever experienced. She tried to take in the dramatic ceiling, the space-age lighting, the shops and restaurants while also keeping up with Abel.

'Good morning Lord Cornfield.'

He stopped by a perfectly coiffed woman in uniform holding a tablet.

'Good morning, Annabel. I hope you are well?'

'I am, sir. Rome should be lovely at this time of year. Not too hot.' She gave Tina a welcoming smile. 'Have a good trip, Mrs Burton.'

'Thank you.' Tina blushed and followed Abel to a check-in desk, seemingly opened especially for them. He produced his phone and offered the screen for scanning together with his passport. The smartly uniformed man looked at Tina and she handed him her passport, which he held under a scanner and then passed back to her.

Abel placed her bag on the conveyor belt. The man fixed a tag and she watched it disappear.

'I thought you'd want our bags in the cabin with us?' Tina said with a smile.

'Don't worry. The airline will ensure there's no delay waiting for them at the other end.'

She followed Abel through security and down a private corridor to a First Class lounge where wealthy-looking people were sitting at tables staring into their phones, accompanied by flutes of Champagne and tiny espresso cups. To one side was a long, luxury bar leading to sound-proofed picture windows that brought the vast expanse of runways, taxiways and Boeing airliners into the room.

They settled at a table and were immediately offered Champagne, which they both declined. 'May we have coffee and orange juice, and...' Abel looked at Tina with an enquiring expression.

She smiled up at the waiter. 'Do you have almond croissants?'

'Yes madam.' He turned to Abel.

'Make it two.'

'Thank you, sir.'

The waiter headed for the bar and Abel looked at his watch, which Tina recognised as a Piaget.

'It's so nice in here,' she said. 'We could forget time and see our plane take off through the window.'

Abel laughed. 'Very true, except they know where we are and when the time is right, will invite us to board the aircraft.'

She looked away and took a breath. The experience was already overwhelming. What was to come? She felt Abel's hand on hers.

'I want you to relax. It's special for me, too. Arrogant men talk about creating their own luck – but, did they create their parents, the era they were born into, their country, their trust fund that provides a safety net, enabling them to take extraordinary risks? There's a cliché which holds true today – the first million is far and away the hardest. The man, or woman, who risks the family home to pursue a dream, is the one with true courage.'

Tina liked the way the conversation had turned. Until she had met and married her policeman, she had been very ambitious, but the move to London swiftly followed by Gary's disappearance had snuffed out much of her lust for success. But meeting this smart, sensitive and supremely successful older man had reignited her ambitious flame.

'I have something for you,' Abel said. 'It's a gift, not an inducement. I've also had it engraved, so I can't take it back. Please accept it as a simple thank you, with no strings.'

Tina looked at Abel and wondered what the gift was. 'May I see it?'

He reached into his jacket pocket. 'Before I show it to you, I want you to understand how important it is, for perfect running, to have it serviced every five years.'

She kept still, held her breath, her excitement building.

Abel placed a red leather box on the table and she immediately spotted the brand name: Patek Philippe, Genève. She glanced at her wrist and at the watch her parents had given her on her eighteenth birthday.

He smiled. 'I know what you're thinking. *I already have a watch.*'

Almost involuntarily, Tina placed her right hand over her left wrist.

'Today, you're travelling in trainers,' Abel continued. 'But, for dinner, you'll probably select another pair of shoes. That's how you should think about this watch.' He pushed the clasp and opened the box.

She gasped. She couldn't help it.

'This is a travel timepiece, a Calatrava Pilot by Swiss watchmaker Patek Philippe, to record your first flight in a helicopter. As you can see, the styling is aeronautical and incorporates a second time zone little hand, set to Rome time.'

She tried to control her breathing.

Abel took the watch out of its box. 'But, most importantly,

it is self-winding. No battery to run out. It is also water resist-
ant down to thirty metres. That's about a hundred feet – pretty
deep. The case…' He rubbed the watch between his thumb and
forefinger. '…is made of rose gold, and the strap is calfskin.'

Tina's mouth was dry.

He held out his hand. 'Please try it on.'

'What's the engraving?' She heard her voice crack.

'Take a look.'

Gary shivered. This was the end game, of that he was sure. His
one consolation was that Tina was ignorant of his existence
and so not in immediate danger. A tear crept out of the corner
of an eye and he swiped it away. He would not beg. He had no
belief in a God or an afterlife. When his time came, he would
embrace oblivion. At the moment, all he could embrace was a
hard floor and a long chain coiled around old water pipes in
the basement room. A little daylight came through fixed, thick
glass high windows that were a little above ground level.

The bolts slid back and the door opened. Eamonn recoiled. 'A
bit of a stink, eh?' Gary said, sprawled on the stone floor.

Eamonn edged his way in and grabbed an old metal bucket
containing body waste.

'What about food, or am I to be starved to death?'

'You'll get it when it suits me, you feckin' bastard!'

'I could've killed you, Eamonn, but I didn't.' Sprawled on the
floor, Gary looked up at the big man and hoped he wouldn't
empty the bucket's contents over him. 'Help me and I'll make
sure you're in the clear. No jail time.'

'Me. Help an Englishman? A policeman? Save your breath.'
He reached for the door.

'Leave it open, Eamonn. Please. I'm chained. I can't move.
Please.'

Eamonn stared down at him. 'Now you know how we feel.
Ireland has been chained to Britain for centuries. What mercy
did you show us? We starved but did you send food? No. When
we fought back, you hanged us.'

Gary looked at the man's angry face and chose his words

carefully. 'I apologise for all the hurt we've caused.'

'Still. Mustn't dwell on the past.' Eamonn's mouth curled up. 'At least your wife is safe in the arms of the rich bastard who's buying this place.'

Gary tried not to betray any emotion.

Eamonn's expression softened. 'Tina's a nice person. Beautiful. Me and the dog scared the shit out of her but she's got courage, I'll give her that.' He walked away, swinging the stinking bucket, but leaving the door open.

Tina sat back in her seat and watched the world rush by. She felt a surge in her back as the nose lifted and the jet soared into the sky. She turned to Abel who was looking at her. 'I like travelling First Class.'

'And you will. This is Business Class... they don't have First Class on this flight. But, when we go to New York for Christmas, we will fly First Class, although the seats are a bit too far apart for my taste.' He smiled and rested his hand on hers.

She enjoyed his touch and wondered what sex with this handsome, wealthy man would be like. She'd really fancied Dermot who had an enigmatic charm, laced with massive sex appeal. Abel was different. He was completely deferential, was scrubbed, manicured and polished, but behind his smile and perfect white teeth he clearly had a spine of steel.

She looked out of the window at the wisps of cloud scudding by and wondered about her own judgement. The death of her parents had driven out the last vestiges of balance. She knew she was out of control and that she was vulnerable. But, she wasn't scared. There was nothing bad about Abel on the internet, just his business successes, estimates of his vast wealth, and the small matter of his marriage.

She turned back to him. 'I Googled you.'

Abel smiled. 'So that's what it was. I thought I felt something.'

'I didn't realise you're a widower. I thought you were divorced.' She waited for his response, but it was slow coming.

He took his hand away. 'We met in a restaurant. Claudia was

studying English at university and was out with friends. I was also a student celebrating my first business deal. We were nineteen and, I'm embarrassed to say, it was love at first sight.'

She looked into his eyes and knew she liked this man. 'What happened?'

'Claudia was about your age. Felt terrible, went to bed early. At midnight, I called an ambulance. By morning she was on life-support. Her parents and her sister came to say goodbye. She died.'

'Why? How?'

'Sepsis.'

Tina had heard of it but wasn't exactly sure what it was.

'They didn't know what caused it. It could've been something as minor as a scratch having her nails done. She went into septic shock. Her organs failed one by one. They fought the virus as best they could but she was overwhelmed. I have never felt so helpless.' He took a deep breath and smiled. 'It taught me to live in the moment. Have an eye on the future, but not live there.'

Tina felt her new watch with her fingertips. 'Thank you for my present. And thank you for taking me out of myself.'

Lunch arrived in white ceramic dishes. Tina wanted to tuck in but there was a bit of turbulence and she was anxious about spilling food on her top.

'Timing is everything in life,' Abel laughed. 'May I help you?'

She allowed him to cover her top with a cloth napkin. 'Thank you kind sir... sorry, my lord.'

He chuckled. 'I'm still not used to it.'

'Is your father an earl? Or a duke?'

'He was a tailor. Originally from Lithuania. His parents were shot by collaborators but a non-Jewish family managed to hide him. After the war, a surviving uncle took him to the new State of Israel and then in the 1950s he came to England, ostensibly on holiday. Thanks to help from the Jewish community in Finchley, he was able to evade deportation and learn the rag trade. He met my mother in the mid 1960s. She was a fashion model. They married. My sister arrived, and then me.'

'Is your mother alive?'

'Lung cancer took her. She smoked as a model to help keep thin and it killed her aged thirty-nine. My dad has never really got over it. He's had three wives since but they didn't stand a chance. He's in his late eighties and has decided it's time to hang up his gun.'

Tina smiled. 'My dad always used cowboy analogies. If a business meeting went wrong he'd sometimes describe it as Custer's last stand. For years, I thought he said *custard's* last stand. As in, he had a bit of a wobble.'

'I've had meetings like that.' He touched her hand. 'I am so sorry about your parents. At the very least, I hope Rome will give your mind a break, a chance to rest.'

The journey from Fiumicino Airport took longer than Tina expected. Sitting in the back of the taxi with Abel she felt a bit awkward. They really knew so little about each other and lived in very different worlds. But, as Audrey had reminded her, opportunities like a luxury trip to Rome come but once and she was determined to treasure every minute. And judging by the increasingly beautiful buildings they were passing, there was an awful lot to attract her estate agent's eye.

The taxi entered a large cobbled piazza. Encompassing the entire square was a low wall adorned with countless marble statues. Within the pedestrian centre were two highly intricate fountains where gargoyles spouted water, boys blew horns, and giant naked men with bulging muscles and strange animal heads prepared for battle. Most striking of all was a commemorative column, exquisitely carved, rising out of a mass of writhing serpents. Tina couldn't quite see who or what was standing at the top.

'Almost there,' Abel commented.

'It's stunning. Everywhere I look it is unbelievable.'

He turned to her. 'I hope you will come to love Rome as much as I do, and that this is the first of many trips we make.'

She didn't know how to respond, so took his hand.

The driver turned into a narrow street, turned into another, turned again, and halted the taxi. He got out and opened Abel's door.

Tina pushed open her door and looked at the classic Italianate facade. *Massive kerb appeal*, said her estate-agent brain.

'Buona giornata, signore e signora,' welcomed the liveried doorman. 'Spero tu stia bene, Lord Cornfield.'

'Very well, Luciano. I hope life is good for you, too.'

'I live in Rome and I have a wonderful job. Seriously, sir, my life could not be better.'

Tina spotted Abel slipping a couple of hundred-Euro notes into Luciano's hand.

'Signore, we are honoured that you have chosen the best hotel in Rome for a vacation with la tua bellissima moglie.' He gave Tina his most winning smile.

Abel turned to look at her. 'Luciano, I would like to introduce you to un'amica molto buona, Christina Burton.'

The doorman bowed his head. 'Welcome to Hotel di Santa Benita, signorina. I hope your stay will be very happy.'

Tina smiled. 'Thank you.' She looked through glass doors into the extravagant reception and imagined the wealth of beauty within. She was confident about how she looked, albeit a bit on the thin side, but her clothes were chain-store stylish rather than high-end designer.

The driver removed the bags from the car's boot and wheeled them to a uniformed porter.

Abel gently put his arm around her shoulder. 'Let's get settled in.' The glass doors opened and he guided her to a large reception desk and to a beautifully groomed, smiling receptionist.

'Lord Cornfield. How lovely to see you. My name's Gabriella.'

'Thank you Gabriella. Have we met before?'

'I don't believe so. This is my first week.'

'Congratulations.'

'Thank you signore.' She placed two glossy folders on the counter. 'Is this your daughter's first visit to Rome?' She smiled at Tina.

'Mrs Burton is a friend, not my daughter,' Abel said. 'È anche una vedova.' He handed her his passport.

'Many apologies, signore.' Clearly embarrassed, Gabriella placed his passport on a scanner and returned it to him avoiding eye contact. Tina handed over hers with what she hoped was a reassuring smile.

Gabriella scanned her passport and gave it back. She turned to Abel. 'I think Signora will enjoy the Augusta suite.'

'I agree,' Abel said.

'Mario will take you to your rooms and your luggage will be with you, shortly.'

A young, liveried valet guided Tina and Abel towards the only lift in the ancient building. The doors slid open and Tina entered, followed by Abel and Mario. They stood in stiff silence until the lift came to a halt. The doors slid open and they followed Mario down a short corridor. He removed a white entry card from one of the folders and put it in a door slot. A light turned from red to green and he pushed the door open. He looked at Tina and she and Abel entered.

'Signorina, it is necessary to put entry card in slot for lights to work.' She watched Mario place the card in a wall-mounted slot. 'When you leave, take card. All lights go out. Simple. Save planet.'

Abel peeled off a fifty-Euro note and gave it to Mario. 'I can take it from here, thank you.'

Although Mario looked pleased to see the large tip, he could not hide his disappointment. He turned to Tina. 'I can show you how to work everything.'

'That's all right,' Abel said. 'I've stayed here many times.' He relieved Mario of the folders and ushered out the flirtatious young man.

Tina looked around her room with its luxuriously embossed wallpaper and extravagantly gilt-framed oil paintings. There was a button-back, silk-covered sofa and matching armchair; there were low-level tables bedecked with cut flowers in decorative vases, or with exotic lamps; and a large wall-mounted TV. On the screen appeared a message: *Welcome Signora Christina Burton to the Hotel di Santa Benita.* She smiled. 'But where's the bed?'

'Next door. It's a suite.'

He guided her through to an even larger room with an enormous double bed, side tables with drawers, fitted wardrobe units and another widescreen TV. A silk rug depicting classic Roman carvings covered much of the carpet. She spotted her borrowed suitcase sitting on a raised stand and thought it looked distinctly shabby in comparison.

Abel picked up the TV remote control. 'There's a simple menu for ordering room service et cetera and we can also message each other via the TV. Of course you can also dial my room from the phone by the bed.'

'Or I can use my own phone.'

'Exactly.' He smiled. 'My suite is just next door. Relax, have a drink, there's Champagne and chocolates; unpack if you want and I'll come back in, say, thirty minutes? We could then go for a stroll, look at some world-renowned shops and stop off for a little light refreshment. Tonight, I suggest we dine in the hotel, get a good night's sleep, and explore the cobbled streets of the old city in the morning.'

'Fabulous.' *When were they going to make love for the first time?*

'I'll freshen up and see you in about half an hour.'

'Great.' She watched Abel leave the room and a moment or two later she heard him close the door to the suite. She took a few seconds to take in the five-star surroundings. The furnishings were high-end and everywhere she looked was another little touch of luxury. No need was left unrequited. She unzipped Audrey's suitcase and quickly hung up her clothes in the large wardrobe. She had been unsure as to what to bring and was still not certain she'd made the right choices. However, she was confident about her underwear, which was almost unworn. Gary had loved seeing her dressed all in white, but he had disappeared so soon after their marriage that much of her smooth satin lingerie had remained in her bottom drawer, untouched.

She took her toiletries and make-up to the en-suite bathroom, beautifully appointed in Italian marble and with concealed lighting. Snow-white towels, perfectly rolled, were displayed on recessed shelves with matching monogrammed bathrobes and slippers.

Her new watch, displaying the hour in Rome, told her she had time. She removed it, read the inscription, then kicked off her trainers, peeled down her jeans and removed all her clothes. She looked at her naked form in the tinted mirror. She had forgotten about her complete wax… and smiled at the memory.

She stepped into the large shower and stood back before turning on the tap. Within a few seconds she was cascaded by lovely warm water from a giant-sized showerhead as she lathered her whole slim frame in luxurious, complimentary Nuxe body wash.

Wrapped in the softest towel she'd ever felt against her skin, she stepped onto an equally soft bath mat, warmed by underfloor heating. Once dry, she used Borghese body cream, another high-end courtesy product, to moisturise her arms, legs and torso. She dug in her toilet bag for a toothbrush and gave her even, white teeth a good going over. Happy, she ran a comb through her damp hair and carefully touched up her make-up, to preserve her natural look. Finally, she used the hotel's powerful hairdryer and added volume to her thick, blonde locks. She picked her clothes up from the floor and hung them in the fitted wardrobe. Her briefs she balled up and placed in a pocket within her suitcase. She selected a pair of white satin knickers and slipped them on. They felt good. She put on a long T-shirt and looked at herself in a full-height mirror. *Too thin but still pretty hot!*

A sudden thought. She hurried back to the bathroom and retrieved from her toilet bag a small plastic bottle of lubricating gel and a top of the range packet of condoms. She hated using them but she had given up the pill following Gary's disappearance. She placed both items in a bedside drawer.

She was ready. She glanced at the TV to check the time, then heard a soft knock. She took a deep breath and tried to keep her cool as she walked through the suite and opened the door.

Abel, wearing a lightweight suit and tie, stood tall and

very handsome. For a moment, he seemed lost for words. She reached for his hand and took it in hers. 'I thought you might like a little rest before we go out.' She smiled. 'Work up an appetite.'

'If we go out now, I can show you the famous Spanish Steps and the Pantheon. Or, we can do a bit of shopping. Stretch our legs.'

Had she got the whole situation wrong? The first clue was Abel booking two suites. Putting aside the cost, most men would not be so considerate. 'Come in. I'll pop on some clothes.' She hurried through to the bedroom. What to wear? Her jeans? No. She put on a bra, changed her satin knickers for comfortable cotton and rolled on a pair of tights. She lifted a pleated tartan skirt that Gary had loved off the rail in the wardrobe and chose a top that was not too clingy, in case they went into a shop and she had to try something on.

Shoes.

Trainers were ideal for cobbles but were definitely not the look. High heels were also out. Luckily, she'd had the sense to pack a pair of leather ankle boots. She pulled on a jacket and reached for her bag, which had a long shoulder strap.

A full-height mirror confirmed she looked good. Abel clearly wanted to treat her before getting his wicked way.

She smiled.

Patience, girl!

Patience.

32

The doorman bowed his head as Tina and Abel stepped out of the high class hotel. She slipped her hand through Abel's arm and they strolled down the narrow cobbled street. The sun was on its way to setting but it was still full daylight and pleasantly warm. She marvelled at the beauty of the historic buildings, with their stunning facades, sculpted stonework, and pastel shades.

'Wow… what a lovely street.'

'Historic Rome is as big as it is beautiful. We could walk for days and only see a tiny part of it. It's my favourite city. Stunning. Every visit I'm amazed. On each corner is a church with magnificent carvings, statues and paintings, often by renowned masters.'

'Have you seen the Basilica?'

'Yes. If you think it looks big on TV, wait till you get inside. It's beyond description. We will have to queue in St Peter's Square but it doesn't take long to get in.'

'Fast track?'

Abel laughed. 'No. It's not like Disneyland.'

'I can't imagine you in a queue.'

'Tina, I'm a man of the people. I suppose I could donate to a Vatican charity and buy my way to kissing the papal ring, but who knows where that chunk of precious metal's been?'

'God knows, I presume.'

He chuckled.

Her arm through his, they strolled along cobbled streets lined with fabulous little restaurants, ice cream parlours, boutique hotels, and guest houses with large oak doors set in pale pink stone facades. Almost on every piazza corner was a church named in memory of a saint. They went in one; dimly lit, the peace in the vast enclosed space was awe inspiring. Everywhere she looked were unbelievable examples of intricate artistry.

'I have no words,' she whispered.

Abel smiled. 'We are not even scratching the surface of what this incredible city has to offer. Tomorrow, we have tickets for the Vatican museum. I have only been there once and could take in just a fraction of the Renaissance art on display. It is almost beyond belief. I also found it hard to get my head around that I could walk right up to giant-sized statues, in perfect condition, that were carved before Jesus even walked this earth. As for the Sistine Chapel… forget swimming with dolphins. Michelangelo should be on everyone's bucket list.' They stopped strolling and looked up at a vast painting of the Mother and Child.

'I'd like to swim with dolphins,' Tina said.

'Then you shall.'

She turned to him. 'Have you?'

'Tame ones in Florida.'

'Is there anything left on your bucket list?'

'Yes.'

She waited for him to expand. 'May I know?'

'It's what we all want.'

They strolled into Piazza di Spagna and Tina stood for a moment to take in the enormous square with its tall palm trees, boat-shaped fountain, exquisite shop fronts, horse-drawn carriages, and seething mass of tourists. Her arm through Abel's, they meandered past colourfully dressed people towards the north end of the piazza where they paused and looked at a white-stone facade. Above each of the small windows was a little white awning, and above the modest entrance was a bronze plate, stamped with the name, *Versace*.

They entered a world that Tina, or Christina as Abel liked to call her, really appreciated. The decor was style perfection, from the beautiful, tiled flooring to the soft-white curved shelving, subtly lit, displaying the finest leather accessories.

An hour later, after trying on the most expensive clothes Tina had ever worn, all her sadness had evaporated. Every time she came out to model another outfit for Abel, the shop seemed to have swelled in numbers. Tina was catwalk thin, and her good posture and innate style carried the designer clothes off to perfection.

When she finally put her own clothes back on, they felt cheap, almost shabby, but the applause she had received every time she came out of the changing room wearing another beautiful outfit had pumped her full of confidence.

It was dusk when they left the shop. Tina gripped Abel's arm and gave him a very long peck on the cheek. 'That was fun,' she whispered.

'You looked gorgeous in everything.'

'Thank you.'

'Let's go via the Spanish Steps then swing by the Trevi fountain. Photos cannot convey its scale and beauty. You have to see it. The Spanish Steps, on the other hand, are slightly underwhelming but they're en route.'

'I feel so spoiled.'

Abel placed his hands on her upper arms. 'Nothing and nobody can spoil you, Christina. You are the most remarkable young woman I have ever met. You appreciate the finer things in life but they don't turn your head. You have integrity. Grace. Charm… I admire everything about you.'

Tina's heart was pounding as she tried to control her breathing. She didn't know how to respond. Abel offered his arm and she took the cue.

They walked in silence.

She was the first to speak. 'Computers. What attracted you? It seems at odds with your appreciation of culture and art.'

'There's a part of me I cannot control. It's a gift for recognising talent in others. Believe you me, it's the only skill I possess. I was eighteen, at university studying maths, and I met a guy who told me that one day we would all have our own phone, our own individual phone number. At that time, phones were so big and heavy it seemed a preposterous idea, but I knew the guy was clever. I asked him if he could design a computer program that could anticipate currency movements. He did. I bought it. I made my first thousand pounds playing the market... in one hour. I sold the program to a commercial bank for a million. I asked my friend to design an accounting program. I gave him all the parameters but what he produced was so much cleverer. In fact, it was a financial modelling tool the basis of which is still used by leading software packages today. I didn't sell that. I sold licences and by the time I was twenty-five I had about fifty million. So did my friend. I used some of the money to buy property and land. But I was over-confident and invested in start-up businesses during the first dot com bubble. I lost a few million but learned a lot. I kept on investing, backing ideas, and gradually built a portfolio. I've been lucky. I have good instincts. I have no talent but I recognise talent, and I back it.' Abel stopped walking and turned to face her. 'As soon as I met you, I knew you were special. You have a gift. You attract others to you. Look at Versace today. People waited, paused their shopping, to see you model the next dress.'

Tina had always believed in herself but she was embarrassed by the level of his praise. In most circumstances, she would write off compliments as solely a ploy to get her into bed but Abel had already passed-up the first opportunity.

'Are we nearly there, yet?'

He laughed and did a grand gesture to a wide, high, flight of steps. In the twilight, people took selfies with the steps behind.

'Shall we run up?' she asked.

'Let's...' He grasped her hand and they ran to the base of the steps.

She took a deep breath and looked at her would-be lover. 'Thank you Abel.' She let go of his hand and started running up the steps. Her feet pounded the old stone as she rejoiced in the exuberant exercise. For the first time in oh so long, she felt happy.

The cold really bit into Gary's bones. He was already thin but now he knew he was seriously malnourished. His skin lacked thickness and was scarred and bleeding from where the cuffs rubbed his wrists and ankles. He felt beaten. They couldn't let him live if they were to escape justice. He was a loose end Stacy would ensure was squared away. How could somebody who looked so angelic be so ruthless? If she wasn't a psychopath she certainly bore most of the traits.

He looked up at the high window and saw a little dwindling daylight poking through into the basement room. There was no escape. He was not dealing with amateurs. He was a slave waiting for the end. And it would come soon, very soon.

'I love these narrow streets,' Tina said. 'I love the little alfresco restaurants, and the food market we just passed. And I love the enormous piazzas with their amazing dramatic fountains and bizarre, erotic statues.'

Abel laughed. 'Rome does boast a lot of naked men.' Arm in arm they ambled-on as the sun set. Long shadows were cast by tall stone buildings with dark alleyways lit by ancient street lamps. They entered another historic square and joined a horde of tourists from almost every nation on the planet.

'Fontana di Trevi,' Abel said, 'is without question the most beautiful fountain in the world.' He took her hand and weaved her through the craning visitors to the edge of the fountain. She looked up and saw a vision of such magnificence it almost stilled her heart.

Abel continued in tourist guide mode. 'The fountain is fed by fresh water brought here by an aqueduct constructed by the Romans, nineteen years BC. These days, I think the water's re-cycled so it's not wasted.'

Tina pressed herself closer to the man she was falling for, big time. She relished his body heat and knew that the feeling in her heart was real.

'Every time I come here,' he continued, 'I am astounded by the artistry. The scale is mind-blowing. The facade behind the fountain with those columns and statues is mightily impres-sive in itself, but those winged horses galloping through the water touches something deep inside me.' She felt him fishing in his pocket. 'Throw these in.' He handed her a few coins. 'They say it will bring us luck, and the money goes to a good cause.'

She looked at the Euros in her hand and threw them into the frothy, white water. His arm slid around her shoulders and she snuggled into him.

'I think we can squeeze in one more item,' he whispered into her hair.

She took his arm and he led her down Via delle Muratte, another cobbled street with stylish shops and pizzerias. The route they were taking seemed complicated and, at times, Abel was forced to consult the map on his phone. And then they arrived at Piazza della Rotonda. Tina looked up in awe at the majestic stone colonnades that line the entrance to Rome's famous, former pagan temple.

'Wow.'

Abel smiled at her. 'Wow indeed. It was commissioned in the second century by Hadrian, the Emperor who built the wall in the north of England. The reason it looks so good today is that Emperor Phocas gave the temple to the Vatican early in the seventh century. Of course, it would look even better if Pope Urban the eighth hadn't robbed the temple of most of its bronze. Let's take a look inside.'

'Can we go in?'

'Yes. It's the perfect time of day.'

He took her hand and guided her past the towering Corinthian columns and through the giant-sized doorway and vestibule into a rotunda that was beyond imagination. She looked up in awe at the domed roof. 'Oh my God.'

Abel pointed to a hole at the top. 'The oculus is lined with Roman bronze and is the largest of its kind in the world. Its size allows the sun to light the Pantheon by day and for us to view the stars at night.'

She tried to soak up the magnificent artistry and geometry of the Pantheon's coffered dome. 'Is the oculus covered over with glass?'

'No, it's open to the elements. When it rains, it falls onto the floor. If you look carefully, you'll see it's concave with numerous holes for draining the water into original Roman waste pipes. When it snows, I understand it looks incredible.'

She turned her attention to the square and circular-patterned marble floor then lifted her eyes to take in the granite columns, elaborate tombs, and many ecclesiastical statues.

'Shall we sit?' He guided her to several rows of wooden pews in front of the altar. She sat down and he slid in beside her.

'It's so peaceful,' she said.

'There's something about the perfect symmetry of the spherical interior that relaxes the mind.'

In the still, cool, evening air she closed her eyes and tried to shut out the conflicting emotions that tore at her heart. Was she betraying Gary? His voice echoed inside her head and his face was so clear, so alive, she had to snap her eyes open to erase his image. She stole a glance at Abel and immediately felt a deep longing to be in his arms, to be protected by him, to be loved. But was it him or his wealth she found so intoxicating, so alluring? Could she ever love him with the same intensity she had loved Gary? She took a breath and leaned against him.

33

Dermot O'Hanlon lay back in the king-sized bed and luxuriated in the fine-cotton sheets. The White Hart Hotel in Undermere had good ratings online. He hated splashing the cash but giving a convincing performance was essential if he was to protect the woman he truly wanted. There was nothing he could do to save her husband and he pushed the thought of what was to happen to him out of his mind. In truth, he should never have got involved with one of the most violent and crooked criminal gangs in England, let alone Essex. But, lust and greed had got the better of him. Now, all he wanted was to wriggle out of the situation without jeopardising Tina's life.

The door to the bathroom opened and he felt a stirring. Backlit by the bathroom light, Stacy looked exquisite in her sheer nightdress. How could somebody have the face and figure of an angel, yet be so cruel, so lacking in empathy? He could understand why Gary had let his guard down in the presence of such a woman. He felt no love for her but his desire to consume her bountiful body was as great as ever.

'Hello, my sweet,' he said. 'You are beyond delicious.' He saw Stacy fight a smile. 'I swear, in all the places I have travelled, never have I seen, let alone met, anyone who can hold a candle to your beauty.'

'Do you love me?' Her voice was husky.

His response had to be convincing. 'Enough to make you my lover, my betrothed, my wife, until death do us part.'

Stacy laughed and Dermot felt a chill that wilted his erection. She hurried across the plush carpet and hurled herself at him. Her arms wrapped around his neck and he felt her gym-trained sinews.

'What a team we make, my lover,' she said. 'We'll rule the world.'

'Rule the world? Not getting banged-up is enough for me.'

She pulled away and looked into his eyes. 'What's the problem? Tell me and daddy will deal with it.'

That was the problem. Gary's dick had ruled his head and Dermot had fallen into the same trap. He looked into her sparkling eyes. 'I may have to disappear for a while.' He saw her sparkle turn to flint, but pushed on. 'I thought we'd have longer but Cornfield looks set to buy the old school.'

Stacy lay down on the bed. 'Daddy has dealt with bigger problems than Cornfield.'

'What can he do?'

She turned her face to him. 'Please. Don't pretend you're not part of the game.'

All sexual desire evaporated. The Cottees had a fearsome reputation for a very good reason and the apple of her father's eye had not fallen far from his violent tree. Getting out from under her high heel without incurring daddy's wrath, or attracting the attention of the authorities, was going to require some very fancy footwork.

He felt the tips of Stacy's long, manicured nails on his chin. 'Kiss me.' Her fingers traced a line down his neck and bare chest.

He took her hand and kissed her palm.

'Wait,' she said.

'I'm not sure that I can.'

She went to her suitcase and from a pocket removed a blister pack. He watched as she popped a pill into her mouth and swallowed. She smiled down at him. 'I want an all-nighter.' She threw the pack onto the bed and opened a glass bottle of sparkling mineral water, standing on the bedside unit. She took a sip and held out the bottle for Dermot. He took it and watched as she peeled off her nightdress.

'Holy Mother of God, I don't need any blue pill.' He put the open bottle and blister pack on the bedside unit. He moved across the bed and she lay down beside him. He pushed her onto her back and kissed the firm mounds of her perfectly created breasts. He caressed and kissed her golden, toned skin, working his way down to her sheer thong. He pulled a tie string and pushed the fabric to one side.

'Go for it, lover. Go for it.'

A sweet smile framed by blonde locks floated into his mind's eye.

'Come on, sweetheart. Don't keep a girl waiting.'

Tina felt Abel's arm in the small of her back as they followed the liveried waiter to a square table with a white cloth, laid with highly polished silver cutlery and sparkling crystal wine glasses. The head waiter pulled out a padded chair and she sat down as he pushed the seat under her. As quick as a magician he placed a pristine white linen monogrammed napkin on her lap. Meanwhile, Abel helped himself to the chair opposite.

Two waiters, each holding a glass bottle, came up to the table. 'Frizzante o naturale, signora?' asked the more senior of the two.

'Naturale per favore,' she said, smiling encouragingly.

He picked up her glass with a white-gloved hand and poured the still mineral water.

'Lo stesso per me, grazie,' Abel said.

The waiter glided around the table and filled a second glass with the same careful attention.

'Champagne?'

She looked into Abel's hazel eyes and Gary smiled back. His no nonsense, defined features were immediately dismissed only to be replaced with Dermot's phenomenally attractive mishmash. Abel was different. He had clean, even features that were sculpted to perfection. Perhaps they had been, but it was not a question she was about to ask.

'Christina? Champagne?'

'Thank you. A glass would be lovely.'

He turned to the waiter. 'Please ask your sommelier for a bottle of Louis Roederer Cristal.' He grinned at Tina. 'A glass is never enough.'

She smiled. 'I feel intoxicated by Rome, already.'

'Christina, you look stunning.'

Following their excursion, Tina had taken her time to freshen up and moisturise her body. After selecting her very best lingerie, she had opened her wardrobe door to decide what to wear and discovered, hanging on the rail, three of the dresses she had tried on in the Versace store and had loved the most. How had they got to her room, her suite? She tried on all three and found it almost impossible to choose. Finally, she settled on an almost-sheer dress that hugged her contours. When Abel knocked on her door to escort her to dinner, she had glanced into a full-length mirror and knew she was at her peak; she would never look better than she looked tonight.

'It's thanks to Donatella,' she smiled, and sipped some water to deflect the compliment. Her parents' union had created two children whose looks had always attracted attention, even when they were very young. From his late teens, men had been drawn to her brother. He was cool, calm, collected and deeply sensual in a wholly masculine way that had broken many hearts until he had found the man for him. In her late teens, Tina had put her career, her ambition ahead of love until she dated a good-looking inventory clerk she'd met whilst measuring up a property. There was a lot about him that had appealed to her but his love of football outbalanced any desire he may have had to build a career or business. A brief dalliance with a Russian property developer ended that relationship.

'A penny for them.'

It took a moment for Tina to drag her mind back to the present and to understand what Abel was saying. 'A penny? I can assure you they're priceless.'

He laughed. 'I bet they are.'

She smiled and contemplated the man seated across the table. Baron Cornfield of St Mawes plied the aphrodisiac of power in a body that told its own story. He was tall but not too tall with the kind of lean, athletic torso and limbs that were toned by gym machines and masseurs. Everything about him was polished, complemented by a ready quip and self-deprecating humour. Despite his enormous wealth and power to influence, he shrugged off his status as purely his ability to capitalise on lucky throws of the dice. Well, tonight, he was going to have a very lucky throw of the dice.

'The menu is yours for the eating,' Abel continued. 'Don't hold back.'

'There are no prices.'

'I should hope not.'

She laughed and chose the lightest food as she did not want to make love with her handsome suitor for the first time on a full stomach. 'For starter may I have the asparagus and parmesan salad?'

'Good choice. And for your main course?'

'I think I'll be fine with just a starter.'

'You may think that now, but when you smell the aroma of my veal ossobuco, I'll hear your tummy rumbling across the table.'

She grinned. 'You're probably right.' She picked up the menu and ran her eyes over the choices of fish. 'Turbot with morels and escarole sounds good.'

'It does.'

'The only problem is, I don't know what morels and escarole actually are.'

'I was once asked that question and pretended I had to take a call so I could Google the answer. Morels are wild mushrooms, I believe, and escarole is a type of bitter lettuce, like chicory.'

'Were you on a date?'

For a moment, he looked puzzled. 'No. It was a business lunch with a Japanese client. To this day I have no idea why I didn't just ask the waiter.' He reached across the table and took her hand in his. 'Christina, thank you for coming with me to Rome.'

She felt a warm glow glide through her body.

'I have a proposal,' he continued.

What was coming next? The air sucked out of her and her head began to spin. She wasn't quite ready for marriage yet, but it would only be a matter of time.

He squeezed her hand. 'Thanks to your initiative, I am starting a great new venture in a part of the world that I had never
visited. You have an instinct for what people want, even if they
don't know it yet, and I cannot think of anyone who will do a
better job.'

What was he talking about?

'I want you to mastermind the development of my new hotel
and leisure complex at the old school. It won't be easy, and it
will take several years of your life, but if you accept, I know it
will make a massive difference to the success of the project...
and to your own financial wellbeing.'

She breathed out, slowly. Shouldn't she be thrilled by the
offer? Why wasn't she? She looked into his eyes and knew
what she really desired. 'Thank you, that's such an honour. I'm
deeply touched.'

'Don't give me your answer now.'

She smiled to hide the disappointment that washed through
her. 'Lord Cornfield...'

'Please, don't call me that. To be frank I am ashamed of it. I
contributed an eye-watering amount of cash to a certain political party that needed the money and was rewarded with a
peerage for...' he did quotation marks in the air. '...services to
computing.' He laughed at his own joke.

'You bought your title?'

'Like a car, all shiny and bright. I'm a cross-bencher. In other
words, I don't, officially, support any political party. But it
proves that wealth can buy almost anything.'

She pulled her hand out from under his and placed it on her
lap, out of his reach.

He looked at her intently. 'I am forty-eight, twice your age,
Christina. I am active, but with each passing year, I will get
older as you climb to your prime.'

What had brought this on? She was completely puzzled.
'Why did you bring me here?' she asked, her mouth, dry.

'When we arrived at the hotel, the receptionist mistook me
for your father. Rich man with woman half his age is not news,
but I care for you too much to exploit you that way.'

'Nobody exploits me unless I want them to.' She felt tears spring to her eyes as the sommelier showed Abel the bottle of Champagne. He nodded.

She stood up and spoke directly to the wine waiter. 'Signore, please don't open it.' A tear escaped much to her annoyance. 'Goodnight Abel.' She hurried out of the hotel's restaurant, feeling several pairs of eyes on her.

34

Abel nodded to the waiter who took the Champagne and ice bucket away. He looked at Christina's recently vacated chair. Could he have handled it any worse? Simply put, he had fallen for the beautiful, charming, smart, grieving young widow and wanted nothing more than to wrap his arms around her. If she were any other beautiful young woman, he would have already bedded her several times. Usually, at the end of a long weekend, he'd had enough and was keen to part-company. But Christina was different. Of course, she was expecting to have sex and he would have enjoyed it, but he would also have been ashamed. If he were his usual self, he would show her off to his chums in London by escorting her to his favourite clubs and restaurants. As much as people would smile and as good-looking for his age as he was, everyone would know that Christina was on his arm and in his bed solely because of his wealth. He could delude himself that he could have pulled her even if he were... what? An accountant? After all, Christina's late husband had been a police officer, so her head wasn't turned by money. But, an accountant? No, he wasn't that good looking, or witty.

He placed his napkin on the table and stood. Several diners looked in his direction. He took out his wallet and dropped a hundred Euros on the white table cloth and strode out of the restaurant.

Standing in the lift, as it took him to the fifth floor, he tried to form a plan. He was falling in love with Christina, of that he was sure. The doors opened and he strode down the corridor towards her suite. What could he say or do to repair his clumsiness? He tapped on her door and waited. He tapped again. He knocked. He knocked harder. He banged. He pulled out his phone and swiped the screen. He waited for her to answer her mobile phone but all too quickly it went to voice mail. He dialled again. Voice mail. He tried calling her room phone via the hotel operator. He could hear the phone ringing. He held on.

Tina tilted her tear-stained face up to the large shower head and the hot water cascaded over her.

She'd been a fool.

How could she have ever imagined that someone so famous and important as Abel Cornfield would be interested in her, romantically? He wasn't even interested in sleeping with her! Had he brought her to Rome simply to seduce her into accepting his job offer? She wanted to talk to her mum, as she always had, but her mum was dead. Her daddy, who was her anchor in all things, was dead, too. She sank to her knees as the tsunami of grief overtook her. She tried to imagine Gary taking her in his arms, looking so handsome in his uniform, but she couldn't summon the image. Her life that had started off so well had peaked when she married aged twenty-two, then shattered into a million pieces. She was sliding backwards to a place where all light was gone.

Abel ate, sitting at the dining table in his suite. The food in the hotel was second to none, but his mind was far away from haute cuisine. He had been so crass. Christina was expecting to sleep with him and all the job offer had done was act as a rejection. He'd only felt this way once before in his life and sepsis had stolen her from him. He loved Christina but more than that, he admired her and wanted to protect her from the advances of a man twice her age; a man who had used his wealth to woo her at a tragic time in her life when she was at her most vulnerable. All it had taken to prick his conscience was the receptionist referring to Christina as his daughter.

What a mess. He had allowed his conscience to overrule his heart and destroy his second chance, perhaps his only chance, of finding happiness.

He called down to reception and asked for the food to be removed. He tried Christina's numbers again but she wasn't picking up. He got ready for bed and switched on the TV. He flicked from Italian show to Italian show then checked out the movies. None of the new ones appealed to him. He was about to turn it off when Roman Holiday came on the screen starring Audrey Hepburn and Gregory Peck – they had a big age gap, didn't they? He turned out the lights and let Christina's sweet and beautiful face fill the screen in his mind. In the morning he would take her hand and tell her how much she meant to him. How much he loved her.

A valet opened the door to Tina's suite. It was still early but, after a sleepless night, Abel was desperate to be with her.

'Christina. It's Abel. I was worried about you.' He listened for a response. Hesitantly, he entered the sitting room and looked at the half-open door to the bedroom. 'Christina? Are you there?'

No response.

He pushed open the bedroom door. The first thing he noticed was that the bed was fully made and had not been slept in. Now he was worried. His eyes flicked around the room looking for her suitcase. It was gone. He slid back the door to the closet and saw the three dresses he'd bought for her. He checked the bathroom. No toiletries.

She must've snuck out without anyone noticing.

He tipped and dismissed the valet then sat down on the edge of the bed and put his face in his hands.

35

Malcolm didn't much enjoy driving into Undermere. In the last few years the traffic seemed to have doubled and there were now cameras everywhere, ready to ensnare the unwary driver. He swung into the station car park and saw Tina standing near the taxi rank. He pulled on the handbrake and leapt out as fast as his ageing muscles would allow.

'Thank you, Malcolm.' There was a note in her voice that spoke volumes. He opened the boot and Tina slid in her bag. She looked up at him. 'I'm in trouble.' He saw tears gush into her eyes and he wrapped his arms around her.

'You will get through this, darling. It won't be easy, but you will.' He felt the young woman shake in his embrace.

Audrey heard the bell, hurried down the hallway and pulled the door open. Standing on the step was Samuel.

'The coroner has released their bodies.' She guided him into the cottage and sat on the sofa next to him. 'I should've been home,' he whispered. 'I left this country for selfish reasons. I should never have gone.'

She squeezed his shoulders. 'We all feel guilt when someone dies. My mother never got over the guilt of sending my brother to a boarding school from which he never returned. Malcolm feels guilt. I feel guilt. But remember this… your parents would not exchange their lives for yours. They would not want you to feel any guilt. It was an accident.' She looked up at Malcolm standing in the doorway to the hall.

'She's asleep,' he said. 'Absolutely exhausted.'

Audrey nodded.

'I'll make a pot.' A few seconds later, she heard the clatter of crockery coming from the kitchen.

'Sam.'

The young man looked at her.

'Malcolm and I are here for you. We can help arrange the funeral. Please let us.'

The Reverend William Longden entered the Methodist Church from the vestry, wearing a long, plain black robe. He had already checked that there were enough order of service pamphlets in each of the pews. Aged eighty-nine, once over six feet three inches tall but now stooped, with a bald pate and a hooked nose, he put his sharp mind down to his love of language.

'Reverend Longden.'

He recognised the voice immediately. 'Mr Cadwallader, you're here early.'

Malcolm approached with his hand outstretched. 'You know me, William. Just in time is late.' They shook hands. 'Difficult day ahead.'

'It is. I will do my best to provide a crumb of comfort but only time can ease the tremendous sense of loss. Of course, what is truly tragic is the terrible fate of young Gary.'

'What a glorious wedding that was.'

'I've married many young couples but that late summer's day in your beautiful memorial garden I mark as my finest.'

Malcolm laid a hand on the older man's arm. 'If we're not careful, we'll both be weeping.'

William offered a tight smile. 'Without doubt.'

'How is the church?'

William looked around the interior. He saw plain walls, plain Victorian windows with plain Victorian panes, contrasted by surprisingly decorative cast-iron pillars supporting galleries for additional worshippers, rarely required, on each side of the church. 'Thanks to Audrey's largesse the decor is much improved but we've had to invest in a new bucket as the constant rain has found a way of entering the ladies' facilities.'

'What about the gents? I hope there are no unintended leaks there?'

William chuckled.

'Here's another thought,' Malcolm continued. 'Have you considered crowd funding to improve the heating? I don't know about you, but these days I can detect the merest wisp of a cold draught.'

William glanced down at a metal vent in the plain flagstone floor. 'Are you suggesting that the warmed air pumped under the floor is inadequate?'

'It may have been good enough for Victorian worshippers used to hardship but oldies like you and me need more wrap-around comfort.'

'Well, I'm astounded. I'll have to take your complaint to a higher authority.'

'I hope you do, Reverend, as a schooner of sherry prior to the service simply doesn't cut it anymore.'

Audrey was seated in a funeral car between Tina and Sam, holding each of their hands as they followed the two hearses to the front of the Methodist church. She was not surprised to see so many people standing outside. Malcolm hurried up to the car and opened a rear door. He took Tina's hand and helped her out. Meanwhile, the driver opened the other passenger door for Sam and Audrey.

Tina exchanged Malcolm for her brother and Audrey took her husband's arm. They followed Tina and Sam through the arched entrance into the Victorian church. Most of the pews were full but four spaces had been reserved at the front.

They sat down on crushed felt cushions that provided scant protection from the cold, solid-wood pew. Elgar's solemn masterpiece, *Nimrod,* was being played by Eleanor, usually seen wearing an apron in the Olde Tea Shoppe, now all in black, hands and feet working the traditional piped organ.

Audrey picked up the order of service. On the front was a photograph of Tina and Sam's parents on their wedding day; below were their full names and against each the date of birth and the date of death. She opened her bag and removed a pressed, linen handkerchief, one of Malcolm's she'd sneaked from his drawer. She stemmed the tears that spilled out and then snuck a sideways glance at Tina, who was sitting bolt upright and wringing the lace hankie Audrey had given her.

The organ music swelled and there was a ripple from behind as the congregation stood.

Audrey turned and saw the first of the coffins brought in, carried on the shoulders of four men in dark, formal suits. The coffin, of light wood veneer, was placed on one of two biers at the front of the simple church. Once both coffins were in place the pallbearers retreated and the congregation watched the Reverend William Longden, dressed in a full-length cassock and white surplice, climb the few steps that led up to the wooden pulpit.

His church was packed. People were pressed together in pews, several stood by the entrance and a few had ventured upstairs to sit in the galleries. William surveyed the expectant congregation but took little pleasure from their numbers. As the organ music came to an early conclusion, he looked down into Tina and Sam's tear-stained, upturned faces, each gripping the other's hand; and at the two boxes containing the remains of two people William had grown to like. On each coffin was a beautiful bouquet of fresh flowers, rich in vibrant colours, their heady scent imbuing his soul with renewed energy.

In front of him on the lectern were a few notes, but he didn't need them. He knew precisely what he wanted to say. The eulogy had taken longer than usual to write but he hoped his words would bring some comfort. He opened his mouth to speak but before he could make his first utterance, the air was filled with the pulsing chop-chop of rotor blades.

Abel Cornfield peered out of the helicopter's side window as it circled above the Methodist church. A dozen people were crowding around the entrance, shielding their eyes as they stared up. In the church's graveyard were two freshly dug plots, with duckboards on each side and straps coiled ready to lower the coffins into the ground.

Christina's parents.

He should be with her, supporting her, but despite all his efforts, they had not spoken since Rome. He signalled to Graham, his regular pilot, to fly off and within a few seconds they were approaching the old school standing in solitude on the moor. Abel caught a glimpse of a handful of men carrying pot plants to a curtain-sided truck. The pilot circled the helicopter above a number of caravans and assorted vehicles. A man with a large dog on a leash emerged from the side of the building.

'What the...??' The pilot forced his stick over and the helicopter lurched to the left hurling Abel into the side panel. The pilot regained full control and guided the helicopter down to the flat patch of grass in front of the gravelled apron. 'Sorry about that, sir. Bloody drone.'

Abel waited for the rotors to come to a rest. The man with the dog stood some way off but everything in his demeanour seemed threatening. Abel was now the legal owner of the old school and grounds and his lawyers had given Dermot O'Hanlon notice to vacate. They had a month. If the travellers didn't comply, Abel could take them to court but his preferred Plan B was to pay them to go.

'It's safe now, sir,' the pilot said through the headphones.

'Thank you, Graham.' Abel removed his headset, reached for the door handle and pushed it open. The strength of the wind caught him by surprise. He looked back at the pilot. 'I don't know how long I'll be.'

'Take your time, sir. I have coffee and a whole moor to piss on.'

Abel laughed and stepped down from the helicopter. He carefully closed and secured the door. The rotor above was turning slowly. He stood upright and walked over to the man with the dog. 'Mr Dermot O'Hanlon is expecting me.'

'He's said nothin'.' The man snarled the words, almost like his dog.

'That's your beef,' Abel replied. He stepped off the grass onto the gravel and strode towards the front door. As he approached, it opened and he was met by Dermot's scowling face.

'I thought you were coming tomorrow?'

'It's not a problem is it? I'm not expecting you to have tidied up!' Abel laughed at his own joke.

Dermot didn't smile.

Abel felt his blood pressure begin to rise. 'I own this place. I've been generous with your notice to quit.'

'Come back tomorrow.'

He looked into the Irishman's eyes and knew the man had something to hide. 'As you've been here for a considerable amount of time I, politely, ask if you would act as my guide.'

'Didn't Tina show you around?'

'I was a bit more focused on her than the building. With you I won't be.'

Dermot stepped aside and gestured for him to enter the grand hallway.

The first thing Abel noticed was the smell. It was a mix of aromas; that of an old institution and something else he couldn't readily identify.

The pallbearers lowered the second of the two coffins into its final resting place and pulled up the straps. The area around the two open graves was carpeted in green to protect the assembled shoes. At the head end of each grave was a large mound of earth and, a short distance away, was a small mechanical digger. The bouquets of flowers that had been placed on the coffins were now at the foot of the open graves.

Tina gripped her brother's hand. This was it. This was real. This was when she had to grow up. This was the goodbye, the farewell that Gary's disappearance had denied her. The pallbearers bowed their heads to the deceased, and slipped away.

The Reverend Longden stood slightly to one side. In his hands he held the Methodist Prayer Book but, when he spoke, he didn't refer to the text open in front of him. 'God of all grace, we pray for one another, especially for Helen and John who we commit to your immortal care. In our loss and sorrow be our refuge and strength, and enfold us in your everlasting arms.'

36

Stacy looked up from the mass of green plants to the ceiling as she listened to the receding chop-chop of the helicopter. Good. Dermot had got rid of Lord Cornfield. His sudden arrival had interfered with the removal of the marijuana, which was to be processed in a drying facility in Essex before the weed, pot, grass, ganja, skunk, bobo bush, whatever... was to be distributed via a network of dealers.

Unfortunately, the workers could not be distributed quite so easily. They were all men from Vietnam, illegal migrants who knew that if they went to the police their families would suffer back home.

But what to do with them now?

Not speaking English was a positive. Perhaps they could be transported to Scotland and let loose in the Highlands? Stacy hated involving her father especially when she knew he disapproved of her associations. Sleeping with the enemy had been embarrassing for both her and her father, who had genuinely liked Gary. Although Dermot was on the right side of the law, as far as her father was concerned, the involvement of so many Irish travellers in the Cottee family business could end up being a costly mistake.

She didn't want to undermine Dermot's authority; she fancied him like hell and wanted to be Mrs O'Hanlon, but she had a job to do and that was to clear the old school of all the incriminating evidence, including the rat chained to a water pipe in the basement pantry.

'Jesus said, *do not let your hearts be troubled.*'

Tina listened to the wonderful Reverend Longden and wished her heart was not troubled.

'*Believe in God,*' he continued, his voice strong, almost theatrical. '*Believe also in me for I am the way, and the truth, and the life.*'

'Amen.' The word came out louder than Tina had intended. It was immediately repeated by those closest to the graves.

A pallbearer approached her with a copper bowl and matching trowel. Her vision blurred by tears, she scooped up a little earth and took a careful step forward. She looked down at her mother's coffin, appreciably smaller than her father's. Audrey's hand rested gently on her shoulder. More than any words, it gave her the maternal comfort she needed as she tossed the earth onto the box below.

The chop-chop of rotor blades lifted all their eyes to the sky and she watched as Abel's helicopter disappeared from view into low cloud. A few spots of rain splashed her cheeks.

'I cannot believe how many people have come, despite the rain.' Sam had not responded positively when Audrey first suggested the Methodist Church Hall as a possible venue for the funeral wake.

'I told you.' Tina gripped her brother's arm at the head of a mass of local people queuing to pay their respects. Inside the entrance was the tall, imposing figure of the Reverend Longden who had spoken so movingly, so powerfully, about their parents.

Huddled under umbrellas, old friends and acquaintances had the good grace to introduce themselves to Sam, to speak words of consolation, briefly, and to move on. But, Tina took her time with each guest and very quickly she and Sam had to seek shelter inside the hall so that people were not kept standing out in the rain.

Hair slicked by the deluge, Tina was delighted to see one of Hawksmead's greatest champions. 'My sincere condolences, Sam,' said Andy Blake. 'My wife and I got to know your parents well over the last few years. We are profoundly saddened by your terrible loss. If there's anything I or my paper, the Hawksmead Chronicle, can do, please let me know. My office is just down the High Street.'

'Thank you. I'm so grateful for all the support Tina and I have received, today.'

'I meant what I said.' The tall man looked intently at both Sam and his sister. 'Wherever you go, however long you are away, Hawksmead is your home and will always welcome you.'

Tina leaned across and gave Andy a kiss on the cheek.

'Last point,' Andy said, 'then I'll leave you two alone. I know you have the inquest to get through but if you need any help sorting out wills and probate, I have experience in that area and would be more than happy to help.'

'Thank you,' Sam said. He held out his hand then changed his mind and gave Andy a surprise hug.

Cloud encased the AgustaWestland helicopter in an impenetrable blanket of white, compounded by torrential rain. It had been particularly bad over Elstree Aerodrome where Graham had tried to land. He had sought permission from Air Traffic Control to head south to Redhill Aerodrome, where the helicopter was based. He hoped the rising heat from London's buildings would at least lift the cloud base. Through the murk he made out the meandering River Thames and followed it downstream, which was the specific flight path for private helicopters.

Keep cool.

All he had to do was follow the river, between low and high water marks. The problem was, he could barely see the grey ribbon. If he flew too low, he risked flying into offices and apartments, built near the river's edge. Then there were the cranes. At night, their warning lights were easy to see but in thick cloud during the day, by the time he saw a warning light it would probably be too late to change course. He was tempted to go higher, away from lethal obstacles, but the risk of getting lost over south London, outside of official helicopter lanes, was too great.

Keep cool.

Magdalena wrapped her arms around Tina and squeezed. 'I love you, my sweet. I would give anything to take pain from you.' She held Tina's face in her artisan hands and kissed her on each cheek. 'May God bless you and protect you. And if he's too busy, I am here.'

Tony Blake accompanied by his wife, Eden, interrupted Magda's flow and Tina felt quite relieved.

'We are so sorry about your parents. Your father calmed my nerves on your wedding day. I was terrified of giving the Best Man speech.' He took both her hands in his. 'I was very fond of Gary and was honoured to be at his side on such a special day. He adored you, as we all do. When you left Hawksmead for the bright lights, Eden and I talked about uprooting our family and following you south. Then Gary... disappeared. I should've come to see you. But I didn't want to impose. It's my biggest regret. I'm so sorry, Tina.'

She saw tears in his eyes and released her hands. She blinked hard and looked at his voluptuous wife.

'Please come and visit, as soon as you can,' Eden said. 'Georgiana remembers being your bridesmaid as though it were yesterday. She loves the dress she wore even though she's way too big for it now. That summer preparing for your wedding was so very special.' Eden's eyes brimmed over.

'We can't turn back the clock. I wish we could.'

'No. But we can go forward, together. We want to be here for you, to help you build a new, happy future. So many people have come today because they care. We all really care.'

He was sweating. His shirt clung to him. The cloud base was zero and it wasn't even truly winter yet. He couldn't see a damn thing. The radio was tuned to Air Traffic Control. He pressed the transmit button. 'Cornfield requesting permission to divert to Battersea HeliPort.'

'Request pending. Maintain holding.'

Graham held position but decided to go lower to try and get a bearing. It was a great risk as the helicopter may have drifted away from the river and the rotor blades could easily clip a tower block or crane.

The radio burst into life. 'Cornfield. Diversion approved. Contact Battersea on 122.9.' At that moment, through a break in the cloud, Battersea Heliport appeared, stretching out into the river. He couldn't believe it. Relief flooded through him. He tuned into the new frequency and was about to open his mouth to speak when the helicopter jerked and jolted and spun in circles like a winged sycamore seed.

The party was in full swing. There was no other word that could accurately describe the wake. Tea had turned into wine, and black ties were loosened as people relaxed and laughed, albeit suppressed. The last time Tina had seen this many friends and acquaintances was at her wedding in the neighbouring memorial garden. Three years later, her parents' funeral had brought the same wonderful folk together again and, for a brief while, she could park her grief. Deep down, she had hoped Abel would come to the wake but when she heard his helicopter fly back south, she was disappointed but not surprised. The man had done all he could to reach out to her, but she had given him nothing in return. Was it too late?

'I expected to see your young Irishman here.'

Tina looked into Harry's florid face. The last time she'd seen him was when she and Dermot had dined at the Rorty Crankle. That seemed such a long time ago.

'Thank you for coming, Harry. Is Cathy with you?'

'Yes. We shut the pub and jumped the condolence queue as we were both in need of a drink. She's chatting to Audrey and Malcolm. We are both so sorry for your terrible loss.'

'Thank you.' She kissed him on the cheek.

'And the Irishman?'

'He had a previous engagement... with another woman.'

'Ah, I see.'

'There is somebody I like, but I cocked it up.'

'I think, my dear, you are permitted multiple cock-ups.'

She nodded slowly. 'Would you excuse me? I need to give

that someone a call.'

Tina moved away from Harry and smiled at guests as she sought a private place. She would have gone outside but it was bucketing with rain. She opened a door and felt for a light switch. It was a storage room with old items of furniture. Feeble daylight probed the grimy window pane. She took her phone out of her small handbag and scrolled through her contacts.

Graham refused to accept that all was lost. He used his training and innate skill to regain control of the helicopter, which was no longer plummeting but still spinning like a Frisbee. Thank God he was alone.

'You get on back before the weather closes in. I'll catch the train.'

He was so pleased his best client wasn't with him now. Not only was he about to sink several million pounds in the grimy brine below, he'd be lucky to escape with his own life, let alone also that of a trusting passenger.

'Christina!'

The moment she heard his voice her heart flipped. There was something in his tone that enveloped her soul. She opened her mouth to speak but couldn't find any words.

He continued, 'I owe you an apology. I acted like a fool.'

'No. There was only one fool, and that was me.'

'Where are you?'

'The Methodist Church Hall. The funeral wake is still in full swing.'

'May I see you?'

'I would like that.'

'Tonight?'

'Aren't you in London?'

The tail rotor which Graham had given up on slowed the spinning helicopter and he managed to regain some control. Almost crab-like, he edged the cumbersome machine towards the helipad and it spun slowly as it descended. As soon as the tyres touched the deck he altered the pitch of the blades spinning above and cut all power.

It took a few minutes for the rotors to come to a stop. By that time, a fire tender was standing by, and a tow truck. He opened his door and stepped onto terra firma – at least it felt like that to his rubbery legs – and walked down to the tail. The damaged rotor blades were stained with blood.

'Geese,' he confirmed to himself.

Sofie leant back against the storage room door and placed a Viceroy between her lips. She fired up a Dunhill lighter and sucked in the smoke. 'I hope you don't mind. I can't get on with e-cigarettes.' In the two years since Tina had last seen Sofie in London, she had bulked-up.

'What are you doing here?'

'I wanted to make sure you're all right.'

'I can assure you I am far from all right, no thanks to you.' She gave her old neighbour a long hard stare.

'It was Gary's decision. He wasn't forced. He knew the risks.'

'Did he? Did he really know the risks?' She took a breath. 'Why are you here, Sofie?'

'I'm sorry about your parents.' She stepped closer to Tina. 'I am really sorry.'

'I can't blame you for what happened to them, so thank you. How's Miroslav?'

'He's well.' She took another long drag.

'You weren't really a couple, were you?'

'No.' The admission came out with the smoke.

'And your name's not really Sofie, is it?'

'No.'

Tina reached for the doorknob. 'I have to go.'

'I am happy for you, Tina. Abel is one of the good guys.'

'So you were in a relationship?'

'There was a terrorist attack on London Bridge. I happened to be passing and was cornered by an attacker with a knife. Abel fought him off.' She looked around for somewhere to stub out her cigarette and selected an old inkwell. 'He's a special man. Very special. A knight in shining armour, but we didn't have an affair.'

'I saw you kissing that day in St James's.'

'What you saw was a goodbye kiss. He had much too high a profile for me to get involved. But I had hoped when I left the service we could reignite the spark. Unfortunately for me, his interest lies elsewhere.' There were tears in her eyes as she rested her hand on Tina's arm. 'Be happy.'

'Can you deputise for me?'

The ageing former photographic model and ballerina turned her kind face towards Tina who whispered, 'I have to go.'

A frown wrinkled Audrey's brow. 'Go where?'

'The old school. Abel's waiting for me. I'm going to pick him up.'

Audrey gripped her hand. 'I'm so pleased.'

'I'm sorry to leave you in the lurch.'

'Go. Malcolm and I will take care of everything here. You get your man.'

Tina felt herself bubbling over with nervous excitement. 'I may not be home tonight.'

'I'd be disappointed if you were. Take every happy, blessed moment.'

'I will. I promise.' She looked at the Patek Philippe watch on her wrist.

'I'll find Malcolm,' Audrey said. 'He'll drive you. His motor is parked by the entrance to the memorial garden.'

'Thank you, but I rang Station Cars. There's a taxi on the way. We're going to be staying the night at the White Hart in Undermere.'

Audrey smiled. 'I know it well.'

'Have you seen Sam?'

Near the rear of the deserted Methodist church Sam was seated in a pew. He wanted to stand by his parents' graves but the torrential downpour had driven him to seek shelter. Now he was alone. Truly alone. God was not with him.

Many times he'd been told by Christians and those of other

faiths that being homosexual was a lifestyle choice. That God had given him free will and that he had chosen to disregard Leviticus, chapter eighteen, verse twenty-two: *Thou shalt not lie with mankind, as with womankind: it is an abomination.* For the avoidance of doubt, he had checked other versions of the Holy Bible. They were all full of Don'ts: *Don't have sex with your mother* – no problem there. *Don't have sex with your sister* – no problem there, either. *Don't have sex with another man's wife* – he never had the desire. *Don't have sex with an animal* – never in his wildest dreams. *Don't have sex with a man* – why not? He looked across the empty wooden pews to the plain cross sitting on a simple wooden table.

'Why not!' he shouted. His voice bounced around the walls. 'Why not, God? Jehovah? Allah? Whatever you care to call yourself.' He stood and gripped the back of the pew in front. 'Why can't I have sex with the man I love? Why? What harm does it do? You don't have to look, you all-seeing being. Turn away. Focus on something else, like all the misery dished-out to honour your name.'

'Brutal.'

Sam turned and saw a tall man standing near the entrance. 'I'm sorry. I was having a bit of a moment.'

The man walked down the side aisle towards him. 'No apology required on my account.'

'Do I know you?'

'I knew your parents. I was at school with your Uncle Mark. He was a couple of years below me.' The man came up to Sam and held out his hand. 'My name's Vincent. I guess I've missed the funeral.'

Sam shook his hand. 'Yes. But the wake is still going on.'

'I just wanted to pay my respects. I'm sorry for your loss, Sam.'

'Thank you.'

'I've seen you in the Falcon.'

'Ah, yes, I remember.'

'Drink does get the better of me. I er… I agree with your sentiments. I've not said this out loud, before, ever.' He swallowed.

'I was married… to a woman. Divorced. I should've owned up a long time ago.' He paused. 'I'm gay. Homosexual.'

'Vincent, coming-out is not owning-up. '

'I've not been honest. I loved a boy, once. He was thirteen, I was fifteen. We were in a school play, together. I was Cyrano de Bergerac and he was Roxane. He was so beautiful, so tender.'

'You were in love with a girl, not a boy.'

Vincent shook his head. 'No. I was in love with Robert, not Roxane. He will always live in my heart.' He sat down and wept. 'He didn't have a life and I've wasted mine denying who I am.'

Sam put his arm around the elderly man. 'It's not too late, Vincent. It really isn't.' For the first time since coming home to Hawksmead, Sam felt strong.

Tina hurried out to the waiting taxi and climbed in the rear seat of the Toyota Prius. 'Sorry to keep you.'

The driver did not respond but pulled away from the kerb before she had a chance to click her belt, and headed out of the small town.

'Dreadful weather,' Tina said, trying to make small talk.

'Perfect for a funeral,' replied the driver.

She recognised his voice immediately. 'Sean?'

The driver glanced over his shoulder. 'Hello Tina. My condolences. Terrible.'

'Bridge!'

Sean turned back to look at the road as the wipers frantically swept the downpour from the screen. They were approaching the humpback bridge over the River Hawk and going too fast. He slammed on the brakes and the car snaked. He managed to straighten it up and Tina's stomach flipped as they bumped down on the far side.

'Sorry about that.'

'Take it easy, Sean. No rush. How come you're a taxi driver?'

'I got bored with inventory work; bored with freezing my nuts off in cold houses; bored with photographing chips and mould. It was driving me crazy, and when Gemma got pregnant, I decided to chuck it in.'

'Gemma?'

'Someone who appreciates me for who I am.'

'I always appreciated you. Don't forget to turn right.'

'You're the passenger not the driver.' He swerved right and entered the mile-long drive that led up to the former school. The rain came down even harder.

'I'm sorry if I hurt you, Sean.'

'Hurt me? You stuck in a knife and cut out my heart.'

'Slight exaggeration.'

'First you left me for a Russian property developer, then you ran off with a cop. The fact you preferred a lousy traffic cop to me said it all.'

'Well, you've got Gemma, now, and a baby.'

'Chelsea.'

'As in King's Road, London?'

'I dunno. We heard the name on TV and liked it.'

They approached the old school. Several vehicles were parked close to the back entrance near the abbey ruins including a curtain-sided lorry. Sean swung around the large gravelled apron and brought the taxi to a halt near the main entrance, where several cars were parked including the Porsche Spyder.

'What's going on here, then?' he asked.

'I found a buyer so the travellers are leaving.'

He pulled on the handbrake and looked at her. 'You sold this?'

'Yes. Would you wait here while I get the buyer? We're going on to Undermere.'

'Undermere? Is that where he lives?'

'He's staying at the White Hart.'

'I get it. No need to explain further.'

'Please, Sean.'

'So who is the rich bastard?'

Tina sighed. 'His name's Abel Cornfield and he's a decent man. He'll give you a good tip, I promise.' She gripped her handbag and opened the door. Heavy rain pounded the front of her black dress. 'I'll be back in a few minutes.' She wrapped her raincoat around her and ran as best she could in her heels to the front entrance.

37

Gary stank. He was amazed at how quickly a human could sink to a putrid mess. Something was going on, of that he was sure. They would have to get rid of him soon, one way or the other. As far as Tina was concerned, she was widowed a long time ago. He didn't want her to go through it all again on top of her parents' death. What about his family? He had a brother and a sister. He was the bonus, his mother always said. A lovely pre-menopause surprise. He wondered how his elderly mother was coping. His brother and sister both had their own families, one living in Exeter and the other in Bristol. He hoped they were all well and happy. Occasionally, a tear would sneak out but Gary wasn't going to feel sorry for himself. There was nobody else to blame. Calling Frank Cottee's beloved daughter Tina instead of Stacy, in the age of the all-will-be-revealed era of the internet was suicide, as it had proved to be.

The door opened and it was the woman herself. 'Jesus!' she gasped.

'No, Stacy. It's Gary. I've just not had a shave for a while.'

Abel followed Dermot up the wide wooden stairs to the top floor. Every instinct told him that something was fishy. He'd started his wanderings of the Grade II building in the basement rooms but some woman called Stacy had gripped his arm with steel talons in her determination to steer him away from certain parts. As soon as she opened her mouth, he recognised her for what she was but decided to keep his own counsel. The victor in almost every fight is the one who gets to choose the battleground. Occasionally in his business career he'd come across dodgy individuals who'd tried to launder their ill-gotten gains through one of his businesses. There had been times when veiled threats were made but he'd always stayed firm and, fortunately, his own security team had kept him safe. He had considered bringing a personal protection officer with him to the school the first time he visited, but he'd communicated with Christina on Zoom and had been attracted to her, immediately – a minder would have cramped his romantic overtures.

Dermot opened a door to a large dormitory and flicked a bank of switches; neon strips hummed into life revealing a long room with innumerable beds and old school blankets, and three large chests of drawers down the centre.

'This is where the migrant workers sleep. They are moving on tomorrow,' Dermot said.

Abel walked into the room and the boards creaked. 'The floor feels warm, even through my shoes.'

'We keep the heating on. These men have suffered enough, already. Plus, most come from a tropical country. There are two dormitories on this floor, shower and toilet facilities, and various smaller rooms. I presume you'll want to gut the whole place?'

Abel looked intently at Dermot. 'Let's go down.'

They went back the way they'd come, down the flight of stairs to the landing. Abel gestured to a pair of double doors. 'What's in here?' The wired glass was blocked-in by black material.

'A few classrooms. Nothing of interest.'

'Everything's of interest.' He tried the doors.

'They're bolted,' Dermot said. 'The floor's not safe to walk on. We can go via the back stairs and enter at the far end, if yer like.'

Abel took a couple of paces back and ran at the doors, slamming the sole of a handmade shoe against the metal fingerplates. The doors flew open. Immediately ahead was a wooden frame encased in black plastic sheeting. He looked at Dermot, questioningly. Coming up the stairs, behind, was the oaf with the big dog. At that moment, his phone rang. 'Christina. Where are you?'

'Looking for you,' came her reply.

'Listen to me. Get back in your car and I'll meet you a bit later at the hotel.'

'I have a taxi waiting.'

'Good. Go now.'

'I'm happy to wait.'

Dermot snatched the phone out of Abel's hand. 'Tina, it's Dermot. Lord Cornfield is going to be tied up for quite a while. You go. Bye.' He terminated the connection, dropped the phone on the floor and stamped on it. He looked at Abel. 'Shall we go?'

Abel was pushed through an overlap in the plastic sheeting and was met by a forest of green, almost luminescent under the abundant overhead lighting. As they walked, the cloying odour was overwhelming. At the far end, men were carrying away plants.

He was pushed through more plastic sheeting and entered a smallish area with windows on each side. Rain was still lashing down. The door ahead was opened and he was shoved through plastic sheeting into an almost identical room where only a few plants remained. A steady stream of silent young Asian men and teenage boys, dripping from the rain, passed them as they walked, each carrying a plant rich in foliage. By the time the trio had reached the far end, Abel felt sick. The pungent smell was nothing like the whiff of grass he'd occasionally caught on the breeze when at university.

Where was Sean and the taxi? Getting soaked, Tina ran in her high heels across the gravelled apron searching beyond the parked trucks for the Toyota Prius. The sun was setting, although it had barely made an appearance at all during the miserable day.

'*Bastard!*'

Drenched, she made her way back to the entrance, stopping, momentarily, to admire the Porsche Spyder. She entered the hallway, took her phone out of her handbag and tried Abel's number. It went straight to voicemail.

Abel was pushed through into another open area at the far

end of the building, and towards a stone staircase, narrower than the one in the main entrance hall, and made narrower still by the air-conditioning pipes trailed along the side. He followed Dermot down with Eamonn and the dog panting behind. When they reached the ground floor, he expected to follow the air-conditioning pipes out into the rain but a shovel of a hand told him he was to go on down to the basement. Here, the stairs were even narrower, and the way ahead dark. At the bottom, Dermot flicked a switch and old neon strips flashed and hummed into life, revealing a large bare room, lined with shelves which must, at one time, have stored the farm's produce. They walked on through another door into a boiler room.

'Impressive,' Abel said, pausing to look at a large, barrel-shaped boiler.

'It's a Paxman,' stated Dermot. 'A classic. It should be in a museum. I hope you won't sell it for scrap. But, if you do, give me a shout and I'll take it off your hands.'

Their conversation was interrupted by the dog barking and scratching at the door ahead. Dermot gripped Abel's arm and guided him through into a room with old wiring, a stench of diesel fuel and an incredibly noisy engine.

Dermot shouted into Abel's ear as though explaining something interesting to a friend. 'Yer see, we needed extra electricity to keep the marijuana plants happy. Can you imagine my surprise when I found this little monster? It's a diesel powered, water-cooled old Lister generator from the 1970s. It means we didn't have to draw extra electricity from the national grid and attract the attention of the authorities.'

'Move on.' Eamonn's command was followed by a shove in Abel's back. More rooms came and went. Below ground level, in almost darkness, he wondered whether he had arrived at his final resting place.

A vast ancient kitchen opened up and to one side he spotted a dumb waiter, a lift on a pulley system for taking food up to the refectory above. His old boarding school had had a similar system.

Ahead was an arch and a long passage, with doors to the left and right. At the far end, barely discernible in the gloom, stood a figure he recognised from earlier.

Two bolts, top and bottom of a solid oak door were thrown back and Dermot pulled it open. Despite all the smells Abel had experienced in the last ten minutes, he was completely unprepared for the stench that assaulted his senses.

The dog barked, making him jump, and pushed its way past Abel with such force even Eamonn couldn't maintain his grip on the leather lead. The dog bounded in and smothered the stinking occupant's face with licks.

'Hello Hector. How are you, old boy?'

The man was English and Abel was touched by the reunion.

Eamonn picked up the lead and pulled hard. With the help of his brother, they hauled the yelping hound out of the room.

Abel had considered trying to fight his way out of the building but had been confident that he would be freed once all the evidence of illegal activity had been removed. Christina was his main concern, but as crooked as the travellers may be, he did not believe they would harm her, although he began to have his doubts when the door was slammed shut, the bolts rammed home and he was locked in with a stinking, bony, bedraggled man. Luckily, the light worked.

'My name is Abel Cornfield.' He looked at the long chain and cuffs binding the man's thin, bleeding ankle to an old iron pipe. 'I will get us out of here.'

The response was a chuckle that was profoundly disturbing. 'I am Detective Constable, Gary Burton.'

The Gary Burton?

'The Irish are fine,' he continued. 'They will sweep this place clean and move on, as they always do.'

'That's good to hear.'

'But not Stacy and Frank Cottee. They can't afford to let me live, or you.'

Tina was soaked through following her fruitless search for her wretched ex-boyfriend taxi driver. She was also puzzled by the way the phone call with Abel had ended. What was going on?

She decided to wait in the main hallway for him to finish his tour of the school before ordering another taxi.

'Hello.'

She swung round and looked at a figure standing by the open door to the basement stairs.

'Stacy?' She was wearing a black, double-breasted trench coat, high-heeled ankle boots, and a Gucci shoulder bag with a long chain looped over her head.

'I'm here to help Dermot with the move,' Stacy said. 'By the way, he's with Lord Cornfield.'

'Could you take me to them?'

'They're busy.'

'Doing what?'

'Looking around.' She came up to Tina and gripped her arm. 'I'll walk you to your car.'

Tina recognised the threat in Stacy's pressing fingers and shook her arm free. 'I can walk myself, thank you. I wouldn't want you to get wet.'

'You're very considerate.'

Tina looked beyond Stacy across the hallway to the main stairs. 'Please ask Lord Cornfield to call me when he's finished here.'

'No problem.'

'Thank you.' She walked back through the porch and out of the main entrance into the torrential rain.

Dermot and Stacy were still an item.

She felt a surprising pang of jealousy as she hurried around the end of the building and found shelter with a few rusting bicycles. She tried Abel's number again – voicemail. She tried Dermot's and a recorded voice stated, *'The mobile phone you have called is not available'.*

She called Station Cars. *'All our drivers are out at the moment. We'll get one to you as soon as possible but it could be as long as an hour.'*

She shivered. She was getting cold, very cold. Her thumb hovered over Malcolm's name.

38

Audrey and Malcolm had taken over the roles of host and were standing near the entrance within the Methodist Church Hall, thanking people for their good wishes on behalf of Tina and an absent Sam. Gradually, as the hall emptied, they spotted their friend who had played the organ earlier.

Malcolm leaned close to Audrey and spoke quietly in her ear. 'I'm relieved that Tina and Sam resisted asking Eleanor to play the modern classics.'

'Yes, there was no *Wind Beneath My Wings*,' came her whispered response.

'No *Flying Without Wings* either.'

'No *You Raise Me Up*.'

'No *Angels* from Robbie.'

'*Morning Has Broken*, usually hits the spot.'

'Not this afternoon.'

'*Time to Say Goodbye* always makes me sob.'

'Me too,' Malcolm agreed. 'As soon as I hear the strings followed by Sarah Brightman, I'm doomed.'

'I can usually hold it in until Andrea Bocelli goes from singing Italian to English. And then I'm awash.' She reached for Malcolm's handkerchief in her bag.

'On such a sad day as today,' Malcolm added, 'I fear the church would've been flooded.'

Audrey dabbed her eyes and then called to her friend across the room. 'I hope the Olde Tea Shoppe hasn't lost too much business, today.'

Eleanor came over and joined them. 'My loss is inconsequential and I did manage to hand over a few "two-cakes-for-the-price-of-one" cards.'

'Any spare?' asked Malcolm.

'Agnes does not approve of my promotions,' Eleanor said. 'She also thinks I allow customers to hang around for far too long chatting over a cup of tea. I've had to ask her more than once not to slam the bill down on the table in front of them.'

Audrey laughed. 'Agnes? Is that what you call her?'

'She thinks it sounds more English than Agnieszka. I tell her that more English is allowing people to change their minds after placing an order. She's really tough on the customers but they still seem to like her.'

'And what about you?' Malcolm enquired 'How are you getting on?'

'Still manless. Apart from that, I'm hunky-dory.'

'Have you tried any of the apps?' A smile hovered at the corners of his mouth.

'I'm tempted. Agnes meets loads of boys that way.'

'Perhaps you should consider dating men!' interjected Audrey.

Eleanor burst out laughing. 'Ah, it's so good to see you both. I've really enjoyed today, catching up with everyone. Is that terrible to admit?'

'It's why we have a wake,' Audrey said. 'We all need a rest from grieving. None more so than Tina and Sam.'

'Where is he, by the way?' Eleanor asked.

'I'll check on him,' said a familiar voice. 'I saw him enter the church.' They all looked at Reverend Longden. 'The young man has quite a bit to work through.' He turned to Eleanor. 'Thank you for playing, today.'

'My pleasure.'

He looked pointedly at Malcolm. 'Eleanor has become one of our regular organists at Sunday matins.'

Eleanor laughed. 'At the end of each service William very kindly reminds the congregation that the tea shop is open. His sermon is a small price to pay!'

They laughed but it was swiftly suppressed by guilt.

Malcolm offered his hand to William. 'Good job, Reverend. I think you'll pull in a big crowd after today. Your eulogy was spot on.'

'Thank you Malcolm. I find in life that one is never too old to accept praise.'

They all laughed, again.

'The caterers will clean up in the morning,' Audrey said, gesturing to the hall. 'After, they'll call by the church and drop off the keys.' She stepped forward and gave William a kiss on the cheek. 'It was a lovely service.'

Bedraggled, Tina climbed the stairs to the first floor, pushed open the double doors and faced the long corridor with classrooms to one side that she had first seen when escorted by Dermot. She searched for a light switch and neon strips all the way along flickered into life.

'Abel?' She listened for a reply. 'Dermot? Stacy?'

She let go of the door and headed up the stairs to the next floor where she was met by an overwhelming smell coming through the open doors. Beyond was black plastic sheeting, partly ripped. She stepped forward and peeked through the gap. Where partition walls had once stood, there were umpteen waist-high tables bedecked with lush foliage. At the far end, migrants were carrying potted plants out through the doors. The tropical heat was welcome as she was chilled to the bone, but the smell made her feel sick as did the realisation that Dermot dealt in drugs and was not simply a petty criminal bending the rules to survive. What a fool she had been.

Where was Abel? It was clear he was in danger. She had to find him. But first, she had to call the police. She opened her bag and with a shaking hand removed her phone. She had a signal, not great but good enough.

Manicured talons snatched it from her and twisted her arm up behind her back.

'Ow!! You're hurting me.'

'Walk,' snarled Stacy. 'Or I'll break it.' She shoved Tina in the back and forced her to walk past the marijuana plants.

39

Gary, in their short marriage, had taught Tina two things: fight hard from the get-go and emit the loudest, most annoying, ear-piercing scream as possible.

At the far end of the second vast room was another set of doors leading to the back stairs. The men removing the pots of marijuana plants kept their eyes averted, but a couple of teenagers were brave enough to steal a glance in her direction.

Tina bided her time until they were mingling with the migrants. As they exited the growing room, she screamed loud enough and sharp enough to almost rupture eardrums, and wrenched her arm free of Stacy's grip. Rage poured through every muscle and with nails manicured by Magdalena, she scored Stacy's left cheek. The shocked woman screamed, adding to the cacophony. Tina kicked off her high heels and barged her way past the plant-carrying men down the back stairs to the floor below. She contemplated going to the ground floor but she'd seen too many travellers near the entrance by the abbey ruins. She decided to run down the two long corridors where the classrooms were located towards the main stairs at the far end. Without shoes, she ran fast but bits of grit and discarded classroom tools scattered on the worn linoleum caused her to yelp as they dug into her soles.

Where was Abel? She had to find him. If she'd been more thorough when she first took on selling the school and less enraptured by Dermot, she would have discovered the marijuana. It was her fault Abel was in danger and she was not going to leave without him.

Just before she pushed open the final set of doors, she stopped. Barking was coming up from the entrance hall below.

She was trapped and it wouldn't be long before they would come looking for her.

She had to do something.

But what?

She opened the nearest classroom door. It was the science lab with its old work benches, wooden stools and aged equipment. She grabbed a high stool and rammed it under the door knob. At least it would buy her a few extra seconds while she thought what to do.

Below each workbench, were several gas cylinders, some attached to rubber pipes leading to Bunsen burners. She could try and blow-up the school but that could kill her, kill Abel and all the other poor souls. But, if they smelled gas, everyone would clear the building and in the confusion she could escape outside and hide in the dark until the taxi arrived. She squatted down to a cylinder and tried to undo the tap at the top but it was too stiff. She tried another and it gave. After a few turns she heard the hiss of gas.

Stacy barged her way into the Headmaster's private toilet facility on the ground floor and switched on the light. She hurried to the mirror and stared at her face in horror. Her entire life, people had complimented her on her stunning looks, which she valued almost above everything else. Smoking had etched a few fine lines, but she was still a to-die-for stunner. But now she had three deep scratches that had penetrated the epidermis and would take weeks to fully heal and months for the marks to fade – perhaps they never would entirely disappear.

Scarred!

The vile, little bitch had scarred Stacy Cottee, the daughter of Frank Cottee, known as King Cottee for his absolute rule of every strand of his business empire. She searched her bag and removed a tube of hand cream. It would have to do. At first it stung but after a few seconds it soothed the pain and she felt better, though no less bitter.

Her hand shook as she searched her bag for a pack of Newport menthol cigarettes and placed a filter tip between her lips.

She flicked back the lid of a Ronson flip-top lighter and put the flame to the tobacco.

'Stacy,' said familiar, warm, enticing Irish tones.

She turned to the handsome face. 'Look what she did to me!' She pointed a talon at her cheek. 'I'm going to destroy her for this.'

'No you're not. You're not going to touch a hair on her head.'

She felt the heat of rage turn into the arrow of pain. 'What? You like her. I knew it!' She spat the words.

'More than that. What you and I have done to her is evil. Sure, Gary was nosy filth but it's no excuse. I see that now. I'm letting the migrants go. I'm letting Cornfield go. I'm letting the policeman go.'

'Daddy will never forgive you for this.'

'Daddy sets foot in Ireland, or any of his oikish thugs, we'll take their kneecaps first.'

She recoiled. Dermot's words, full of bile, spoke to her the way she'd rarely experienced before. She wanted to hurt him. Really hurt him and there was only one way to do that.

She took Tina's phone out of her bag and tossed it into the lavatory bowl. There was a satisfying plop. She smiled. 'Well lover... I'll be off.' She expected him to grab her arm or to try and make peace, but all he did was wait for her to go.

40

Audrey looked around the Methodist Church Hall and was pleased with the work that Malcolm, Eleanor and she had put in to make it look respectable. The caterers would come in the morning to pick up boxes of dirty plates, glasses and tea cups.

'Shall we go to the pub?' Audrey smiled at her own words.

'That's an invitation I've not heard for quite a while,' Eleanor said. 'Actually, for a hell of a long time.'

'We'll find you a man, yet.'

'I'm in my sixtieth year. I've more chance of winning the EuroMillions. Any man my age wants a woman half his.'

'More fool them,' responded Audrey, emphatically.

'She has a point,' Malcolm said as he stacked a final chair. 'I went for a younger woman.'

'Not half your age,' Eleanor laughed.

Malcolm approached the two women. 'Yes she is. At least, that's what she told me.' He cocked his head to Audrey. 'It's the big four oh coming up isn't it?'

'More like the big seven oh!' Audrey kissed her husband.

'You two love birds are just making it worse.'

Audrey turned to her friend. 'Once Tina is back on an even keel we're going to scour the planet for the perfect man for you.'

'One thing's for sure,' Eleanor said. 'You ain't gonna find him in Hawksmead!'

'Audrey found me in Hawksmead.'

Eleanor and Audrey both looked at the tall man pulling a mock-offended comical face, and laughed.

Abel rattled the door to the basement pantry.

'It's bolted on the other side,' said the bedraggled younger man. 'There's no way out.'

'You think they're going to dispose of us?'

'I know it.'

'Two years on, you're still alive.'

'That's Stacy Cottee for you – keeping me alive is the greater punishment. I'm the mouse to her cat. She likes playing with me.'

'At least Christina's in the clear.'

'She's in danger until Stacy and Frank Cottee are behind bars.'

'Then I have to get you out of here. You're the one person who can give evidence in court.'

'Good luck with that.' He rattled his chained ankle.

Working as fast as she could, Tina dragged five heavy cylinders towards the door. She undid the valve to each one and soon the gas made her feel heady. Taking great care, she opened the door and looked both ways. No person or dog was about. She dragged the first cylinder into the corridor.

It was almost dark when Stacy stepped out of the school's main entrance. 'Eamonn,' she called. A deep throated growl from the bullmastiff startled her.

'Going already?'

In the fading light she looked at Eamonn's bulky figure sucking on a cigarette and holding his snarling hound in check.

'I was looking for you.'

'And why would that be?'

'We've lost Tina. Do you think your dog could help me find her? She's hiding somewhere in the school. Probably in one of the classrooms on the first floor.'

'Have you anything of hers he could sniff?'

'Will a shoe do?' She held out one of Tina's discarded shoes.

'Okay, we'll give it a go.' He took the shoe. 'Come with me.'

She followed the man and dog back into the school hallway and watched as he squatted down and placed the shoe under the drooling jaws.

'Now listen here, Hector. We've got a pretty girl to find. You know, the one with the blonde hair and those fabulous long legs.'

'Not that fabulous.'

Eamonn looked up at Stacy. 'Don't interrupt.' He turned back to the dog. 'Listen to me, Hector. Here's her shoe. That's right, have a good long sniff. Find the pretty girl and I'll give yer a big, juicy, meaty, bone.'

The dog barked, making Stacy jump, but Eamonn didn't seem bothered at all.

'She's probably hiding in a storage cupboard wetting her knickers,' Stacy smirked.

'Hector'll find her.' He stood up and Stacy followed the man and dog as they ran up the wooden stairs to the first floor.

Tina barged her way past the men carrying marijuana plants and hurried down the back stairs to the ground floor. She opened the internal double doors and looked down the long corridor. She knew that one of the rooms towards the far end was the headmaster's study where she'd nearly given all to Dermot. Perhaps she should thank Stacy for interrupting? Could Abel be locked-in down there? She had no choice but to check every room.

'Come on, Hector!' growled Eamonn.

Stacy stood back from the double doors to the first floor corridor as Eamonn tried to coax his whining dog. Far from being a ferocious hound, the beast looked scared.

'What have you got there? A bloody poodle?'

Eamonn turned to her and she didn't like the expression in his eyes. 'Call Hector a poodle again and I'll set him on yer. Do I make meself clear?'

'Crystal.'

'Something's spooking him.' Eamonn almost did a pirouette as Hector ran in circles wrapping the long lead around him.

Bored with waiting, Stacy pushed open one of the double doors and recoiled. 'Whoa! Gas.'

'That's what he's smellin'.'

'It's not the mains supply, just gas from some old cylinders.'

'Come on Hector. Let's get out of here. This whole place could go up.' He led the dog back down the main stairs.

Stacy called after him. 'Where are you going?'

'To find me brother.'

Tina banged open each room door on the ground floor and called out for Abel. She waited five seconds for him to reply, and then moved on. Her torn, stockinged-feet were sore and bleeding.

She came to the headmaster's study and opened the door. The light was on but the sparsely furnished room was deserted. She hurried across the worn carpet to the toilet facility and looked in.

Empty.

'Daddy, I can't do that.'

'Listen girl,' Frank said to Stacy all too clearly out of her iPhone. 'This is your mess to clear up. I said I would deal with it when we found out what your lover-boy was really all about. But you wanted your plaything. You wanted to make him suffer. I told you it was a massive risk. You assured me the gippos were tough enough to handle him. It's clearly gone tits-up. Deal with your mess and get the hell out of there.'

'It's not just Gary,' Stacy said, putting on the little-girl's voice she saved for her daddy when she needed his help. 'There's someone else we have to top as well.'

'Spit it out, girl.'

'His name's Lord Cornfield. He's locked up with Gary.'

'Geezuschrist!'

'Daddy, the scrambler app on our phones is making it very hard to hear. Shall I come home?'

'Don't you dare! At the very least get rid of Gary. Anything he's told Lord Cornfield is hearsay in court.'

'How? I've never killed anyone.'

'Dealer's choice, sweetheart. Just do it. And don't come home till it's done.'

Stacy heard her father end the call. She was standing by her Porsche wanting desperately to get away but knowing she had a job to do first. She never batted an eyelash when her father spoke of clean-up operations but actually doing it herself, and to a policeman she had slept with and had sort of loved, was a very tough gig.

What about Tina? Where was she?

And what about Dermot? It was his fault she was in this mess. One way or another he and the blonde bitch were going to suffer.

Gary heard approaching footsteps before Abel and braced himself for what he felt sure was the inevitable. The bolts were pulled back and the door opened to reveal Dermot. Gary watched him recoil at the smell before regaining his composure. He kept his distance as he threw a key ring at Gary. It bounced on the floor. He turned to Abel. 'Lord Cornfield. I apologise for any inconvenience we've caused you. You're free to go.'

Abel rose to his full height. 'I think you owe Mr Burton a great deal more than an apology.'

'I do,' Dermot said. 'It's a debt that can never be repaid. All I can do now is ensure Gary is reunited with his wife.'

'Where is she?' Gary asked.

'She's here. Somewhere. She's looking for Lord Cornfield. I think she has a soft spot for him.'

Abel met Gary's gaze. 'I assure you, nothing happened between us.'

'Unlike between you and Stacy Cottee, eh Gary?' smirked Dermot.

Shamed, Gary looked at the stone floor.

Dermot continued his punishment. 'Both me and the good Lord here, we did all we could to make Tina our own, but she held her ground. There's a tiny part in her soul that always believed you'd come back to her.'

Gary picked up the key and struggled to release the handcuff. 'There's something wrong with the lock. The key's not working.'

Abel slipped on his jacket and squatted down beside him. 'Once this is off, I think your first port of call should be the shower.' He tried to turn the key in the lock. 'There must be a technique to getting this open.'

'Well gentlemen, I'll leave you be.' Both Abel and Gary looked up at Dermot standing in the doorway.

'Dermot, please don't leave me like this,' Gary implored. 'Can we at least part as gentlemen? I was sent to help bring down King Cottee. We're not interested in you or your family of travellers. As far as I am aware, you don't have blood on your hands.' He hoped his words would have some impact.

'Lord Cornfield, please step away and not by the door,' Dermot requested.

Abel moved to the back wall below the high window.

Dermot entered the room and squatted down. He turned the key and the cuff snapped open. Gary whipped the linking chain around his neck. 'Help me!' he yelled.

Abel rushed forward and threw his weight on Dermot who fought with sinews toughened from generations surviving on the road. He clawed at the chain blocking the air to his lungs as Gary pulled with all his diminished strength.

'Are you going to kill him?' Abel gasped.

Gary gritted his teeth and continued to pull on the chain.

BANG!!

Both men looked at the door which had been slammed shut. Abel leapt to his feet but before he could cross the room they heard the first bolt slide home. Within moments, the second was also slammed into its keep.

41

Tina couldn't find Abel anywhere. She'd tried calling the police from the landline in the headmaster's office, but it was dead. The work emptying the forest of marijuana plants was still going on and from the sound of engines starting-up outside, some of the travellers were already making a move. Perhaps Abel was trapped in one of their caravans or trucks?

Dermot.

She had to find Dermot. He liked her and she was confident he would protect her from anything that Stacy was planning, and would draw the line at hurting Abel.

She had put off searching the basement level as it was dimly lit with many, dark, windowless rooms, sealed by heavy oak doors with solid iron bolts. In her torn and bleeding stock-inged-feet she walked into the main entrance hall – no one was about – and hurried across the stone floor to a battered door, twisted its iron ring and pulled it open. Stretching down into the darkness were stone steps and an old, worn handrail. She ran her fingertips over the dirty wall and found a switch. A bulb struggled into life.

'Tina.'

Stacy's voice cut like an ice pick. Standing in the middle of the hallway, she was still very beautiful despite Tina's best at-tempts to scar her face.

'What are you doing?' demanded the voice from Essex.

'Where is Abel? What have you done to him?'

'He's fine. He's with his mates, Dermot… and Gary.'

It was a sucker blow.

'Did Dermot tell you about Gary?' Stacy moved a couple of steps closer. 'I introduced them. Me and Gaz screwed our way to heaven but then I found out he was filth spying on me dad, and had to be punished.'

Tina's mouth was dry. She couldn't speak.

Stacy laughed. 'Cat got your tongue?'

'Is he… alive?'

'Who? Which luvver-boy are you talkin' about? Posh Abel? Gypsy Dermot? Or Gary the cop?'

Tina couldn't catch her breath. 'You're evil.'

'No Tina. I'm not evil. I'm an angel. Daddy says so.'

Tina looked at her feet. Without shoes, she could not outrun Stacy. 'Where is Abel? Please tell me.'

Stacy opened her mouth but her words were cut short by an explosion from above.

'Oh my God!' Tina turned and looked towards the main stairs.

'That'll be one of the gas cylinders,' Stacy said. 'If Abel's dead, it's your fault.'

Tina whirled round. 'What are you saying?'

'He's upstairs in a top floor dormitory, tied to a bed.'

'Show me. Please.'

Stacy smiled. 'Goodbye Tina.'

'Where are you going?'

'Home.'

Tina rushed up to her and gripped her arms. 'Please Stacy. Help me find him.' She looked into her eyes and saw only victory.

Stacy peeled off Tina's fingers. There was another explosion followed by pops and cracking. 'Oh dear. Poor Abel. The Cornfield is on fire.'

Malcolm opened the passenger door to his Honda and Audrey climbed in. Once he was sure that her coat was fully clear, he closed it and walked to the driver's door. As he clicked in his belt he looked at Audrey. 'Well done. Congratulations.'

'I don't feel I can accept congratulations for a funeral.'

'You should. It went off very well. Everyone enjoyed catching up with old friends.'

He saw Audrey reach for her bag and remove his borrowed handkerchief. She dabbed her eyes.

'Are you okay, my sweet?'

'I love that girl,' Audrey said. 'My tears are for her, for all the pain she has suffered these last couple of years.'

Malcolm slid the key into the ignition. 'I'd better get driving before you set me off too.' He started the engine.

'I hope she's having the most wonderful evening with Lord Cornfield.'

'In my dealings with him re the sale, he came across as a fair and honourable man.'

'Well I trust he's going to be very dishonourable tonight.'

Malcolm laughed. 'I don't know what you mean!' And he pushed the lever into drive.

Stacy pressed her car's fob and her beloved Porsche Spyder sparked into life. Daddy had wanted her to have a more solid vehicle, one higher off the ground with decent fenders at the front and rear, but as soon as she'd seen the beautiful soft-top car, she'd fallen in love. Daddy hated the idea that she was driving around with a *"rag top"* instead of toughened steel, but in the summer, cruising down London's fashionable streets, for all the envious women to see and all the men to admire, gave her the kind of buzz she craved. The car was fast, too, and incredibly responsive. She'd taken it to Brands Hatch race circuit and burned so much rubber, all four tyres had to be replaced. Daddy had not been pleased when he'd seen her credit card bill but it had been worth a few minutes of his ire.

She fired up her throaty beast, switched the lights on full beam and thrust the gear lever into reverse. The wheels spun on the wet loose gravel as she backed up. She stamped the sole of her Christian Louboutin boot to the brake pedal and the tyres skidded as the discs locked. She depressed the clutch, found first, and stamped the accelerator so hard the rear wheels spat grit.

Ahead, one of the travellers' trucks had the audacity to block her path. She blasted her horn and turned onto the marshy grass, sliding sideways before her spinning wheels secured enough grip for the Spyder to leap ahead of the truck. She glanced in her rear-view mirror and hoped the fiery glow would turn into a mighty blaze that would consume the whole building and solve the problem of the three men locked in the basement room.

She tugged at her seatbelt but the strap was caught in the door. She'd sort it out when she stopped at traffic lights. All she wanted to do now was get home. She accelerated and the Spyder tore down the mile-long drive to the Old Military Road.

Tina pushed through the plastic curtain at the entrance to the first long growing room and was shocked by the intensity of the fire. On the floor above were the dormitories and judging by the ferocity of the flames eating up the old timbers it wouldn't be long before the whole top floor and roof would be ablaze. Was Stacy lying when she said Abel was trapped up there? Tina had firsthand experience of what smoke and heat can do when Audrey was trapped by fire in the old school boarding house.

Stacy liked driving at night in the countryside; she could see whether vehicles were oncoming and there were fewer speed cameras to spoil her day. She had lost her licence more than once and despite being forced to attend two speed awareness courses, driving fast gave her an exceptional thrill.

Her xenon headlights lit the hedgerows on each side of the mile-long drive. She took a risk and averted her eyes to set the satellite navigation system for home. By the time she was back with daddy, all her problems should've gone up in smoke.

She came to the T-junction at the end of the school drive and the sat nav instructed her to turn left. She swapped gears with great precision and the alloy wheels spun the car to more than sixty miles per hour in just a few seconds. The speed of the Spyder ensured Stacy had plenty of work to do holding the car on the wet, meandering road, lined with dark-shadowed ditches and solid-looking hawthorn hedges. A road sign warned her she was approaching the humpback bridge spanning the River Hawk at the north end of the little town. She'd seen no other vehicles so kept her smooth leather sole pressed against the accelerator pedal.

The Honda headed up Hawksmead High Street, turned the corner at the top end, and drove towards the humpback bridge.

'Look at that.' Audrey pointed at the windscreen.

Malcolm glanced at her. 'What?'

'There's an orange glow in the sky.'

He kept driving as he peered through the windscreen. 'It could be the travellers burning their rubbish. Let's go up there and double-check.' He turned onto the humpback bridge and was blinded by xenon headlights.

Tina ran up the wooden stairs to the top floor where the dormitories were located. She shoved open the double doors and searched for the light switch. Neon strips flickered on, lighting the long room, divided into sections by wooden partitions. She ran down the dorm looking at each of the narrow iron beds with their thin, stained mattresses. Some were made up with sheets and old school monogrammed blankets. The floorboards beneath her almost bare feet were getting hot, and she saw the first trails of smoke.

She pushed open the doors at the far end, looked left and right, and slammed back the double doors ahead. It was another dormitory. She found the light switch and neon strips revealed an even longer room, with more partitions and many more beds. She ran down the long room, dancing from foot to foot, as she desperately sought Abel. Thickening smoke made her slow and caused her to cough. A flame licked her toes.

Stacy stamped her foot down on the brake pedal and her discs responded immediately, but the recent heavy rain prevented the rubber on her low-profile tyres from gripping evenly. The car skidded sideways causing the rear to bounce off the stone wall lining the bridge. The nose shot forward with such force into the opposite wall, the rear end of the car lifted and the inertia flipped the vehicle over.

'*Daddy!*'

The soft top crushed as it hit the water and the air was driven out of her lungs.

Malcolm brought the Honda to a halt on the north side of the bridge.

'What happened?' Audrey looked over her shoulder into the darkness.

'I think we've had a miraculous escape.' He reached into the glove compartment and removed a torch. 'I'll have a look. Wait here.'

'Take care. There may be other cars.'

'I will.' He opened his door, switched on the torch, and walked carefully in the dark towards the bridge. Sections of wall on each side were dislodged and badly scraped but had held. He leaned over the side and his beam picked out the underside of a car, held by one of the arch supports, but almost entirely submerged in the fast-flowing river.

'Good grief!'

Tina felt sick and light-headed as she worked her way to the far end of the dormitory. Flames, no longer tentative, were voraciously eating up the dry floorboards and decades of debris. The heat became too intense for her feet and she was forced to jump onto one of the narrow beds. To protect her soles, she wrapped each foot in an old school sheet. The dorm was now properly on fire with flames licking to the ceiling. Abel was not up here. He was either trapped in the basement, taken prisoner by the travellers, or already dead. She had to put the last thought out of her mind.

What about Gary? She didn't believe a word Stacy had said. But she was from Essex and she knew that was where Gary had been working undercover. Could he still be alive?

And what of Dermot? Where was he? Or had he driven away with the other travellers, together with their illicit organic hoard?

She heard a crack and watched in horror as part of the wooden floor fell into the former growing room below, followed by several iron beds and burning mattresses.

'The school is definitely on fire,' Audrey said as Malcolm got back into the Honda.

He closed the door. 'There's a car lying upside down in the river.'

'Did you see anyone get out?'

He returned the torch to the glove compartment. 'No. I don't hold much hope for them. The police are on their way. I said I'd wait.'

'I'm worried about Tina.'

'Have you tried calling her?'

'Straight to voicemail. I think we should get up to the school, just to make sure she's not there.'

'I said I'd wait.'

Audrey opened the glove compartment and handed him the torch. 'You wait here for the police and I'll drive up to the school.'

Malcolm took a breath. 'I don't like the sound of that.'

'You didn't jump in the river and I'm not about to run into a burning building.'

'You promise?'

'I give you my word.' Audrey eased herself out and hurried around the nose of the car. Malcolm held the driver's door open for her. She put her arms around his neck and gave him a kiss. 'Be careful.'

'*You* be careful.' They both looked towards the orange glow across the moor.

'Your phone has battery?' she asked.

'Yes. I only turned it on to call the police.'

'Good. Keep in touch.' She slipped into the driver's seat and reached for the handle to adjust the position. She turned to her husband. 'You'd better call the fire brigade, just in case nobody else has.'

Tina dragged a couple of school blankets into the washroom. She entered the communal shower area and was so relieved to feel the cool water. She soaked the blankets and soaked her feet, each wrapped in a sheet. She kept thinking about Audrey and what she had had to do to escape a burning building. But Tina was not ready to escape. Before she got out, she had to find Abel.

The soaked blankets felt heavy as she draped them over her wet hair and around her body and face. Gripping them from within, she looked through a narrow gap.

Shuffling in her sheet-wrapped feet, she opened the door and was shocked by the amount of smoke. She gripped the blankets tighter and through eyes, barely open, shuffled to the stairs. The sheets around her bare feet almost caused her to trip and so she decided to kick them off. Luckily, the flames weren't licking through the stair treads yet although the wood felt warm to her tender soles.

As she approached the floor below, the smoke was more dense, more acrid, more damaging to breathe. Everyone appeared to have left the building. The only company she had was the roar from flames voraciously eating up the old wood. The heat was intense and even though she filtered the smoke through the blanket, each breath hurt her lungs.

She carried on down to the first floor where she had released the gas from the cylinders. The air was now unbreathable, even through the blanket. She could argue that her hasty plan had worked as she was sure help was on its way, but at what cost?

Abel's life?

Her life?

The heat in the storage room was getting intense. It glowed down from the ceiling. Surprisingly, the light bulb still worked. Abel had tried to smash the high window and only succeeded in bruising his elbow to such a degree he was sure it was fractured. Dermot lay on the floor, his ankle chain-linked to Gary's.

'Let's all look on the bright side.' Dermot's voice was hoarse following his near strangulation. 'At least the woman we all love is not in here with us.'

At that moment the power went, plunging the room into darkness.

Dermot chuckled. 'There is one thing I'm sad about.'

Abel waited for him to continue, then got impatient. 'You can't leave us hanging, Mr O'Hanlon. What is the one thing? I can think of plenty.'

'Dear Lord, I'm sad that Gary's is the last face I'll ever see. Of course, it's different for him and for you, 'cause I'm so bloody handsome.'

Abel decided he had to take control. 'It's clear we're about to be roasted. We're locked in a room with a solid door, bolted from the outside. Even if we could break the window, the gap is probably too narrow for us to squeeze through.

'I'm thin enough.'

Abel was pleased that Gary had an edge of hope to his voice.

A burning ember fell from the ceiling.

Too late. They were out of time.

42

Audrey indicated she wanted to turn right off the Old Military Road onto the mile-long drive up to the school, but the stream of vans, four-by-fours towing caravans, trucks and lorries prevented her, whilst the red glow in the sky got more and more intense.

She hooted her horn to no effect.

'Enough is enough.' She flicked her lights to full beam and swerved around the nose of a curtain-sided truck, almost ending up in the water-logged ditch beside the mile-long drive. With two wheels on the verge, spinning on wet grass and mud, she forced her way back onto the tarmac, making the on-coming stream give her room. After passing a few more vehicles the way ahead became clear and she pressed the accelerator. The last time she had seen the old school was when Malcolm and she walked out together on their first date, over four years ago. It was not a place she enjoyed visiting. Within forty seconds, she was confronted by a blaze that dwarfed what she had experienced a few years previously. The size and power of the conflagration was truly shocking.

She parked the Honda on the furthest reaches of the deserted gravelled apron and got out of the car. The blast of hot air and the appalling smell of burning triggered terrible memories she had tried hard to forget. The skin on her scarred legs tightened, and her breathing became raspy and short. She fought to quell her growing panic but the more she tried the more memories of acrid smoke tearing at the fabric of her lungs, and ferocious flames stripping her calves and thighs, brought the whole terror back into sharp focus.

Tears poured down her cheeks as she stood and watched

the Victorian building crackle and roar. Small explosions on an upper floor added to the cacophony of sounds. Soon the school would be little more than a burned-out shell, unlamented by the many generations who had had the misfortune to reside within its walls.

Tina knew she should get out. She couldn't see, she couldn't breathe, she couldn't hear. Something large rubbed against her and she would have screamed but the fear of the acrid smoke and burning heat was far greater. She reached out a hand and felt sharp teeth.

'Oh my God!'

The dog barked. Whimpered. What should she do? Unable to see, she tripped over the air-conditioning pipes and fell on the hard floor. The dog licked her face and she grabbed his collar. She tried to get up but lost her balance and was dragged down the stone steps, landing in a bruised heap in the basement. The air felt cooler, at least not as hot as it had been, and less smoky, although it was almost pitch black. The dog rubbed against her and she felt for his collar, more scared of being alone than of his fangs. Almost blind, she allowed herself to be led through the bowels of the building, banging into all manner of hazards, pulling open doors and lurching into blackened rooms.

Suddenly, she could see. She was in a kitchen, lit by the light of flames coming through high windows. Burning embers were falling all around her and one fell on the dog. Without a second's thought, she swiped it away. The dog ran ahead through an archway and barked and clawed at a closed door.

Staccato cracking made her turn her head as part of the kitchen ceiling fell followed by a crashing dining table from the room above. Flames, where there had been none before, suddenly appeared and within seconds the whole kitchen was a raging furnace as more wooden tables and benches crashed down.

Malcolm could not see the face of the young police officer without shining his torch into her eyes, and he was sure that would not go down well.

'What speed were you travelling?'

'About ten miles an hour. Needless to say the other car was going considerably faster.'

'How long ago did the accident happen?'

'Ten minutes, possibly twelve.'

The police officer leaned over the stone parapet and shone her torch down. She spoke into her radio but the sound of rushing water from the river below drowned out her words. Malcolm assumed she was asking for help – a tow truck with a winch, maybe, and divers to retrieve any bodies.

Finished with her radio call, she approached Malcolm. 'Right, Mr...' She shone her torch on her notebook and the reflected light gave Malcolm a chance to see her face, which looked as young as she sounded. 'Mr Cadwallader. I'd like to examine your vehicle.'

'Ah, yes... my wife has it.'

'She drove away from the scene of an accident?'

'The car was unscathed.'

'The car is evidence.'

'Exactly my thought, but my wife is worried about a friend.'

'Worried. In what way?'

He turned his head and gestured to the bright orange glow clearly visible across the black expanse of moorland.

Abel was the first to hear the bolt. Or was it the sound of cracking embers as they fell to the floor?

Clunk!

He was sure it was definitely a bolt. He pushed open the door with his good arm and was shocked by the intensity of the heat. The giant dog almost leapt past him and felled Gary in a canine embrace. The room immediately filled with burning, acrid smoke and his eyes were seared by the heat. A figure shrouded like an Egyptian mummy staggered into the room and collapsed in a heap of blankets amongst the burning embers.

'Christina!' Abel bent down and tried to pick her up but the pain in his elbow was too great. 'Gary. Help me,' he shouted above the crackling wood and roar of the flames.

Gary pushed away the amorous hound as burning embers from the ceiling continued to float down, and scrambled to his feet.

'I'll carry her.' Dermot shouted to Gary. 'Unchain me.'

'You're joking,' Gary said. 'She's my wife, I'm carrying her out.'

'For the love of God, Gary, release me.' Dermot shouted and then coughed. 'The chances of us getting out are almost nil, but I'm far and away the fittest person here. The good Lord has a broken elbow and you're not up to the job. Release me and I'll carry her to safety.'

Abel hugged Tina's wrapped body to him. 'Do as he asks, Gary. I promised Christina, she would one day swim with dolphins, and I'm keeping that promise.'

In the blazing light from the flames, Gary removed Dermot's ankle cuff. 'Don't try to escape,' he shouted into his face.

'I thought escape was the plan,' Dermot retorted. 'Although cremation is far more likely.'

Both Abel and Gary helped lift the unconscious Tina into Dermot's arms, making sure that the blankets protected her body as much as possible.

'Gentlemen, it's been a pleasure,' Dermot said and coughed.

Abel looked at Gary. 'You lead us out. You know this place much better than me. I'll follow Dermot.'

Abel waited for Gary to push back the door and as he did the heat and brightness of the flames terrified him. The dog, their saviour, stuck close to them as Dermot staggered through the thick fog of toxic smoke. Gary led the way down the corridor, constantly looking back to check that Dermot and Christina were close behind. Abel admired the young man's determination and bravery. There was almost no chance they were going to make it out.

43

Audrey watched the firefighters working in twos as they manned the large hoses. There were three tenders and count- less men in protective gear carrying breathing apparatuses on their backs. Some could have been women but she couldn't tell. Despite the power of pumped water aimed at the ground floor, and at the end of ladders fitted to turntables, it was clear to her that the fire was going to win and destroy the entire building. Thick black smoke was billowing out of the main entrance, with the rest of the former school burning with a ferocity that Audrey had not witnessed before.

She retrieved her phone from the Honda and tried Tina's number again.

Gary had been down to the basement many times and was quite familiar with its umpteen rooms sealed by heavy doors. Fortunately, the main entrance hallway had a stone floor and stone steps leading down to the basement. Other rooms on the ground floor had wooden floorboards which were clearly already alight and dripping embers. The great hound had an instinct for survival but also a love for Gary, so kept hanging back. Burning embers had scorched the dog's coat and Gary had burnt his hands dealing with them. Soon the fire raining down would turn into a storm.

Sharp, blue flashing lights penetrated high, ground-level windows on the far side of a former changing room, and cut through the thick, acrid smoke that was so searing and toxic. After all that time hoping, help had finally arrived, albeit just too late. The room swam and swayed and Gary fell backwards as black sheets enveloped him.

A drop of water splashed on Audrey's cheek. She looked up and several more drops landed on her face. The weather had been atrocious for weeks thanks to a stream of Atlantic storms, but she welcomed the rain. Within seconds it was coming down in torrents. Would the pelting rain preserve some of the building? She hoped not.

Out of the school's main entrance bounded a large dog, its fur singed and smouldering. The now lashing rain was a mercy for the whimpering beast as it coughed and vomited onto the gravel. She wanted to encourage the dog to get further away from the ferocious flames. As a child she grew up with Lhasa Apsos, and would normally avoid getting close to big dogs, but the poor animal was in such distress she felt compelled to comfort it. She hurried over and gripped its collar, and felt something attached to it. In the blazing light she saw a Patek Philippe watch.

This was it. For all his wealth and considerable achievements in school, university and in business, Lord Abel Cornfield lay down to die. In one hand he gripped Gary's and in the other he held onto Tina's. His last act had been to remove her watch and strap it to the dog's collar. At least there was a chance the firefighters would realise someone was trapped in the building. He couldn't breathe, he couldn't see, he couldn't move. He vomited.

'The police want you back here.' Audrey listened to Malcolm's words and wondered how she was going to break the news. 'They've got lights on the car but the river is too fierce for divers to fix a tow hook. The rain's not helping, but it has to be good your end.'

'Tina's in the building!' Audrey heard Malcolm's intake of breath. 'The firefighters have gone in with thermal imaging equipment to try and locate her. Malcolm, I think we've lost our little girl.' Her words came out in a massive sob. 'The school is all but destroyed.' She looked at the entrance. Surely, nobody could survive such an inferno? And then, out of the dense smoke appeared a firefighter in full breathing apparatus, dragging a body by the shoulders. 'They've brought someone out!'

'Is it Tina?' Malcolm's voice shouted out of her phone.

'I can't see. The firefighters are fitting an oxygen mask. The Chief Fire Officer has ordered me to keep away.'

'What about medics?'

'They've not arrived, yet.' The heat was beyond intense as she hurried to the person lying on the gravel, whose face was covered by an oxygen mask. She shuddered with disappointment. 'It's a man,' she shouted into her phone. 'I don't recognise him.'

'Is he alive?'

'I think so.' She looked towards the entrance where the firefighters were pointing their hoses. 'There's someone else being dragged out!'

'Who?'

'I can't see.' She watched as two firefighters dragged a second person away from the entrance.

'Is it Tina? Audrey!! Is it Tina?'

'I think it's another man.'

'Can you talk to the fire officer? See if they've located her.'

'I will, but they're busy saving the two they've brought out.'

Two more firefighters appeared, one dragging a man and the other carrying an inert body, wrapped in blankets, as if it weighed nothing.

'There are two more.'

'Tina?'

She watched the firefighter carry the person to a safe distance followed by another with an oxygen tank who fitted the mask.

'I can see her blonde hair. It's Tina!'

'Is she alive?'

Audrey rushed over, her wet clothes steaming from the blazing heat.

'Madam. Keep back!' shouted the Chief Fire Officer.

The rain continued to pound down. 'Where are the ambulances?' she shouted, trying to make her voice heard above the incredible roar.

'We have to wait,' said the breathless man. 'A massive pile up on the motorway has sucked in every paramedic in the region, not helped by the weather. There should've been more tenders here.'

'I'll take them to A&E in Undermere. Put them in my car. You can radio ahead.'

'I can't allow that. It's outside my remit.'

'This young woman saved my life when I was injured in the fire at the old school boarding house. I am not leaving her here to wait in the pouring rain.' She pointed to the youngest-looking and most raggedy of the three injured men. 'And he looks like Gary Burton, the policeman who's been missing for over two years.'

The Chief turned to his men and touched their shoulders to get their attention. 'Right, lads. Get them in the lady's car, with oxygen.'

'I want Tina in the front with me.' She spoke into her phone. 'Malcolm, are you still there?'

'Right here.'

'Tell the police officer that I have PC Gary Burton, and three others, all seriously injured by fire, and I need to be escorted as fast as possible to Undermere A&E.'

'You mean, our Gary is alive?'

'Yes, but only just.'

She heard Malcolm cough several times. When he was able to speak, his voice sounded strained. 'Audrey, take the Old Military Road across the moor. A tow truck's arrived and the bridge is entirely blocked.'

44

Heather brought over a glass of brandy and placed it in front of Sam before sliding into the booth seat, opposite.

'Thank you.'

'Have you heard from Tina?'

'She's in good company. Certainly, better than mine.'

'We all need a rest from grieving, including you.'

He nodded and took a sip of his drink. 'Wow, that is good.'

'Finest cognac we have. You deserve nothing less after the day you've been through.'

'Tina's had it rougher than me.'

Heather reached across the table and took his hand. 'It's good you're home.'

Tears filled his eyes. 'Everybody's been so nice to me. I don't deserve it.'

'People care about you. About Tina and what your family has suffered. Please allow us to support you through these troubled times. What about your husband?'

'I asked him to stay away. I didn't want to embarrass anyone.'

'Hawksmead has open arms, especially since the arrival of a certain special lady. She sat in this very booth the first night she arrived in Hawksmead and, frankly, changed all our lives for the better.'

'Audrey and Malcolm are beyond words.'

She smiled. 'They don't see themselves that way. Audrey came to lay to rest a family tragedy and in so doing found a new home, new friends, and a new husband, in many ways all thanks to your sister.' She squeezed his hand. 'Hawksmead is a special place, not because of the bow-fronted shops, or the humpback bridge, or the moor, or this wonderful pub...'

Sam grinned.

She pressed on. '…but because of people like you, and Tina.'

The rain was exceptional. Low pressure had scooped up water from the Atlantic and was dumping it on a little Japanese car trying to negotiate an unlit, twisting strip of slicked tarmac across a sodden moor. The road had hidden brows and steep drops into small lakes that the Honda aquaplaned across. Bends came with little warning, causing the car to slide more than once before the tyres gripped.

Four lives depended on Audrey's driving skills. The smell of smoke, and singed skin, was almost overwhelming but if she opened a window she knew the heavy rain and cold air could bring on pneumonia to smoke-damaged lungs.

They rounded another water-filled bend and dived into a flooded dip. Blinding lights filled Audrey's vision and she had no choice but to jam on the brakes and hope the anti-locking system would prevent her from skidding off the road. Headlights on full beam, she focused on the narrow strip of wet tarmac, all the time trying to slow the car until it came to a slithering halt.

A man shone a torch through her side window, which she lowered an inch.

'A bit of an accident.'

'Eamonn, is that you?' Dermot's voice from the back of the Honda sounded pained and raspy.

'Dermot, where the feck were you? We're in a ditch. The Asians have scarpered and the marijuana plants are all over the place. If the deer eat it they'll be higher than a kite. I think we should abandon the haul and take this car.'

'Good plan.'

Eamonn pulled open the driver's door as Audrey slammed her foot down on the accelerator. The front wheels spun as his giant paw reached in and tried to turn off the ignition.

Once the car had gathered sufficient speed and left Eamonn sprawled in the pouring rain, Dermot spoke again from the rear. 'Thank you.' His voice was little better than a croak. 'I hoped you'd do that, but I couldn't ask you in front of me brother.'

'How is Tina?' Abel asked, his voice even more pained than Dermot's.

Audrey didn't reply. What was the point? She had to keep focused. Through her swiping wiper blades she saw the faint orange glow of streetlights in the far distance.

Malcolm had done his best to explain to the young police officer what was happening up at the old school and that Audrey was in no position to come back and give a statement.

'It's about saving lives. Whoever was in that vehicle, now upside down in the river, is without doubt dead but inside my car are four people in urgent need of medical attention. I know you have your job to do but surely you can see why my wife had to take the Honda?'

'You were involved in a fatal car accident and then your wife removed a vital piece of evidence from the scene. It does not look good.'

The grinding of the tow truck's chain interrupted their terse conversation. In the bright spotlights aimed at the dripping vehicle it was clear that whoever was driving had long since been swept away.

'Look at that,' Malcolm said.

'What?'

'The driver's seat belt is caught in the door.'

The police officer noted the car's index number and put a call in via her radio to have the driver identified.

The rain continued to pelt down. Malcolm ventured to ask a question. 'Would you mind if I ordered a taxi to take me home? I'm rather chilled. You have all my contact details.'

'Fair enough. But, crime scene investigators will be examining your car so don't put it in for repair.'

What a relief to be back in civilisation. As Audrey followed the main road that led to Undermere General's Accident & Emergency, three ambulances with sirens wailing and lights flashing whizzed past her.

'Follow them,' came Gary's croaked command from the rear seat. The sign ahead made it clear that only ambulances and other emergency vehicles could turn right and go up the tree-lined drive to A&E.

Audrey didn't care about her driver's licence or a fine. Her sole concern was cutting safely across the oncoming traffic, not easy without blue emergency lights and in pelting rain. But flashing her headlights seemed to do the trick and she was soon across the road and heading up the one-way drive. Ahead, she saw paramedics wheeling broken people from the multiple car crash into A&E. Would there be anyone available to help her passengers?

And then she saw him as if it were preordained and slammed on the brakes. 'Wait here,' she called over her shoulder. She pushed open her door and splashed through the rain towards a tall man in a stylish raincoat sheltering under a large golfing umbrella. 'Mr Bisterzo! Mr Bisterzo.'

The man walked away fast. Perhaps the pounding rain on his umbrella had obliterated her voice. In desperation, she launched herself forward and grabbed his arm. He turned and scowled down at her.

'Doctor, please can you help me?' She knew that she either looked like a drowned rat or a woman released too early from an asylum.

'Mrs Willat?' He remembered her! Willat had been her surname when she first came to Hawksmead.

'Yes. You helped me recover after I fell in the river.'

'Have you fallen in again?'

Malcolm was drenched and exhausted. It had been a long day, not helped by the appalling weather and a near head-on collision with a sports car. He sat back in the rear of the taxi and allowed his eyes to close. His thoughts immediately turned to Audrey and Tina, and her Gary, seemingly back from the dead. He hoped he hadn't misheard.

'Would you mind putting the heat on?' Malcolm asked the

driver as a chill rippled through his body. Standing exposed in the rain had been crazy at his age and he feared there could be health repercussions.

'You heard about the fire?' The driver asked over his shoulder.

Malcolm could do with some of that heat now. 'Yes. The old school is no more.'

'I wonder what will happen?'

'It's probably good news for the man who bought it.'

'How's that?'

'He can apply for planning permission for his new enterprise with a clean slate.'

The driver nodded. 'Perhaps it was him that started the fire.'

45

Hector cowed in the darkness as he watched the firefighters tackle the blaze. His back hurt but he couldn't reach it to lick and rolled over on wet moss to get relief. He was cold and tired and hungry, but he lacked the strength to chase after a rabbit. Keeping to the shadows, he skirted the blazing building and walked amongst the ruins of the old abbey. He'd hidden here in the past, when he'd managed to escape the man who often kicked him. Only hunger had forced him back into his clutches. This time, when the man took off the lead, he wrenched himself free from his grip and went to find his friend. But, now his friend was gone and he was in pain and all alone.

She shivered. She'd tried drying herself by standing close to the hand dryer in the ladies but the airflow had been so pathetic she'd had to give up. Feeling damp and cold, Audrey emerged from the washroom and walked down the long corridor towards where the beds were curtained-off. A&E Consultant, Mr Bisterzo, caught her eye and approached. She'd liked this man when he'd treated her years ago and, for some reason, he'd remembered her.

'Mrs Willat.' She decided not to update him on her latest married name, Cadwallader. Her birth name was Oakes, but it was almost fifty years since she'd been Audrey Oakes.

'Mr Bisterzo.' She smiled at the handsome Italian doctor.

'I think you should get home,' he said. 'Have a hot bath and a hot drink, and get warm. At a certain time of life, it's all too easy to let pneumonia take hold.'

'I would normally object to the phrase "at a certain time of life" but, on this occasion, I am more than happy to take your professional advice.'

'That's not my professional advice. My professional advice would be to confine you to a secure ward. The last time we met you had endured near drowning and hypothermia in the freezing River Hawk. You then suffered smoke and flame injuries from a fire and, today, you show up with no fewer than four seriously ill people.'

'In mitigation, there's been a gap of nearly four years.'

'Four years? Unbelievable. Well it's very nice to see you again.'

'How are they? Tina in particular.'

'She's stable, but the damage the hot smoke and chemical asphyxiates have done is considerable, and worrying.'

'How worrying?'

'Short term, there is risk of a heart attack but longer term the prognosis is not especially good. We're looking at the possibility of pulmonary disease, recurring bronchitis, asthma, even emphysema. Her system was already compromised from prolonged exposure to carbon monoxide.'

Audrey dabbed her eyes. 'What about the three men?'

Mr Bisterzo blew out his cheeks. 'The smoke was clearly incredibly hot and definitely toxic. I'm not even factoring in burns from falling embers. Lord Cornfield has a scorched oesophagus and a fractured ulna. I understand he used his elbow to try and break a toughened glass window. It must've bloody hurt. Mr O'Hanlon, part of the travelling community, has similar throat and lung injuries but is responding well to treatment, although his head and face are badly burned. Most serious of all is Mr Burton. He's emaciated, vitamin deficient and has suffered burns both in and out. You made the right decision bringing them in.'

Audrey felt her tears flow.

The consultant lifted his arm and it hovered over her shoulders. 'May I?'

'I think I need it.'

He placed his arm around her. 'I'm driving you home.'

'Oh, I have my car.'

'Long gone I'm afraid. Hoisted and carried to a secret pound we call Fort Knox.'

'Fort Knox?'

'It costs more than its weight in gold to get your car back. All proceeds go to the consultants' benevolent fund.'

Audrey laughed and dabbed her cheeks with a hankie from her bag. She liked the Italian doctor, whose skill and courage had saved her life. He was giving her a comforting arm as he would to an elderly aunt.

Dermot luxuriated in the clean sheets. He was the first out of the four to be wheeled from Accident & Emergency to an acute ward on one of the upper floors. He thought about what possessions he had – his wallet and his phone, but no charger, and clothes that were unfit to wear again. There would come a moment when he would need to slip away. He'd managed to elicit from Enya, a sweet nurse from his homeland, that Gary was in a bad way and may not make it. That could be good news, albeit unfortunate for Gary. But when he enquired after Tina, Enya's graphic description of her physical state left him deflated. She was the first woman he'd ever had such strong feelings for. Somehow, he had to protect her from Stacy, in particular her father's henchmen, without endangering himself. He was convinced it was Stacy who had bolted the three of them in the basement room, and then set the building on fire.

On the other hand he could pray that Gary got well and, if Dermot gave evidence in court against the Cottee family, he said he would speak up for him. Sure, it was not the way travellers did business, but the Cottees had to be stopped to protect Tina from the avenging angel. The downside was the risk of him spending his prime years in prison.

Audrey looked at the doctor in the driver's seat of the Mercedes SUV Coupé and could understand why so many patients would fall for the man. He had the heady mix of a classic Roman profile topped with neat, wavy hair; good posture, lightly tanned Mediterranean skin, and long legs.

Chilled and shivering, she was a bit embarrassed that she

still appreciated a handsome man with such a good bedside manner at her age.

She spotted Tina's Golf parked on the road outside Malcolm's cottage and thought about the awful day the poor young woman had endured. The passenger door was opened from the outside and Audrey looked at the consultant with surprise as she had been so absorbed by the day's events.

'I don't need to pay a single penny for your thoughts.'

She smiled and accepted his hand as she climbed down from the SUV. Fortunately, the rain had stopped. 'Yes, it's been quite a day that began sad and, without your expertise, would have ended in tragedy.'

'We're not out of the woods yet.' He looked at the cottage. 'The lights are on. Have a hot drink and a warm bath and keep wrapped up.'

'Yes doctor.' She smiled and gave him a kiss on the cheek.

Audrey closed the front door and kicked off her shoes.

'Malcolm?'

She listened for his reply, and then walked up the stairs to the landing. The light was on and their bedroom door ajar. She pushed it open and was about to switch on the light when she saw Malcolm's shape under the covers.

Pulling the door to, she crossed to the bathroom and decided to follow doctor's orders by running a bath. As she cleaned her teeth, she wondered how a single day could deliver so much.

Tina was awake. She knew exactly where she was thanks to her stay following the carbon monoxide poisoning at her parents' house. But how and why was she there? If she lay still, and did nothing, she felt quite comfortable. Covering her mouth and nose was an oxygen mask and almost within seconds of her pulling it away from her face, a nurse appeared and gently told her to keep it on. If she took a deep breath, her lungs tightened and she was forced to take her mask off to cough. It hurt her lungs when she did and frightened her, as mixed in with the blackened phlegm she coughed up was dark blood.

When thirsty, a nurse would help her drink water from a tall cup with a straw. She'd already drunk quite a bit and had wondered why she didn't need the loo, until her fingertips told her she had been catheterised.

She felt for her watch and discovered a plastic hospital band in its place. The nurses must've put it somewhere safe. She hoped so.

Her head ached and her eyeballs felt incredibly sore. What had happened? She tried to think back but all she could grab were flashes. She was at the school. She was looking for someone. Stacy's face, so sculpted, so beautiful, so fearsome, filled her vision, and she shivered.

And then the face most important of all, thin and bearded. She pulled at her oxygen mask and through vocal cords scorched by hot particles she croaked his name.

'*Gary.*'

Warmed-through from her bath and almost overwhelmed with tiredness, Audrey slipped into bed, trying not to disturb Malcolm.

'Goodnight darling.'

All she heard in response was the slight wheeze of his breathing.

46

Weak sunrays through a wall of windows in the small ward told Dermot it was morning. He pulled on a hospital dressing gown and shuffled in his hospital slippers into the main reception area. A young woman was sitting behind the raised counter, her eyes fixed on a computer monitor.

'Apologies for the vision before you, me darlin'.' Dermot spoke in his broadest and most charming Irish brogue. 'Any chance you could point me to your facilities?' He saw her look up at him with a smile that immediately froze. She gathered her composure and pointed to a unisex lavatory. 'Thank you. One quick question. The friends I came in with last night – Lord Cornfield and Gary Burton, do you know where they are?'

The receptionist looked at her computer. 'Lord Cornfield is in Acute Ward Two but there is no record of Mr Burton. He may be in intensive care.'

'Intensive care? Is that where they've taken Tina Burton?'

'I'm sorry, I couldn't tell you.'

Dermot nodded and shuffled to the lavatory. Once he was sure the door was locked he looked in the mirror... and recoiled.

To his certain knowledge, Abel had never slept in a National Health Service bed until last night. He was quite impressed. When he decided a little tweak was necessary to his nose as a result of a fist from a prop forward in an opposing school rugby team, the experience within a leading private hospital was much less interesting than the activity in the acute ward. Sleep had eluded him so, at the start of the new day, he was happy to observe all the comings and goings. Most extraordinary of all was the man in the bed opposite who had talked to himself all night and who, suddenly, sat up and yelled, '*This Champagne is bloody awful!*' The exclamation made Abel laugh – and it hurt, it really hurt, but it was worth it.

A handsome nurse came to quell the man's diatribe about the poor standard of service and then he came over to Abel and asked if he was comfortable.

'Thank you. I'm impressed with this establishment,' Abel said, not recognising his own croaky voice. His face felt so tight it was as though his skin had endured a chemical peel. 'A glass of Champagne, even one not to the standard acceptable to the gentleman in the bed opposite, would be most welcome.'

Ari laughed. 'Would you care for it to be accompanied by a selection of our canapés, vol-au-vents, tartes-au-Francais?'

Abel could not resist breaking into a smile and it hurt again. He tried to sit up but could only use his left arm as his right was in a plastic splint, supported by a sling. He knew he looked a mess but was resisting a visit to a mirror. He would let his personal assistant know that for the next few days he was out of commission and that his phone, the finest money could buy, was no longer in his possession. In some ways, it was quite freeing, but it also felt like walking across a tight rope without a net. Nobody went anywhere without their phone.

'Is it possible for me to take a shower or bath?'

Ari examined Abel's chart. 'I think it would be best if you see the doctor first.'

'When will he come?'

'She generally begins her round at about ten.'

Abel looked at his left wrist but his watch was gone. 'What time's it now?'

Ari checked the watch clipped to his tunic pocket. 'Six forty-five.'

'Are you telling me that I have to sit here and simply wait for three and a quarter hours?'

'Probably a bit longer as she'll be starting her round in Acute Ward One.'

'Any chance I can make a phone call?'

'You can use the phone at reception.'

'Thank you.'

'Right, well, I'd better sort out your Champagne.'

Abel sank back onto the NHS pillow. He would've laughed, but it wasn't worth the pain.

47

Audrey woke with a start. Something was wrong. She looked at the bedside clock and then looked at the body lying beside her. He was usually up and pottering around for at least two hours before she lifted the corner of her eye mask.

'Tea, my darling. It's time to get brewing,' she said, sotto voce.

No response. She gently rested a hand on his shoulder and his pyjamas were wet.

'Malcolm?' She flung back the covers, leapt out of bed and opened the curtains, filling the bedroom with weak morning light. For a moment she stood, motionless, and then she heard a bubbling croak. She hurried to Malcolm's side of the bed and knelt down to look at his face. His breathing, barely discernible, was short, shallow, raspy. His face was drained of blood and the heat from his brow was like touching the hot plate on a stove.

Breathing deeply herself and trying to quell her rising panic, Audrey reached for the landline phone sitting on a bedside table. Memories flashed through her mind of when her first husband had died following a heart attack. *Please God, not again, not yet.*

'Emergency. Which service?'

'Ambulance please.'

Massimo Bisterzo looked down at the beautiful young woman on a ventilator. Dr Manson, his favourite registrar, handed him the chart and he suppressed the rage against his God that erupted almost every day working to save very sick people. He always talked to himself in Italian, allowing the words to trip off his tongue freely, confident that only a very few would be able to understand his diatribe, hopefully nobody in the medical team accompanying him.

There was nothing he could do for the angelic woman lying before him. At least she was comfortable or, at least, oblivious. Every terminal patient he had treated, despite all their brave words, was a little afraid of death.

He wanted to believe in God, to believe that there was an unimaginably beautiful world that envelops the soul but, in his heart, he believed death was a total wipeout.

He replaced the chart in its slot, checked the vital signs monitor, took a last look at the sleeping beauty and led his team into the neighbouring unit. Here there was a chance for some sort of life, albeit one reduced by malnutrition, smoke inhalation, and burns. The man was receiving oxygen and was breathing on his own.

Bisterzo looked at the vital signs monitor. His heart rate was satisfactory, but his blood pressure was too low for comfort. On initial examination, there were signs of thermal injury of his upper airway and trachea which could lead to obstruction but, at this stage, Bisterzo didn't want to intubate as the very process could exacerbate the damage. He was feeling tired from his late night treating a high number of patients with life-threatening injuries. It wasn't so bad when a patient was getting on in years, but when still young, as the man in the bed before him, he found it disturbing.

Audrey held Malcolm's hand. His skin felt thin and cold, barely covering his long fingers. She'd followed his bed when it had been wheeled out of intensive care to an acute ward. She knew she looked a mess. At least she'd had a bath last night but she'd not had time to brush her hair or teeth before the ambulance came. It had been out on another emergency where a person was treated at the scene and by brilliant good fortune had almost been passing the cottage when they took the call. A swift check of Malcolm's temperature, his sweating and wheezing, pointed to pneumonia and within three minutes he had been helped downstairs and, wrapped in a blanket, wheeled out to the ambulance. Meanwhile, Audrey had grabbed clothes that were robust but not exactly matching and just had time to set the alarm, and grab her handbag and keys. She had sat by her husband in the ambulance and held his hand for the somewhat rocky and bumpy journey to hospital.

At one point, Malcolm had pulled away the plastic oxygen mask and rasped, 'My car. Where's my car?'

'It's all right, Mr Cadwallader.' The paramedic had gently replaced the mask and turned to Audrey. 'Pneumonia can cause some confusion.'

'He's not confused.' She leaned towards Malcolm. 'Darling, your car is at the hospital, safe and sound. We'll pick it up when you're better.' In truth, the car was safe but far from sound. At the very least it would need a deep clean to rid it of the vast array of odours that had accumulated during the helter-skelter drive across the moor.

Sitting beside her husband's bed in the acute ward holding his hand, she looked at the monitor and checked his vital signs. His heart rate was ninety, his respiration twenty-four, albeit a bit wheezy, and his blood pressure was one hundred and thirty-eight over eighty-two. His blood oxygen saturation was ninety-one per cent, thanks to the extra oxygen he was receiving. Malcolm was slim and fit and, although he was less mobile since his accident falling downstairs a few years ago, he took great pride in being active in his eightieth year. She looked at the monitor again; the numbers confirmed that the intravenous antibiotics were already having a positive effect.

She eased her hand away from his but was surprised by the sudden grip of his fingers. 'Darling, I'm not going,' she said, gently. 'I just need to use the facilities. I'll be back in a jiffy.' She got up from her chair and looked about for her handbag. She retrieved it from the floor and stepped through a gap in the curtains drawn along a track. She took a moment to take in the small acute ward which had eight beds, then walked into the communal corridor.

'Audrey.'

She turned on hearing the refined, albeit husky voice, speak her name. Abel had clearly showered since the trauma of the fire and although he was unshaven and his skin a little blotchy, and his arm in a sling, all in all he looked pretty good, if a little odd, in his NHS gown and slippers.

'Lord Cornfield. How are you?'

'Lungs hurt a bit and I have some sort of malevolent vice gripping my head but, apart from those two inconveniences, I've never felt more relieved to be alive, for which I thank you.'

Self-consciously, she ran her fingers through her unkempt hair. 'I look a mess.' He seemed slightly puzzled by her statement and she felt a bit of a flush coming on.

Good God woman, you're not trying to pull him!

'My husband was out in all that rain last night following an accident with another vehicle on Hawksmead bridge. He has pneumonia.' She saw immediate concern in his eyes. 'Thankfully, he's responding to antibiotics.'

'Let me get this straight; while you were at the school rescuing us, your husband was getting soaked?'

She nodded.

'Would you care for a cup of coffee? There's a drinks machine down the corridor.'

'I would love a hot chocolate but I have to pay a visit, first.'

48

Abel sat at the end of the corridor in the acute unit nursing two rigid paper cups containing hot chocolate, despite one arm being in a sling. He would have liked to be dressed, but his clothes were fit for nothing but the bin. He had no phone, no money and no access to a computer. He was sure Mrs Cadwallader would be happy to help him. It was a long time since he'd been in a position of need. Money bought most people, although Abel had made it a point in his life not to throw his cash around.

He looked up as Audrey came to sit near him. She'd clearly taken a bit of time to sort out her hair and face and it was to good effect. She was a fine looking woman who, in her prime, would have been drop dead gorgeous. She still looked pretty good to his forty-eight-year-old eyes.

'Chocolate.' He handed the cup in his left hand to her and relieved his injured arm of the other.

'Thank you.'

'Dermot, the Irishman, is in your husband's ward. He looks pretty beaten up, but he's tough. He carried Christina so his hands weren't free to swipe away the burning embers that landed on his head. He carried her all the way up the stairs to the entrance hall before collapsing. I know he's a criminal, but Christina owes her life to him. Of course, Dermot's heroic effort would've come to nought without the firefighters and you.'

'We were lucky, Lord Cornfield.'

'Abel, please.'

'If Tina hadn't told me she was meeting you up at the old school, I would not have gone there to check she was all right when I saw the fire. I would not have seen the watch you gave her strapped to the dog's collar. That was a life-saving stroke of genius.'

'It was my last throw of the dice. Thank God the dog made it out.'

'Indeed.'

'Where is the dog, now?'

'I don't know. I have to confess, once I saw Tina's watch I forgot all about the dog.'

'Of course. Have you seen Christina… or Gary?'

'Not since last night.'

'One of us should check on them.'

'I really want to but I don't think I can leave my husband.'

'This is a bit of an imposition but, would you mind if I borrowed your phone for a while?'

He watched as she took her phone out of her bag. She checked the screen. 'There's no pass code to get in and the battery is almost fully charged.' She placed it in his hand, supported by the sling, as his left hand was holding his drink. 'If anyone calls, please tell them where I am and what's happened.'

'Thank you.'

She stood and finished her hot chocolate. 'It's been a pleasure to meet you, Abel.'

'The pleasure is all mine, I can assure you.'

'Tina has very good taste.'

'She is a truly remarkable young woman.' He saw her eyes fill with tears.

'Shall I take your cup?'

'Thank you.'

He watched her drop the paper cups in a rubbish receptacle and head back to her husband's acute ward. Her phone was at the budget end of the spectrum but it gave him a vital link back to his world of power. Although, using his left hand to tap and swipe the screen felt awkward.

49

Time passes incredibly slowly in hospital, so when there is any movement, it's a drama that attracts attention. A vacant bed was removed from Malcolm's acute ward and ten minutes later another bed put in its place, this one with a patient. Audrey noted a bottle collecting urine attached to the side of the bed. There was an oxygen cylinder and pipe to a mask covering the man's face, and a bag of clear liquid was dripping intravenously into his arm.

'Is that...?' Malcolm's voice was croaky but there was more life in it than Audrey had feared. She gripped his hand. 'How are you feeling?'

'Warmer. I did get chilled.'

'I told you not to leap in the river.'

Malcolm chuckled, but it was more of an audible wheeze. 'Any news on the driver?'

'Not that I've heard.'

'That bridge. What can I say? It has form.'

Audrey looked down the ward at where the new arrival was curtained-off.

Malcolm squeezed her hand. 'I hope the Honda is not racking up horrendous parking charges. If you need to go and re-park the car, I'm perfectly fine.'

She looked into his warm, loving face. 'Darling, I think I need to come clean about your motor.'

Gary looked up at the hospital ceiling and admired the modern engineering. Undermere General Hospital was a good place to be ill and, boy, did he feel ill. He had first dated Tina when she was visiting Audrey following her escape from the boarding house fire. Audrey had survived due in part to her own determination, due in part to Tina refusing to stop for Gary's police patrol car, and due in a major part to the skills of the medical staff.

Gary had no idea how he'd escaped the fire in the old school. His last memory was the stink of the smoke, the impenetrable darkness and the scorching heat. He vaguely remembered being in the back seat of a car being tossed about as the driver skidded around bends; and then faces looking down at him, a few weird dreams and waking this morning and speaking to an Italian doctor. He looked at the intravenous drip and felt the oxygen mask. He knew he needed them both but the policeman in him wanted to take action.

'Hello Gary.'

He looked up into the face of the woman who had changed so many lives for the better and pulled away the oxygen mask. 'Hello Audrey.' He was shocked by the sound of his voice. 'It's good to see you.'

She smiled and squeezed his hand. 'It's more than good to see you.'

'Tina. Have you seen her?'

'Not since last night. I will try and find out how she is. Lord Cornfield told me that Mr O'Hanlon's actions saved her from getting badly burned, and worse, at his own cost.'

Gary replaced the oxygen mask and took a deep breath as he digested the information. He pulled it away again. 'Audrey,' he whispered. 'It's important that the press and TV do not get wind of the fact that I am still alive until the criminals I was investigating can be arrested.'

She leaned closer to him. 'What do you want me to do?'

'Can you make sure that O'Hanlon does not tip them off. Could you find him and see if he's fit enough to come and see me. I think it's time he and I made a deal.' He reached for her hand. 'Someone drove us to hospital. Was it you?'

Audrey smiled. 'Across the moor. No cameras, no red lights, no chasing police car – I was able to really pump the gas.'

Gary laughed and it hurt his lungs.

Audrey raised her brows. 'Malcolm doesn't know that his

pride and joy was hoisted up onto the back of a flat bed and now resides in a very expensive car park.'

'Priceless.' Gary smiled and that hurt, too.

'Not quite priceless, but a king's ransom to get released.'

'Never mind. You can sell your story. I'm sure the Hawksmead Chronicle will buy it.'

'You rest. I'll see if I can locate Mr O'Hanlon.'

50

He ordered his driver to pull up outside the main entrance to the hospital, not caring that the car was in a no waiting zone.

'Keep your phone on. Take a piss. Get something to eat. I'll be at least an hour.' He opened his rear passenger door and slammed it shut behind him. He felt stiff from the long drive and needed to take a piss himself. He pushed the revolving door that was determined to control his pace and entered the main reception area. He looked for male toilets and hurried towards the sign, pressure building with each step. He had always prided himself on keeping fit, and often worked out at his local boxing gym. As a young man he'd been known as Frank the Punch – landing a solid right was always a pleasure.

'Your phone.' Abel looked at Audrey, sitting by an elderly patient.

'Thank you.' She took it off him. 'This is my husband, Malcolm.'

Abel turned his attention to the man who appeared to be enjoying a deep sleep. A half-full bag hung from a stand, dripping into a clear tube that led to his arm. 'How is he?'

'He's on the mend but he'll need a week, or possibly two.'

'If there's anything I can do please let me know. If he'd be more comfortable in a private facility, no problem.'

'That's very kind of you. We're fine here at the moment. Any news of Tina?'

'All I've been able to glean is that she's still in intensive care. Only a relative can get to see her.'

'What about her brother? Does he know?'

'I presume the hospital has already contacted him. I'll check. I fear she's in a pretty poor state.'

He pushed down the nozzle to the wall-mounted hand sanitiser and cursed as a jet of foamy liquid shot past his hand onto his cashmere jacket.

'Bollocks.'

At the reception desk, a doctor was occupying the focus of two receptionists. He approached the high counter and patted it with his hands as though playing bongo drums.

'Frank Cottee to see Stacy.'

The doctor ceased talking and looked at him. It was what Frank liked best – respect.

'Mr Cottee, my name's Mr Bisterzo. I have been caring for your daughter.'

'No offence, *Mr* Bisterzo, but I demand to see the doctor in charge.'

'That is me.'

'Really?'

'Please take a seat.' He gestured to an alcove with two chairs.

'I've been sitting in a car for three hours plus, I don't need a seat.'

Bisterzo smiled. 'I understand. I'll take you to your daughter.' They walked side-by-side down a wide corridor.

Frank sniffed. 'So, what's the story?'

'I'm afraid Stacy's in a bad way. When she was brought in, the paramedics had fought to revive her, first on the river bank where she had been spotted by a dog walker, and later in the ambulance, pumping her heart all the way. We managed to get her heart beating on its own, but her brain was starved of oxygen during her time in the river. We've conducted several tests to determine -'

'You said her heart's beating,' Frank interrupted. 'So she's alive?'

'Her heart will stop beating once we take her off the ventilator. She can't breathe on her own as there is no brain activity.'

'So, you're saying she can't breathe without a ventilator but her heart's pumping, regardless?'

'The heart in a way has its own brain, its own inbuilt

pacemaker. All it needs is oxygen to continue to beat and the ventilator is providing the oxygen.' Bisterzo led the way into a room full of what looked to be up-to-the minute monitoring and technical equipment. A young female nurse was writing on a chart. Bisterzo stopped by the foot of the bed and looked intently at Frank. 'This is the worst situation any parent can face.'

'But she's still alive?'

'Yes, but only with our help.'

Frank walked away from the doctor and went to look at his girl, kicking aside an upright chair. Fixed to her mouth was a tube, pumping air into her lungs. Other wires were connected to her and their numbers displayed on a monitor. Rage rose from deep within. He turned to the Italian doctor and almost spat at him. 'What are those marks on her face?'

Bisterzo looked momentarily confused. 'I, we don't know.'

Frank approached the younger man. 'I do. Someone scratched her.'

'Mr Cottee, I think we are at the point when Stacy's mother and siblings should come and say goodbye.'

'I'm all she's got.' He looked hard at Bisterzo, desperate to blame the doctor for his daughter's predicament. 'Listen to me, you keep my daughter alive until I tell you not to. Got it?'

'It must be a terrible shock. Take your time. I can bring in colleagues. You don't have to accept my word. I'll leave you in peace.' He walked out of the unit, followed by the nurse.

Frank went back to the bed and picked up Stacy's lifeless hand. 'I'm here sweetheart, Daddy's here. I'll look after you. Now, who clawed your face? Tell me darlin'. I know you can't talk right now 'cause of that thing in your mouth but I promise I'm gonna make 'em suffer. I promise. I love you. I love you.' He could not hold back the tears and Frank felt his whole body overwhelmed with grief as he sank onto the chair. He cried like he'd never cried in his life before. The pain was beyond anything he could have ever imagined. *His princess, his baby girl, his sweet angel.*

A hospital porter pushed Gary in a wheelchair down a corridor and after quite a wait, they entered a lift. The saline drip had been removed but an oxygen bottle rested on his lap and he was grateful for the pure air. Audrey had done her best to smarten him up but he was a far cry from the cocky police patrol officer who had chased after Tina in more ways than one. And now he had to be brave. He had to brace himself. He hoped he had the strength to conceal any shock or emotion when he saw her, but he knew Tina was too smart to be easily taken in.

The porter used his pass to get them through a multitude of locked doors, and with each roll of the chair's wheels, his nervousness increased.

Did Tina still love him?

Even if she did, would she still love him once he'd told her the whole story? He had to tell her, didn't he? Sooner or later she'd find out. Timing was the key; first and foremost they had to get well. Not until they could both stand and breathe could they begin to think about their future.

They entered Intensive Care and Gary steeled himself. He was pushed through the open entrance to her unit and the porter locked the chair's wheels. He looked at Tina, her head and shoulders propped up with a multitude of pillows. An oxygen mask covered her nose and mouth, a drip was in her arm and a bottle was hung on the side of her bed collecting urine. Earlier, Gary had had to use all his persuasive charm to get the registrar doctor to remove his catheter. He lifted the oxygen cylinder. 'I don't need it for a while, thanks.'

The porter turned off the tap and once Gary was standing, placed the bottle on the seat of the wheelchair. Gary took a step towards Tina and her eyes opened. In that brief moment, not even as long as a second, he saw the truth.

51

'Mr Cottee.'

Frank turned his head away from his sleeping angel and looked towards the Italian consultant. Standing beside him was a woman wearing a dark blue jerkin top and baggy trousers. Around her neck hung the usual photo ID.

'Mr Cottee,' continued Bisterzo. 'I would like to introduce you to my colleague, Laura Duffy. She's a specialist nurse who helps the unit to support families during particularly difficult times.'

'Are you Irish, Ms Duffy?' Frank got up from the bedside chair.

He saw her smile and was surprised by the small resurgence of his long-dormant lust.

'My husband is, I believe, although I think the bloodline is a little tenuous.'

There was a pause and it annoyed Frank that the Italian doctor felt compelled to fill the void.

'Mr Cottee,' Bisterzo said. 'As I mentioned earlier, we undertook certain brain-stem tests to determine the level of activity.' The doctor took a deep breath. 'Unfortunately, we concluded that all Stacy's brain function is irreversibly lost and that when we remove the ventilator, she will slip away.'

Laura Duffy stepped forward and Frank was able to get a closer view of her pretty face. He estimated that she was in her late thirties and probably had children. There was a look in her brown eyes that told him she understood what it meant to be a parent of a sick child.

'Frank… may I call you Frank?'

He nodded.

'I would like to discuss with you something that you may

find initially disturbing but in time you will derive great pride and comfort from the decision you make today.'

He straightened his back. Frank knew when he was being softened up for a killer punch. 'You want to turn off her life support so someone else can use this room?' He looked down at Stacy. 'No way.'

'That's not what this is about.' She laid her fingertips on his left forearm and he felt a charge. He had to get a grip.

'I have money.' His voice came out surprisingly husky. 'I presume this hospital has a private wing? Move her there and then this room is free for the next mug.'

'Frank, today you and Stacy have the chance, the opportunity to transform the lives of up to eight people.'

'You want a donation?'

'Mr Cottee,' interjected Bisterzo.

Frank turned to the consultant. Why was he still here? Couldn't he see that Frank and Laura were having a moment?

'Mr Cottee.' Bisterzo spoke in a tone of voice that Frank marked down as classic ristorante Italiano. 'I would like to assure you that every decision we have made with regard to Stacy's treatment has been based one hundred per cent on what is best for her. We have done all we can.'

Laura touched his arm again. 'Frank, do you know what Stacy's thoughts were with regard to organ donation?'

Frank stepped away from her. So, that's what the soft sell was all about. 'You want, while her heart is still beating, while warm blood is passing through her veins, to cannibalise her body for spare parts?'

'You and Stacy,' Laura continued in a soothing tone, 'have the chance to help others receive the greatest gift of all – an independent life.'

'Mr Cottee.' Bisterzo interrupted again. 'Stacy has moved on. She cannot suffer anymore. The retrieval procedure is undertaken with total respect and dignity.'

The image of what the doctor had just said hit home and Frank felt his knees going. He reached for the chair, slumped down, and grasped Stacy's hand.

'Frank,' Laura said in her enticing tone. 'Your beautiful daughter will always live in your heart and her heart can live on in the body of another.'

'Get out.'

Laura pulled back. 'Please think about it. There's no rush, but time is short for those who Stacy can help.'

'Get out!'

Audrey watched the uniformed police officers leave the ward and hurried to her husband's bedside. 'Everything all right?'

'She was a young woman.' Malcolm spoke sombrely. 'She *is* a young woman. She's on life-support in this hospital. They've gone to examine my car. I told them it's in the pound. When I explained that you'd had to rush one of their own to hospital, I was suddenly their best friend.'

'I'm sorry about the young woman.'

'I am too.' Malcolm squeezed her hand. 'How is Tina?'

'She's still in ICU but well enough to see Gary.'

He took a deep breath and coughed. The sound was horrible and he had to reach for a box of tissues. Once he had recovered, he looked at his wife. 'After two years apart, too much water may have gone under the bridge. Poor choice of metaphor.'

Audrey nodded. 'I hope you're wrong.'

'I hope I am, too. They've both suffered terribly.'

'How are you feeling?'

'I love antibiotics.'

'Don't we all. Have they said when you can come home?'

'I think it's going to be a couple of days. Are you going to be all right?

She forced a smile. 'I'll be fine.'

He paused a few seconds before responding. 'You don't like being on your own, do you?'

'Not anymore. When I first came to Hawksmead, I was happy to be alone in the old school boarding house, living within its Victorian walls. But, when I realised I had fallen in love for the second time, I felt vulnerable, fearful that I could lose someone who is very precious. I get nervous when we're apart.' She gripped his hand tightly. 'You scared me.'

He nodded. 'I think I'm going to quit driving.'

'But it wasn't your fault. I was there. You didn't even hit the other car.'

'It wasn't my fault when I skidded on black ice fifty-four years ago and killed your brother's best friend. I'm old. It's time for me to pass the key on to you.'

She couldn't fight back the tears.

Frank emerged from his daughter's unit and stood to gather his emotions. He saw a medical orderly push a youngish, dishevelled, bearded man in a wheelchair out of another unit and was sure that he recognised him. He stood back and watched the orderly take the man out through the controlled entrance and exit doors.

A loud, demanding beeping sound filled the ICU. A nurse hurried out of the unit the bearded man had just left to join several other medical personnel who rushed into another intensive care unit, one wheeling a trolley with hi-tech electrical equipment which Frank had seen being used in TV dramas but couldn't remember what it was called.

He waited a few moments then checked the patient's name written on the wipe board.

Christina Burton.

The scum police officer was visiting his wife! It was only a matter of time before police would come knocking on Frank's door. The pieces that led up to his daughter's race from the boarding school were falling into place. And the scratches on her cheek were typical of a bitch. Now was his chance. His last act to avenge his angel. Without his beautiful Stacy there was no future. The policeman who had deceived him, who had lied through his teeth, who had defiled his beautiful daughter, who had betrayed Frank Cottee's trust, would serve a life sentence.

He entered Christina's unit and stared at the blonde-haired young woman lying with her eyes closed on the raised bed, surrounded by sophisticated equipment, her mouth and nose covered by an oxygen mask. He looked up at the beeping monitor displaying her vital signs.

'Hello.'

Her voice startled him. It was husky but with an endearing silky tone. She had lifted off the oxygen mask and he had a much clearer view of her fine-boned features.

'I was visiting my daughter down the corridor.'

'How is she?'

'Not good.'

'I'm sorry. At least she's in the right place.'

He nodded. 'And how are you?'

'A bit battered. But they tell me I'll live, barring the unforeseen.'

'My daughter has three score lines on her cheek.' He saw a retraction in her eyes and moved closer. 'Gary lied his way into the bosom of my family, he made love to my daughter, promised her marriage, and then betrayed us.' He watched as his words sunk in. The girl held his gaze. She had courage, he'd give her that.

'I was jealous of Stacy,' she admitted. 'Gary told me on a brief visit home that our marriage was over the moment he met her. He may have been working undercover but he was in love with your daughter. Stupidly, I hoped he'd come to his senses, and then waited for him to come back to me, but even after more than two years held as a prisoner, he told me he still loves your daughter and wants a divorce.'

Frank looked intently into the young woman's eyes. 'Why aren't your parents here?'

'They're in heaven. They liked Gary. They trusted him to look after me. They were very disappointed.'

'So you have no one?'

She reached out her hand and touched his fingers. 'In this moment, all I have is you.' He took her hand in his and felt her fine bones. 'Please tell Stacy,' she said, 'that I'm sorry I hurt her.'

He nodded. 'Get well, my dear.' He let go of her hand and hurried out of the unit. The corridor was empty apart from a young woman sitting at the reception desk. He returned to Stacy's unit and looked at his beautiful girl. He had loved her mother and raged against the cancer that had robbed him and Stacy of so much. He had fought hard to protect his little girl, but angels have wings and she'd wanted to stretch hers.

He walked around her bed and gripped the electrical cable leading to the ventilator in his scarred fist. He pulled down with all his power and there was a blue flash and a surprisingly loud bang. An alarm sounded almost immediately. He switched the power off at the socket and pulled out the plug. There would be no cranking open her chest and plundering her organs.

Within seconds a young doctor and nurse were in the room attending to Stacy. The nurse turned off the alarm. Another arrived pushing the trolley with the electrical equipment.

Defibrillator.

That was the word Frank had been seeking.

'Extubate.' Everyone stopped what they were doing and looked at Mr Bisterzo. 'Remove the tube,' he ordered.

Frank watched as the young doctor gently unclipped the mask and pulled the tube out of Stacy's trachea. There was no gagging reflex. The nurse used a tissue to wipe around her mouth.

'Mr Cottee,' Bisterzo continued, 'would like some private time with his daughter.'

Frank watched the medical personnel leave the unit. He looked at Stacy and up at the vital signs monitor. Her heart was still beating. 'I am here, angel. You are about to go on a journey to a beautiful place, far, far away where your mum is waiting for you. And, if you need me, just call. I'll always be close.' He gripped her hand as he fought to hold back his tears. This was a fight he couldn't punch his way out of. He heard another alarm and knew her heart had stopped beating.

Tina held her husband's hand as he sat by her bed wearing a hospital dressing gown and pyjamas. She had been moved out of the Intensive Care Unit and was now in an acute ward. Much nicer. There was more to see. She had hated being alone in the ICU surrounded by all the equipment.

'There's an arrest warrant out for Dermot but he's disappeared.'

'Abel told me he saved my life.'

Gary nodded. 'Yes. But we mustn't forget Hector the dog. Then there's the firefighters. And, of course, Audrey, and the medical staff. All the drugs and specialist equipment. But, yes, Dermot protected you at his own cost. Without him, you wouldn't be here.'

'I hope, one day, I'll be able to thank him.'

'And when that day comes, I'll be waiting with handcuffs.'

'Gary, shall we usher the elephant out of the ward?' She saw him stiffen. 'Did you love her?'

'No.' He shook his head. 'I want to say she seduced me but that would be a lie. I got too close. It was a role. Method acting. I was consumed by lust. Nothing more. I give you my word.'

Tina felt a wave of exhaustion sweep over her and closed her eyes as she pulled her hand away from his. He had slept with Stacy within months of their marriage. Could she forgive him? Could she ever trust him again? Did she want to?

She opened her eyes. He was gone.

When Sam received Audrey's call and she had given him a potted account of what had happened since the funeral, he was stunned and immediately called his husband via WhatsApp.

Luke responded assertively. 'Sam. Get in a taxi and get to the hospital. See your sister. She's your priority.'

'I will but there is one other thing. I don't want to return to New Zealand.'

'What are you saying?'

'I want you to pack up our stuff and come here. I can't deal with my parents' estate from the other side of the world. Once their house is sold, we'll be able to buy our own place.'

'In Hawksmead?'

'Or Undermere. I've been made to feel so welcome. You'll feel it too.'

'What about my job?'

'You'll get a good job here.'

'In London, yes, but Hawksmead? I don't think so.'

'What do you want me to do?'

'I want you to see your sister – then we'll talk.'

52

William Longden climbed up into the pulpit of his church. He looked across at the sea of expectant faces and rejoiced in their presence, whether they were here to celebrate or to worship. Everyone was always welcome. He took particular delight in seeing Gary Burton sitting beside William's dear friend, Malcolm; and Tina holding the hand of Malcolm's remarkable wife, Audrey. The reuniting of the estate agent and her policeman had been rejoiced by the whole of Hawksmead. To help their recovery, the young couple were staying in Malcolm and Audrey's spare bedroom where they were receiving the kind of care that only love and good cuisine can provide. However, he was surprised by the urgency of Gary's request, coming so soon after being released from hospital, but he understood the young man's reasoning.

He waited for Eleanor to finish playing *Wind Beneath My Wings* and took a deep breath. 'There's a structure to sermons that most preachers tend to follow.' His voice carried to the back of the pews, without the need of a microphone. 'It's a structure typical of what we often see on TV. It starts with a problem, what writers call the inciting incident. As in drama, the preacher explores various approaches and dead ends until, almost despairing of a solution, we pull out our Ace in the hole, our trump card – *God*.'

He smiled as a few in the congregation tried to control their laughter.

'Detective Constable Gary Burton agreed to work undercover to bring down a ruthless gangland leader. In the line of duty, he was uncovered and held captive for more than two years, and for some of that time up at the old school with migrants who had been trafficked from Vietnam. A brave young man, whose marriage to Tina I officiated, was suffering not much more than a mile or two from here, as the crow flies.

'Was his rescue and the rescue of his wife and others from the subsequent conflagration a miracle? An act of God? Or simply the result of firefighters doing their job? You tell me.' He paused and waited for a response. Of course, all responses were unspoken. He smiled again. 'Today, we are here to celebrate and show our support for a young couple who were torn apart and through Manus Domini Dei, or sheer good fortune, have found each other again.' William stepped down from the pulpit and gestured for Tina and Gary to stand in front of the Lord's table.

Gary stood and offered his hand to Tina. His suit was a size too large and, William thought, was probably one of Malcolm's.

Tina did not take the offered hand. 'What's going on?'

'Please. It'll all become clear.'

She stood and studiously avoided his eyes.

'I want to say something.'

Reluctantly, she looked at him and allowed him to take her hands. He turned his face away to give a little cough. It clearly pained him. 'I, Gary Simon Burton, broke the vow I made to you on our wedding day to forsake all others.' His voice was croaky and he tried to clear his throat before continuing. 'I do not deserve a second chance. But, if you have it in your heart to forgive me, I promise, before God and all these witnesses...' He coughed again. '...I promise to love you, comfort you, cherish you for the rest of our days, in sickness and in health, forsaking *all* others, whatever the circumstances, whatever the temptation, and shall be faithful for as long as we both shall live.'

A strange, shuffling silence almost like a Mexican wave, rippled through the congregation as they all waited for Tina's response.

Silence.

The Reverend spoke quietly to Tina. 'Would you like to say a few words, my dear?'

She took a deep breath and stared at Gary. 'Who else knew you were going to do this?'

'Almost everyone who came to our wedding.'

She pulled her hands free and looked at Audrey.

Gary interjected. 'Both Audrey and Malcolm thought it was too soon, but I made them promise to keep quiet.'

Tina scanned the congregation and saw many puzzled faces she recognised. She sat down beside Audrey and closed her eyes.

Gary coughed. He looked at William and then at the people who almost filled the church. 'Thank you for joining my wife and me, today. Once the service is concluded, you are all invited to the Falcon pub where there is an open bar and food courtesy of our dear friend, Lord Abel Cornfield.' He sat down and hung his head.

William waited patiently for the cacophony of whispering to quieten. Finally, he was able to utter the words, 'Let us pray.'

53

The Falcon was heaving. Tina parked the sadness of her parents' passing and her annoyance at Gary's unwelcome surprise and relished the company of so many old friends in their Sunday best; people who had been such a part of her life before she and Gary had left for London. She was particularly pleased to see her brother openly displaying his love for his husband, Luke.

'Sweetie, let me see.'

Tina offered her hands to Magdalena. 'Wow, Mags, you look stunning.'

'And you look beautiful.' She examined Tina's nails. 'Nice job.'

'My mother always said, self-praise is no praise, but you do do very good nails.'

'Darling Tina.' Both women looked at the source of the melodious voice.

'Eleanor!' Tina joyously shouted her name. 'You played the organ so beautifully.' She turned to Magdalena. 'I take it you two know each other?'

Magdalena gave Eleanor a kiss on each cheek and then held her at arms' length. 'You should fire Polish girl who work for you in tea shop,'

'Fire Agnieska?' Eleanor replied. 'Why?'

'She is very rude to Polish customers.'

Eleanor looked puzzled. 'I don't understand.'

Magdalena laughed. 'Of course you don't. She speak in Polish!'

'*Christina!*'

All three women turned as one to Abel whose right elbow

was still supported by a sling. There were a few marks from the fire on his handsome face; and his great head of hair looked a little patchy, despite a recent trim.

Tina wrapped her arms around his neck. 'You should have warned me.' She kissed him tenderly on the cheek.

'I sent the three Versace dresses to the cottage as a clue. I thought Gary would crack and tell you.' He looked at what Tina was wearing. 'Gianni would be truly honoured.'

She smiled. 'Thank you.' And she kissed him again.

'Will you think about my offer? With your help a fantastic phoenix can rise out of the ashes.'

'I will. I promise.' Reluctantly, she pulled away from him and saw that Magdalena was now in deep conversation with the owner of the Hawksmead Chronicle, but Eleanor was standing by, looking on. 'Abel, I would like to introduce you to Eleanor Houghton, Hawksmead's finest cakeologist and organist.'

Eleanor laughed. 'Lord Cornfield.'

'Abel, please. You have a theatrical air. Were you ever on the stage?'

'I was,' Eleanor responded, smiling.

Tina chipped in. 'Eleanor has sung in London's West End. She has a beautiful operatic voice.'

'I knew it!' Abel responded. 'I do not have an artistic bone, but I have a great nose for talent.'

Tina gently backed away leaving Abel and Eleanor immersed in conversation. She really liked Abel. He was incredibly exciting company. No. She felt more than that. A lot more.

'He is very handsome.'

She looked at Audrey. 'But way too honourable.'

Audrey laughed. 'There's a man outside who lives to a very different code of honour. He wondered if he could have a few words.'

The man was wearing a long rain jacket with a hood. Tina wondered who it was.

'Geezus, it's good to see you.' He turned his smiling face to her and she fought an instinct to recoil. 'Not a pretty sight, I grant you.'

She leaned forward and pushed back his hood. His once thick hair was in clumps and tufts with skin that was raw and seeping. His face looked as though he had suffered a severe bout of eczema, with red-raw patches, scabs and weeping wounds.

'It's not a problem. I'm wanted by the British police but with this face I can move around with ease. I'm unrecognisable even to facial recognition cameras. There's a plus to everything.'

'I will never forget what you did for me.'

'Gary will never forget what I did to him. I hope he will forgive me, one day. I hope you will, too.'

She took his hand in hers and held his palm against her cheek. 'Farewell my travelling friend.'

'Till we meet again.'

54

Hawksmead Chronicle

King Cottee Captured in Rio

Self-styled King of Essex, Frank Cottee, who disappeared following the death of his daughter and the resurrection of undercover police officer, Gary Burton, has been captured on the phone of a tourist filming his girlfriend sunbathing in Brazil. Sightings of the ruthless gangland mastermind have resulted in many *GotCottee* viral videos. He has been, allegedly, spotted in almost every corner of the world but despite an international arrest warrant, remains at large.

Tina pressed her accelerator and felt Gary stiffen in the seat beside her.

'Relax... my mother was a member of the Institute of Advanced Motorists.'

Gary laughed as the white VW Golf zoomed up the long drive. After so much rain, the early winter's sun was a welcome visitor. Within little more than a minute the tyres scrunched on the gravel as Tina swung around in a circle before bringing the car to a halt as far away from the old school as the apron would allow. She turned off the engine and they both released their belts. Without speaking they climbed out of the car and stared in awe.

The once forbidding edifice was a hollowed shell of blackened bricks and timbers, held up by scaffolding, peppered with large signs warning people to keep away from the dangerous structure.

'How did we get out of there?' Gary murmured.

'Burly firemen,' she replied. 'Do you really think he could still be here?'

'I do. But whether he's alive or not, I don't know. Audrey said he was hurt pretty bad. We should've come sooner.'

'We weren't in the best shape.' She looked away from him and coughed.

'Still,' Gary said. 'He was good at catching rabbits.' He turned to her. 'What about Abel's offer? Are you going to accept? I could help you.' He waited for her response. 'Tina?'

Roff! Roff!

'Hector!' he called.

The great dog bounded towards them from the abbey ruins. Gary moved away from the car and knelt down to welcome their saviour. The once ferocious-looking hound was all sharp bones but so happy to see him. 'Hello boy. My heroic friend.'

Tina watched as her husband hugged the dog that had played such a pivotal role in saving their lives.

'I prayed he'd still be alive,' he continued, 'but I didn't really think it possible after all this time. We must take him home and feed him up.' He looked at her. 'Audrey and Malcolm said they were looking forward to the patter of tiny feet.'

'With the best will in the world, I don't think those paws can be described as tiny.'

Gary continued to hug and kiss the dog as Hector covered his face in sloppy licks. 'Look what I've found.' He twisted the dog's collar and revealed the Patek Philippe watch. 'It's still attached. I don't believe it.' He undid the strap.

'I'll take that, thank you.' Tina approached her husband with hand held out.

'It's still working.'

'It's automatic. Doesn't need a battery.'

He turned the watch over and looked at the back. 'There's an inscription.'

'It's a private message, Gary.'

'*To a most remarkable woman.*' He handed her the watch. 'My thoughts, entirely.'

'Thank you, Hector,' she said, as Gary helped her fix the weathered leather strap to her wrist.

'What about giving Hector a thank you hug?' He turned to the dog and stroked both his ears. 'You would like a hug, wouldn't you boy?'

Tina glanced at the face of her new-found watch. 'Well, I'll be off.'

'You're going?'

'I've seen all I need to see.' She slipped back into the car.

'You're leaving without us?'

'I can't have those big claws on my leather seats.' She started the engine. 'I'll see you at the cottage. There's a shortcut across the moor.' She closed the door and quickly drove off. In her rear-view mirror she saw Gary cuddling the excited dog. As she approached the start of the long drive she swung the steering wheel and accelerated back to the reunited couple.

She pushed open her door and held out her arms. 'Hector!' The dog bounded over to her and tried to cover her face in happy licks.

The chop-chop of a helicopter's rotor blades attracted their attention and the familiar sight of the AgustaWestland AW109 came into view. Hector barked with great enthusiasm as the flying beast circled over the school's burnt-out shell and disappeared from view. The dog gave chase, barking happily. Gary followed. Tina grabbed her handbag and ran in her trainers as fast as her damaged lungs would allow. As she rounded the far end of the school, she saw that the helicopter had landed on the playing fields. Hector was some way off, bouncing around, barking.

The rotor blades were still turning as the front passenger door opened and Abel eased himself out, his arm no longer in a sling. He slid open the rear passenger door and removed what looked to be a cool bag. Hector barked with even greater enthusiasm. Tina watched Abel slip on a blue chef's glove and pull out a large hunk of red meat, which he tossed in Hector's direction.

'I don't believe it,' Gary said, breathlessly, to Tina. 'He's been feeding Hector.' Abel peeled off the blue glove and waved as he came out from under the slowly rotating blades. They hurried over to him.

'Abel!' Tina out-paced Gary and gave him a hug. 'It's so good to see you.' She broke away and looked at him, her heart pounding. 'I've got my watch back!'

He smiled. 'So I see. I tried to get it off Hector's collar, but even though Graham and I regularly flew up here to feed him, he never let me get close.' He looked at the dog enjoying the raw meat. 'I'll take care of him. Keep him fed.'

'He's my dog.' Both Abel and Tina looked at Gary. 'Hector means the world to me,' he continued. 'I hope you understand. When we were both chained to this place, he gave me hope.' They all watched as the scarred hound gulped down a chunk of steak. Gary spoke directly to Abel. 'Will you keep your promise and take Tina to swim with dolphins?'

Abel looked from Gary to Christina and back again. 'Of course. When you are both free to go.'

Gary opened the cool bag and used the blue glove to pick up a hunk of red meat. 'Hector!' The dog came bounding over and gulped it down in one. He turned to Abel. 'Tina is free to go now, if she wants to.'

Abel took a moment before responding. 'What about you?'

'Hector needs me to take care of him.'

Tina stared at Gary. 'What are you saying?'

'Take some time. Have a holiday. Swim with dolphins. You deserve it.'

'We both do.'

Gary approached her, tears rolling down his cheeks. 'Thanks to my actions, you lost more than two years of happiness.' He sniffed hard and wiped his eyes with the heel of his hand. 'I was wrong to think we could simply pick up where we left off.'

She touched his arm. 'I can't go. I have to sort out my parents' house.'

'Sam and Luke can handle that. I'll help.'

She turned to Abel. 'What's the weather like in Florida at this time of year?'

He smiled. 'Pretty good.'

'My passport is in Malcolm's cottage.'

'I'll send a car to pick it up.'

She looked from Abel to Gary and back to Abel. 'I don't have anything with me.'

'I'm quite sure our friend, Audrey, can pack a bag for you.'

She stepped close to Gary. 'I think you and Hector had better move into my parents' house. They have... there is a lovely big garden at the back.'

'I'll talk to Luke,' Gary said. He stared into her eyes and took her hand in his. 'Goodbye... Christina.'

'Goodbye.' She kissed him on the cheek and hugged him for all her worth. 'You will always be in my heart.'

'I never doubted that.'

Tears pouring down her cheeks, she pulled away and walked swiftly to the helicopter.

'The car key?' Gary called.

She stopped and used both her hands to wipe her eyes. 'It's in the ignition. But Hector has to go in the back. And tell him not to dribble on the front passenger seat.'

Gary laughed. 'I'll be sure to tell him that.'

She climbed into the rear of the helicopter. The pilot, wearing headphones, turned and smiled. 'Mrs Burton, it's really good to see you again. Welcome aboard.'

'Thank you, Graham. It's good to see you, too.'

A few moments later, Abel sat in the seat beside her and clicked his seatbelt. 'All good?' he asked, as he handed her a set of headphones.

She nodded. 'All good.' And she put them on.

The rotor blades spun in earnest and a few seconds later they lifted the helicopter off the ground. Tina watched Gary as he walked with Hector around the hollowed shell towards the front of the old school. He looked up as the helicopter circled and then opened the Golf's rear door. Hector leapt in.

She turned to Abel and squeezed his hand. 'This time you came to collect me.'

'I was determined to get your watch back.'

She looked at her Patek Philippe. 'The second hour hand is still set to Rome time.'

'Florida is five hours behind the UK.'

She unclicked her seatbelt and removed her headphones. Abel copied her. They leaned towards each other and their lips were about to meet for the first time when the helicopter jolted. They fell apart, laughing. Both clicked in their seatbelts and put their headphones back on.

'My apologies, Mrs Burton,' the pilot said. 'A small air pocket.'

She held Abel's hand and looked into his eyes. 'I love you.' She mouthed the words so the pilot wouldn't hear; then turned to look out of the window. Through wisps of cloud she could see the quietly flowing River Hawk and its historic humpback bridge.

~

If you have a moment, please leave a review. Your help
to spread the word is very much appreciated.
Amazon.com / Amazon.co.uk

~

For B.
I'll never forget the moment I met you.
I didn't know how fortunate I was going to be.

Romola Farr first trod the boards on the West End stage aged sixteen and continued to work for the next eighteen years in theatre, TV and film, and as a photographic model. A trip to Hollywood led to the sale of a film script and a successful change of direction as a screenwriter and playwright.

'Bridge to Eternity' and 'Breaking Through the Shadows' are the first novels in a planned series, set in the fictional town of Hawksmead.

Romola Farr is a nom de plume.

romolafarr@gmail.com
@RomolaFarr
www.wildmoorpress.com

~

The illustration 'Breaking through the Shadows' is by Lucy Perfect.
lucyperfect.com
instagram.com/lucyperfect

Printed in Great Britain
by Amazon